Apron Strings

Mary Morony

ISBN: 0615951791
ISBN 13: 9780615951799

ACKNOWLEDGMENTS

Thank each and every one of you for all of your help.
Hilary Jackson
Ralph Morony
Melissa Parrish
Susannah Shepherd
Sarah McCollum
Annie Morony
Katherine Kane
Ross Howell
John McAllister
Colin Dougherty
Sara Sgarlet
Alison Abel

Chapter 1

———

Sallee

Change; not even the quarter, nickel, or dime type was appreciated in our house. I don't remember ever seeing a spare coin atop a table or amid the dross in the back hall drawer where everything that didn't have a place ended up. No jar sequestered on a corner of a bureau collected dust and pennies. The thin dimes the tooth fairy brought, once discovered and delighted over, were promptly deposited in our sterling silver piggy banks; each with initials engraved in script. It was as if change didn't exist. I wonder if coins in a pocket would have been eschewed if they had been called anything else.

My mother, Virginia Stuart Mackey, understood her biological duty was to nurture us children. She found the job difficult. Tall, angular, pale, and blonde, my mother spit my brother, sisters, and me out in her image, and then proceeded to whirl about our lives like an icy comet in an orbit rarely intersecting our own.

Our maid, Ethel, would puff up with pride whenever she said, "Miz Ginny done made a good-looking bunch of chil'ren." I guess she was right. Each of us had our mother's hair and blue eyes, although in varying shades. Not one of us had exactly the same color hair or eyes; but there was no question who our mother was. We each, in our own way, had something of her looks.

Soft and round, Ethel was the color of coffee with cream, with big freckles dotting her broad nose. Her wide set eyes were light brown, and her lips were thin. Short, just over five feet tall; she weighed well over two hundred pounds.

I grew up thinking that Ethel and my mother were as close as any two friends could be despite the fact that it was 1957. Even to a child that seemed unbelievable considering they were so different in color, shape, and attitude. Friendship had to be next to impossible: in Virginia it was against the law for a colored person to drink from the same water fountain as a white. Yet, for as long as I could remember, thirteen hours a day, six and a half days a week, my mother and Ethel shared their lives. Well, that's not quite true. My mother shared her life. Ethel listened and edited her own life. And despite their disparate worlds, their views were remarkably similar; their thoughts intertwined like neglected perennials in an old flower bed.

Each of us children was named for somebody else. My sister Stuart was the oldest and the prettiest, she'd just turned fourteen. She hated her name, though I don't know if that was because it sounded like a boy's name or because it was my mother's maiden name. Next oldest to Stuart was my brother, Gordy, just nine at the time. Gordy was named after my mother's brother, Gordon Stuart. Then there was me, Sallee; seven and named after Daddy's father, Sallee. It was an unusual and unfortunate name for a man as far as I was concerned. I was happy to be a girl. Helen, at just four and a half, was the baby of the family and was named for my father's mother who died days before Helen was born. It was lucky that Helen was a girl; I think my parents would've gone right ahead with the name even if the baby had been a boy. I can't imagine a boy on earth who would have been able to tolerate Helen as a name.

The house we lived in was big like a mansion of the old South: butter-colored stucco with enormous fluted columns and dark green almost black shutters on the floor-to-ceiling windows in the front. It sat in one of the treelined neighborhoods that rimmed the University of Virginia where my father had gone to law school. It was the prettiest house on the street. My mother said that if it hadn't been she would never have allowed Daddy to buy it because of the tacky houses that ran down one side of the property line.

"Not charming like slave quarters," she'd say to most any visitor. "Just tacky post–First World War housing." I didn't know why she thought slave quarters were so charming. The ones I'd seen had been nothing but old, rotting, weed choked, falling down sheds. She definitely wouldn't have wanted those right next door. I think the thing she hated most about those houses was their proximity. When our kitchen door was open, you could hear the neighbors talking; the houses were that close. So unless it felt like it was a million degrees inside, she always insisted that our kitchen door stay closed.

A few weeks after her birthday, Stuart decided to have her hair cut short, almost like a boy's. She made the appointment herself, convincing the barber that our mother knew all about it. When we pulled up in the car to pick her up, my mother took one look at my sister's head and started screaming. She left the car idling with us inside while she stalked into the barbershop to give the barber a lecture. Clear out in the car we heard her demand in her most offended tone, "How dare you ruin my little girl's looks?" Still fuming when she got back into the car, she slammed the door and said, to no one in particular, "Cutting girls' hair without their mothers' approval. How dare he?" Stuart sat mute in the front seat. She had been acting pretty smug up until then, but I could see she was trying not to cry. As for me, I squirmed with humiliation.

Stuart, especially as she got older, looked more and more like my mother. Adults loved to compliment her on the resemblance; Stuart loathed it. Anything that had to do with my mother was like poison to Stuart, it seemed. She and my mother got along about as well as beets and mashed potatoes. You had to keep them on opposite sides of the plate if you didn't want to create a big pink mess.

My mother was a beautiful woman and we all knew it; my mother most of all. She wore her long golden hair up in a loose bun, or in a braid wrapped around her head for parties. Her features were delicate. She always wore jewelry that shimmered and jingled when she moved. We were lucky to have such an attractive mother, people said. It boded well for how we would turn out. Sometimes I would look in the mirror and study my face, searching for signs of my mother in it. But I'd ended up with my father's square face and round nose; features that suited him just fine, but made me look boyish in spite of my long hair.

That long hair was a Mackey girl trademark, as far as my mother was concerned. She took pride in it, delighting in the variations among us, even running her fingers through Helen's soft curls sometimes. I think that's why she was heartbroken when Stuart lopped her's off.

When we got home from the barber, my mother announced that Stuart was grounded for a month. No longer fighting back her tears, Stuart ran up to her bedroom, passing a stunned Ethel on the stairs.

"Lord a mercy, whaddidya do to yo' head, chile?" Ethel asked.

There was another change my mother was none too happy with. My father had started wearing blue jeans and work boots on weekdays. For years Daddy had been a lawyer, leaving and coming home from work in nice gray suits and handsome wingtip shoes. But he quit his job at the law firm to start building a shopping center. "The way of the future," he called it. My mother called it an ugly atrocity, at least when she was speaking with her friends. I think Ethel was inclined to agree with her. More than anything though, I think my mother missed the suits. Thing is, I'm not sure my father even needed the jeans and work boots. They stayed nice and clean. And he still wore his suits some days when he had meetings. The way Ethel told it, my father worked on the "business" side of the project. I could see he liked his new clothes, but I wasn't sure the jeans and boots were worth all the fuss.

Whenever my mother complained about Daddy's attire, Ethel would reassure her. "Miz Ginny, ya know good as me he'll be back in dem suits afore too long," she'd say. But he never was. I think that was why Ethel never said anything to my mother about Stuart's haircut. Ethel seemed to have a sixth sense about what could be said and what was best left unsaid.

I know it can't really be so, but looking back, I believe the events of that morning when Stuart had her hair lopped off marked a tipping point. Things had never been perfect in our house, and at the age of seven I was just beginning to consider the possibility that other families might have it better or worse. Until then, things were simply the way they were, and they didn't seem likely to ever change—boy, was I wrong about that. I see now that thinking that way gave me a sense of security, like the way a recipe arms you with the notion that a dish will turn out the same every time you make it. As the winter of 1957 gave way to spring, it seemed that the Mackey household was about to have a whole new menu.

A few weeks after Stuart cut her hair, I almost died. At least I thought I was dying. The Saturday morning started off like any other. Ethel arrived for work, and the kitchen filled with her clean, earthy scent, which was alive with wood smoke, farmyard animals, hay, and grain. She lived on a farm with her husband, and finished chores there while I lay dreaming in my warm bed. She hummed spirituals as she set about fixing breakfast. Coffee perked on the stove. Bacon fried in the big black skillet. She softly sang, "*Gwine to chatter with the angels, Sooner in the mornin', O Lord have mercy on me.*" Halved oranges waited on the counter, ready for squeezing as soon as my mother's footfall was heard at the top of the stairs. Then she would help Gordy, Helen, and me get dressed.

Ethel stopped singing and started squeezing orange halves when she heard my mother start down the stairs. I always thought it was strange that my mother hated singing so much. If you wanted to really get under her skin, all you had to do was sing along with Ethel. "*Dem Bones, dem bones, dem dry bones,*" we'd shout along.

"Gordy, Sallee!" she'd snap at us. "Stop that this instant." Then she'd look at Ethel and shake her head. "Please, Ethel, those songs are just too sad."

"The past is the past," Ethel would reply, looking my mother dead in the eye.

On Saturdays Ethel often brought Gordy, Helen, and me Three Musketeers candy bars in a too-dressy-for-everyday worn black purse that she parked on the counter behind the kitchen door in front of the folded paper bags. One particular Saturday she arrived with no such offering. Gordy and Helen didn't seem to notice, but I felt a pang of dismay when she didn't mention the candy. I decided to check her purse, just in case she'd forgotten.

I lingered in the kitchen after we'd finished breakfast. My mother left to run errands. Ethel went upstairs to make beds. I tiptoed to the bottom of the stairs and listened. When my mother was away from the house, Ethel would start belting it out. *"Leaning, leaning, on the everlasting arms,"* thundered down the steps. That morning Ethel was in full voice.

I crept back into the kitchen to the back door. I clicked open the beaded, silver catch of the purse and peered inside. There was a single dollar bill folded over three times and a black change purse that had long lost its luster. A gold ball clip was missing from the latch, but the hinge still held. Inside the change purse were a few pennies, a couple of nickels, and another carefully folded square dollar bill. I replaced the change purse, and then pushed aside a wadded up tissue and two scraps of paper covered with Ethel's distinctive cursive to get a better look.

Reaching into a little zippered pocket on the side, I found a small glass bottle half full of what looked like water. I unscrewed the cap and smelled it. Phew, was that some awful stuff! I screwed the cap back on and zipped it into the pouch. There were no candy bars to be found, but at the very bottom of the purse was a thin turquoise box labeled "Ex-Lax" in red letters. Inside were tiny, precise rectangles that smelled and looked like chocolate. They didn't taste as sweet or as chocolaty as I had hoped, but because of the clandestine nature of my search, I was in no position to be choosey. I ate only two or three; not because I was worried I might be depriving Ethel of her treats, but because I thought such a small theft might pass unnoticed. Later, Ethel found me in the bathroom hunched over with stomach cramps.

"Honey don' ya'll know ya'll shouldna be goin' into other peoples' thangs wit'out askin'?" she asked with a chuckle.

"My stomach hurts. I think I'm dying," I groaned.

"Ya ain't dyin'. Ya just ate somethin' you shouldna, and Lord now you a mess. C'mon, let's gitcha cleaned up." I guess she'd taken inventory of her purse and knew why I was in such distress. Mercifully, she didn't tell on me to my mother.

Anything my mother deemed valuable she kept under lock and key. Not jewelry, furs, or money, mind you, but food and drink; mostly sweets and liquor. Getting caught taking something that my mother would lock away was a mistake you only made once.

A month or so after the Ex-Lax incident, I was playing dolls with Helen when the doorbell rang. Ethel answered the door. A Girl Scout dropped off six boxes of chocolate mint cookies, my personal favorite. Ethel put them on the shelf in the pantry. When my mother got home, she would lock them in her "cabinet." Helen and I decided with the impeccable logic of a four- and a seven-year-old that if we took an entire box, no one would miss it. My mother not only missed the box, she asked everyone in the house where it was. We answered her query with puzzled looks, not anticipating that the empty Girl Scout cookie box under the bed in our shared room would convict us.

"What kind of children have I raised?" my mother shrieked. She loomed over us with a wooden, boar bristle brush in her hand, her eyes cruel and hooded. "I'll teach you to steal and lie to me about it." She grabbed Helen by the armpit. Holding her up off the floor, my mother swatted my terrified sister as if the force would knock the larceny right out of her dishonest little heart.

Helen wailed, "Mama, please don't hit me." Her light curls plastered to her tear-stained face.

I scrambled to the safety of our closet. My mother followed, grabbing my hair and yanking me out into the bedroom. Twice the brush stung my thigh, creating angry red welts. "I'll teach you to run away from me, you little brat. Were those your cookies?"

"No...I don't know..." I howled as I thrashed about, scrambling to the back of the closet. She lunged at me again.

"Don't hit me! Please don't hit me!" I shrieked. I held my hands up to protect my head and to keep my hair from being pulled again. Helen, discarded like a worn sock, cowered in a corner, wedged in tightly for protection from my mother's fury. Then, like ash in the wind, our mother was gone; leaving both of us gasping and weeping.

One spring evening, after what seemed like a very long winter for the Mackey household, Gordy, Helen, and I were playing outside. Ethel stood on the back porch and hollered, "Come on in, now, chil'run. I need to get ya'll cleaned up 'fore yo' momma get home. Come on, now!"

Gordy and Helen went right in. Since I had just learned to skip rope, I decided to test my growing agility by continuing to play.

"Salleeee, git on in he'ah," Ethel bellowed. Ethel's temper had a fuse longer than my mother's, but she kept a switch behind the kitchen door that could make you dance..

"I'm coming. Hold your horses," I said as I skipped rope to where Ethel stood. The next thing I knew, she was bearing down on me with her switch at the ready. I dropped the rope and started to run. She chased me around the rose garden and through the back gate.

"Ethel, stop!" I shouted. "I didn't mean anything."

My favorite climbing tree was by the kitchen door—one of two hemlocks that stood like sentinels on either side of the driveway. Gordy and I had each claimed a tree as our own. We'd climb up the trees and call back and forth like crows for hours. I climbed my tree as fast as I could.

Ethel circled the trunk, her chest heaving for breath. She glared up at me. From a branch just out of her reach, I tried to reason with Ethel. She was having none of it.

"You better get down off that tree *righ'* now," she said.

"Ethel, I was coming," I pleaded. But I wasn't making any headway. Ethel circled the tree for a good ten minutes, puffing and muttering; whipping her switch in the air.

"Yo' momma gon' have my hide if dinner ain't on the table on time. If you don' get down here right now I'm gon' come up there after ya."

I knew that was impossible, but I climbed a little higher just to be safe; higher than I had ever climbed. I wedged myself into a crook of the tree. Finally, Ethel went into the house. I heard her calling my brother.

"Gordy, climb up dat tree 'n brang yo' sister down," she said.

Gordy appeared at the base of the tree and started climbing. With Ethel in the house, it seemed safe to descend. I turned my body to shimmy down, but my foot was caught. I couldn't turn around or look down. I couldn't quite reach a branch below me with my free foot. I was stuck. A cold wind picked up pulling strands of hair from my long braids, sending hair into my eyes and mouth along with bits of bark from the tree trunk. As I was too afraid to let go of the tree to wipe my hair out of my eyes, I crouched in the crook of the tree, choking back tears.

Gordy could tell I was frightened. He didn't say one smart alecky thing to me as he scampered up the tree as easily as any squirrel. He tried gently to guide my free foot to the lower branch. I felt for purchase, but my foot wouldn't reach. Gordy's exhortation, "You're almost there!" only infuriated me.

I kicked at his hand in frustration. "Leave me alone!" I wailed. Our hound, Lance, came over to inspect the situation. Red eyebrows knitted together on his black face. He gave a look of keen interest to the goings-on above. He barked and brayed as if making suggestions then sat and watched. Ethel came back outside, thankfully, without her switch. Evidently she had abandoned all hope of having dinner ready on time. She looked worried. I continued to wallow in self-pity.

"I can't get her down. Her foot's stuck. She's not helping, either," Gordy called down to her. He leaned his weight into the tree, and then looped one leg around a branch trying to reach my trapped foot.

"Would you quit?" he asked. "I can't get you down if you're gonna be kicking. You're almost there."

"Gordy, stay right there wit' 'er 'til I get somebody to help," Ethel yelled.

"Ethel, I wasn't talkin' back, I promise," I cried. That wasn't exactly true, I knew, but I was desperate. I began to imagine I would have to stay up that tree forever. Then it occurred to me that I might not be alone. Who else might be sharing my perch? I peered around, looking for a bird or varmint nest. Gordy said you could always tell if a rat lived in a tree because a squirrel would have nothing to do with that tree. I racked my brain trying to remember if I had ever seen a squirrel here. I didn't think I had. It was too early in the spring for snakes, or was it? Last summer Gordy and I had watched a snake scoot right up the trunk of a tree slick as anything.

"Please, get me down," I pleaded. "Please."

"Oh, don' cha worry, darlin'. Ol' Ethel'll git'cha down."

Ethel comforted me as best she could while the sun set in glorious orange hues all around me. The clouds were tinged with brilliant streaks of pink and purple, as beautiful as the shimmery colors of butterfly wings. But I was terrified of the dark night that was to come.

Gordy patted my leg. "It's gonna be OK," he said. "You wanna try one more time?"

"No, I can't. I'm scared," I wailed.

"OK. I'll just sit here then. Don't worry," Gordy said. Ethel shook her head and put her hands on her hips. Lance flopped down at the base of the tree with a groan and soon began to snore. Darkness fell.

We heard my mother's car coming up the drive; the headlights made eerie shadows on Gordy's face. "She'll be able to get you outta this tree," he said and started to laugh.

"What's so funny?" I asked.

"She's gonna have to climb up here to get you. Do you think she knows how'ta climb a tree?"

Did she? I wondered. *What if she couldn't? What would happen to me, then?* There was no telling when Daddy would get home. I moaned. "Gordy, have you ever seen a squirrel in this tree?"

I heard the thunk of a car door and Ethel anxiously telling my mother what happened. Gordy scampered down to the ground. Before I could get any more worked up, I saw my mother gingerly climbing the tree. She reached the lower branch.

"Put your foot here," she cooed. Her voice enveloped me like a soft blanket, comforting and warm. She patted the branch. "Put your foot here," she said. "I've got you. I'm not going to let you fall." Her calm, sure words, and the way she stroked my leg reassuringly either shocked or soothed me into complying. I had never before heard that calmness in her voice. It was magical. I still can't piece together *what* or *why,* just that it *was.* Daddy drove up just as my mother and I were inching our way down the tree.

"What's all this?" he asked.

Gordy, practically delirious with excitement, explained the situation. I heard Ethel and Helen talking inside the house. Then Ethel, ever the brooding hen, peered down from the kitchen porch while she made a great show of putting out a bowl for Lance who was already up and on his way to his dinner. She wiped her hands on her apron before disappearing back into the kitchen.

Just then our closest next door neighbor's porch light flashed on. Mr. Dabney lurched out, the screen door banged behind him. He stood swaying slightly in the harsh light in a stained sleeveless undershirt and dirty trousers with barely contained wisps of hair, and fat sticking out wherever there was a gap in his clothing. He held a beer can in one hand and stabbed the air in the direction of our kitchen with the other.

"I saw that nigger of yers chase that child up the tree and she weren't gonna let'er down. If you hadn't come home when ya did I was 'bout ready to call the cops on her," he spewed. There was a flash of white behind him. I thought at first that was it was Miz Dabney until I heard what he said. "These nigger lovers think they're too good for us. We'll show'em won't we boy?" I saw a much younger man in a white T-shirt take a swig from his beer and laugh—a real low, mean laugh. Mr. Dabney sorta laughed too, then turned his head back to us and tried to focus. As he stood there pointing and swaying, closing one eye then the other, he looked more comical to me than threatening, though his young friend's laugh chilled me to the bone.

"Thank you for your concern. Everyone is just fine. We'll take care of it," Daddy said. There was steel in his voice. He turned, scooped me from the bottom branch, wrapped his arm around my mother, and gave her a squeeze.

"Well," he said to my mother, "aren't you the heroine of the hour!" A broad beam replaced the concern that Mr. Dabney's words had produced on my mother's face. I wiped my eyes, suddenly pleased with my little escapade, and held my father tight. I burrowed my face into his neck, savored his earthy scent, and gently rocked against his chest as he and my mother walked hand in hand up the stairs and into our house.

"Dabney's an ignorant fool," my father whispered to her. He put me down and pointed me toward the kitchen with a pat on my behind. "Don't pay any attention to him."

Chapter 2

On my Easter vacation from school I trailed along after Ethel as she worked: I sprawled in piles of sheets as she pulled them from the beds, or pushed a dust rag around in imitation of her. Ethel, ever practical, shoved dirty clothes into a pair of pants or a buttoned-up shirt rather than haul around a heavy laundry basket from room to room.

"Lemme help," I pleaded as she stuffed Daddy's pajama bottoms, making them look like an overfed scarecrow.

When the pajamas looked as if they would split a seam, she put the bundle on the floor. "Roll it to the stairs an' giv'er a'push," she directed.

I watched the pajamas tumble down the stairs. "Look, Ethel, Gordy's drawers spilled out in the front hall," I said with a laugh.

"Go'n down an' pick 'em up now, 'fore somebody gets home. Ya can push it down to the basement stairs, too, big as ya is," she said. "I'm goin' up to the attic to put away these winter clothes and get out yo' spring thangs. Ya c'mon up when ya get done, hear?"

"Oh goody!" I cried. I loved this ritual of going through my old clothes, rediscovering dresses I'd forgotten, and noting how much I'd grown since the year before. I called up to Ethel, "Wait for me!" I tore down the stairs, picking up bits of laundry along the way. Restuffing by myself wasn't as much fun as working upstairs with Ethel, but I was happy to help her do anything. Grunting and groaning, I heaved the pajama bottoms, now ballooned to twice my size, to the basement door. I switched the basement light on as soon as I opened the door—you never could tell who or what might be lurking down there in the dark. With one last push, I stuffed the laundry through the small door and down the stairs. Just as I was about to turn out the light, I noticed broken glass and a rock on the basement floor. I quickly flicked the light switch off and slammed the door shut, sliding the bolt to lock it. I ran upstairs to the attic, listening for the safety of Ethel's tuneless humming.

The smell of mothballs, and the presence of rounded top steamer trunks and hanging bags gave the attic the feeling of a world far removed from the rest of the house. I was grateful for the haven it provided. As Ethel folded clothing and sorted through hanging bags, I plied her with questions about my family. When my mother was out of the house, Ethel seemed to relish my questions, as if the mere asking of them validated her. I counted on her to fill me in on the history of my parents' lives before I was born, or, as she would say, "When ya'll was down da river count'n sand." I took her accounts of my parents' history as gospel. My father's past was shrouded in mystery; my mother's in a kind of confused awe. Her brothers—my uncles—were disagreeable individuals, I thought, but people always seemed to defer to them. They comported themselves as though oblivious to their social shortcomings—secure in the confidence of their good breeding. Likewise, my maternal grandparents were presumed to be infallible—paragons of southern culture whose legacy we should strive to uphold. It was understood that my father's family lacked the standing of my mother's, though neither my siblings nor I quite understood why. We adored our father with a reverence that was intensified by how rarely we saw him. It only made sense to us that, if our mother was descended from southern royalty, our father must be descended from nothing short of the gods. The fact that the scales apparently tipped the other way confounded me. Asking my parents about it was rarely fruitful—"bad blood" between relatives made for raw nerves, and so they had to be in a really good mood to tolerate my questions. Fortunately, Ethel seemed to know more than anyone else. She didn't mind sharing what she knew and making up the rest.

"Mista Joe's daddy was one good lookin' man. He coulda been in da picture shows." She stopped folding clothes, shook her head side to side, and smiled like she was remembering something fine.

"Did you know him? Did he ever come here?" I asked as I plowed through a pile of last summer's shorts.

"No, he lived in New York. I ain't never seen him in person...did see a pitchur of 'im, though. He died just after yo' daddy got back from the war, 'bout a year or so later."

"How'd he die?"

"Was a big fire that killed 'im. He weren't no real doctor, I don't believe; his lab blowed up."

I shuddered at such a dramatic demise. "Why wasn't he a real one? Did he just pretend to be a doctor?"

"He was one of them PhD doctors, not the kind ya go to when you's sick—a scientist."

"He must have been mad," I deduced from my Saturday morning television shows.

"I 'spect he was. Ya mama tried to git Mista Joe to go to da funeral, but he wouldn't do it. He never said another word 'bout his daddy. The two of 'em had a fallin' out, and after that, Mista Joe didn't pay him no mind; even when the man died. Ain't right if you ask me."

I was trying on my Easter bonnet from last year, which was too small. "Whadda they fall out about?" I asked. Then I spied one of Stuart's bonnets. I took it over to an old mirror leaning up against the wall and placed it on my head. I spun every which way, hoping I looked as beautiful as I remembered Stuart did when she wore it. "Think I can wear this one?"

"Is too big. I 'spect Stuart gonna be fighting with ya mama 'bout wearing it again dis here Easter."

"What were you sayin' about why Daddy fell out with his daddy?"

"The fallin' out mighta had somethin' to do wit' Mista Joe decidin' that lawyerin' wasn't for him no mo'. I don' rightly know all of it...I just know he got this big shoppin' center idea after he come back from the war." She sighed and heaved open another trunk. "He been working on it for a good while and he asked his daddy for money to help him along with it. I 'spect the old man said no. Mista Joe came back from that trip fit to be tied."

When I asked such questions of my mother, she would snap, "Mind your own business, Sallee!" Often she'd say I was rude or even *impudent*, though she never told me what that meant. Given her tone, I was pretty sure it wasn't good. With Ethel it was different. She let me push and prod about the past and told me endless stories; which always seemed to leave me with more questions.

"What exactly is a shopping center, anyway?"

All I knew about shopping was our twice-yearly drives with my mother to the big Thalhimers and Miller and Rhodes department stores in Richmond. I couldn't imagine buying anything here in Charlottesville except shoes or groceries.

"Honey, I wish I knowed, much trouble as it's caused in dis here family." She shook her head and bent over to pick up a bundle of clothes. "Pick up that stack an' let's get on downstairs. Yo' mama'll be back 'fore long, and I gotta get lunch started."

I gathered the stack of clothes and followed her down the steps, "Oh," I said, "I almost forgot to tell you. There's broken glass all over the basement floor and a rock, too."

"Huh," Ethel said. When Gordy came into the kitchen for lunch, she put her hands on her hips and asked, "You ain't been throwin' rocks at de house, has ya?"

Gordy looked at her like she'd hit him in the head with one. "I know better than that," he muttered. He continued to munch on his peanut butter sandwich.

"Hum, I hope so," she said.

One morning shortly after school had let out for the summer, my mother swept into the kitchen. "Ethel!" she called. "Miss Dorothy, Miss Della, and Miss Emily are coming over this afternoon. Make sure the children are presentable. It's just a small tea. A few sandwiches and some of those marmalade tarts will be all we need." She checked her new diamond watch. "Oh, and Ethel, put out some sherry glasses. You know how Miss Emily likes her sherry," she laughed. "I'm on my way to the car, Stuart. Your tennis lesson starts in ten minutes. Let's go."

"Can I go?" I asked.

"I suppose so. We'll be back in time for you to get cleaned up," she said. Stuart, who was always late, had to run back to her room to get her racket. "Come on, come on," my mother grumbled while we waited in the car. I sat in the back seat. "Oh Lord, there's that dreadful man again," she groaned. "Come on, Stuart."

"What dreadful man?" I asked. I glanced about seeing no one but Mr. Dabney sitting on his back porch. He waved and I waved back. "Mr. Dabney? He's OK. 'Sides, his wife is really nice. She makes…"

"Sallee, you stay away from those people. Do you hear me?" She glared at me over the back of her seat. Stuart jumped in the car and we roared out of the drive.

"For once I'm glad I've got a stupid lesson this afternoon," Stuart said. As soon as the words tumbled out of her mouth, I knew she was in for it. My forehead was pressed against the window. I looked up to watch my mother's reaction in the rearview mirror.

"Why on earth would you say such a thing, Stuart Mackey?"

Stuart shifted a little in her seat. "Cuz I hate those parties. I don't get why we have to go. They're not our friends."

"Darling," my mother's voice took on a sugary tone, but her eyes narrowed. "How are you going to learn how to behave in polite society if you don't practice? It's important."

"Important? To you maybe."

"Not just to me. If you know how to entertain, you will be a tremendous asset to your husband." She reached over and pinched Stuart's arm playfully. Stuart writhed away. "Why, a wife who is comfortable in any social situation…"

"What if I don't want to get married? What if I don't want to be anybody's wife? Then I don't need to know all that stuff." Stuart glowered at my mother and rubbed her arm. She fished a kerchief from her pocket and tied it around her head. "Who's coming anyway?" she asked.

My mother sighed, casting a sharp look at my sister. "Mrs. Mason, Miss Eades, and Miss James." She glanced at the kerchief. "I wish you would let your hair grow. You are so much prettier with your hair longer."

"Just what I want to be—a miniature you," Stuart muttered. "Maybe I should wear it up just so and wear sapphires too," she added. I noticed Stuart had moved a bit closer to the car door.

When Stuart talked to our mother that way, I always battled the feeling of being in class and having to pee, but the teacher won't let me go. It made me feel fidgety and downright uncomfortable. *Did she always have to be looking for a fight?* I wondered. "Don't you like how it makes your eyes look?" I asked Stuart, hoping to avert the coming storm. When I saw she was about to direct a sneer at me I quickly added, "I think it makes you look pretty—longer hair, I mean."

Stuart rolled her eyes. "And it's so important to look pretty. Right, Sallee?" Then she turned on my mother. "You seem to be getting what you want from Sallee. Congratulations, another convert to the Happy Homemakers' Club."

Again my mother sighed. I couldn't quite tell if Stuart had just said something bad about me.

My mother was silent, but the storm was still brewing. I tried to change the subject. "Hey," I piped up, "why does Miz Mason always wear gloves and long sleeves even when it's hot outside?"

"Hay is for horses, Sallee," my mother said crossly. My diversion had worked. I was so relieved I barely listened to her answer.

"I can't remember what it's called, but she has some type of pigmentation problem—sun damage or something," my mother said. She glanced from the red stoplight to her wristwatch. "Her doctor warned her never to go outside without being covered up. She is very sensitive about it. Apparently nothing can be done, and it is only going to get worse, poor dear."

"A pig?" I said. "Miz Mason?"

"What? Sallee, hush! I can't even think." Gravel crunched under the tires as we pulled up by the tennis courts. "Stuart," she said, "You're coming home with Kathy." Stuart leaped from the car. "If my guests are still there when you get home I would appreciate it if you would come in and speak to them," my mother called as Stuart's back disappeared behind the fence. "Good luck, make me proud and don't forget your manners!"

Ethel had laid out my pink and white party dress on my bed. It had a stiff crinoline that made it stick out. After she buttoned me up, she started pulling my hair back into a ponytail. "Chile, wouldcha hol' still?" She squeezed my head in both her hands like she was testing a melon, then gave it a yank to make me face straight forward.

"Owww, don't pull so hard. It hurts."

"Stop jumpin' round."

"I can't help it. This dress itches, right here." I pointed to my waist. She pulled the skirt up to inspect the waistband.

"Ain't nothin' but yo' petticoat and I ain't got time to fix it now. The way you dancin' and wigglin', you ain't gonna be in it that long, no way." Ethel knew as well as I did that my squirming would be a sure invitation for dismissal from the party.

After she was finished with my hair, she sent me into the parlor. I flopped on the sofa with Gordy while my mother greeted her guests in the front hall. Gordy had already stuffed two of Ethel's famous marmalade tarts in his mouth.

"You better not eat all those," I warned as I rubbed my back against the sofa cushions.

"Why don't you save your scratching 'til the party starts?" he asked while spitting crumbs from his mouth. "Then we can get out quick and take a look at Mr. Dabney's slingshot. I don't think he's home."

"What's he doing with a slingshot?"

Gordy screwed up his face and shrugged. "That's what I'd like to know," he said. "I saw it on his porch the other day. It's a really neat one, fits over your wrist to hold…"

My mother thought her children talking with each other when she entertained was impolite and strictly forbidden. Miss James's entrance into the room ended our conversation. Gordy sprang from his seat. "Why hello, Miz James," he said. "It's so nice to see you again." He extended his hand taking the lady's and shaking it like a pro. "How have you been?"

Tall and wiry for his age, Gordy sounded like a fifty-year-old man who'd been entertaining ladies all his life, though he was barely two years older than me. I envied him his ability to do so easily just what he was told. Unlike me, he almost never argued with anything my mother told him to do. At just one of these afternoon parties, Gordy would garner more approving smiles from our mother than I would in a whole month.

Even little Helen, expertly guided from one old lady to another older one by my mother, was more successful than me. She smiled just so while delicately holding on to her carrot stick. She had just the right amount of shyness. "Darling," tripped off every set of crimson lips in the room.

"She is *precious*, Ginny. You must be so proud," Miss James gushed in her raspy cigarette voice. She patted Helen's head with a gnarled, ring-decked hand, her cigarette ash poised overtop my sister's curls while she balanced her sherry, napkin, and tart in the other. When she smiled, the skin on her cheeks stretched and the skin around her mouth dissolved into a series of cracks and lines. Her perfume crawled into the back of my throat so I could almost taste it, thick and sweet—and I was clear across the room. Her blue hair was just visible under a little black hat shaped like a mushroom with netting sticking up all around. Small diamond shapes festooned the netting, which came down just below her eyes. The netting and diamonds bobbed up and down like a swarm of flies whenever Miss James moved her head, something she did every time she spoke or took a drag off her cigarette. She was a tiny woman, not much bigger than me, in a gray suit with turquoise and orange bumps all over. Draped around her shoulders were three dead minks that looked like they were biting each other's tails just as they were run over by a car.

Helen was having a hard time maintaining her precious smile with the cigarette waving around her head, cutting invisible lines through the cloud of perfume. Smoke hung around my sister's head like words in a cartoon. "I just think this shopping center idea that Joe has is so exciting," Miss James was saying. "I hear they are the rage in Connecticut. My great-niece says that everybody in New Canaan shops in shopping centers now. It is just so *exciting*."

Helen pulled on my mother's dress and looked up at her, pleading without a word. "Excuse me, Emily," my mother said. "Helen, honey, would you mind passing the sandwiches?" My mother smiled at Helen as she guided her toward the tea table. "That's a good girl. Emily, could I get you some more sherry?" she asked as she refilled her own glass.

While Gordy and Helen followed the script, I straightened, clawed, squirmed, and straightened again, attempting to relieve the misery of my dress. The ladies jabbered away. Gordy nodded like a slinky toy going down a staircase as Miss Eades talked about her godson. I knew she was talking about her godson because that was all Miss Eades ever talked about. Ethel said Miss Eades was "stout." I thought she was just plain fat. She wore the same kind of stockings Ethel did: the ones that roll up just under the knee. You could see the rolls when she sat down and her dress hiked up. Miss Eades didn't just spill out of everything she wore; she spilled *on* everything she wore, too. Stuart swore he once saw a whole cucumber sandwich stuck in Miss Eades's pearl necklace. The pink frilly dress she was wearing showed food stains when she walked in the door. Her purse looked like it might have been a better size for Helen. The tiny little thing was stuck on her wrist like a rubber band and swung about as she sucked from her teacup. I watched as she stuffed a sandwich in her mouth and blew crumbs on Gordy's shirt. He looked mournfully over at me. I started to laugh, which made my dress start to itch again.

I should have already been mingling. When my mother asked her usual question—"Have you spoken to everyone?"—I would need an affirmative answer before there was any hope of being dismissed; squirmy or not. In the throes of what must have looked like a mild fit, I had failed to pay attention to my surroundings. Mrs. Mason's approach startled me. I swallowed and tried to remember the crucial steps of the "first greeting" my mother had drilled into each of us: *look them in the eye, remember their names, smile and be pleasant, and above all—no dead fish handshakes!*

"Why, Sallee, you are getting prettier and prettier, turning into quite the little lady," Mrs. Mason said, sitting down next to me before I could jump up and shake her hand. She reached over and patted my knee. I didn't know if I should stand up and shake her hand or remain seated and smile.

"Thanks...I mean thank you, Miz Mason," I said, caught in an awkward crouch. I limply reached out my hand to shake hers. She took my hand in both of hers; an action decidedly absent from the script my mother had drilled. Her charm bracelet jingled. My eyes grew wide with admiration. "Oh, can I...I mean, may I...look at your charms? I love charm bracelets. I can't wait to be big enough to have one," I gushed. It wasn't so terribly difficult to greet someone, especially someone like Mrs. Mason. But my mother insisted it must be done properly, and there were so many rules that only she seemed to know. Mrs. Mason held her gloved hand out for me to inspect the bracelet.

"This charm came from Russia. Look what it does," she said. She felt around the small golden sphere for an invisible catch. The charm sprung open to reveal six tiny picture frames. The pictures were so small the people could have been anyone. Mrs. Mason said they were her children and her grandbabies.

She let me inspect the pictures for some time. Of all of my mother's "tea party" friends, Mrs. Mason was my favorite. She was pretty, but old—probably around fifty—though she didn't act that old. She smiled more than most old women, and her smile never seemed fake. She didn't smell old, either; more like loose powder and faint flowers.

She lit a cigarette. "What are you doing to keep yourself busy this summer?" she asked. Mrs. Mason exhaled smoke over my head as she tilted her's to catch my response.

"I don't know," I replied absently. "Nothin'." I tried to think of another topic that might interest her. I patted her arm gently. "Well, Miz Mason," I said, "how's your pig?"

A trail of smoke escaped her lips. She smiled, her forehead crinkled with confusion and amusement. "Pig?" she asked. "Honey, I don't have a pig. Where on earth would you come up with a notion like that?"

I blushed, flustered. I tried to recall details from my mother's conversation. "You know, the one that gets all sunburned," I offered. "The one the doctor said you can't take outside anymore unless she's wearing a hat and gloves." Mrs. Mason's expression was still puzzled, but no longer amused.

She laughed nervously. Just then my mother appeared. "A pig, Sallee?" Mrs. Mason asked. "I don't have any idea what you're talking about." She eyed my mother suspiciously.

"Sallee Mackey, you apologize this instant!" my mother commanded. She looked earnestly at Mrs. Mason. "Dorothy, I am so sorry. I don't know what I am going to do with this child. There are times when she can't tell fact from her own stories. I don't know how she comes up with this stuff."

Mrs. Mason stubbed out her half-smoked cigarette, the charms of her bracelet jingled and banged against the ashtray. "No doubt she is only repeating something she has heard," she said, not looking at my mother. "Ginny, it's been a lovely party, but I really must be going." After she gathered up her purse and cigarettes, Mrs. Mason turned to me. "In the future, young lady, you would be well advised not to ask so many questions."

"I'm sorry," I sputtered. Mrs. Mason brushed past me. The other guests hadn't noticed a thing. My mother swooped down, grabbed my arm, and escorted me to the parlor door hissing like a mad goose. I scurried upstairs in shame. In that instant I was jealous of Stuart. She didn't care what our mother thought of her. I wished somehow I had her distance, her cool detachment.

When my mother walked into the kitchen later that night as we were eating dinner, I noticed Ethel quickly tipped out the contents of a tin cup into the sink. The cup must've been nearly full. She refilled it with water from the faucet and took a sip. She placed the cup back beside her on the sink and continued washing the tea party dishes. My mother leaned against the counter.

"I love those old girls," she said, "but dear Lord, it is getting harder and harder to entertain them. And Betty Chambers, who calls herself my best friend, won't even come." She mimicked Miss Chambers in a high-pitched voice. "'Oh, Ginny, you are such a darling to keep inviting them, but who has tea anymore, really?'" Then she answered in her own voice, "Della Eades, that's who, though she gets more food on her dress than in her mouth, poor dear."

Ethel chuckled as she finished drying the teapot. She began to stack the cups and saucers on a tray.

"Well, I guess I'll have to consider it my civic duty," my mother said. "But we don't have to do it quite so often, do we? I wish they could play bridge." She folded an arm across her chest, leaned her opposite elbow on it, and held her chin in her cupped hand. She tapped her cheek lightly as her cigarette smoldered between her fingers. "Emily said shopping centers are all the rage in Connecticut—as if she'd know. The old dear is just trying to be sweet. This whole shopping center business is getting so messy," she sighed. "I wish Joe would just give it up. Why can't he leave things the way they are?"

"Mm-hmm," Ethel answered from the pantry as she carefully placed the china back in the cupboard.

Gordy, Helen, and I sat at the table, silent as sheep.

Ethel came back into the kitchen. "You and Mista Joe havin' supper tonight?" she asked. "I ain't had time to fix nothin' for ya yet, but I can whip up a Welsh rabbit if'n ya want. I think Stuart'll eat that."

"She made a sandwich when she came back from tennis," Helen offered. "She went up upstairs and told us to leave her alone." She looked at Gordy and me for affirmation.

"No, Joe's not coming back 'til late," my mother said. "I'll get something then." She went into the bar. We could hear her pouring herself a drink. She came back to her spot by the counter. "You'd think he was in love with that construction site by the way he—"

"You chil'ren get on upstairs an' put yo night clothes on. I'll be up in a minute," Ethel said, cutting in.

I jumped up and ran out of the room. I heard Ethel say to Gordy, "You don' need no mo' sweets, boy, ya already had enough. Now go'n wit' yo' big self 'fore I get me a switch."

I heard my mother giggle; the ice clinked in her glass.

Summer had blossomed in all its glory and agony. One day—so hot having skin touch me was just plain annoying—I walked around holding my arms away from my body and keeping my legs as far apart as I could. Ethel had the afternoon off. Gordy was playing with a friend and Helen was napping. Stuart, who could never be counted on for entertainment, was "out." With no hope of finding companionship, I resigned myself to a dull, hot afternoon watching TV.

My mother was working on a jigsaw puzzle on the table in front of the sofa when I entered the den, my arms and legs akimbo. She greeted me with a forced smile; as if it was my fault that Ethel had the day off.

"Is Ethel coming to fix dinner?" I asked.

She nodded her head without so much as a glance in my direction.

"It's so hot. Why don't we go to the beach anymore?" I whined, irritated by the heat and her acting like having to stay home with us kids was the end of the world. "Remember how much fun we all used to have? Remember?"

She nodded again.

"Can we go to the beach? It's too hot here."

She didn't look up from her puzzle. "Mmm, that would be nice, but no, we can't."

"Why not?"

"Because your father's too busy, that's why. You wouldn't want to go without him, would you?"

"I guess not," I lied. At that moment I would've sold the whole family for a bus ticket to the ocean.

Resigned to no beach trip or TV either, I pulled up a chair and sat down to watch her. "Momma, tell me 'bout when you was big as me."

"Sallee you say, 'Tell me...,' oh, never mind." She hesitated a moment then sighed. "When I was your age, I had a piebald pony named Puddin' Head. He was so fat his belly nearly dragged the ground. He looked more like a cartoon than a real live pony."

"Did you ride Puddin' Head to school? I think it would be so fun to ride to school."

"No, we had cars just like we do now."

"You had those old-timey cars without any windows like in the *Little Rascals*?" It was always a mistake to mention television to my mother— you could never tell if she was going to say you watched too much and put an end to it forever.

She laughed; it sounded like beautiful, tinkling chimes. "My daddy's cars were the finest money could buy. One day when your Uncle Gordon was a few years younger than you, he decided that, if horses ran on oats, cars must too. He put a whole big scoop of oats in the gas tank of one of Daddy's brand new cars. He ruined that car. Try as they might—and believe me they did try—they were never able to get that car to run right after that."

"Boy, oh boy, Granddaddy musta been mad about that!"

"You know, Daddy laughed and laughed," she smiled. "He never once raised his voice in anger."

I wondered about that. It certainly never seemed to be that way in *our* house.

"He thought it was the funniest thing. I remember he bragged about how smart his son was," she said.

He doesn't sound so smart to me, I thought, but I knew better than to say so.

"Daddy boasted to everybody who would listen, 'My son is barely five-years-old and already he's using deductive reasoning. That boy is going to go far.' He was so proud of Gordon. He was proud of all of his children. You would've loved your grandfather. I'm so sorry you never got to meet him." She sighed.

"Did your daddy like my daddy?"

"Oh, he died when I was in my teens. I hadn't met your daddy yet."

"You didn't know Daddy when you were little? I thought Uncle Gordon was his friend."

"They were friends in college—Uncle James, too—but not when we were children. Your daddy came from up north. He came here to go to college. That's where he met Uncle Gordon, in law school."

I looked at one of the jigsaw pieces and tried to find a fit. "What was it like to have your very own pony?"

"It was the grandest thing. After the fire—remember, I told you my parents' house burned to the ground when I was just a little older than you?—we moved to Appin, my father's home place out in the country. You know, beyond Belfield School? Remember where Granny Bess used to live?"

I laughed. "That's silly. Granny Bess didn't live in the country."

"It was country then," she said. "After we moved, Daddy bought me a much bigger pony, twice the size of Puddin'. He was beautiful, black as pitch, with a white heart shape on his forehead. I named him True Love. He could run like a racehorse. Our stable boy, Cy, took such good care of Puddin' and Lovey." She paused for a moment to turn a piece of the puzzle between her fingers. She put it in place.

"There are no pictures," I said. "How do you put this together?" I inspected another tiny piece and peeled my sticky arm off the table. "Aren't you hot?"

She nodded her head slowly. "Don't think about it."

"This is harder than my puzzles. I don't think I could ever do one of these."

"Each piece is part of the picture. You can't see the picture until the whole thing is done." She took the piece I was holding, examined it, and then fit it into the puzzle.

"But I've got to have pictures. Did you play with Cy?"

"Lord, no. It wasn't allowed. I learned that quickly. I had put Cy's picture in a locket Daddy gave me for Christmas. It was the prettiest little locket, heart-shaped with a small diamond. I told Daddy I put Cy in my locket because he took such good care of Puddin' and Lovey. He told me to take it out. He said it wasn't right to have his picture in my locket. What did I know? I was just a silly little girl."

She glanced up at me looking almost embarrassed. She picked up her pack of cigarettes and lit one, holding it in her mouth as she undid all her work on the puzzle and knocked all the pieces back into the box. She told me to go help Ethel in the kitchen. I didn't bother to remind her that Ethel was off.

Chapter 3

———

Ethel
1927

I was fourteen-years-old when I come to work for yo' granddaddy's family, Miss Sallee. It was just a few days a week when I didn' have nothin' to do at the boardin' house; helpin' my mother in the kitchen, mostly. Folks say I was tied to mamma's apron strings, but I never did much mind what folks say. Turned out to be one of them little decisions that don't seem like much at the time, but ends up changing yo' life.

First day they puts me to work pluckin' and dressin' the chickens for that evenin's dinner. It was summertime and the kitchen was pipin' hot, what with bread bakin' in the ovens all morning long. I had sweat rollin' off me; but it was the kind of work I's used to. I hadn' been there two hours when in breezes a blonde headed white girl, all smilin' and flushed. And she ask' me, well, she tol' me—like I'd been there all her life—to cut up some carrots for her pony. Didn' ask me my name (white people never did), just said, "Little pieces; he likes little pieces." I said, "Yes'm, I'll bring 'em to the stable for ya," and she was out the door 'fore I'd even finished my sentence.

And that was the first time I ever laid eyes on Miz Ginny. Now, she was the prettiest girl, white or colored, you ever would see: so slim and graceful, with hair that didn' seem to fall out of place no matter how fast she rode that pony; and always smilin', or so I thought. Even though she acted all high and mighty about them carrots, I liked her right off. Course, I was gonna learn she could be a difficult lady to please.

"Particular," my mother called her. Reckon she come by that trait honest; both her folks had mighty particular ways.

Her daddy, Gordon Ulysses (musta been a Yankee in that woodpile, some ways) Stuart, was one of the *cussedest* men ever drew breath—least that's what my Mama said. I don't know. He never had much to say to me. He sho did love yo mama. But my own Mama said that big boned, red-faced, beast of a man could turn sweet milk sour with a look. Mista Gus waited 'til he was neigh in ta forty-five afore he married. His wife, Mary Bess Stuart, was good as two saints. She had to be to put up with his ornery self—least that's how Mama seen it. My way of seein' Miz Bess was that she liked to look like she was good. Lord knows she stood by her man, but come time for judgment day she's gonna have to pay for leavin' her children out to dry. Mama said it's a shame a good woman like Miz Bess would be saddled with the likes of Mista Gus, bein' that she was a lady through and through. I kept my thoughts to myself on that score. She didn' drink a drop of alcohol and was kinder than three pews full of church ladies, so everybody thought. Mama would walk barefooted on broken glass for Miz Bess; but if there was a way she could avoid Mista Gus, she would take it even if she had to walk a mile outta her way. Mama could *not* abide that man.

Mista Gus filled up a room with his voice, his laugh, even his silence, and when he was crossed, he had a face on him would stop water freezin' in January. Miz Bess, on the other hand, was a little bird-like woman. She spoke soft and sweet, and hardly took up space atall 'cept when a thing didn't suit her. Then she could give even Mista Gus a run for his money. Mama said he burnt down the house he and Miz Bess was livin' in before so after his parents done died they could move into in the big house where he growed up. Miz Bess didn' want to live in the big house, but after he burnt the other house down, she didn' have much of a choice, folks said.

Appin was in Mista Gus's family since his great-granddaddy's time, and most folks that worked there was born on the place. The big house didn't look as big as it was. There was a porch wrappin' min'near 'round the whole house, covered in jasmine, climbin' roses, and honeysuckle vines. I 'spect it was the way you come on the porch that made the house look smaller than most the houses around. There weren't no big columns. It sat up on a slope with a brick walk lined with box bushes. Behind them was lilacs and crape myrtles. With all the vines and bushes you couldn't really see the house. Made it real cool in the summertime, and smelled sweeter than I 'spect even heaven in the spring.

Miz Bess liked to sit out on the screened in part of the porch in a rocking chair and read while Mista Gus played patience at a card table he made Cy set up right outside the floor-to-ceiling parlor window. Mista Gus could pretty much see all the goings on in the house without being seen his own self.

Sometimes Miz Bess had to take Mista Gus up to the Annex if he'd been drinkin' too much. The Annex was a house on the farm out near the dairy. Nobody much went near it 'cept Wilson and Cy, and then only when they was milkin'. Had its own drive, and unless you knowed different, you mighta not thought it was even part of the Stuart's place. Miz Bess'd stay up there with him and nurse 'im 'til he sobered up. Ever'body in the house had to pretend to Miz Ginny and her brothers that Mista Gus was off on a business trip and Miz Bess done gone along with him. But they couldn't keep that lie up forever, not with Miz Ginny askin' questions the way she did.

I don' rightly know what Mista Gus done to make a livin'. Miz Bess sho didn' let him outta her sight for long. Some men folk come up to the house on occasion and I heard tell Mista Gus had himself a business partner, but I didn' know what sorta business they was up to.

As far as Miz Ginny was concerned, I wasn't the only one thought she was pretty neither. That boy, called hisself CL—delivered the groceries from Sikes's Store—piled excuse on excuse to stay in the kitchen, hopin' to get a glimpse of her. It was right comical how he'd nod and wink at Miz Ginny when their paths crossed. She didn' pay him no mind. Annoyin' didn' go half way to describin' that boy. He was always givin' his opinion, no matter who was talkin' or what about. Mama shooed him away every chance she got and I can tell you he didn' take to that, no way. He finally struck up a friendship with Mista Dennis. Them two was trouble looking for a reason to be mean. I, for one, was glad when

Mista Dennis went off ta school and CL didn' have as much reason to hang around. His head still spun like a whirligig ever' time he step foot in the kitchen, thinkin', I suppose, he might catch a peek at Miz Ginny.

All dem Stuart boys was a handful. I know that the two oldest ones was sent off to school and summer camp. Mista Dennis, he stayed at home, along with Miz Ginny. That is, 'til he gots himself into a heap of trouble with that no count delivery boy CL. I know'd Mista Gus told Mista Dennis any number of times to stay way from that devil CL, but Mista Dennis didn' listen none. Every chance he'd get, if CL wasn' mooning around after Miz Ginny, Mista Dennis would hightail it off to the store and wait 'til CL was done with his chores. Then the two of them would get up to the most awful mischief. I heard tell once they'd built theyselves a big fire and tossed in gunnysacks filled with kittens and stray cats, laughin' like fools. That did it for Miz Bess. She had enough, and was ready to send Mista Dennis off. Roberta say she heard tell that CL and Mista Dennis didn't just burn cats. She say them two did some terrible, terrible things to a boy that lived over near Mama's and then tried to burn him up so nobody know, but I ain't never heard from anyone else 'bout such a thing. One thing I do know shortly after Roberta told me her tale Mista Gus done sent Mista Dennis off to some kinda school for special children. Shoulda been *reform* school, you ask me. And Mista Gus say CL ain't never to step foot on his place again. CL didn't pay it much mind. He still did the deliverin' for the store. I 'spect he did his share of keepin' outta Mista Gus' way, even so.

Miz Ginny was alone most of the time. Her daddy doted on that child and you could even say he watched her like a hawk. I heard him say more than once he never, ever goin' to send his little girl away. Miz Bess, I heard tell, thought Miz Ginny ought to be sent to school up north, but Mista Gus wouldn' hear none of it. I 'spect Miz Bess wasn' all that crazy about sharing Mista Gus with nobody; including his own chil'ren.

As ornery as he was, Mista Gus was good enough to the peoples who worked for him, if you didn' mind the show he was always putting on. He paid pretty good, and was regular about it. Mama got a whole day off ever' other week, besides a half day weekly.

We'd line up, at least the household help did, every Friday and Mista Gus handed each one of us our pay. We'd stretch out a hand and he'd put our money in it and we'd smile and say, "Thank ya, Mista Gus."

And he'd say, "Thank *you*." Then he'd call each of us by our name. He did that ever' single Friday except when he'd been drinking. Miz Bess would give the money to ol' Black Sam those times and Black Sam'd do the same.

Black Sam and Mista Gus was about the same age, though I reckon Black Sam musta been just a hair older. Black Sam's mama nursed Mista Gus when he was a baby, and she took care of him until the day she died. Black Sam didn' do much. He'd got the bad arthritis, and mostly he just filled in when Mista Gus had been drinkin'. Black Sam's son, Wilson, and his grandson, Cy, did most of the work on the farm. Don' make much sense to me why they call him Black Sam. He weren't much darker than me, and his grandson, Cy, could pass for white easy wit' no questions asked. But the old folks had some ways that no amount of thinking could make sense of, so most times I didn' even try. But it did cause a body to wonder.

Miz Pansy, she used to be Miz Ginny's nursemaid. After Miz Ginny was grown, Miz Pansy helped wit' the cleanin' and laundry. I used to hear Mama and her talk 'bout how if Miz Ginny was one of them's daughters she wouldn' feel like sittin' down for a week after sassin' back to her mother the way she did. Miz Bess didn' seem to have no notion about how to raise a child. It's a shame, too, 'cause Miz Ginny had a real sweet side to her if somebody woulda just made her mind. The shame is there weren' nobody to do it: Miz Bess couldn' and Mista Gus wouldn'.

I'd been working in the kitchen with Mama off and on 'bout two years. One morning Mama hollered, "Ethel, get on out an' look for Cy. Tell 'im I wants 'im in he'ah now!" She was wavin' a spoon, lookin' to beat the band like she was goin' to make somebody pay. I knew better than to ask her any questions. "I'd 'spect he be in de pony barn mucking out, but he might be out with Wilson. I needs him right away. So you go'on an' get ta lookin'."

"Yes'm, I'm goin' right now." I wasn' payin' attention and let the screen door bang shut behind me.

"Ethel, how many times does I's haft tells ya?" I shuddered as I turned to look. She was standin' in the door lookin' like she was gonna throw that spoon and wasn' plannin' on missin' neither. "You bet' not be doin' dat agin!" she said.

"Yes'm." I took off toward the barn in a dead run, wonderin' what had gotten her so riled up. I was just glad I was the one doin' the lookin' and Cy was who she wanted.

It being summer time, I was barefooted. I don't 'spect I made a sound when I ran down the aisle of the horse barn and out into the small log barn in the back where Miz Ginny's ponies was. It was more like a shed than a barn, but then Mista Gus, he liked ta give a thing a name. So it was called the pony barn by all and sundry.

As I ran in, I saw two folks at the other end of the barn, but I couldn't tell who they was. Sunlight was streamin' in so bright, I stood inside the door catchin' my breath and givin' my eyes a chance to adjust. I couldn' see much, but I could tell them two folks was kissin'. One of 'em sure looked like Cy. I'd learned a long time before interruptin' somebody kissin' could get you in a heap of trouble. I slipped back outside the door and hollered, "Cy, where is you? Mama wants ya in da kitchen *right now*. Cy, ya in he'ah?"

Then I pretended to come in the door and ran right smack into Cy. He jockeyed with me to keep me from comin' into the shed. I seen Miz Ginny was leadin' her pony out the far door.

"Mornin', Miz Ginny," I said. She didn't pay me no mind atall. She climbed on that pony and trotted off toward the far field. I commenced to deliver Mama's message to Cy. He took off to the big house at a good trot hisself. I stood and watched Miz Ginny ridin'. Always so perfect—and there she sat on that pony with straw danglin' in her hair. I bet she wonderin' to beat the devil what I's goin' to do or say 'bout it. This here couldn' stand. Cy was too good a boy, too much like a brother to me for me to let him get hisself killed over no white girl. I shoulda knowed right then this day was all topsy-turvy. Nothing happenin' as it oughta; everything outta kilter.

What with my uneasy feelings about Cy, and Mama's mad bear mood, I took my own sweet time gettin' back to the house. I kicked at dried mud clods in the road and daydreamed 'bout what it would be like to be in love. I lay down in the shade of a hibiscus clump with my hands behind my head and stared up at the white summer sky. I couldn' help tremblin' when I thought of what'd happen to Cy if he got found out. The pitchur of him beat up and bleedin' kept creepin' into my mind. I couldn' shake it. I got up and went on to the house. I had to step out of the way 'fore that devil CL run me over comin' down the path with a toothpick hangin' out his mouth and sneer on his ugly puss, he looked me dead in the eye and didn't give up no ground atal. God amighty, I hated to think what woulda happened if he seen what I'd just seen.

Mama looked up from her cookin' when I walked in, but she didn' say a thing 'bout me takin' so long to get back. I pitched in, tryin' my best not to think 'bout what I seen. It musta been two hundred degrees in that kitchen. I stood over the cook stove boiling eggs. The afternoon was hummin' along 'bout as usual.

Then Wilson come runnin' in the house. "Miz Bess, Miz Bess! Bertha, where Miz Bess?"

"What de matter wit' you, fool, hollerin' like that?" Mama snapped.

"Where Miz Bess? Des been an accident down by the river. Mista Gus's car...Call a doctah."

Mama looked at me, "Go'n git Miz Bess. She on the porch I think. Tell her I needs 'er. Then you take Miz Ginny upstairs and you stay wit' her. We sho' don't need her getting' all worked up. Oh, an' tell Pansy to get on down he'ah. Imma need all the help I can get." She wiped her hands on her apron.

When she turned and seen Wilson still standin' idle, she boomed out, "Wilson, git on back there an' see what you can do! I'll call the doctah. I be right behind you wit' Miz Bess. Lorda mercy, man, stop yo' blubberin'!"

Wilson kept right on cryin'. He wiped his face with his hand, "Bertha," he said. "Daddy an' Cy's in dat car wit'em."

Mama looked at me. "What you standin' there for? Git on outta here an' do what I tol' ya."

The crystals on the candlesticks in the dinin' room set to jinglin' as I ran through the swingin' kitchen door. I slowed down on the front porch so I wouldn' scare Miz Bess. I tapped on the open door and peeked out on the porch.

"'Scuse me, Miz Bess, Mama say she need you in the kitchen real bad. You gotta come quick."

Miz Bess looked up from her sewin' like I'd run up on her naked as a jaybird. "What?" she said. "Ethel, what is the matter with you?"

"Miz Bess, I's sorry but she say she wantin' ya, direc'ly. She say it's real important."

Miz Bess pursed her lips and stood up. She set her sewin' in the basket and started for the kitchen. Mama had already come as far as the dinin' room. I heard them whisperin' and then Miz Bess let out a gasp. The crystals commenced a terrible racket, and I heard Mama and Miz Bess go in the kitchen. I stole a look at Miz Ginny in the parlor. She was workin' on one of her jigsaw puzzles. I went in. She cocked her head at me, and then studied the puzzle.

"What's so important that my mother has to run to Bertha's beck and call?" she asked. She glided one of them pieces over the puzzle not lookin' up. I stood there dumb. She fitted the piece where it should go then looked at me hard. "I asked you a question, girl. What is going on?" All I could do was shrug. I don' remember when I felt a bigger fool. Here I was, a good year older than Miz Ginny, and I couldn' find nothin' to say. Her blue eyes felt like they was borin' holes in me. She'd combed her blonde hair out of her face with her fingers. Right then, I hated myself. I never felt so ugly. Miz Ginny was tall, pretty, slim, and cream white. I was short, plump, nappy headed, with brown skin and freckles. I couldn' think of nothin' to say to her.

"Miz Ginny, you don' know where Miz Pansy is at, do ya?"

"Why in the world would you think I'd know where Pansy would be?" she asked. "Probably sitting upstairs with her feet propped up in the guest room. That's usually where she hides. Why?"

"Oh nothin', I jest wondered is all. You wouldn' wanna help me find her, would ya?"

"Are you out of our mind? Why in God's name would I want to do anything with you?"

I was makin' a mess of this. I couldn' see my way clear how to do what Mama tol' me. How was I supposed to get this smart alecky girl off her backside and up the stairs out of the way, and find Miz Pansy to boot? The good Lord musta been smilin' down on me 'cause jus' about then I heard Miz Pansy hummin' a tune. She was dustin' the banister. I ran into the hall and motioned her to come down the steps.

"Girl, you crazy, wantin' me to come down there?" she said. "If you got somethin' to say to me, say it, 'cause I ain't got no time to be runnin' up and down these stairs for the likes of you."

"Miz Pansy, Mama say she need you in the kitchen. She say if she ain't there, she be along directly. You 'pose to wait for 'er."

"Since when Bertha tell me what to do? I be there directly. You go on an' tell 'er."

I ran up the steps to where she was workin'. "They's trouble," I whispered. I was out of breath and excited, but I told her all I knew. She dropped her dust rag and bustled her big self down the stairs and off in the direction of the kitchen.

Miz Ginny was standin' in the doorway of the parlor, watchin' me. "Damnation, Ethel, you tell me what is going on right now." Bein' so scared myself, I couldn' tell if it was fire or fear in them blue eyes.

"Miz Ginny, you needs to come up here with me right now." I marched up the stairs with as much authority as I could manage, prayin' that she would follow. I stopped on a step and looked over my shoulder. Thank the good Lord, there she was. "I gotta talk with you and I don' want no one hearin' what I gotta say," I said.

I marched to the head of the stairs and took a right turn and stepped on into her room as if it was my very own. When she come in after me I said, "Shut the do'. You and me's gotta talk." I patted the pink bedspread across from where I stood. "Sit down on this here bed." I was surprised she wasn't putting on any of her high and mighty ways—she looked for all the world like a scolded puppy. She sat right down where I had just patted my hand and waited. I sat down next to her.

It probably was only a few moments, but it seemed like my whole life had passed when Miz Ginny finally said something.

"You saw us didn't you? Ethel, promise me you won't tell." She had tears in them big eyes, looking as scared as a hare caught in a snare. "Please, Daddy would kill me. You don't have any idea."

"Miz Ginny, I got mo' idea of it than you know. But yo' daddy won' kill you, he'll kill Cy, and skin 'im 'fore he do. I can promise you that."

"I love him and he loves me."

I shook my head, just lettin' it hang there, rockin' back and forth; thinkin' about what kind of mess I done got myself in. And that slip of a white girl sittin' next to me with no more sense 'bout the world than that bed she was sittin' on.

"Lord have mercy," I said. "You ain't got no more idea what love is than my left shoe." I looked down and seen I was barefooted. She did too and we both sorta laughed. "Lord, Miz Ginny, if you loves that boy you best be leavin' him alone. I'm tellin' you dey still string colored men up around here for touchin' white women. You ain't doin' him no favors lovin' him, if that's what you wanna call it." Miz Ginny was cryin'. Her shoulders shook as she sat on that bed lookin' like I done kicked her good.

"But Cy looks as white as I do."

"Yes'm, he might do, but he ain't, and ev'rybody 'round these parts know it. He gon' be lyin' in his grave wit' you to thank in no time if'n you keep up like you was today. Ya'll lucky it was me that come lookin' this mornin'. Anybody else and they woulda called out the dogs."

The last ice in her seemed to melt away and she near collapsed. She throwed herself at me and wrapped her long arms round my shoulders. She started up bawlin' like I never heard. "What am I going to do, Ethel? We weren't hurting anybody. He loves me, too. I just know he does."

I sat there with that girl draped over me thinkin' to myself, *That damn fool Cy oughta know better*. Cy was Mama's sister's boy, and after she passed, Mama took him in. Cy and I was the same age; he had been living with us since as long back as I could remember. Mama told him, more times than I can count, he best be keeping his hands to hisself with all his girl cousins round, and don't be trying to charm her or no body else with them spirituals he was always singing.

One day Mama sat us all down—Cy, too—and told us how you get babies. Cy started up singing and she cut him a hard look. "I can't help it. De jest bubble up," he said, with that quick smile of his that would melt butter on a cold day. Then she say she better not be gettin' no baby surprises from the likes of us. She was lookin' Cy square in the face when she said it, too. Weren't too many peoples that wanted that look more than about once.

"Miz Ginny, it ain't none of my bid'ness what you and Cy be up ta. But I loves him like a brother my ownself and I gots ta know if'n ya been at more than jest kissin'."

She looked like I done throwed hot milk at her. "Kissing, that's all. Ethel, what kind of girl do you think I am?" She sat up straight and started takin' on some of her high and mightiness again.

Well, Miz Ginny, I thought, but didn't have the courage to say, *that's 'xactly what I'm tryin' to figure out.*

"Ethel," she said, like she had just snapped out of a trance, "You didn't get Mother out of the way so that you could talk with me about Cy. What's going on?"

Chapter 4

———

Sallee

Sometimes Ethel would take us children with her on her errands. Those trips occurred when my mother had made plans to be out and there was no one to leave us with; or she was feeling blue and didn't want us around. So Ethel would suggest that she had an errand to do, and couldn't we come with her? We'd always take the bus since Ethel couldn't drive. Few adventures were more alluring than riding the bus to Ethel's appointments.

One Friday afternoon a few days before school started, Ethel was scheduled to have her half day off. But my mother suddenly asked her to stay, saying she had something important to do away from the house. Ethel told her that she couldn't because she had a dentist appointment that afternoon, but she could take us with her. My mother hemmed and hawed then finally gave her permission.

In preparation for our adventure, Ethel gathered all her possessions: her purse, her sweater—despite the blistering heat—her hat, and her ubiquitous brown shopping bag. She walked from the house with the folded bag tucked under her arm, her purse dangling, and Helen planted high up on her ample hip. She instructed Gordy to hold my hand, and then grabbed my other hand. As we left the yard she said, "Gordy, don' you let go of 'er hand no matter what. If'n I gotta let go, you hol' tight, ya hear?" Gordy nodded and squeezed my hand harder. I did my best to shake free. Before we'd even gotten to the bus stop at the corner in front of our house, Ethel stopped twice: once to adjust Helen, her purse, and her bag, and again to ask Gordy and me, "Does I have to git a switch?"

"He's squeezing my hand too hard," I whined.

"But Ethel told me to," Gordy protested, his face screwed up with earnest responsibility.

"Honey, jest hold 'er hand an' don' let go. Now hurry on, here's de bus."

Like a monstrous green and yellow dragon spewing diesel fumes, the bus hissed to a stop in front of us. Its enormous doors sprang open, revealing steps. A uniformed driver at the wheel peered down at us.

"How did it know we wanted it to stop, Ethel?" I asked, mesmerized by the vehicle's enormity.

"Cuz it's a bus stop," she said. I didn't think that was much of an explanation since I'd often watched from the house as bus after bus drove up and down the road never stopping. But I let the subject drop. I'd learned that even with Ethel questions sometimes weren't worth pursuing, and you could never tell which ones they might be until it was already too late. I learned that the hard way the time I asked her how Lil' Early could be her grandson when she didn't have any children of her own.

"He be Big Early's son's boy," she said.

"How come Big Early has a son and he's not yours, too?"

"Big Early was married befo'."

Then I went one question too far. I had heard my mother say that Big Early and Ethel were only married *in common-law*. I had no idea what the phrase meant, but I remembered it, so I said, "Common-law, like you and Big Early?"

"What you know 'bout dat?" Ethel shot back, giving me a cross look that ended my questions.

Boarding the bus proved to be awkward. Ethel, juggling Helen and her purse on one arm, let go of my hand to pay the bus driver. The driver had a mean look on his face like he didn't like us. I glared at him. He kept putting his foot on the brake pedal then taking it off so the bus jumped and bounced as Ethel tried to pay him. I was going to help, but Gordy took it upon himself to be my sole protector while Ethel was otherwise occupied. After we had a small skirmish at the head of the steps out of Ethel's line of sight, I wrested my hand from Gordy and tripped to the vacant seat at the back of the bus. Gordy trailed after me doing his best to follow Ethel's orders.

"Leave me alone," I hissed. "I can't get lost on the bus. There's no one on it but us anyway." With the fare paid, Ethel plodded down the aisle then plopped herself breathlessly down next to me. She placed Helen on her other side. She sat there on the wide back seat, legs splayed, fanning herself with her brown bag, sweat pouring down her face.

As the bus rattled and lurched its way downtown, Gordy and I stood on the seat and waved at the drivers following us. The honk of a car horn or the friendly wave of a hand through the great cloud of black diesel exhaust behind us provoked squeals of delight. We stopped several times to pick up passengers along the way. Just before our stop, Ethel said, "Gordy, reach up there an' grab hold'a that cord. Give it a yank." With great self-importance, Gordy climbed up on the seat and grasped the cord. A little bell down near the driver rang and rang. "Let it go, boy," Ethel directed. I could see the driver scowling at Ethel in his big mirror.

The stop was across the street from Ethel's dentist's office, a worn red brick house with a crooked roof next door to the taxi office. Ethel gathered up her belongings, including Helen. I scampered ahead down the aisle toward the front of the bus, Gordy following. The back door swished open. Ethel stood at the top of the steps, jostling her load. "Com'on now, you two, git back here," she said. Several passengers stood up between us, blocking the way.

As Gordy and I were swept toward the front door, he clung to my hand so tightly my fingers turned white. "Cut it out," I said, trying to loosen his grip. "You're hurting me." As we stepped down, we were greeted by an out of breath Ethel who'd already made her way from the rear exit up the sidewalk to us. She glared at the bus driver as if he were solely responsible for our being separated from her. She helped Gordy and me down to the curb. The driver flashed us a nasty smile as he shut the door and the bus roared off in a cloud of fumes.

"Let go a'me," I said, shaking Gordy's sweaty hand from mine.

"Honey, you hol' his hand, now. We gotta cross the street right chere. Now," she said. She grabbed my free hand and proceeded across the street, dragging me like the tail of a kite.

From what I could see, Ethel's dentist must have lived in his office. The building looked like someone's house. It had a crusty porch that was as lopsided as the roof, barely clinging to the front of the red brick structure. The gray floorboards were scarred and rotten. They looked as if they'd been gnawed on.

"Sit on the stoop an' don' let me catch you off it when I git back," Ethel instructed us.

Gordy and I perched on the edge of the porch and dangled our legs over the side. Ethel disappeared with Helen into the darkness of the office. Every so often we could see someone peering out the door glass to check on us. We watched from the porch as people walked by. Only if a passerby called out, "Morning," would we say hello.

The taxi office next door offered up considerable interest. Drivers sat behind the steering wheels of their cabs with the windows rolled down, talking to a man inside the office. He was smoking cigarettes and complaining about the heat. When he wasn't reporting about how much he could drink or who he saw somebody out with last night, he was answering the phone then shouting destinations and instructions out the window. After a driver received an address from the man in the office, he'd pull away in his cab. But there didn't seem to be any pattern. One cab and driver sat idle the whole time we were watching from the porch, while another, which had just pulled up, left moments after the man shouted an address out the window.

I moved over and stood up in the weeds just off the porch. Gordy, his pale eyes filled with concern, warned, "You better get back here before Ethel catches you." I slouched back onto the porch and scowled at my older, wiser brother. But his advice was good. Just then Ethel emerged from the door with Helen.

As we walked downtown, Ethel released my hand and let me skip ahead with Gordy, giving a cautionary grunt if we ventured too far ahead. I had to tug on Gordy to get him to do much skipping, but after a while he acquiesced. We skipped along as high and as fast as our overseer behind us would allow.

Our next stop was a tiny office with a large metal and glass door. Big white letters read, "Public Finance Company." Metal venetian blinds covered the windows like aluminum foil: all dull, dirty, and bent at the edges. My mother said venetian blinds were tacky, but I liked them. I'd play with them whenever I got the chance, snapping the slats up and down to cast ribbons of sun and shadow over a room. I was wise enough to gather that the blinds in the public finance office were off-limits to children. Ethel grunted as she pushed open the big door to the office.

There was a man in a shortsleeved shirt and a greasy tie sitting behind a massive ugly, gray desk that bisected the room. The fabric of his shirt was so thin you could see his sleeveless undershirt through it. Two gray metal chairs sat on our side of the desk. There were magazines scattered haphazardly on the windowsill along with a couple of dusty looking plants. Gordy and I stood in front of the desk beside Ethel. She set Helen down and pulled out a frayed little book, just like the little books my daddy had. He called them our "saving accounts." Ethel's book was wrapped in a rubber band. She also pulled out her change purse and took out some money. After removing the rubber band, she handed the book and her money to the man. He unfolded the money, counted it, and then wrote something in Ethel's book. He picked up a stamp from his desk, smacked it down on a big black pad, and stamped the book at a precise spot. As he returned it to Ethel, his thin mustache twitched like a horse's back when a fly lands. There was an ugly black stain on the edge of his hand from the inkpad. He placed the money in a drawer. Ethel carefully rewound the rubber band around the book and said something pleasant to the man. They both laughed, though he didn't look like he thought it was funny.

Even though the room was so small that you could sling a cat from one end of the room to the other, the man pretended not to notice that the door was proving to be problematic for us to open. Ethel had her arms full of Helen and her belongings. Gordy and I weren't big enough; try as we might, we didn't have the heft to move it. Ethel tried to pull the door without disgorging herself of her load, but she couldn't. She put Helen in a chair, pulled the door open, instructed Gordy to hold it, picked Helen up again, grabbed my hand, and went through, checking herself to make sure she had everything she came with. As we emerged, Gordy stood still as a post, holding the door. She told him to come along, muttering and fussing as we walked down the street.

Then a friend of Ethel's spotted us. "How ya doin', Miz Ethel?" the woman said. "Is them Mr. Mackey's chil'ren? Mighty fine lookin', they is! Ya keepin' pretty good? Hot, ain't it?" Ethel held Helen on her hip as she chatted. Whenever Gordy and I ventured farther down the sidewalk than she thought we should, she'd grunt in midsentence to call us back. Before long, we were on our way again. The bus stop was in front of the bakery, and this was always our last errand. No trip downtown was complete without a cookie for the four of us to share on the bus ride home.

As we looked over the counter, mulling over just which cookie to buy, Mrs. Dabney walked into the shop. "Hey, Miz Dabney," I said, skipping over to her. "Are you gonna be riding the bus, too?"

"Well, what a surprise," Mrs. Dabney said. She smiled and patted me on the head, then ordered a half dozen dinner rolls. "My darling little neighbor children, what brings you down this way?"

I heard the bus hiss to a stop, and then Ethel hustled us outside with barely a glance in Mrs. Dabney's direction. Mrs. Dabney waved to me as she came out of the shop and the bus door smacked closed behind us.

A week or two later it had, thankfully, cooled off a bit. While Ethel made mayonnaise, I watched with my head nestled in the crook of my arm and my legs swinging lazily up against the chair legs. "Was it 'cause my granddaddy gave her the locket? Did he git to decide whose picture is in it? Was he the boss of everything?"

"What you talkin' 'bout?" she asked as she worked the mayonnaise churn up and down.

"Momma told me that she put Cy's picture in her locket. You know Cy what took care of Momma's horses, True Love and Puddin'?"

Ethel chuckled. "Whew wee, I bet them was some fireworks," she said. "Ol' Mista Stuart would have been righ' smart hard on Miz Ginny 'bout that had he known. Miz Ginny was hiz prize n' joy. He spoilt that child rottn'."

"That's why she thinks he's so great?" I asked.

"Yea, honey, that man thought the sun rose an setted on yo' mama. Ya know she was his only girl. Mista Gordon and Mista Jimmy worried yo' granddaddy and Miz Bess sick with the shenanigan day gots up ta. And Mista Dennis, he weren't never right in the head, po' soul."

"Why was he mean to Granny Bess?"

"Who was mean to Miz Bess?"

"Granddaddy."

"Who say he was?"

"I don't know. She lived in that little house. He didn't give her his big one when he died. That's mean, isn't it?"

"He'd done lost all his money."

"Why?"

"He was a drunk," she said, finishing the mayonnaise. She put it away in the cupboard and walked over to the sink to peel eggs. "Befo' the accident he used to hole up in the Annex on a drankin' binge. Nobody'd see 'im fo' weeks, 'cept Miz Bess. She'd tend 'im and you'd hear him yellin' an' cussin' clear down to the kitchen. After a while he'd give it up. You know—clean hisself up an' go on 'bout his bid'ness. Then somethin' would set 'im off again. I don't 'spect ya can hang on to yo' money an' keep that kinda livin' up fo' long," she said philosophically.

"What accident? I never heard about any accident."

"Never you mind, girl…just talking through my hat, thas all. Go'n out and play, now." She said as she bustled a bit more than was her nature.

"What's for dinner?" I asked as I slipped out of the chair while gravel crunched in the drive. I slunk off to the window to check; sure enough my mother was just getting out of the car.

Later that day Ethel took a rare afternoon off. That left us at home with my mother. I found her alone in the sitting room playing solitaire.

"Don't you have to go riding today?" I should have known better than to have asked, but I wasn't thinking.

"Ethel had something she had to do at the last minute and she couldn't find a sitter." She rolled her eyes and sighed, sounding exasperated.

"Oh, you wanna play war?" I asked as I looked for another deck of cards.

"Sallee, it is—*want to.* The question you are asking is: Do I want to play war?" She looked at me intensely as if her look could somehow make me speak properly. Then she acquiesced, "If you'd like," she gathered the cards up into a deck. "How do we play?"

"You cut the deck in half if you don't have two decks, and give me one, and you put down a card and then I put down a card and the highest one wins. If they are the same then you spell 'war', and then the highest one wins."

"Who taught you how to play this game?" she asked as she handed me half of the deck.

"Daddy taught me and Gordy."

"Gordy and me," she corrected.

"Daddy taught Gordy and me. We play it with him all the time. Do you want to play?" I turned a card over and looked up at her expectantly as I rested my chin on my arm.

She placed a king on my six. I asked, "Didn't you play this with Granny Bess when you was little?"

"You were," she corrected. "No, Mother didn't play cards."

"I was what?" I looked at her quizzically, then shrugged and continued. "Did you play with Granddaddy then?"

She shook her head, "He only played bridge and solitaire. Not games for children."

"Two twos," I exclaimed, "this is when you spell w-a-r and ... don't turn 'um over, you put'm upside down like this." I slipped three cards off the stack in front of me and arranged the cards face down, carefully stair stepping them just as I had seen my father do, then waited while my mother followed suit.

"My brothers played cards with each other, but not with my father. My parents didn't play games with their children." Her perfect red nails clicked on the table as she placed each card down exactly as I did.

"Now you turn this one over. I win!" I shrieked as I struggled to gather up my winnings. In my triumph, I carelessly picked up my line of questioning again. "At least not when they was in the Attic, right?" As soon as I said it, I could have kicked myself. I had just broken Ethel's unspoken law. I braced myself for the reaction.

"What? Attic what are you...? Is it over?" she asked as she went to gather up all the cards. Her gold bracelets jingled while her long elegant nails clicked on the cards; her movement was at once both graceful and tense.

"No, we still have lots of cards." Relieved, I let out a long slow breath. "See," I pointed to our stacks. "Did you have any friends in the neighborhood you could play with?"

"We didn't live in a neighborhood. We lived on a farm. Daddy had a good friend who lived on the next farm over. He had a daughter ten years older than me. She wasn't much of a playmate."

"Ethel lived there, didn't she? You coulda played with her."

"Ethel's mother, Bertha, had worked for my parents for some years in the kitchen. I didn't know Bertha like you know Ethel now. It was different then. All I remember of her was that she had a kind voice..." My mother's voice trailed off as she played with the edges of the cards I dealt her, looking thoughtful. Finally, she continued, "I don't remember meeting Ethel until just before I married your father. When she was a child, she worked at a boarding house. Later on she worked for another family, and then she came to work for your father and me."

"I thought..." I started and then remembered that it was Ethel who told me "...uhh that you um played—that you and Ethel were friends like Lil' Early and me."

"I never played with Ethel. Where would you have heard such a thing?"

"I guess I just thought it up," I lied knowing that Ethel told me that she had known my mother since she was a young girl.

After a double war that she won, my mother scooped up all of the cards and dealt out a game of solitaire. "Why don't you go outside and play with your brother and sister?"

"It's raining."

"Well then don't go outside."

I left the room as the cards clicked on the table.

Before everything changed, my mother spent most of the day at luncheons or meetings or horseback riding with friends. Whatever she did took her away for most of the late morning and afternoon, and just before our dinnertime she would rush into the house, race upstairs and change into a pretty dress. She must have taken a bath first, but I don't know how she had time. She always smelled sweet and flowery. Her gold bracelets jangled on her arm, and her lipstick was freshly applied like she was going to a party. It must have taken some serious time, but it seemed like magic. Her soft blonde hair would be done up in a chignon; pearls encircled her long graceful neck. One minute she was in a suit or riding clothes and then, as if her fairy godmother had waved a wand, she was all dressed up. She would greet my father in a cloud of sweet perfume with a drink and a kiss as he came in the door.

Usually, he entered with one, if not all three of us in tow. We would wrap ourselves around his legs and stand on his feet. He'd heave us all in the door while wondering out loud why it was so hard to walk. A favorite thing for us to do was to wait for him at the bottom of the driveway. As soon as his big, black Cadillac pulled into the drive, he'd throw open the door. We'd clamber onto the doorjamb, oftentimes before the car came to a full stop. He would hold us tightly while he slowly drove up to the house with the door wide open. The tiny breeze felt like wind as it whipped through my hair. Knowing how forbidden this would be if my mother knew heightened every sensation. I gazed up into the bright blue sky as I leaned against my father's strong sure arm, arching my back and pointing one foot as I had seen an aerialist do at the circus. As we came in the front door, my mother shooed us away like flies. "Run along, children. Your daddy's tired. I'm sure your dinner is about ready."

Sighing, he hung his jacket over the dining room armchair.

"Go on now, do what your mother says," he said, patting one of us on the backside.

My mother called into the kitchen. "Ethel, Mr. Joe is home," as the two of them disappeared into the living room.

Ethel, wiping her hands on her apron, ushered us upstairs where she stripped us down and started our baths. More often than not, she would bathe all three of us at the same time. All lined up in the claw foot tub, we

waited our turn to get scrubbed, rinsed, dried and dressed before return-
ing to the kitchen to eat our dinner. After dinner, we trooped into the
living room to kiss our parents goodnight.

Stuart managed almost every night to get home just before dinner
was on the table. I felt sorry for her because she had to eat in the dining room with Daddy and our mother. She'd slip out as soon as she
could, sometimes in tears, go up to her room and close the world out.
Sometimes Daddy would go up afterward and they'd talk, but I never
knew what about. I think she would have happily stayed downstairs if my
mother weren't around. They couldn't say a word to each other that the
other one wouldn't jump on. It seemed the more Stuart grew up, the
less she had to say to any of us.

Not that it took much in those days, but it seemed like everytime
Daddy went up to talk with Stuart afterwards my mother and he would
get into a big fight. Doors slammed and sometimes I could hear glass and
china smash against the wall. One morning we came down for breakfast
and Ethel was cleaning plaster out of the sink and her big black skillet
was covered in paint and plaster chips. "The shouting and cursing was
flat out terrible last night." I said. She didn't say anything but stopped
what she was doing and bent down and hugged me tight.

"I didn't hear anything." Helen mumbled with her mouth full of
thumb.

Ethel let me go and patted Helen on the head. "Honey, go on and sit
down. Ethel gonna make you some hot chocolate with marshmellows.
How 'bout that?"

"I had to put my pillow over my head and pray that they wouldn't kill
each other last night." I said. "I just hate it when they do that."

"I know, darlin'." Ethel said shaking her head, "I know."

Chapter 5

"Have any plans today?" Daddy asked my mother as they sat at the breakfast table reading the newspaper. I was playing at being a waitress and clearing the table.

"No, I hear it's going to be hot, so I thought I'd stay home and enjoy that new air conditioner. Why? Do you have something in mind?" She folded her paper and placed it neatly by her plate. "Sallee, tell Ethel we'd like some more coffee, please. Oh, excuse me, I meant to say, Miss, may we have some more coffee?" She looked at Daddy to confirm.

He shook his head. "None for me, but I'd like the check, please." He winked at me.

As I left the dining room with their plates, I heard Daddy say, "I thought we could take the children for a picnic up to Crabtree Falls. I remember how much you used to love hiking there. It ought to be much cooler in the mountains."

I put the plates down by the sink with a loud clatter. "Ethel, Mama wants some more coffee!" I shouted, turning on my heels as quickly as I was able. I was half way out the door when Ethel's head shot up from her task. "Mind them dishes!" she said. "Where you goin' so licktey split? Ain't you gon' to carry your mama her coffee? You can pour it like a real waitress do, from the pot."

"No, I gotta go." I danced from one foot to the other.

"Well, you can take it when you get back from the baffroom. Don't forget to wash yo' hands."

"Will you do it?" I didn't wait for an answer. I rushed from the kitchen. I had to find Gordy and tell him the news.

As I passed the dining room, I heard my mother say, "Oh, it's much too hot for me to go." I stopped dead in my tracks. "But why don't you, if you want? I'll stay home with Helen. She's still too young for that hike. Ethel can make the three of you a picnic before she takes the rest of the day off."

"She's already working on it," he said. "I asked her first thing."

I gave a delighted little hop. Taking two steps at a time all the way to the third floor, I was gasping in deep gulps by the time I reached Gordy's room. *Not here, darn. Where could he be?* I wondered out loud. I slid down the bannister, ran around the second floor landing, and slid down the main bannister to the front hall. Gordy came running out of the dining room and met me as I slid to a stop. "Guess what?" he shouted. "We're going on a picnic to Crabtree Falls!"

"I know," I said, bouncing up and down like the red ball on that television show, *Sing A-long with Mitch*.

"Settle down, you two," Daddy said as he walked out to the hall. "You need to get ready. Put on old clothes and tennis shoes." As I turned to go back upstairs, I heard my mother talking softly to Helen. She was sitting in her lap with her thumb stuck squarely in her mouth. Big tears ran down her face.

"Don't you worry," my mother cooed. "We'll do something special, too. I promise."

Minutes later Gordy flopped himself on my bed dressed in a pair of tight shorts and a T-shirt that barely covered his belly button. "Too bad for Helen, huh?" he said. "Bet she'll have to take a nap most of the day."

Helen and my mother waved goodbye from the front door. I felt guilty about Helen's misfortune for about as long as it took me to reach the car. Gordy raced ahead and then ran back to help Daddy with the picnic hamper. "It's all right, son, I've got this. You get in the car."

Mr. Dabney banged out onto his porch. He waved to me then sat down in a chair and stared at us like he was watching *Leave It to Beaver* on TV. I waved back. Daddy nodded first toward Mr. Dabney then for me to get into the car.

"I'll go get Lance," Gordy volunteered. He yelled frenetically, "Here Lance, here boy, here," over and over as he ran to the kitchen porch to get the leash.

"Gordy, come back," Daddy called. "We can't take the dog." Gordy and Lance trotted around from the other side of the house.

"Aw shucks, why?" Gordy whined. Lance cavorted up to the car, barking and wagging his tail.

"Remember the last time? He ended up in Greene County."

"But..." Gordy's glee was instantly dashed. He rubbed Lance's broad head. "Sorry, buddy. You can't come," he said then crawled onto the front seat next to me. He swung the car door closed. "Stay, Lance. You hear?" The big dog sat down with his back legs splayed out then he flopped to the ground with a grunt and began to pant.

Daddy climbed in behind the wheel and reached across me to rub Gordy on the head. "It's better this way, son. You know how he is when he catches a scent." Daddy started the engine and patted Gordy again, this time on the knee. "When he puts that head down and starts baying, he's gone for who knows how long. He's a bloodhound, son. It's what they do."

"Sure, but..." Gordy started.

"Remember how upset you got when we couldn't find him? And we had to leave cuz it was getting dark? Remember you cried?" I added.

"Did not!" he retorted.

"Did too," I said.

"Enough!" Daddy bellowed. Then, just as loudly, he started singing "There's a Hole in the Bucket."

An hour later Daddy pulled off onto the side of the road and stopped the car. "That Henry must be really dumb," I said.

Daddy shoved the gearshift lever into park and opened the door. "Who's Henry?" he asked as he got out of the car. "Coming this way?" he asked with a tilt of his head.

I scooted over the seat to the driver's side and hopped out onto the gravel. "Henry in the song. Why didn't he just fix the bucket? He could've carried water in something other than the bucket, like his hands. I don't think he needed Liza to tell him all that unless he was just plain dumb."

Daddy tousled my hair and laughed as he pulled the picnic basket from the trunk of the car. "That head of yours doesn't stop spinning, does it?" he chuckled. He put the basket on the ground with a grunt. "Ethel must've thought we'd be gone for a week. This thing weighs a ton. How 'bout we walk to the stream and eat? Then we'll hike on up to the falls. We can have a swim when we get there. Here Gordy, you take this blanket."

Soon we were spreading the blanket on a warm rock, pulling fried chicken, potato salad, deviled eggs, and cherry tomatoes from the hamper along with a thermos of lemonade, and forks, plates and napkins. Daddy whistled. "Ethel sure can pack a mean picnic," he said.

"She sure can," Gordy concurred, stuffing chicken in his mouth. He had a smear of deviled egg on his lip.

Daddy sat, leaning against a tree trunk with one knee up, eating slowly and watching as Gordy and I scarfed down our food. He held a chicken leg loosely in his fingers, his right hand draped causally over his bent knee. Smiling, relaxed in his madras shirt and khaki shorts, Daddy looked like a man in an ad on television.

With cookie crumbs flying from his mouth, Gordy said, "Race you to that rock over there."

"I'm too full," I groaned. I lay down with my head on Daddy's outstretched leg. "I wish I hadn't eaten so much. Ugh, I'm never going to eat again, ever," I complained as I spread my hands over my stomach.

"Ever?" Daddy asked with a laugh. He laid his hand lightly on my shoulder. "Take a little rest. We don't have any place to go—plenty of time."

The last thing I heard was Gordy complaining, "Oh no, she's not going to sleep, is she?" I drifted off.

When I awoke, Daddy and Gordy were both asleep. I stared up into the trees towering overhead and thought it might be the very best day ever. I slipped in and out of daydreams, wriggling to get more comfortable. I thought about how Daddy's laugh made me feel good, like Ethel's laugh. Not like my mother's. I never knew with her. Daddy laughed when he thought something was funny and he never laughed at me.

I saw Daddy was looking down at me and smiling. "Daddy?" I smiled back., "Do you love me?"

"What do you think, you goose?"

"I think you do," I said.

"I think you think right."

"Will you love me no matter what?" I asked.

"Of course, forever; no matter what. Scout's honor." He held up two fingers. "Are you planning on doing something dreadful any minute, or do I have time to steel myself for it?" He laughed and moved to get up, poking Gordy with the toe of his sneaker. "Come on, buddy! We've got a date with a waterfall."

As we climbed, Gordy and I must have taken thirty steps to Daddy's one; we ran ahead, then back to him to show off whatever treasure we'd discovered. We galloped over fallen branches like ponies, and ran down to the icy stream, splashing our faces with water, and then scampered back up to the trail. By the time the climb grew steep, we had worn ourselves out and trudged behind Daddy like pack mules, huffing and puffing; sweat streaming down our faces.

Gordy stopped. "Come on, slow poke," I said.

"Do you hear?" Gordy shouted. "The falls, do you hear?"

"I might be able to if you'd quit yelling!" Daddy stopped too and we all listened.

"It must be pretty close," Gordy said. "At least, I hope so."

"It's a while still, Gordy. Do you need some help?" Daddy reached for Gordy's hand and began to tug him up the hill.

"Me, too!" I shouted and stuck out my hand.

When we finally made it to the falls Daddy was dripping with sweat. Water cascaded down shelves of rock and pounded the stones in the pool below. Even the air around the falls was cooler.

"That water is going to feel pretty good," Daddy said, letting go of our hands. "Race you in!" Daddy splashed into the pool, still wearing his clothes and sneakers. Gordy and I followed right behind him even though we had bathing suits on under our clothing. The icy water took my breath. Undaunted, we jumped in and out of the pool until we had scrapes on our knees from crawling over the rocks. In minutes, my teeth were chattering and my fingers were blue. To escape the cold water, Gordy and I began to scout around in the ferns near the falls looking for snakes.

"You two might give up looking for snakes, especially there," Daddy said. "They'll be up in the rocks, sunning." Gordy immediately scampered toward a pile of boulders outside the shade of the trees. "Don't you go up on those rocks, Gordy," Daddy warned. "There might be rattlesnakes up there!"

Of course Gordy kept on going. "Cool! Rattlesnakes!" he shouted.

Daddy leapt from the rock where he and I were sitting and latched onto Gordy like a hawk on a mouse. He snatched him so quickly I hardly knew what had happened.

"Son, I said don't go up there!" Daddy looked scared, but not nearly as scared as Gordy who'd had the wind knocked out of him. "If a big rattler bit you, no more than you weigh, you'd be dead before I could even get you to the car," Daddy said. He hugged Gordy close.

"Daddy, there weren't any snakes," Gordy whimpered when he finally got his breath back. "I just thought it would be cool to see one."

"Way to go, Gordy," I said. "Way to be stupid."

"Now both of you listen," Daddy said. "Snakes up here are nothing to be playing with. They're big and they're dangerous. So watch out."

"Can we go home, Daddy?" I asked. "I'm cold and hungry."

"Hungry? Weren't you just saying you were never going to eat again?" Daddy asked with a laugh.

Certain a deadly rattlesnake lurked at each and every step, I watched the trail down from the falls as carefully as a mother watches her newborn. My soggy clothes clung to my skin, clammy and cold. "I wish I'd just worn my bathing suit. My clothes are all icky," I complained.

"Well, take them off," Daddy said.

"And walk down the mountain naked?"

"No, silly, you have a bathing suit on, don't you?"

"Oh yeah." I whipped off my shirt and shorts and my skin started to feel much better.

"Duh," Gordy said, swinging his damp T-shirt over his head like a lasso. "Don't say I'm the one that's *stupid*."

Gordy and I slept as Daddy drove us home.

My mother was reading in the sitting room as we clamored in. Helen was nowhere to be seen. "Shh, you'll wake Helen, if not the dead," she hushed us. "Looks like you had fun. You're certainly dirty enough."

"Yes, we had quite a trek," Daddy said. He carried the picnic basket into the kitchen.

My mother kissed us like we had a disease, hardly touching our cheeks. "Now go on upstairs and clean up, then you can tell me all about it."

As we climbed the stairs, Gordy poked me. "See, I told you."

"What? Told me what?"

"That Helen would be taking a nap most of the day."

I shrugged. "Guess you did. Too bad she couldn't come with us." I pulled a handful of pebbles I'd collected along the trail from my pocket. "Look at this. I think this is glass; rocks don't come in this color blue." Gordy pulled a handful from his pocket, and we sat down at the top of the stairs admiring our treasure.

"What ya doin'?" Helen asked.

"Where'd you come from?" I said. Gordy began stuffing rocks in his pockets so Helen wouldn't see them.

"I was sleeping. Did you have fun?"

"Yeah, we did!" Gordy gushed. "The waterfall was so loud, and the water was cold, and there were rattlesnakes and cool rocks."

"Rattlesnakes?" Helen looked stricken.

"Well, we didn't see any, but they were there and if one bit Gordy he'd have been dead before Daddy could get him…" I trailed off when I saw the look of horror on Helen's face. "No snakes," I added lamely.

"They were there; we just didn't see 'em. But they saw us. You can bet on it," Gordy insisted. I glowered at him, willing him to shut up.

"What did you do?" I asked Helen. Now it was Gordy's turn to glower.

"She slept," he mouthed over Helen's head, "like I told you before. Shut up."

"I went out to lunch and then shopping with Mama," Helen said. "We went to Timberlake's Drug Store. You know, where they make those really good milkshakes? I had a chocolate milkshake and a grilled cheese."

"Wow, a whole one?" I asked. She nodded yes. "Then what?"

"You drank a whole milkshake?" Gordy asked, letting out a slow whistle.

"Yep. Then we went to that jewelry store with the creaky wood floors and the green rock with the lines in it. Mama bought some pretty gold earrings. She said if I was good she'd buy me something when we got to Tilmen's. I asked her if I was really, really good, would she buy me two things? She said she would. So I was quiet as could be and didn't whine or suck my thumb the whole time. Look!"

Helen pulled her trophy from behind her back: a beautiful Barbie with a dark ponytail dressed as a bride. "See?" she beamed. "A Barbie! And pop beads, too." She held out her arm so we could admire her new pearl-like bracelet.

While I was happy that Helen hadn't spent the day in bed, I was overwhelmed with jealousy and anger. A Barbie! I had only seen one on television. A real Barbie. I knew I had to have one.

"Can I see?" I asked. Helen held the doll up for me to admire, but didn't give it to me. "Can I hold it?" I made a grab for the doll.

"Barbie says she wants to stay with me," Helen said. She stepped back, holding the Barbie to her chest.

"What's the big deal?" Gordy asked. "It's just a dumb doll." He removed the stones from his pockets and eyed my bottle blue stone with the same greedy look I'd fixed on Helen's doll.

"I just want to see," I whined. Helen extended her arms again, holding her doll up for visual inspection. "Hold her, I mean. Oh come on, Helen—just for a minute."

"No!" she announced flatly. "Play with your own." She marched down the stairs with Barbie securely in tow.

"I don't have one," I wailed.

My mother called up from the sitting room. "Sallee! Gordy! You two hurry and get cleaned up so you can come down and tell me about your day. I can't wait to hear."

Gordy and I stood up. "Guess you weren't so right after all," I sneered.

"So what?" he said, toying with the smooth blue stone. He casually lifted it in front of my face. "Do you want this?" he asked. He sounded as though he'd just as soon throw it away.

"No," I snarled. "I don't want any of them. You can have them all."

Gordy took off down the hall before I had the chance to change my mind, leaving me alone to sulk. All thoughts of a wonderful day with Daddy were sullied by my single-minded desire to get my hands on that doll. I turned on the water in the shower. "Helen didn't even know what a Barbie was," I grumbled to myself. "She's too young for one, anyway. Little brat." I stepped out of my clothes and wriggled out of my bathing suit leaving them in a damp heap on the floor. I stepped into the shower. As the warm water ran over me, I made myself more and more miserable.

By the time I'd dressed and gone downstairs, I couldn't think of one good thing that had happened that day. While Gordy spoke volumes about the fascinating things we'd encountered on our adventure, I sat glumly silent with my head in my hand, glaring in Helen's direction.

"How about you, Sallee? Didn't you have fun?" my mother asked.

"Yeah—I mean, yes. I guess it was fun."

"What's the matter, darling? Do you feel all right?"

"Tired, I guess."

"Well, if you're tired," Daddy said, walking into the room, "then you slept too much. You had two really good naps today." He picked me up and sat in the chair where I had been moping and plopped me down in his lap. I smiled despite my foul mood.

"And what's this about you *guess* you had fun?" He wiggled my leg like he was testing to see if it worked. "I distinctly remember you swinging from vines, shrieking like Tarzan, or was that some other little girl?"

I snatched my leg away. "Stop it!" I whimpered.

He felt my forehead. "She doesn't have a temperature," he said.

My mother shrugged. "Helen, tell everybody what *we* did today," she said.

"She already did," I snarled.

"We went to the toy department at Tilmen's and I got a dolly," Helen said. She held the doll up for Daddy to see.

"Very nice, a bride," he said.

My mother said, "I was so touched by this sweet little girl."

My eyes rolled. *Please,* I thought. *Ol' goody goody Helen.*

"Helen said to me, 'Mama, I only want a doll if Sallee can have one, too.' So I bought you one too, Sallee."

"We got you the Barbie with blonde hair cuz I knew you'd like it better," Helen added. "And we got *you* a big box of Lincoln Logs, Gordy!" She was beaming.

"Well, how about that little sugar plum sister of yours, Sallee?" Daddy asked. He leaned over and kissed Helen on the head, and then wrapped his other arm around her.

"Whattya got to say?" he asked as he jiggled my foot with his knee.

Chapter 6

On evenings when my parents entertained, we children had to go to each guest and say, "Hello," and shake the person's hand. Each time my mother would say, as if I were completely stupid, "Sallee, look at Mrs. So-and-so when you speak to her." I wouldn't, mostly because I thought Mrs. So-and-so would be able to see in my eyes how much I hated this little charade. So, I would look just over the person's shoulder, just beyond their ear at something on the wall so that I looked like I was looking at them. Sometimes I would sneak a peek at some of the peoples' eyes and I could tell they knew what I was up to, but my mother fell for it every time. She'd say, "That's better." As soon as everybody said how much we had grown since the last time they had seen us, we were whisked off to bed. Helen and I would sometimes watch Ethel leave from our bedroom window. She'd climb into that rusted Easter-egg-green pickup that her husband, Big Early, drove, and they'd disappear down the drive.

I asked her one day, "Why don't you live with us?"

"Lord, honey! I gotta milk ol' Janice an' Mattie, an' slop the hogs when I gets home. They can't dos for theyselves."

"Couldn't Big Early do that? Couldn't he milk the cows and stuff?"

"And who'd take care o' him? Who'd cook 'n clean and do for him?"

"Can't he take care of hisself?" I asked.

"Chile, that man works hard as ten men! He need me to help 'im."

"But Ethel, I needs you, too. He's big." Ethel took me in her arms and leaned her head on the top of mine. She held me like that for the longest time. It would have been all right with me if she never let me go.

For a good while after I turned eight, Ethel had her grandson, Lil' Early, living with her. On Saturdays, she would bring him to work with her. Only after I grew up did I realize that she didn't bring him to play with us, but to work, because she had nowhere else to take him. Nevertheless, for us it was like a holiday when he came along with Ethel. On Saturday mornings I started sitting by the window hoping to see Lil' Early skipping along next to Ethel as she came up the drive. Gordy and Lil' Early were the same age, although Lil' Early seemed years older to me. He had the best ideas for things to do: climbing trees and jumping out of them into leaf piles, digging to China in the sandbox, and having races around the house or the garden or up the driveway. Rarely did we find ourselves bored on Saturdays when Ethel brought Lil' Early with her.

One particular fall day, leaves covered our entire front lawn. Lil' Early said, "Git a rake and less rake up the leaves." A rake couldn't be found fast enough. Gordy, Helen, and I fell over each other trying to find one. None of us had ever had a rake in our hands, so naturally we waited for Lil' Early to tell us what to do with it and how to do it. He took the rake and pulled it through the russet leaves, clearing winding paths. We were then instructed to find a wagon.

"Helen, go git the wagon," Gordy barked. Lance raised his eyebrows to check that all was in order, and then lumbered over for a closer look.

The blue wagon Helen returned with had almost rusted through from disuse. That afternoon Lil' Early turned it into an Indy car. He flipped the black handle back into the wagon and told us, "Git in the wagon." He went around to the back and pushed us around making roaring car sounds. Holding on to the handle, Gordy sat in the wagon and steered down the green paths through the leaves.

We took turns pushing each other, making more and more elaborate paths. Each time we created a new course there'd be a chorus of, "It's my turn!" The pushers supplied the sounds of roaring engines and squealing tires. Lance played the part of other racecars zipping around us, barking as we shrieked with joy. Whenever we crashed, ol' Lance would bay in his deepest voice then bark at us as we said, "Come on, let's do it again!"

"Would you push me, Lil' Early, and make those motor noises for me? Make the crash sound—you're better at it than I am," I begged. The ensuing pileups left us sprawling, gasping, and laughing in the leaves. Helen, wise beyond her four years, played the starter. She waved an old checkered dishtowel purloined from the kitchen at the start and finish of each race and every pileup.

We played so late in the day that Stanley the yardman showed up while we were still romping around. He just laughed and sat down. He lit a cigarette and watched us play until an oldish rust colored car that was parked across the street suddenly roared to life. It looked like there were three men in it. As it screeched around the turn, one of them yelled what sounded like a threat. All I heard was "nigger." As I looked up, I saw a man in the backseat shake his fist in our direction. Stanley didn't seem to pay it much mind, but we did and were glad to hear Ethel call us. "You kids git inside now and let Stanley do his work," she hollered from the front porch as she stood outside the big front door with her hands on her hips and her dishcloth tucked into her apron. We obeyed in a hurry, and Stanley set about raking over our paths and turning them into neat little piles for removal.

"Golly," Gordy said as we hustled into the house.

"Yeah, that was really scary," I said. All heads nodded in unison. "Should we tell Ethel?"

"I don't think so," Gordy whispered.

We didn't tell her, but we talked about it for weeks afterward. I couldn't shake the feeling that I had seen that car before. All of us had been shaken to our shoes and none of us had any idea why.

Saturdays always flew by with Lil' Early. It seemed like we'd just had breakfast when we'd all be called in for lunch. We all crowded into the powder room to wash up for lunch. Once while washing her hands in the sink with Lil' Early, Helen took the soap he offered. She commented matter-of-factly to him, "You'll never get those hands clean." He looked at his hands, shrugged, and skipped off to the kitchen for lunch along with the rest of us.

"You dummy," I whispered to her, "his hands aren't dirty."

She shrugged. "They looked dirty ta me," she said, putting her thumb in her mouth and leaving the room.

Later the next spring, after Lil' Early had been coming with Ethel almost every Saturday, I passed by the telephone in the back hall on my way outside to play in the yard. My mother was on the phone. It was easy to tell that she was upset about something. Her voice had that high pitch that it got when she was trying not to be mad, but it was pretty clear to me she was failing. I held back a little—tucking myself into the pantry—to see if I could hear who she was talking to. I only caught the name Alice before a maternal glare ushered me out the door, which I left slightly ajar. On the back porch, I strained to hear the conversation. It wasn't often that my mother lost her temper with someone other than us, and it seemed to me that she was on the verge. The novelty of watching a full-blown show of temper that didn't impact me directly was too enticing to walk away from. I perched myself on the back porch— situating my butt on the edge of the wrought iron chaise as quietly as I could manage while the springs groaned beneath me.

Stuart came home from a friend's house just then and gave me a queer look. I put my finger to my lips, silently begging her not to give me away. She rolled her eyes, stepped over Lance's sleeping form, and slipped in the back door. My mother's voice ceased suddenly and didn't start up again until Stuart's footsteps could be heard on the stairs. I held my breath the whole time, waiting for Stuart to tell on me. Once I heard the creak of the top stair, a wave of relief and gratitude washed over me: it might just have been indifference, but sometimes Stuart could surprise you with little acts of mercy.

"I'm sorry you feel that way." The icy tone in my mother's voice made me flinch. Whoever she was talking to had done something bad; something really bad.

"I will not! I wouldn't think of it. Frankly, Alice, I am surprised at this. I would have thought as president of the League of Women Voters you would have a different view." There was a long silence. "It most certainly is appropriate—my children will play—excuse me—as I was saying before…"

Hearing "my children" catapulted me out of the chaise and up against the screen door, holding my breath. What had we done? It must be our back next door neighbor, Alice Giles. I racked my brain trying to think of what we might have done to cause my mother and Mrs. Giles to have a fight.

"I'm sorry that you feel that way. Good day." I was so caught up in trying to figure out what had happened and who had done it that when my mother opened the backdoor I was still standing up against the screen door. "Sallee, were you eavesdropping?"

"No, ma'am, I wasn't eardropping."

"Eavesdropping, not eardropping," she corrected. "I've told you before that it is impolite to listen to other people's conversations. I mean it. Don't let me catch you doing it again."

I assured her that she wouldn't and I meant it. I made a mental note to get better at sneaking around. I sure wasn't going to give up listening. It was the one of the few ways I could find anything out.

"Was that Mrs. Giles you were talking to?" I asked, surprised at my boldness. My mother nodded that it was. "Did we do sumpin' wrong?"

"The word is 'something.' You say 'something.'" She pressed her tongue up against her top front teeth, emphasizing the "th" sound.

"Did we do something wrong?"

"No," was all the answer I got. "What did I just tell you, Miss? Go out, play, and stop listening at the door, young lady."

Pushing wasn't going to get me anywhere, so I made it look like I was doing as I was told and skipped off to find Gordy, Early, and Helen. The three of them were playing on the swing set not far from the wall that separated our house from the Giles's. Having spied them, I had to jump up and down waving frantically to get their attention. I didn't want to make noise in case Mrs. Giles was lurking about. I indicated with a big wide sweep of my arm that they need to come quickly. All three jumped off the swings like paratroopers and ran toward me with Lance trotting behind them. I filled them in as we carefully made our way toward the kitchen porch. I led the charge until I remembered that I had just promised myself to get better at sneaking around, so I fell behind and let the others lead the way. We figured that my mother would be talking to Ethel as she always did when someone upset her. We were right.

An enormous bush that Ethel used as a source for switches was right up against the house by the kitchen porch. Our house had an English basement, making the kitchen porch almost an entire story off the ground. The bush, with its big branches, not only offered us cover, but also made it possible to be within easy earshot of any conversations taking place in the kitchen. Tiny, pearl-shaped blossoms in the spring gave rise to the shrub's name, the pearl bush. We sat in our pearl bush and listened as my mother reacted to the conversation she had with our neighbor.

"I cannot believe the gall of that woman. How dare she presume to tell me whom my children may or may not play with!"

We all looked at each other in amazement.

"Who are we playing with?" Gordy asked, his brows furrowed in confusion.

"Shhhh, you're gonna get me in trouble," I said.

"Ethel, I just do not understand what has gotten into people," my mother's voice wafted through the kitchen window.

"Thas all right, Miz Ginny, I jus' won' bring 'im no mo'."

"Of course you will. No busybody do-gooder is going to tell me what's right or wrong. You and I both know she is wrong, and that is all there is to it. Lil' Early is more than welcome to come play with the children."

The only sound in the pearl bush was the buzzing of bees as we—four wide-eyed children—collectively held our breaths and stared at each other.

Staying home from school when I was sick had the added bonus of giving me an entire day with Ethel. I made up all kinds of ailments. After shattering a thermometer on a light bulb, fevers were no longer a plausible symptom. I relied heavily on headaches until I found stomachaches to be more effective; they were harder to confirm. On any given morning, I writhed around in bed complaining of phantom pains in my gut. After I convinced my mother that I was ill, I would lie in bed listening for the quiet that settled on the house after everyone left. It was my first sign that it was safe to leave my bed. If my mother's car were still in the drive, I had to wait until I heard Ethel singing before I could open my door. The strains of "Rock of Ages" had miraculous restorative powers. My appetite returned; my pale face brightened. I was even able to drag myself to the kitchen where I would instantly be fully healed and eager to chat.

"I knew you was gon' be down here soon," she chuckled. "But if'n you keep it up, ya gonna be behind in school. Ain't a good idea to miss too much, Miz So-sick."

"School's dumb. I'm not gonna miss anything. We do the same thing all the time anyway. Didn't you think school was dumb when you went?" I asked. I pulled out my chair and slumped into it. Ethel turned away from the big kitchen sink while wiping the frying pan with an oil-soaked rag. As the toast popped out of the toaster, she put the pan down on the stove.

"Nope, I loved school. I only went 'til I was 'bout old as Gordy is. Den I went to work in the boardin' house."

"You musta been really smart to be able to get a job when you was as old as Gordy. He couldn't get a job if his life depended on it," I said as I heaped strawberry jam on the buttered toast Ethel had handed me.

"No honey, it wasn't bout bein' smart. It was 'bout bein' able to eat. I had to go to work. Momma had too many mouths to feed for me to stay in school. You is lucky an' you should 'preciate that you can goes to school; not have ta work hard." She scraped scrambled eggs onto my plate and returned to the sink to wash the pan.

"Did you make a lot of money?"

"I made a nickel a day washin' dishes and I was glad to git it, too."

I pushed the eggs around my plate half wishing I had gone to school. The tooth fairy had recently come and left me twice Ethel's boarding house wages for doing nothing more than pushing out a baby tooth.

"Did all your friends work, too?"

"The onliest friends I had was my sisters. We didn't have time back then to be makin' friends. We worked from morning 'til night most ev'ry day." She was standing in the middle of the kitchen with her hands on her hips.

"Did you have a better job than they did? I'd be proud of myself if I had a job. I bet Alberta wished she could have worked at the boarding house like you. I know if I had a job Gordy would wish he could have one just like mine. Were they jealous of you?"

"Honey, you ain't got no notion of what it was like to be po'. Havin' a job and working hard ain't nothin' you know nothin' about. Ya can't help it; it was jest the way you was born. I was proud that I could help my mama put food on the table. And even then there was folks who had less than we did, and some of them was fools that didn't do nothin' all the livelong day. Mama would give up food to help those no-accounts. Used to burn me up good."

"Yeah, I know. There's a girl at school who wears hand-me-downs from her cousin and her shoes have holes in them. She's not very nice. My friend Faye said she was a no-account. I don't like her either." I was trying to understand what Ethel was talking about and to connect any way I could. If there was one thing I knew, it was that snobbery was a linchpin of our particular brand of southern culture. You were nobody if you weren't better than somebody.

Ethel clucked disapprovingly. "Honey, that ain't no reason ta not like somebody, 'em not being as well-off as you."

I'd stepped in it again, so I sought to defend myself with the third highest authority I could reference, after Ethel and my father. "But Mama says all the time that the Dabneys next door are not our kind of people. That I shouldn't go over there. I should leave them alone. She even pretends sometimes she doesn't hear Mr. Dabney call hello. Isn't it because they don't have as much money as we do? And their clothes are old? Isn't that why you didn't like those fools that Bertha gave food to?"

"No darlin', that ain't why. It was cuz they didn't do nothin' to help themselves that I didn't like 'em."

I sighed, frustrated with the injustice of Ethel correcting me. Truth was, Ethel was every bit as much of a snob as was my mother. I knew she didn't like Mr. Dabney anymore than my mother did and in one of our talks, I had asked Ethel about my uncle's houseman. "Why does Leon have gold teeth with little diamond sparkles?"

"'Cuz he low-count people, and they don' know nothin' 'bout nothin'," she'd sniffed. Her lip had curled slightly, the way it always did when my Uncle Gordon's name was mentioned. I got the impression she not only didn't approve of Leon, but that she didn't approve of my uncle either—just like with Mr. Dabney she never said so in words. One of the things I learned early on was that people didn't always say everything they thought, and they didn't mean everything they said. Even when Uncle Gordon would come into the kitchen after a party or dinner and give Ethel some money folded over a couple of times like he always did, she had that look. She would smile and say, "Thank ya, Mista Gordon," but I could tell she didn't like him.

"You don't think much of Uncle Gordon, do ya?" I asked.

Ethel picked up a brown bag, poured something out of it into her usual splatterware mug, and took a big drink. "Why on earth would you axe such a thang?" she said.

"Cuz you look at Uncle Gordy the same way Mama looks at Mr. Dabney, and I know she doesn't think much of him."

"No darlin'...you know, you ask mo' questions than a school full o' chil'ren. Lord have mercy! Now, you go on. I got work to do and I gotta get it done befo' yo mama get back."

Chapter 7

Ethel
1929

That day in Miz Ginny's bedroom I did my level best not to answer her directly. I got up and pulled the dust cloth from outta my apron string and made like I was dustin' as I stole a peek out the window ever now and again. I ain't no storyteller, and for the life of me I couldn' come up with no answer that would satisfy both Mama and Miz Ginny.

"You done made me promise not to tell nobody what I saw today. Well, I'm gonna keep that promise, but you got to do the same fo' me. I'm gonna tell you what's goin' on, but ya gotta promise me to stay right chere afta I do. Ya promise?"

Miz Ginny nodded yes. Before I could get the word "accident" out, she had thrown open the do' and was headin' down the stairs at a gallop. I did the best I could to keep up—no mean trick, considerin' how much longer her legs was than mine.

"Miz Ginny, ya promised," I wailed, breathin' hard. The screen door bounced on the hard rubber ball that Mista Gus had Wilson put on it not two weeks ago to keep the door from making a racket when it was let loose. That thud made a racket in my head as I imagined the beating I was gonna get from Mama when she found out what I had done. "Miz Ginny, wait," I called after her. She was runnin' lickety-split down the drive almost out of sight. I followed, puffin' like an old steam engine.

Around the bend where the river ran close to the drive they was a host of people and trucks, a tractor, a team of horses, and another of mules.

The yellin' and directin' made an awful din. CL was smack in the middle of the goin's on, laughin' and jokin' like he was at a hootenanny—actin' a fool. I spied Mama and Miz Bess over to the side wringin' their hands and lookin' every which way at once. One would be holdin' the other up and then be shiftin' so I couldn't tell who was holdin' who. Miz Ginny ran right up into the fray and almost got run over by a team of mules they'd hitched to the car tryin' to pry it loose from around the tree. Over near CL I could see a body lyin' on the ground covered with somethin'—a blanket, I think. I heard that no-account say to nobody in particular, "One shiftless old nigger ain't no loss." Then he laughed like he thought it was the funniest thing he ever heard. When I got closer I could tell from his shoes it was Sam lyin' under that blanket. Wilson was runnin' every which way looking for all the world like a man who done lost his mind. He seed Miz Ginny, and then he looked right at me as much as to say, git this here girl out my way afore I run her down. He looked mad with grief and fear. Then I remembered what he said in the kitchen: that Cy and Sam both was in the car with Mista Gus.

I grabbed Miz Ginny by the arm and pulled with all I was worth to git her outta the middle of the mess. "Ya come with me," I said, tryin' to put as much steel in my voice as Mama could. "Git on outta de way, girl. You ain't helpin' nobody." I believe if CL hadn't seen her and commenced to makin' his way over to us, I'd still be there pullin' on her. As it was, I still halfway dragged her over to where our mamas was huddled, proppin' each other up. It took most the afternoon afore they could git Mista Gus and Cy outta the car. We went back to the house when we heard they was gonna have to cut off Cy's leg to get'm free. About supper time, six men brought Mista Gus through the front do' and up the stairs to his room on a do' someone done pulled off a shed and made it up like a stretcher. The tired lookin' doctor trailed behind. All the men was covered in blood. I run up and down stairs I know a hundred times that night bringin' bandages, towels, sheets, water, and soap, while Miz Bess directed the goin's on like a field boss. Miz Pansy stayed with Miz Ginny in that very same room Miz Ginny and I had passed time in earlier. Finally, the sedative the doctor gave Miz Ginny took effect. Then Miz Pansy stepped and fetched as much as me. Mama was nowhere to be seen, and I didn't have the time to catch my breath, let alone ask where she was.

Plumb worn out, I fell asleep on the cot in the storeroom back of the kitchen without even botherin' to take off my filthy clothes. Miz Pansy shook me awake a few hours later. "Git on outta here, girl, I need to git off these feet. You best be gettin' on home. I 'spect they gon' need you. Tell yo' sister Roberta git on up here, an' you stay wit' yo' mama, hear?" I nodded. "Well then, move."

If I live forever, I don't expect I'll forget the dreadful sight at home. The room smelled of burned meat and blood. Mama looked a hundred and ten. Cy was lyin' in the middle of the room on a board held up by two sawhorses, his leg still bleedin'. There was no mistakin' that he was dyin', and Mama, by her look, weren't far behind 'im. Wilson, my sister Alberta said, had only just passed out from exhaustion. "Thank the Lord, too," she said. "He 'bout drove us all mad with his carryin' on." Then she added, a little more softly, "Poor soul lost his father and most likely Cy, too." She shook her head slowly back and forth.

"Miz Pansy say Ro best be gettin' up to the big house. They gon' need her 'fore long."

"Hmmph, we ain't no slaves! They jest gon' have to do wit'out," Roberta sniffed.

Alberta said, "We don' need to be runnin' 'round all the time fo' them, no way."

Roberta's face darkened like the sky befo' a storm. She nodded toward Cy. "You see this? Po' boy don' even rate no aspirin, and we s'posed to keep slavin' for them? Ya'll heard 'em, 'Here boy, bite down on this stick, we gonna take yo' leg off.'" She shook her head again, and her eyes lingered on Cy.

"Ro," I said, "you know good as me he was out cold when they cut off dat leg. Stop all the time lookin' at what you ain't got."

"I tell you what *you* ain't got," Alberta started in. "You ain't got the sense of a canary, and po' Mama ain't got no sleep and she 'bout worn out. She won' let nobody do nothin' for 'im, like she can keep the po' soul livin' on the strength of her will. *That*'s what you got, Ethel, but you ain't gonna have Mama or that boy, neither one, if we don' do somethin' for Mama quick."

"Ro, go on up to the big house," I said. "Find the doctor or Miz Bess and axe 'em if we can have one a 'em powders they give Miz Ginny. I'll see if I ken talk some sense into Mama while you gone." Roberta took off at a dead run.

"Mama," I said. "You got to try to rest." She wouldn' even look at me. Roberta was back in no time. "Miz Pansy was in the kitchen lookin' dead on her feet when I gots there. I told her I needed one a 'em powders like the doctor give Miz Ginny for Mama. She reached in her apron pocket and pulled out two packets and tol' me to put it in some warm water. She say, 'Tell Miz Bertha I say drink this, and if'n she don't listen, ya'll tell her I'm comin' down there my own self and makin' her.' Den she say, 'I best be gettin' back up ta da house cuz Miz Bess can hardly stand up herself.'"

It would've been easier to dose a mule than it was ta get Mama to take the powders Miz Pansy sent. Poor Cy died afore we could get anything down her. By then she was so spent she just laid her head down on that boy's chest and cried herself to sleep. Alberta took the sedatives and fell asleep soon as she stretched out. I tried my best to clean the place up a bit. Sam was laid out in the bedroom, so after a while I laid down on the floor next to Alberta and tried to rest.

The Stuart boys come back from camp, and with all the runnin' and fetchin' I had to do for them boys and Miz Bess, I didn't see Miz Ginny. Mista Gus didn't last a month before he was gone, too. I caught sight of Miz Ginny at the funeral. Then, at the end of the summer, she was sent off—along with her brothers—to a boardin' school up north, just like Miz Bess always wanted.

Things changed right smart after that. Mista Gus had been up to his eyeballs in debt, and when the Depression hit Miz Bess didn't have any choice but to sell off most of the farm. She rented out the Annex so the two older boys could go to the university, and let go all the help but Mama, who she kept on part-time since Miz Bess was livin' in an apartment in town. I heard Miz Ginny got a job at a shop in town and Mista Dennis disappeared after he left school. I went back to work for Miz Dupree at the boardin' house. I didn't hear much about Miz Ginny or her family except on the rare occasion when Mama would say somethin' she thought might interest me.

I stopped thinkin' about Cy and Miz Ginny and all that mess, and life seemed normal again; workin' and relaxin' with my sisters. Roberta, Alberta, and me use' to love to dance. Roberta was always goin' out with her boyfriends to juke joints and dances all 'round town. When we was together she'd teach us the latest steps she and Luther, or some other fool she hauled 'round by the nose, had come up with. Roberta was some kind of dancin' trick, and she loved nothin' more than to show off her moves. But it would have been easier to herd cats than for Alberta to get her legs and arms under any kind of control. What she lacked in rhythm she made up in frenzy. Roberta had more music in her toenail than Alberta did all together. The thing about Alberta, though, she didn't give a hoot what nobody thought, long as she was havin' some fun; and she did have some fun. Roberta would show us a step and Alberta would mimic her 'bout as well as a worm mimics a racehorse. It was comical. Thank the Lord I took after Roberta in the dancin' department. I truly loved to dance.

Just after Early and me took up with each other, we was at a juke joint down near the river. We'd been dancin' up a storm. The fact that Early liked to dance like I did was probably what put the icin' on the cake. That man could tear a rug *up*. After a while people stopped dancin' just to look. They was standin' 'round, tappin' their toes, and clappin' in time to the music. Early and me was dancin' the "black bottom." If you have any little bit of competition in yo' blood, the black bottom could wear you out. Early was feeling no pain and it made him bold. He'd dance a phrase, then slap himself on the hind parts and stamp and clap while I danced the same one. Then I'd do a new one of my own, tryin' to outdo his. The place was goin' wild as Early and me hopped, jumped, and gyrated all *over* that dance floor. When the music finally stopped, I had to get me some air.

Early went to fix us a drink and I stepped outside in the cool night air. People was pourin' out of the place, pattin' me on the back and tellin' me what a fine job I'd done. They said they ain't never seen any couple dance as good as me and Early. As the crowd thinned out, I noticed a white couple standin' over in the shadows. The girl took after somebody but I couldn't think who.

"Ethel, that was wonderful!" The girl clapped her hands together and gave a little hop as she stepped up closer to me. Her friend hovered a little ways behind. "I had no idea that you could dance like that!" she said.

"Miz Ginny? Is dat you?" I asked. "Lord, I wouldn't have known if you hadn't said somethin'. Look at how you done growed."

"Golly, Ethel, you'd think you were Mother's age the way you go on. There can't be much difference in our ages."

"I 'spect not. What ya'll doin' here? I bet Miz Bess don't know."

"And Bertha knows you're here?" She laughed and twirled around. Miz Ginny looked happy, and I was glad for that knowin' that the Stuarts had fallen on such hard times. "Ethel, I would love to be able to dance like that," she said. "Would you teach me?"

"Miz Ginny, I wouldn't even know where to begin. All I know is when the music starts, I can't keep my feets still. But Roberta, now, she be a mighty fine teacher. She done taught me near all I know 'bout dancin', and most other thangs besides."

"Come on, Ethel, I bet you could."

Now, I ain't never been able to say no to Miz Ginny. We had us a date to meet at Miz Bess's apartment that next Wednesday while Miz Bess was at her garden club meetin'.

"Make sure Miz Bess ain't gonna be there. I ain't even gonna try to imagine what kinda mad she'd be if she walked in and seen me teachin' you dis here jive." Miz Ginny giggled as she waved goodbye.

"Can't wait until Wednesday," she called as she and her beau disappeared into the night.

Outta nowhere that delivery boy CL come down the path. I don't know if he'd been sneakin' after Miz Ginny or sneakin' after me. He bumped right up against me jest after Miz Ginny left. With a curled lip he snarled, "Makin' sure that ol' bitch ain't home so's ya'll can steal her blind, I 'spect. Girl, you…" I turned tail and walked away like he weren't even there though I felt like somebody done walked on my grave..

Wednesday arrived soon enough. As I was comin' through the kitchen of Miz Bess's place, I ran straight into Mama.

"What yo' doin' here, girl?" she asked.

I hemmed and hawed and hemmed some more until Miz Ginny come into the kitchen. "Oh Lord, what are you doin' here, Bertha?" she asked.

"Well now, I's jest 'bout ta ask you what you was up to when dis here fool rounded the corner," Mama said, pointin' to me. Then she gave us both a good hard stare.

"I didn't know you worked for Mother on Wednesdays," Miz Ginny said, ignorin' Mama's question.

"Has been fo' da last three years," she said flatly. "I know it ain't none of my bid'ness what you be up ta, but dis here girl is mine, so I's gonna axe agin. What ya'll got cooked up?"

"Ethel is going to teach me how to do the black bottom," Miz Ginny said, like we was goin' to study Bible verses.

"Now, dis I gotta see," Mama said, and she followed as we made our way into the sittin' room. Miz Ginny had an old Victrola set up in the sittin' room and all the furniture pushed up against the walls. She had a Bessie Smith record that both Mama and me had a giggle over later.

Miz Ginny was a good deal better at pickin' up the dance moves than I thought she'd be. She was passable at copyin' me, but she couldn't, to save her life, do a move of her own. Mama sat cacklin' at us as we slapped our bottoms and hopped back and forth. I was tryin' to show Miz Ginny how to shimmy and both she and Mama 'bout fell out.

Mama said, "Honey, yo' ain't got nothin' to shimmy, and if Ethel gets ta shimmyin' much more, she might loose control of dem girls! Lord have mercy, where would we be then?"

Miz Ginny looked down at her little flat chest and then at my great big breasts going ever' which way, and she couldn't stop laughin'. Mama and me laughed about that dance lesson for years. And when we got through laughin' at what did happen, we'd start up again thinkin' on what would've happened if Miz Bess had come home.

After that Wednesday, a good few years passed before I heard anythin' at all about the Stuarts. Mista Jimmy did his level best to help out his mama. He went to North Carolina to sell her beach house and came back later with a fortune he had made in real estate, a wife, and a new name. He had grown from Mista Jimmy to Mista James.

After that, Miz Bess moved back to the Annex and Mama was hired again full time. I helped her fix Thanksgivin' dinner for the entire family; except Mista Dennis. Nobody had heard word one from him in eight years. Fact was, the family was feelin' rent apart in all directions, and it was hard to be thankful in those days. It had been a rough time for all of us.

I liked Mista Joe the minute I laid eyes on him. Tall, blond, and good-lookin', he could have passed for one of Miz Bess's own children. He had a real easy way 'bout him. He even could make Miz Bess laugh. All the years I'd known her I could count on one hand the times I heard Miz Bess laugh. Mama noticed, too.

Miz Ginny didn't seem to pay Mista Joe much mind at Thanksgivin' dinner; or so much as say a peep to anybody else, for that matter. She didn't even look at me as I passed the potatoes and vegetables. As far as I could tell, Mista Joe was just one of Mista Gordon's school friends and that was all there was to it. But anyone could see he was already head over heels crazy 'bout Miz Ginny. He made sure to sit next to her every chance he got. And even if they wasn't talkin', he was cuttin' looks her way.

Mista Joe didn't have any sense at all how thangs was done. When I was servin' round, he talked to me like I was sittin', eatin' with the family.

"Hi, I'm Joe," he said, takin' the bowl instead of allowin' me to serve him. He stuck out his hand to shake. "What's your name?" It made me so nervous, I liked to have dropped the bowl when he handed it back. When I didn't take his hand, he put it back in his lap. Round the table I saw every fork stopped somewhere between a plate and a mouth. They was slack-jawed, starin' at Mista Joe like he'd sprouted horns right smack in front of them.

"Ethel," I croaked. I moved on fast as I could.

After dinner Mista Joe came out in the kitchen to thank Mama and me just as we was havin' a little taste of the leftover wine. Quick as a jackrabbit, I dumped mine in the sink and acted like I was washin' up.

"Hi, I understand you're Bertha," he said to Mama, holdin' out his hand. "I'm Joe Mackey. That was the best Thanksgiving dinner I have ever had. Thank you so much. My mother isn't much of a cook, and I don't know when I've had so much good food." He took Mama's hand and shook it. She stood there lookin' at him, dumb as a post. Turning to me, he said, "Thank you, too, Ethel. I'm sorry I embarrassed you out there. I didn't know. I didn't grow up with servants." I kept both my hands in the sink so he wouldn't take hold of one of 'em and shake it like he did Mama's.

Mista Gordon called from the door, "Come on, Joe. We gotta get back."

As he left, Mista Joe turned back to us and waved. "I hope to see you both again soon, ladies." Then he said to Mista Gordon, "I can't go yet. I haven't had a minute to woo that beautiful sister of yours." They both laughed and disappeared behind the swinging door.

After the first of the year, I saw Mista Joe on my way home from work. He was walkin' down the street toward the boardin' house where I used to work. He looked like he was lookin' for somethin'. I wasn't too surprised to see him since lots of university students lived in the boardin' house; that was, until he spoke to me.

"Oh good, Ethel, I thought I was going to miss you again," he said.

I stood there looking at him like he was from the moon. Finally I blurted out, "Why you lookin' fo' me? I ain't done nothing!"

"Calm down. I just want your help with Ginny."

He tried to take both my hands in his, but I snatched them away and gave him a stern look. "My help? How'd you know where I'd be?" I crossed my arms and tucked my hands up under them.

"Your mother told me this was the way you walked home everyday, and about what time. I've been hoping to catch up with you for almost a month."

"Me?" I asked. "You been tryin' to catch up with me?" I looked at him like he was some kinda crazy, which I thought he was.

Mista Joe smiled. He musta understood what my look meant, because he said, "You think I'm crazy, right? Well, probably I am!" He laughed that real easy laugh the way he does. But I was still suspicious.

"Wha' kinda help you want from me?" I asked, checkin' over his shoulder for an escape route just in case he really *was* crazy.

"Would you like to go out and have a beer with me?" he said.

He was crazy all right. Crazy like a fox. I seen what he was lookin' for. "Uh…no, I cain't do that cuz I already got me a man." I looked at 'im steady so he'd understand he weren't gettin' nothin' from me. "Besides, I don't hold stock wit' that kinda foolishness."

"No, I'm not asking you out on a date, Ethel," he said and cleared his throat. "I just need your help. That's it. I swear."

"And where we goin' ta be havin' dis beer?"

"Well, if we were back in New York, we could go to a bar, but here… I guess I didn't think it through. We could go to my room. It's not far." He sounded so innocent, like a little boy. Then he threw his hands up, like he had a gun pointed at him. He crossed his heart. "I swear, Ethel, on my mother's grave, I only want to talk with you." He laughed that easy laugh. "I promise."

I could sure imagine what Mama would say, but I followed Mista Joe to his boardin' house and started up the steps. That beer sounded right good. And besides, he didn't look like he was going to try nothin'.

"I'm sorry yo' Mama died," I said. "You didn't say nothin' 'bout it at Thanksgivin'…musta happened pretty recent?"

"My mother's not dead. Why would you think…oh, on my mother's grave…that's just an expression."

I stopped on the landin' and looked at 'im hard. "Mista Joe," I said, "you can just tell me right chere what you got in mind 'cause I ain't goin' another step wit' a man who say his Mama dead when she ain't."

"Ethel, I'm sorry. It's an expression we use up north. Come on. I promise all of this is on the up and up." He held his door open for me. I went in, but I didn't take my coat off. He went back and forth across the room fetching two glasses and then the beer, and back again for the opener. "It's just that I'm at my wit's end with Ginny, and you know her ways…"

He handed me a glass and poured the beer. "And please stop calling me 'Mister Joe.' It's uncomfortable for me."

Humph, I thought, *uncomfortable for him.*

"Now looky, Mista Joe," I said. "I'm gonna call you what I'm 'spose' to call you, if'n you like it or not. Imma have one beer, listenin' to what ya got to say, an' then I'm goin' straight home."

"Here's the thing, Ethel," he said. "I'm crazy about Ginny and she won't give me the time of day. She acts like she's in a whole other world when I'm around. What do you think I could do to make her see how much…," he hesitated. I noticed red creepin' up around his ears. He had his head bent down, pickin' at his thumb. "How much I love her," he whispered. He looked surprised, like it mighta been the first time he'd said it out loud. Then all excited like, he axed, "Should I push or let things be? Do you think I should send her flowers? Candy? I feel like I'm only going to get one shot at winning her over, and I don't want to miss it. Ethel, what do you think? You know her." He looked at me like he thought I could just hand him the key to Miz Ginny's heart.

"Lord, Mista Joe, I ain't got no idea. I's sorry as I can be." I moved my untouched beer toward him, thinkin' I ain't earned it. I stood up to go. I sho couldn' stand lookin' at the disappointment in his face no longer than I had ta.

"Don't go," he said. "At least not until you finish your beer." He pushed it back toward me. I hesitated then sat back down. "I don't think I really expected you to have an answer. I'm sorry, Ethel. I…she has me turned so upside down. I don't know what I'm thinking." He ran his fingers through his hair, stood up, and then sat down again. "I feel like a damn fool. Truth be told, Ethel, I think I just wanted to talk with somebody who loves Ginny as much as I do." He settled back in his chair and took a pull on his beer. He didn't say anything more. We sat there a few more minutes, but I couldn't think of nothing to help him. I drained my glass and left.

As I walked home, I thought about Miz Ginny kissing Cy in the barn. Was that love? I wondered if Mista Joe had to work so hard to get Miz Ginny's attention, would or even could that be love. Mista Joe was a nice man, but what did nice have to do with love? I was pretty sure Early loved me, but did I love him? Was love the thing that makes you go all weak in the knees? Makes it so you can't think straight so you do stupid things like Cy did, or was it slow and steady? Damned if I could tell.

Love or not, about a year and half later, Mista Joe asked Miz Bess and Mista Gordon for Miz Ginny's hand. They was engaged to be married and was lookin' for someone to work for them. The weddin' was to be in November in Miz Bess's parlor.

Chapter 8

———

Sallee

As colorful and exotic as a trip downtown with Ethel was, a day usually turned into grim shades of gray when we were with my mother. Buying new school clothes always necessitated that we had to be dressed up, mind our manners, stay neat and tidy, be quiet, and generally have no fun. The thrill of pretty dresses and new shoes hardly matched the agony of shopping for them. And as divine as chocolate milk was, it didn't make up for being reminded a hundred times to sit up straight and "don't slurp." My mother didn't like to take us because, as she told Ethel, "They just won't mind me. I don't know why you would want to take them."

She herded us from the brand new five-story Miller and Rhoades to Waddell's shoe store, snapping at us like a collie dog after sheep when they get out of line. We couldn't even think about moving out of her sight; and forget about making any choice in what to buy.

"Mama, I hate these brown shoes. I won't wear them." I tried hard not to cry, but was failing miserably. "Please, can I have these?" I held up a pair of loafers like Stuart wore. "Please?"

"No!" she snapped while the salesman was in the back of the store looking for the right size for a pair of the shoes she had picked out for Gordy. "Your feet are still growing and you need lace up shoes. Stop whining and put the shoes on. Now." Her tone suggested that if I didn't do what she said I ran a high risk of being permanently mortified.

Gordy groaned when the salesman returned with the shoes in his size.

We were just there to try things on to see if they fit. If they fit, we had to get a bigger size. Helen cried, I whined, and Gordy insisted on going to the bathroom even though my mother said under no circumstances were we allowed to use a public toilet.

"But I gotta go," he insisted until she had no choice but to let him. We lurked around the men's room waiting for Gordy for ten minutes. When he finally came out, my mother grabbed him by the ear and hissed that he had better not have touched anything, and did he wash his hands? I was thinking, *How do you wash your hands and not touch anything?* I was about to ask the question when I thought better of it.

The idea of taking us to town was so loathsome to her that once she even said to Ethel, "Leave them with me. There is no reason for you to drag them along with you." On the other side of the door, we listened silently, but fervently prayed for Ethel to find a reason to take us with her.

Ethel answered, "No ma'am, I promised to take 'em to the movies."

Scuttling to get out of earshot in order to give full voice to our joy at the too-unreal-to-be-true delight almost put the trip itself in jeopardy. In our attempt to get outside as fast as possible, Helen was smashed against the doorjamb. She had a tendency to be a crybaby.

"I know it hurts, but please don't cry," Gordy pleaded. "We won't be able to go if you do. Please don't cry."

"Come on, it doesn't hurt that much," I said. "You're not even bleeding."

Helen's lips began to quiver. I grabbed her by the arm and pulled her outside. "Well, if you're gonna cry, at least do it where nobody can hear." Tears began rolling down her cheeks.

Gordy turned on me. "Would you shut up? Look, now she's cryin'" and we won't get to go. It's all your fault."

"My fault? You were the big dummy that ran into her." I pushed him. He pushed back.

Ethel came to the door and bellowed, "Gor-don, Sal-lee, Hell-eeen." Helen wiped her face with her sleeve. We appeared from around the corner as if nothing had happened.

"Ya'll git ready now. We gotta catch the bus. Hurry." She didn't have to say that twice. We were gone and back before she could round up her things. As the kitchen door closed behind us, we heard the bus coming up the road. Ethel was just too big to run. Try as she might, she couldn't propel herself and Helen to the bus stop in time. The bus pulled away, leaving us in a cloud of oily blue-black fumes. Gordy and I were apoplectic. Neither of us was able to stem the bitter tears that welled up.

As we dragged our forlorn selves back to the house, my mother appeared at the front steps, sizing up the situation in a glance. "I'll take you," she said. Gordy and I looked at each other in stunned surprise. Our mother had come to the rescue.

Elated, we raced to the car. The three of us sat in our usual spots way in the back and giggled as we watched Ethel climb into the front seat with our mother. We didn't see Ethel in cars often. She was so short, she could barely see out of the windshield. With our spirits high, we whispered about how little Ethel looked in the car and how big she seemed when she wasn't in it. We got to the movie theater early. The fact that the theater was brand new—a modern, sleek building we'd yet to step foot in—only added to our excitement. My mother dropped us off out front. Ethel walked us around to the alley, looking for a side door, and realized there wasn't one. We came around the front. Our mother had yet to pull out in traffic. She called, "You buy the tickets there," pointing in the direction of the ticket counter. The smell of popcorn wafted out onto the sidewalk as we stood next to Ethel. We peered into the gleaming lobby through its glass front, taking in all the brightly colored movie posters.

Ethel shrugged, went to the ticket counter, and asked where the colored entrance was. "No coloreds allowed," the ticket agent replied.

My jaw dropped. "Does that mean we can't see the movie?" I asked. We looked at each other as if the ticket man were speaking a foreign language.

"You kids can, but she can't." The man gestured with his thumb at Ethel.

My mother got out of the car and came over to the window.

"Excuse me. Is there some misunderstanding? My children and maid came to see the four o'clock movie. I don't suppose you know who I am?" she asked in her commanding tone. "My husband is——"

"Lady, your husband could be the president of the United States for all I care. You can buy tickets for the kids. No coloreds. Do you want tickets? If ya don't, then move along." Obviously, the man had never seen my mother mad.

We stood on the sidewalk in front of the ticket counter in silence. Ethel was resigned; she stood aside with no comment, shaking her head and staring down at the sidewalk.

"What's he mean coloreds can't…?" I whined. Gordy came over and pushed me.

"Shut up," he hissed, and for added emphasis, glared "shut up" with his eyes.

I was dumbstruck that the man hadn't let my mother have what she wanted, especially when she used the tone she had used. That was even more amazing than being turned away from the movies, but none of it made any sense to me. Ethel was the first to turn toward the car. "Well, I guess we ain't gonna be seein' no picture show today." She kept her eyes on the sidewalk as if it were the most interesting thing she had seen all day.

"Oh yes you are," said my mother, fixing her eyes on the ticket agent. "In spite of this man's ignorance." She turned and started walking quickly. "Get in the car."

My mother drove us downtown to the Paramount movie theater. We pulled up to the colored entrance on the side of the building. My mother waited while Ethel bought our tickets. We knew this meant we got to sit upstairs in the balcony. Once she had the tickets, Ethel opened the car door and we scurried inside the theater. She put us in our seats and went back downstairs to buy us treats. Neither Gordy nor I could resist just one spit over the balcony. We had seen some little boys doing it the last time Ethel brought us here. Ethel had said they were bad boys and if she had anything to do with them, they wouldn't be able to sit for a week. When we came back from the railing and sat in our seats, Helen said, "I'm gonna tell."

"If you do, I'll pinch you," I swore.

Gordy said, "I'll share my candy with you if you don't tell."

"You just better shut up or I'll throw you over the balcony," I fumed.

Helen looked at me solemnly. "You'd get in big trouble," she said.

"I don't care. You'd be dead. So shut up." Helen must have believed me. She didn't say a word to Ethel about the spitting. I noticed Gordy gave her a lot of his candy. After the movie, my mother was waiting in her car at the colored entrance.

On sunny mornings light streamed through the big windows in the dining room, helping to start the day. Ethel really shined at breakfast, too. What we had to eat was up to her. She took it personally when my mother bought boxed cereal. In Ethel's mind breakfast, including cereal, was meant to be eaten hot. Pouring something out of a box offended her. "Don' know why ya wants dat," she'd say. "Tastes like cardboard ta me."

Daddy liked to talk with Ethel at breakfast. He'd ask her opinion about things in the news; about the weather, food. They talked to each other as she waited on the table, fixed his breakfast, and oversaw ours. Rarely did she stop to stand and talk, but rather as she served, they conversed. Their conversations weaved back and forth between her trips to the kitchen—the thread would get dropped every time she exited the dining room only to be picked up again when she reentered. Neither of them ever missed a nuance or puzzled over which topic they'd left off on.

"Mornin', Mista Joe," she'd say as she placed his black coffee on the table next to him. "How ya doin' this fine mornin'?"

"I hadn't realized what a fine day it was until I smelled sausage cooking." He flashed her a grin. "I hope it's yours."

"Yes, sir, sure is," she said as she left the room. "Made it last Sat'day evenin'," she said, reentering with a china pot of coffee on a silver tray.

"How many did you slaughter this time?"

"Jest three," she answered over her shoulder. When she came back she stopped. "I ain't gots time to do much more en' that. It takes a right smart while ta gits 'em all cut up and the hams ready fer curin'. We been cutting back. Jest takes too long. Ain't is young as we once was."

"Who are you calling old? I'm older than you, or are you angling for a day off?" He laughed to her back.

"No, sir, I ain't askin' for no time oft. I'm plenty happy doin' for you jest as I is." She chuckled as she reentered the room. "I put more sage in da mix this time. I hope ya likes it," she said, placing a plate of sausage and fried apples down in front of him.

He cut off a small piece of sausage, put it in his mouth, and chewed carefully. "Good, really makes a difference. I like it," he said, stuffing the rest into his mouth. "What do you think?"

"I was waitin' to hear what you had'ta say, but I think it need a speck mo'."

"You know I'm never going to question you when it comes to cooking. If you think it needs more it undoubtedly does, but it's the best damn sausage I ever ate."

"Thank ya," she glowed. "Glad ya likes it."

"Stuart," Daddy said. "Did you try any of this?"

Stuart stopped reading the paper and wrinkled her nose. "I just want toast, Daddy, that's all." He shrugged. Then she turned the page of the paper toward him. "Did you see where the army is trying to draft Elvis Presley?"

Daddy didn't like his music and was always asking Stuart to turn the volume down whenever it came on the radio.

"Why, Stuart," he said, "do you think Elvis should be treated any differently than anybody else? What makes him so special? Because he can hoop, holler, and gyrate?"

Daddy got up from the table and started his imitation of "Elvis the Pelvis," as he called him. It wasn't pretty. Helen and Gordy shrieked with laughter. I had tears running down my cheeks. Ethel came in from the kitchen, a spatula in her hand.

"You go, Mista Joe," she hollered. "Shake it!" Even Stuart was laughing in spite of herself.

"What on earth?" my mother said. Her voice was like ice water. She stood at the foot of the stairs in her riding habit.

Ethel scurried back into the kitchen. Daddy eased back onto his chair at the table as we children fell mute.

Desegregation—a buzzword at the time, a word that had so much power that it rendered my mother speechless around Ethel—came up often in Ethel's conversations with Daddy at the breakfast table. Ethel's opinion had value to him. Often when they discussed the growing firestorm he would say, "That's a good point. I never thought about it that way." And he meant it. On one such occasion my mother was present at the table, her eyes following Daddy's exchange with Ethel over the rim of her coffee cup. As soon as Ethel left the room, she shushed my father. "Joe, what are you trying to do? Don't talk to her about these things," my mother said. "Ethel doesn't know what's going on. Lord knows you don't need to upset her."

My father shot her an exasperated look. "Ginny, Ethel might be uneducated, but she's nobody's fool. Besides, she's right. They are just monkeying around up there in Washington, using this whole race thing to keep people from focusing on the lack of jobs and the stalled economy. It's wrong for Negroes to be treated the way they're treated. It's about time people start changing. Ethel certainly has a right to voice her opinion. Don't you care what she thinks?"

My mother, who had been listening patiently, suddenly bristled. "Ethel and I don't discuss current events."

"Current events? For Christ's sake, it's her life!"

Chapter 9

If by some miracle my parents managed not to fight the night before, Daddy would drive us to school. The mood was always lighthearted. Stuart wouldn't be so argumentative, for one thing. We'd sing and laugh and look for purple cows. Those mornings even Stuart would join in to finish the rhyme, "We'd rather see one than be one." She'd sit next to Daddy and talk about boys and what she was going to do after school.

"Look over there," Stuart would say when we pulled up at her building. "There." She'd point and we'd crane our necks as we strained to see.

"What?" Helen demanded.

"Oh never mind," Stuart would giggle as she climbed from the car. Gordy and I dove into her vacated spot, jockeying with each other to sit next to Daddy. Then Stuart would stick her head back in the window.

"A purple cow!" she'd shout. We'd all laugh as she waved goodbye, as if she'd never played the joke on us before. We'd start singing silly songs and Daddy would whoop and holler as he drove to make us laugh more. We couldn't get through reciting, "Fuzzy Wuzzy was a bear...," without cracking up, as if it were the funniest poem ever written. Then we'd drive by the graveyard on the way to our school from Stuart's. Every single time Daddy would say, "People are dyin' to get in there." We'd all laugh out loud.

But one morning was different. Daddy quietly hustled us out of the house earlier than usual. My mother didn't seem to notice, and Ethel, never a clock watcher, made no comment. As we clambered into the car, there was a sense of excitement, like on a holiday. Daddy hadn't said anything, yet the air buzzed with electricity.

As we left the driveway, Stuart broke the loaded silence. She peered around to look Daddy in the face and asked, "What are you up to?" Her eyes crinkled as she smiled.

"Ohhh," he said, drawing out the word until the three of us were hanging on the back of his seat. "That's for me to know and you to find out." He chuckled.

"What, what, what?" we all shouted, giggling and wriggling with anticipation. He drove along our usual school route, and then turned down a road. Stuart started to laugh.

"Oh, I know where we're going," she crowed. "We're going to…" She mouthed something to Daddy that the rest of us couldn't make out. His face broke into a wide grin.

"What? Where?" Helen and I shrieked.

"Where are we going?" Gordy demanded.

"You'll see," Stuart smirked.

Gordy sat back in his seat with his arms across his chest and started to pout. But he couldn't keep it up for long; the anticipation was just too thrilling. Then, there we were, in the middle of the most dirt I had ever seen in my life. Enormous yellow-and-rust-colored machines were creaking and squeaking, billowing black smoke and red dust everywhere. It looked like our sandbox at home, only a thousand times bigger. In the distance, Erector set-like buildings lined a steep, scarred bank of combed clay.

Daddy shut off the car. Gordy was clawing at the door handle, trying to get out into the fray. His eyes were as big as dinner plates. "Wow o' wow! Golly gee! Oh man!" He piled exclamations on top of whistles and whoops.

"Son, you can't get out now. You still have to go to school. I'll bring you back again, soon. I just wanted all of you to see." Daddy looked out of the windshield. He was every bit as excited and mesmerized as Gordy.

"What is it?" Helen's lip turned up in a sneer. She moved away from the door just in case Gordy opened it; she didn't want to get sucked into the chaos looming outside the car.

Stuart laughed. "The shopping center, silly," she said.

"Oh," Helen and I said simultaneously. We looked at each other as if everyone else in the car had just arrived from Mars. Although I didn't get what all the excitement was about, I was thrilled to see Daddy so happy; happier than I could ever remember seeing him.

Daddy pointed to a huge steel skeleton and gushed. "That's going to be the biggest A&P grocery store in the South. You'll be able to buy everything from fresh baked bread to ice coolers, from socks to seafood in there. And over there, that will be a gift shop and a movie theater." As he gestured from one structure to another, he sounded like a kid reciting a Christmas list.

"Will Ethel be able to see a movie in there?" Helen asked.

"What? Of course, she will, honey. Over there, that's going to be the Western Auto Hardware store. And all of this," he boasted, waving his arms grandly, "is going to be for parking. Can you imagine?"

"Wow!" Gordy gasped. Helen looked at me and shrugged.

"Daddy," Stuart said, "this is great. But you better get us to school or Mom will have a fit."

Daddy looked wistfully at the big machines grumbling in the dirt. "You're right, Stuart," he said and started the engine.

On a weekend just before my ninth birthday, Stuart said to me, "Let me roll your hair up."

"Ok." I jumped up and followed her to her room. I was thrilled with the never even imagined turn of events. "What do you want me to do? Should I wash my hair first?"

"No, it's too long. I'll just spray it," she said, her mouth pursed up like she was thinking about something else. "Wait, sit over there." She indicated her dressing table chair. "I'll be right back." Stuart returned with an armful of makeup and dumped it on the table in front of me. "Your hair's too long to roll up. It would take all day to dry. Let's make you up instead."

As I fidgeted, Stuart attempted to apply makeup, powder and rouge. "If you don't want to look like a clown, you'd better sit still," she grumbled. "I won't be able to put eye makeup on unless you do." I sat as still as I could, only blinking twice. Stuart groaned each time. Every so often she'd stand back to admire her handiwork. Pressing her hand against my head and pulling my eyes wide with her fingers, she tweaked the eye shadow this way and that, smudging and rubbing until she achieved the desired effect. Then she took a tiny little paintbrush and licked it, rubbing it around in what looked like paint. She painstakingly applied the pigment to my quivering eyelid.

"Can I see?" I begged.

"Hang on," she mumbled, brushes and Q-tips bristling from her mouth. "I'm not through." She rubbed a Q-tip as if it were an eraser on my eyelid. I didn't say a word for fear of breaking the Cinderella spell. Finally her work was done. "There," she announced; her voice full of pride. "Now, hold on. I'll be right back. Don't look in the mirror."

I sat as motionless as a sphinx trying not to disturb any of Stuart's handiwork. She returned with a dress, some jewelry, and my mother's highest heels. She grabbed my hair, brushed it back, and pulled it like it was a pony's mane. "Ow," I whimpered, biting my lip hard.

"Sorry," she said. She pulled and twisted my hair on top of my head, securing it with hairpins. It felt like she was sticking them into my scalp.

"Stop, that hurts!" I pulled away as strands of hair fell in my face.

"Just two more; I'll be careful," she promised. "OK, now get up and put this on." She guided the delicate fabric over my head, holding it away from my face. "Stand there." She pointed to a spot where I couldn't see my reflection in the mirror as she pinned up my mother's dress to fit my size. "Shoes," she said. I put my foot in one of the high heels. My foot sank into the toe and I struggled for balance. Stuart caught me by the arm and helped me with the other shoe. She arranged the dress so that I could just see the toes of the shoes under the folds of fabric that drifted onto the floor. She fastened a necklace around my neck and clipped earrings on my ears. "Now," she said." Close your eyes." She positioned the mirror so I would be able to see my full reflection. "Now open. Whattya think?" I saw my big sister's face first. She was looking in the mirror as if she might burst with pride, while I, a creature of exquisite beauty, luxuriated in her rare attention.

"I'm really going to miss you guys when we go," she said, looking unbearably sad. She tucked a strand of hair behind my ear.

"What are you talking about? Where are we going?" I asked.

"Dad and—oh, never mind," she said. She waved her hand casually in dismissal. "Nowhere. Go show Ethel how pretty you look!"

Big Early picked Ethel up every night just after dinner, around seven-thirty. He'd park his old pickup truck outside the kitchen steps and wait for her to finish up, rarely bothering to turn the engine off. While his truck idled, its fenders shook and the engine rumbled, spewing acrid black smoke from the exhaust pipe that jiggled underneath the rusted bed. In the summer months, Gordy, Helen, and I were allowed to play in the bed of the truck among the farm debris while Big Early waited for Ethel. Lance would circle the truck, sniff all the barnyard scents, and then lie down in the dirt, as usual. Meanwhile, I chatted with Big Early about his cows, pigs, and chickens. His even, white teeth glittered in the sunlight when he chuckled at something I said. Even in the hot summer he wore a brown felt hat; only his gray sideburns showed under the brim.

On the evening of my birthday, Gordy, Helen, and I ambled about the house listlessly. My mother had invited several of the neighborhood kids over for cake and ice cream that afternoon. After they departed, the evening hours stretched out before us gray and dull in comparison. When Big Early drove up, we clambered into the truck bed to tell him about the party and show him the small gifts I'd acquired. He observed each obligingly and wished me a happy birthday. Feeling bold and entitled on account of the occasion, I ventured a favor. "Big Early, can you take us for a ride?" I asked. "With us back here?"

"I 'spect it won't hurt nothin'," he said, slipping the truck into gear. "Hang on tight, you hear?" Big Early backed down the drive so slowly that we hardly stirred a breeze. I saw Mr. Dabney sitting on his back porch looking sour and thought I'd cheer him up. I waved from the truck bed. "Hey, Mr. Dabney! Look, we're going for a ride." Mr. Dabney stared at the truck with a mean look on his face.

Gordy kicked at me and hissed, "Leave him alone. You know we aren't suppose to talk to him."

"He's not all that bad. Jest talks a lot, is all. 'Sides you do things all time that Mama says not to do. So leave me alone."

"Mama said…nevermind. Ya aren't gonna listen anyway." He said his nose and mouth all screwed up into a smerk. The oily truck exhaust settled around us as we inched our way down the drive.

"Faster!" we shouted, waving the fumes from our faces. When we got to the end of the drive, Big Early stopped. The gears clunked and the old truck shuddered back up to where we started. Ethel was standing in the drive with her purse draped over her arm and several paper bags tucked around her person. She was smiling at us. Mr. Dabney made a big show of getting up out of his chair on the porch and going in the house, slamming the door behind him.

"Big Early, can we go again?" The truck listed hard to the right on its old springs as Ethel climbed into the cab alongside Big Early. She slammed the door, leaned out the window and said, "Ya'll sit down right back here." She patted the back of the cab. "Don' lemme see you standin' up."

We tittered and giggled as Big Early once again wrestled the truck into gear. This time we backed up, turned around and drove out of the driveway. Wind whipped my braids into my face and Helen's curls blew every which way. We dutifully sat with our backs against the pickup cab, watching the telephone poles zip by. Gordy stood on his knees to get a better look only to receive a warning tap on the cab window and a fierce shake of the head from the ever-watchful Ethel. The only thing missing that would have made my birthday perfect was Lil' Early. The ride in that truck would have been a million times more fun had he been there. We only went around the block, but for months afterward our conversations started with, "Remember when we…"

It had been at least six months since we last saw Lil' Early. I got to wondering where he was, so I convinced Helen to do my dirty work for me. We popped our heads into the kitchen. I poked Helen in the ribs and she finally asked. I held my breath. With her mixing bowl in hand, Ethel paused and told us that he had gone to live with his father in Washington. When she told us we probably wouldn't see him for a good while, I just about crumpled inside.

Helen, Gordy, and I were lounging in the den, still in our pajamas, one Saturday morning a few weeks before Thanksgiving. The good cartoons came on early. We'd been up for more than two hours plastered to the couch. During a commercial break, I went hunting for a snack.

I was standing on the counter checking out the contents of the cabinet when I heard the door open behind me. Two sets of footsteps walked across the threshold. I sucked my breath in. *Not mama, not mama, not mama,* I repeated to myself with my eyes clenched shut. Then I heard it: his voice, now almost a tenor. I spun around just as Lil' Early and Ethel walked past the stove. I shrieked, half-startled, half-delighted to see our old friend again. Lance jumped up to greet him, his tail banging against the cupboard, then spun back around to investigate my shriek and make sure I was all right. Lil' Early stood there for a minute smiling, looking a little uncomfortable. He looked like he had grown too—and not just because his red corduroy pants were way too short. Early was no longer the beanpole I remembered; he was bigger all over. His hair was still close cropped like Gordy's, but instead of blond and silky, Early's was rusty-black and kinky. He was a lot more handsome than I remembered him being. His striped T-shirt looked well-worn but clean. Then he broke out in a big goofy grin and I saw that his teeth had gotten big along with his feet. He had on a pair of high tops that looked every bit as big as Daddy's.

"What ya doing up there? You git on down here this minute afore I tan yo' hide," Ethel snapped, chuckling as she came into the kitchen. "Ya hongry?" she asked. I nodded yes.

I quickly jumped down, bouncing over to hug Lil' Early. "Come on, *Mighty Mouse* is on," I said as I grabbed his hand, tugged him toward the television, and then dropped it like it was a snake. I stole a look to see if anyone saw. "Can we have fried apples?" I asked Ethel, adding, "Please," over my shoulder as we hurried into the television room.

A deep, warm chuckle and a few bars of "What a Friend We Have in Jesus" quickly dissolved into a hum were Ethel's only reply. Then I heard her talking to Lance. "What you doin' in here? You know you ain't 'spose' to be in de house. Go on, git." The kitchen door opened and closed. "Ya'll done let ol' Lance in the house," she mumbled.

Even Mighty Mouse's latest escapade couldn't keep me from noticing the sweet and pungent aroma of apples and cinnamon wafting from the kitchen. "I hope she brought some sausage," I said out loud to no one in particular.

"She did, and I helped make it," Lil' Early piped in. "My granddaddy killed the hog and then Miz Ethel and I butchered it."

"You did what?" Gordy demanded. "You butchered a hog? Yuck." He leaned closer, his nose and lips curled up as he launched into a slew of questions. "Was it all bloody and smelly? Did you get blood all over you? Did it fight back and try to bite you? Hogs are supposed to be mean. Did it try to kill you first?"

"Naw, it was already dead. Granddaddy stuck it in da neck. Miz Ethel and me, we's just cut it up and put it in piles. We took the back legs and cuts 'em up into hams and salted him right good and hung 'im in the smoke house."

"He stuck it? With what? You hanged 'em? How do you hang a hog? Ya go up and say come here little hog lemme put this noose around your neck?"

"I tell ya it was already dead," Lil' Early insisted.

"I can make a hangman's noose. You wanna see? Daddy showed me how. Watch, I'll show you," I said then raced off to find the piece of rope I'd been practicing with the day before.

"Why would you do that?" Gordy continued. "If it was already dead, why would you hang it?"

"I don' know why. Just cuz that's what they says to do."

"Was it bloody?"

"Na, they grabs the hog by the back foot an hangs it up on a branch and all the blood goes away afore you do any butcherin'. Ain't no blood to speak of. Jest a little. It don't smell much 'cept when's you's cleanin' the chitlings. Miz Ethel takes them out an slings em up 'gainst a stump 'til dey might near cleaned out, then she cooks 'em in water for a long time. That smells up ta high heaven like an ol' outhouse in sore need of some limin'."

"What's an outhouse?" Helen asked, taking her thumb out of her mouth and adjusting her blanket around her like a cape.

"A bafroom," he said matter-of-factly.

"Why da ya call it an outhouse if it's a bathroom?" she asked, holding her thumb poised on the edge of her lips, ready to stuff it back the moment she finished her question.

"Cuz dat what it is."

"So how do ya make sausage?" I asked as I held the rope in a figure eight in one hand while I attempted to wrap one end around the other as I'd seen my father do. "Ethel's sausage is the best," I said. "Dang!" The figure eight unraveled in my hand. "I did it yesterday. Just hang on, I'll show you." I put the rope on the floor, made the figure eight, wrapped the loose end around the figure eight, and then pulled gently. The knot came apart the minute I took it off the floor

Lil' Early picked up the rope. Before I could take in what he was doing, he'd handed it back to me in a perfect hangman's noose. "After we git finished cutting up de hog, we takes the leftovers and grinds 'em up in de grinder. Turning de handle was my job. Then we mixes it all up with some spices and thangs and wraps it up in paper. Some of it we freeze and some of it we eat." He puffed up and sat taller.

"Wait," Gordy interrupted, "sausage is hog? I thought it was pork. I don't want to eat a hog; 'specially one that's been put up in a tree. Yuck."

"Breakfast ready," Ethel called from the kitchen.

The warm kitchen smelled of apples, cinnamon, and coffee, with that tantalizingly sharp mixture of spices, hot pepper, and browning pork.

"I brought ya'll some sausages jest like ya'll axt me," she said as she popped two slices of bread in the toaster, then buttered two more with an economy of movement that made the toasting seem as if it were just an extension of buttering the bread.

I was already making my fried apple sandwich by placing the sausage on the toast and piling my apples on top. I was reaching for the cinnamon sugar when I heard a muffled, "I don't want any," coming from across the table.

I put on the last sausage and second slice of toast to top off my sandwich and took a bite. "Are you nuts?" I asked, chewing noisily.

"No, I don't want any," Gordy repeated louder and surer of his conviction. "I don't like hog."

"Pig and hog—they're the same thing," I said as I reached for the sausages on his plate.

"I want some Coco Puffs," Gordy said. He got up from the table, went to the cupboard, pulled down the box of cereal and a bowl, and then plopped back in his seat.

"Ya feelin' all right, honey?" Ethel inquired, putting her hand gently on his forehead. "Ya ain't gots a temperature, do ya?"

He pushed her hand away. "Na, I'm OK. I just don't like hog. Never did," he said matter-of-factly.

"Ain't dat somethin'? I always thought you did. Why, yo' favorite meal is poke chops, ain't it? I ain't got you confused with somebody else now, do I?"

"I do like pork chops. I just don't like hog."

"It's the same, Gordy," Ethel said flatly. "If'n you don' want no sausage, d'ya want some apples?"

"Well then, I don't like pork, and I don't want apples that have been next to hog."

"You are dumb, really stupid," I said, stuffing the last of his sausage in my mouth. I licked my fingers, savoring every delicious, juicy bite of sandwich. "Early, this sausage it is better than ever." I jumped up and gave Ethel's tree-trunk-sized thigh a hug. "What are we gonna do today?"

From his place at the table with his bowl of Coco Puffs, Gordy perked up. "Let's go to the big woods down behind George's house."

"Don' let me catch you in dem woods," Ethel said. "You not s'pose' to be down there. Ya'll got a perfectly good yard to play in—ya don' need to be going acrost the street down in dem woods. Ya hear me?" She shook the spatula in her hand for emphasis.

"I cross the street all the time. My best friend lives across the street," Gordy said.

"Who's your best friend?" I asked as I mentally went down the list of who lived across the street.

"Would you shut up?" he snarled. "Ethel, I walk home from school every day right by those woods. Why can't I play there?"

"Don' be tellin' yo' sister ta shut up," Ethel said. She bent down to look Gordy in the eyes. "Them woods ain't yo' property, is one thing. An' I told ya not to, is the second thing. So don' lemme catch you down there. Now, ya'll go on out an' play. And Mista," she had her beam on Lil' Early now, "don' you be leadin' no wil' goose chases, hear me?"

"Yes'm," was the polite response.

"Sallee, you take yo' little sister and keep an eye on her. Don' be leavin' her behind."

My mouth opened, ready to form a protest, but I saw in her face that it was useless to argue. "Yes, Ethel," I said, resigning myself to a miserable day. Helen was a fine playmate if there wasn't anyone else around, but Early was here and there were always more fun things to do than swing and play with dolls. "Come on," I said to Helen gloomily, hurrying her along to catch up with the boys.

"An' don' cha take her out de yard, neither," Ethel called, ensuring that my Saturday was going to be no fun at all. By the time Helen and I got outside, the boys had disappeared. I stomped down the back steps and as far away from her as I could get. Helen had the good sense to wander off toward the swings. I kicked at dirt, broke twigs, and hurled them into the grass. *Well, Ethel didn't say I had to play with her.* I collapsed on the ground in despair. Lance lumbered over, flopped down next to me, and panted a smile. Then, overcome with the effort, he dropped his great, saggy head to the ground with a massive groan. After I snuggled up to his warmth, I burrowed my nose into his black, fusty fur. He groaned again, let out a huge "humph" of a sigh, and then proceeded to snore as if he'd been asleep for hours. Using his flank as a pillow, I rolled over on my back and looked up at the November sky. It was deeper and bluer than any Crayola sky, no matter how hard you pressed the crayon to paper.

Clouds floated like giant icebergs. As I watched a dragon transform into a fish then a duck, I stuck my hand into the pocket of my dress and pulled out the locket I'd found in my mother's bedroom the day before. I glanced over to make sure Helen was still playing on the swings. I opened my fist and let the locket dangle above my face on its tarnished chain. Flat, gold, and heart-shaped with a little diamond starburst in the center, the locket shimmered against the blue sky. Gingerly, I held it between my fingers, sought the little clasp on the side, and pried it open.

I discovered the locket when I tiptoed into my mother's room and rummaged through her dressing table. I ran my hands under her silky slips and sniffed her perfume bottles. Then I came across a small jewelry box tucked into the corner of a drawer. It wasn't as fancy as my mother's big leather jewelry box where she kept her diamonds—it was plain, made of pressed red cardboard. I pushed the gold latch and peered into a treasure trove of costume jewelry. There were pop beads that looked like pearls, gold bangles and broaches of all sizes and shapes; dazzling glass jewels, earrings without mates, and a wad of chains and necklaces. The locket peeked out from the cluster. I carefully untangled its chain from the others and held the prize in my hand. Just then I heard Ethel singing in the hallway. I shut the box, slipped it back into its place, and closed the drawer as quietly as I could. Ethel never saw me.

Now I looked at the face of a boy in a small gray photograph. The picture was old and cloudy and hard to see, but the boy's face was handsome. I cradled the image in my hands and found myself thinking of Lil' Early. Thoughts rolled like clouds through my head; each one dark with guilt.

I wondered where Gordy and Lil' Early had gone, and what they were doing. I thought about the strange car we'd seen with the mean men inside. For a moment I felt frightened again. I prayed Lil' Early and Gordy were OK. Then thinking I was being silly I let the whole thing go. I thought about them playing catch, about how strong Lil' Early could throw. I thought about him tying the knot for me and how warm his skin felt when I hugged him in the kitchen. I felt myself flush with shame. Why was I thinking these things? Did I love Lil' Early? I wanted to ask someone if that could even be possible. I tried to sort out my emotions. Why did I feel I couldn't even tell Ethel how I felt? Why the shame? What was wrong with loving someone? I didn't feel this way when I loved other boys at school. What was different now? Lil' Early was nicer than any of those boys at school could even hope to be. He was good to look at with those big brown eyes and his beautiful long, dark eyelashes. He was fun. What was it about him that made me want to run and hide? I thought how nice it would be to get a tiny picture of Early and keep it in the locket, hidden from everyone but me. Lance flounced his big head up, and then lolled back down. Clutching the locket, I shifted to my side and pulled my knees up, tucked my hands up under the big dog's warm flank, and fell lightly to sleep.

My head bumped the ground as Lance sat up, surveyed his domain for a moment, and then trotted off. As I became conscious of my surroundings again, I looked for Helen. She was nowhere in sight.

"Great," I muttered. "Where did she go? Helen! Helen, where are you?" I scanned the yard. The swings were empty and still. A quick glance at the sandbox turned up nothing. Lance was nowhere to be seen. Maybe he's with her. I thought I'd better check the house. She might have gone into the bathroom or up to our room, even though Ethel probably would have put a stop to that. No Helen in the bathroom. I heard voices in the kitchen..

Roberta's oldest daughter, Leola, often stopped by to wait while her husband, Johnson, ran errands in town. Ethel kept right on working when Leola came. Her visits were usually on Saturday morning while Ethel was cleaning up the breakfast dishes. Leola, a squat, curly headed woman dressed like she was visiting. She wore a hat and kept her coat on as she sat in the chair talking to Ethel. Clutching her purse up close in her lap, she looked like she thought someone was going to take it. Her black, too shiny hair hung in loose curls, quite a contrast to her Aunt Ethel's four symmetrically arranged knots. Even though Leola was Ethel's niece, she didn't call her "Aunt Ethel" like we would have. She called her "Miz Ethel." Leola was a maid, too, but she didn't wear a uniform. She asked me when I walked in "How you like that school you going to?" and didn't even pretend to wait for an answer before she said to Ethel in a sort of conspiratorial whisper like I wasn't even there, "Johnson saw Miz Sadie de other day. You don't even wanta know who wit'."

I thought about butting in and asking Leola why she'd tell her if she didn't want to know. But I thought better of it, besides, Ethel and I were all ears.

"Who she wit'?" she asked, as she turned from the sink hands dripping, looking like Leola was going tell her she had won *Queen for a Day*, Ethel's and my favorite television game show.

"Ham Bone."

"You don' mean it! Johnson's ain't teasin' ya, is he?"

"I axt. I said, 'Johnson, you ain't pullin' my leg, is ya?' He say to me, 'Sho' as you born, I seen out wit' Miz Sadie.' That no-count ol' dog!"

I didn't know Miz Sadie, and I didn't know why it was such a big deal that Mr. Ham Bone was out with her, but it didn't surprise me one bit that he was up to no good. I was right there with Johnson: Ham Bone was a no-account ol' dog since I was pretty sure he brought Ethel gin.

Ham Bone usually showed up just before Ethel would get sick. He was a creepy, baldheaded, funny looking man. I didn't entirely trust him, though he was always pleasant in that sort of syrupy way that made you think right off he was up to something. I didn't like to stay around if he decided to spend some time. He talked in a hoarse whisper that made my skin crawl. He wore an old-fashioned, baggy suit that looked mussed and dirty, a tie, and a light-colored felt hat, except when my mother happened into the kitchen. That's why I knew he was baldheaded. He'd sweep his hat from his head and almost bow when he said, "How da do, Miz Mackey?" He'd flash a big wide grin. "Fine day, ain't it?" he'd ask even if it was raining like cats and dogs. His gold, wire rimmed glasses made him look owlish. I didn't like listening to him. I didn't like anything about him. He and Ethel must have been doing some sort of business because she always went to her purse and got something out to give him. She wasn't friendly like she was when her insurance man stopped by; she was sneakier, like she was embarrassed. When she acted like that I knew enough not to ask why.

"Speakin' bout no-counts," Leola leaned in like she was telling a state secret. "Yo nevah say that CL was de next-door neighbor over dere. Mama told me he r-a-p-e-d," she spelled, "a colored, a boy, mind you, when was young and never even saw one day in the jailhouse." Ethel looked like she had been hit in the head with a brick as she stole a quick look my way. I didn't need that look to tell me something was up. When grownups started spelling, I knew it was time to pay attention. I pretended like I was leaving anyway, as if I hadn't heard a thing. I positioned myself just out of site in the hall with my ear as close as I could get to the opened door while spelling r-a-p-e-d over and over to myself to make sure I didn't forget how to spell it before I could get to a dictionary.

I heard Ethel demand of Leola, "How you know he CL? You ain't old 'nough ta had knowned 'em. How Roberta know Dabney's CL?

"Mama say she saw him one time when she sat for Miz Ginny. She say she surpised yo nevah say nothing. She say she see 'em from time to time."

I hear Ethel mutter, "I couldn't place his face, but he sho looked famliar." Her voice sounded like it was coming closer so I ducked around the corner just missing being seen as Ethel stuck her head out of the kitchen door and looked up and down the hall. I walked out of the powder room like I had been there the whole time.

"Git on outside wit yo'self an' keep an eye on yo' sister like I's told ya'll to." She turned back into the kitchen. I waited long enough to hear the conversation pick up before I crept passed the open kitchen door and up the stairs. I checked Stuart's room though I knew she'd never let Helen hang around there. The room was empty. A little frantic now, I trotted downstairs and outside, banging the back door behind me. I tried to take in the whole yard at once. Helen was nowhere I could see. I called for Lance. Maybe he had found her and was bringing her home; after all, he was a bloodhound. I rushed behind the garage, around the front of the house, and into the rose garden. No Helen, no Lance.

The cold November air was beginning to sear my throat. Tears stung my eyes. "Helen!" I called, even though it hurt. "Helen, where are you?"

Lance was stretched out by the kitchen steps, but no Helen. The only place she could be was the street. She must have tried to follow Gordy and Early. I started to run down the drive when Mr. Dabney spoke up from his porch. "Hi there, missy! Where you off to in such a hurry?"

I remembered my mother saying that Mr. Dabney was not a nice man and I should stay away from his house. But maybe he had seen Helen. I stopped running. "I'm, umm... You haven't seen Helen, have you?" I asked.

"Well, let me see," he said, trying to draw me in. "I think I saw her. Was it yesterday? Or maybe this morning. I'm not quite sure."

"So, she didn't come through your yard?" I asked. That man could talk, and I didn't have time for it.

"Now, let me think. She might have. I mighta seen her this morning with your brother and that nigger boy. Or maybe it was..."

"When?" I shouted. I was becoming impatient.

"Now, look here, missy, don't you take that tone me with me," he snapped.

My face grew hot with embarrassment and frustration. "I'm just looking for my sister Helen and I can't find her and I'm supposed to be watching her and I'm going to get in big trouble and..." I started to blubber.

"Now, now, you calm down," he shushed. "She's right inside the house with Miz Dabney eating some of her blueberry muffins, I reckon. I suspect a muffin might taste pretty good right about now, wouldn't it? Why don't you go on in? Mabel!" he shouted.

Mrs. Dabney yelled back from inside the house, "Yeah, Luther."

"Got any more of them little men?"

Mrs. Dabney came to the door and broke out in a wide smile. She wiped her hands on the little yellow, frilly apron she always wore. It seemed so out of place on her stocky, country frame. "Well, hi there, Sallee," she said. "Helen and I were just making the beds. Then we're going to sit down and have some little men; blueberry. You want one?"

I was so relieved I burst out crying. "What's the matter, sweetie? Come here. Let ol' Miz Dabney make it all better. Come on in here with me. Don't you cry now." She cooed and clucked like an old hen. Helen emerged from the pantry, her mouth stuffed with raisins. I couldn't decide whether to hug her or hit her.

"Why didn't you tell me you were coming over here?" I yelled. "You scared me half to death. I've been looking everywhere!"

"You were asleep," she said. She climbed up on the stool Mrs. Dabney had set by the counter. "We're going to make some more little men; with raisins this time," she said. She looked up at Mrs. Dabney and smiled. "Aren't we?"

"Yes, sugar, we are," Mrs. Dabney said. "And Sallee can help, too." Helen scowled at that information, but shrugged it off. She stuck her thumb squarely in her mouth.

"Angel, don't suck your thumb. It'll give you buck teeth and then you won't be pretty. A girl wants to be pretty so she can get married and have a family," Mrs. Dabney said. "That's a good girl." She eased Helen's thumb from her lips.

Helen's hand hovered in the air in front of her face, thumb at the ready. Three fingers curled around her upper lip and the fourth was cocked, ready to wrap around her nose in an instant. She looked as if she were contemplating which pleasure she would rather forego: her thumb or the raisin muffins. I could see it was complicated. She touched her thumb to her lip, nibbled at it, then pulled it away. But the prospect of never tasting the thumb again seemed to overwhelm her. A big tear welled up in her eye, then another, and another.

"Miz Dabney, I can't just stop," she whined. "I don't want to be ugly, but I just can't help it. Please, can I suck my thumb a little, just a little?"

Mrs. Dabney's bewilderment melted into a smile. "Oh well, I don't s'pose a little would hurt. But honey, you are going to have to try to stop. Promise me?"

Helen's thumb was back in her mouth before Mrs. Dabney said "s'pose." Helen nodded her promise. It was clear that she had no intention of keeping it.

We spent the rest of the morning making muffins, some with raisins and some with blueberries. Helen's thumb left her mouth only long enough for her to lick a spoon or eat an errant raisin. Mrs. Dabney seemed to give up on worrying about Helen's buckteeth and marriage prospects.

While we waited for Mrs. Dabney's blueberry "little men" to finish baking, Helen fell asleep. She had eaten three or four raisin muffins and countless raisins. Mr. Dabney had gone down into the basement. Mrs. Dabney and I sat in her musty parlor waiting for the oven to ding. She wanted to talk about Ethel.

"Do you like having her tell you what to do?"

"Well, no, but she's supposed to. I mean, that's what she does. My mother tells her some things, yes. No, she doesn't tell her everything. She does what she wants sometimes..." The more Mrs. Dabney plied me with questions, the more confusing our household seemed. Frustrated, I began to answer, "I don't know." Mrs. Dabney soon changed the subject to school.

"What's your favorite subject?" she asked.

"I like writing stories," I said proudly. "I can write a story quick as anything. Why, just the other day Gordy forgot he was supposed to write a story and asked me to write one for him before school and I did too."

"Honey, I don't think you should be doing your brother's school work for him."

"Oh, it's OK. He isn't very good at school. When I help him he gets better grades. That makes him feel better. He gets really sad when he gets bad grades. Then my mother and Daddy get mad at him, so I help him out sometimes."

Mrs. Dabney gave my hand a little squeeze and sighed.

I decided to take the gesture as an invitation. I couldn't talk to my mother about love. Stuart was never around, and talking to Ethel was completely out of the question. Mrs. Dabney was old but she had to have been in love at some point in her life because she married Mr. Dabney. In a serious voice I asked, "Miz Dabney, does being in love hurt?"

She laughed. "Now, what in the world would make you ask such a question? Of course it doesn't." She sank back into her chair, crossed her arms over her bosom, and got a faraway look in her eyes as if she were remembering something. "Well, maybe sometimes it does; but not at your age. Why? Is some little boyfriend being mean to you? I know they don't ignore you, you're too pretty."

"No, ma'am, I don't have a boyfriend."

"I wouldn't think so. You're a little young yet. Is there something I can help with? Something about your momma and daddy?"

I decided she was too fast with her questions. "No, no, I was just wondering. Thanks, though."

"You know you can tell me anything any old time. There! I think that was the timer. Let's go check the little men, shall we?"

I skipped ahead into the kitchen. Mr. Dabney was sitting at the breakfast nook smoking a cigar. He had on shorts, and his legs were as white and skinny as the pipe cleaners Daddy used to dig around in the bowl of his pipe. As he sat splayed on the bench, Mr. Dabney looked a lot like a white rat with his pasty skin, tufts of hair, and pink face.

"Hello to you, missy. Ready for some of those little men?" He patted the bench next to him. "Come on, sit next to ol' Mr. Dabney and give me a hug."

"I don't think I have time to stay and eat," I stalled. "I promised Ethel I'd get home as soon as I found Helen. She'll be worried, you know."

"Where'd she get off to?" he asked, looking around for Helen.

"Oh, she's in the other room. I'd better go get her."

"Oh, don't wake her up," Mrs. Dabney interjected. "I'll give your mother a call and tell her you'll be home as soon as Helen wakes up. Go on, give Mr. Dabney a hug. He loves little girls." She hurried to the phone and started dialing.

"Hello, may I speak with Mrs. Mackey? Oh, well, this is Mrs. Dabney from next door. I just wanted Mrs. Mackey to know that the girls are over here, and as soon as Helen wakes up from her nap we'll send them right home. Oh no, they're no bother at all. Mr. Dabney and I love having them visit—our pleasure."

"Come on over here and talk to an old man," Mr. Dabney said. He held out his arms, flesh sagging like wet sheets on a clothesline; his nasty old cigar clenched between yellowed teeth.

Mrs. Dabney came into the room shaking her head and clucking her tongue. "It's none of my business," she said, "but I don't know why that woman lets that…that…" Her eyes fell on me and she shrugged.

Mr. Dabney "humphed" in agreement then turned his attention back to me. "Come over here and sit on ol' Mr. Dabney's lap."

I moved closer, standing next to him with my arms down by my sides. Then I leaned into him, praying that would suffice as a hug. I could smell his sour breath. His crooked teeth were all chipped like he ate rocks or something. There was no way I was going to sit on his lap. The smell of his sickly sweet aftershave caught in the back of my throat and made my head spin. He wrapped his hairy arms around me. The thick cigar smoke curling around his pink face made me even woozier. I pushed away and started to cough. Waving the smoke away, I coughed my way to the other side of the table.

"Phew, I'm allergic, you know," I gasped with my hand still waving at the offending cloud. Mrs. Dabney was busy with the muffins and bustling about with plates and potholders.

"I have to use the bathroom," I said, adding a cough for good measure.

"Around the corner," he said, indicating with his cigar stub and looking a little less jovial than before.

In the bathroom I coughed sporadically, played with the water taps, and then stood on tiptoe to see out the window. I waited for a few minutes before opening the door. I let it bang against the stop, hoping the noise would wake Helen. No such luck. As I peeked around the corner, I saw Mrs. Dabney with her back to me. Mr. Dabney was gone, so I crept over to the sofa to shake Helen as hard as I could. Just as I was about to hiss, "Get up," Mr. Dabney spoke from the chair across the room.

"What are you doing? Didn't Miz Dabney tell you not to...?"

Startled witless, I shrieked. Helen woke up terrified and let loose a war whoop. Mrs. Dabney ran in from the kitchen, her silly yellow apron bunched in her hands.

"The little brat woke her up!" Mr. Dabney shouted as he pointed at me.

Mrs. Dabney yelled back at him, "Luther, don't call the children names."

Helen and I were shrieking and crying. Then, as quickly as it all started, it stopped. There was a banging at the kitchen door. Standing there was Ethel with her hands on her hips. "You two git on home, ya hear me?" she said before Mrs. Dabney hardly had the door open. Ethel glared at the Dabneys. They sneered back at her. No one spoke. Ethel shook her head from side to side and left without a word.

Helen and I ran crying into our house. When we burst into the kitchen, we saw our lunch ready on the table. Gordy and Lil' Early had almost finished eating theirs.

"Don' ya'll be botherin' them folks again," Ethel said as she huffed through the kitchen door after us.

"You aren't going to have to worry about that," I said, relieved to be home. I glanced at Lil' Early as he shoveled the last bites of food into his mouth. I was curious to know what he and Gordy had been up to all morning. I wondered if Lil' Early ever missed me the way I missed him. I reached into my pocket and touched the locket.

The next week, just after Daddy had pulled out of our driveway to take us to school, three tires started flapping at about the same time. They were kicking up a terrible racket. Daddy pulled over quickly. "You three sit still for a minute," he said. He got out and inspected the tires. Boy, did he look mad. He opened the passenger door. "All right, then," he said, "we'll have to go back to the house."

As we walked the several hundred yards back to our drive, Daddy sputtered and muttered about "irresponsible carpenters" dropping nails all over the shopping center construction site. Delighted at this turn of events, Gordy, Helen, and I skipped and laughed alongside him.

"Boy, too bad for Stuart that she went to school on the bus," Gordy remarked.

"You can't tell with her," I said. "She seems to like to go to school these days. Who knows?" I shrugged my shoulders. When we turned and started up the drive, Helen tripped and landed on her knee. Daddy leaned down and picked her up. He wiped Helen's tears. "Aww, honey, I know that hurt." He went down on one knee. "Let me see."

"Owie, owie! Daddy it hurts," she sniffed, hopping up and down; blowing and waving her hands over her knee. When she saw blood trickling down her leg, she dissolved into a full throated wail.

"Come on, sugar, let me see. I think you're going to be all right," Daddy said. He pulled a fresh handkerchief from his pocket and gently wiped the dust and gravel from the tiny wound. After mopping her face and coaxing her into blowing her nose, he puckered his lips. "Can I kiss it and make it all better?" he asked.

Helen nodded with a little smile.

Leaning over, he hesitated for just a second to tease her, and then quickly kissed the knee. "Gordy," he said with a funny edge to his voice, "take your sisters home and tell your mother to come down here. And be quick about it."

"Yes sir!" Gordy said. He puffed himself up with pride as he assumed his newly bestowed responsibilities. I rolled my eyes. Helen took a step gingerly on her injured leg. Like a sheep dog, Gordy began herding us up the driveway.

Because I never wanted to be outdone, I ran ahead of my brother and sister. "Wait!" Gordy yelled after me. "He told *me* to tell her. Sallee, wait!" He tried to move Helen into a faster gait. Then he just grabbed her by the hand and started dragging her.

I burst through the front door, banging it against the mahogany card table on the adjacent wall. The blue and white Chinese vase perched on the table was rocking back and forth as my mother's eyes widened from shock to anger. "Sallee, what on earth?" She hurried over to steady the vase before it toppled over. "Young lady——"

"Daddy wants you!" I broke in breathlessly.

Just then Gordy repeated my entrance, nearly smacking my mother in the face with the door as he and Helen plowed into the front hall. My mother stood in stunned silence, holding the vase as Gordy, in between great gasps for air, attempted to relay our father's message. Bending over with his hands on his knees, he managed to get out, "Flat tires."

"A whole bunch of nails," I interjected, "in the tires."

Gordy shot me a scathing look. "Daddy wants you to come now. He's with the car out on the road near the end of the drive."

"He sounded really serious," I added, interrupting Gordy.

Ethel must have heard all the commotion. She came out to the hall and exchanged a worried look with my mother. Then she took Helen, who had started crying again, by the hand. "Come on you two," she said over her shoulder as she patted Helen's back as she led her to the kitchen. "Miz Ginny, don' be goin' out wit'out yo' coat, it's cold out there. I'll git it fo' ya." She dropped Helen's hand and bustled to the coat closet. "Sallee! Gordy! You two git in this kitchen!"

Ten minutes later my mother was back in the house scurrying to the phone. I heard her ask for a police car and then give our address. "New nails," she said, "like someone scattered them in the gravel. Yes, my husband will meet you."

That afternoon, as my mother was reading the *Daily Progress*, she shook and rattled the newspaper, then refolded it to the editorial page. She got up and fixed herself a drink. That was pretty unusual since Daddy hadn't gotten home. When he finally arrived, my mother didn't even let him get all the way in the door before saying, "Joe, look, there were two more today. That makes eight in the last month."

"Hello to you, too," he said as he breezed past her. He took off his coat and dropped it on the nearest chair. "Drinking already?

Did you make one for me? I could really use it. God, what a day!" he sighed.

"Here, look at the editorial page," my mother said, dropping the paper onto the seat of his favorite chair. "I'll get you one." She left the room. My father sat down, glared at the television for a moment, and then picked up the paper.

Gordy and I could see that whatever my father was reading wasn't improving his mood one bit. We turned the TV off and sat quietly, hoping we might find out what was in the paper before we were dismissed. My mother returned with his drink.

"What in the hell is wrong with people?" he sighed. "Jesus, you would think I'd suggested we burn all the churches and build strip joints in the ashes! It's a shopping center...just a shopping center." My mother sat on the edge of the love seat and watched him read. "Robbing old ladies of their land!" he ranted. "Who writes this stuff?"

He stood, slammed the paper against his knee, and stormed from the room. My mother followed. I jumped up and peeked down the hall. I could see him bent over, dialing the phone. He straightened. After a moment he began to yell into the receiver. My mother put her hand on his shoulder, but Daddy kept yelling.

A few weeks later, just before Thanksgiving, the day was cold and wet; the kind that Ethel says "gits in yo' bones." Gordy and I had our noses pressed to the window. We watched Lance thrashing up the kitchen steps, slobber flying every which way. Daddy had found him wandering in circles in the backyard. Now he was behind Lance, driving him toward the kitchen porch.

"Ethel!" he called. "Ethel! Open the door!"

Ethel scurried out and swung open the screen door. She pressed herself against the stair rail, trying her best to stay out of Lance's way. His big head swung toward her as he passed, and he growled, showing his teeth. Spit and foam flew all over her.

Ethel let the door clap shut and latched it. Daddy herded Lance into a corner of the porch with his arms spread, holding trash can lids like shields. "You go on into the kitchen," he told Ethel. "I'm coming right behind you." Just then Lance lunged at Daddy, teeth bared. Ethel leaped in the air and landed in the kitchen, a good five feet from where she'd taken off. It was a sight to behold. Daddy scrambled in after her, slamming the door behind him. The door shuddered as the big dog threw himself against it with all his weight.

"Lord, Mista Joe, you thank he got the rabies?" Ethel asked. "Po' thang don' even know us."

Daddy rubbed his jaw, looking concerned. "I don't think so. He must've eaten something. I'll call the vet. He can take a look." The spectacle of Lance gone mad kept all of us riveted to the kitchen window. The vet showed up quickly, like it was an emergency, but he didn't venture out on the porch.

As the vet and Daddy stared through the screen door, puzzling over the possible causes of Lance's madness, the vet suddenly changed the subject. "I hear tell you're the one building that shopping center over yonder," he said, gesturing with his head toward the stove. "I was thinking I might open up an office there. Do I talk to you 'bout that?"

"I'll give you my rental agent's number before you leave," Daddy said, his voice a little edgy. "Right now I'd like it if you'd check out my dog."

"Dog's in bad shape. Nothing I can do for 'em," the vet said. "Gonna have to put him down. I wouldn't be surprised if he was poisoned. Symptoms look like it—dehydration, delirium. I'll take a closer look, but like I say, probably poison. Could be antifreeze; plenty of that around."

"Poison!" Gordy and I chorused.

Daddy glared at us, indicating that we had better be quiet or get the hell out of there. "Who'd do such a thing?" he asked.

"Coulda just gotten into some. Ya let him run loose?" the vet asked. "People aren't real careful about how they dispose of the stuff." He hemmed a little. "Course, that shopping center of yers has a good many people riled up. But you know that, don't you?"

"I knew there was an element that didn't approve," Daddy said as he placed his hands on our heads and pointed us to the door. With a little push and another glare, he indicated we should go. We scurried from the room.

"Poison! Who would do such a mean thing?" Gordy blubbered. He gave the door a good kick on his way out. "Son of a bitch," he said.

"You better shut up," I warned. "If Ethel…"

"*You* shut up," he roared then stomped up the stairs and out of sight.

I could hear my father and the vet talking. "To poison someone's dog, though…" Daddy said.

"I'm not saying it was on purpose," the vet said. "I'm just saying it wouldn't be the first time some lowlife took his rage out on a dog."

"Can't you look at him? Do something?" Daddy said. Then he muttered, "Jesus, it's just a goddamn shopping center."

I heard a big crash out on the porch. I ran to see. I heard Gordy coming down the steps, taking two at a time.

Poor Lance had flung himself against a big metal locker Ethel used to store cleaning supplies. It had come clanging down on top of him, pinning him. The vet hustled out on the porch, but came right back in.

"He's dead," he said. "Crushed his skull. I can send his body down to Richmond for an autopsy, if you want. That'll tell us whether it was antifreeze or something else. It's against the law to poison a dog, if that's what happened here."

Daddy raked his hand through his hair and then stood real still. "I guess it can't hurt to find out," he said.

"Mind if I use your phone, then? Gotta call the sheriff."

"No, go ahead. It's down the hall."

Two mysteries! The shock of Lance's death and the unexplained flat tires on Daddy's car battled for dominance inside my head. I hardly knew what to think. I nudged Gordy in the ribs with my elbow and indicated with my head that we should go somewhere else. "Ya'll git on outta here now," Ethel spoke up. "Ya don' need to be seein' all dis. Go on, now." Daddy patted each of us on the head as we left the kitchen.

"I don't want you two to worry," he said. "Nobody is going to hurt you. Promise."

The thought of being in danger hadn't occurred to me, but there was one thing I knew—when a grown-up told you not to worry, you had better start. We ran up to the third floor and flopped down on Gordy's bed.

"What do you think?" I asked. "Poor ol' Lance. Gosh. What a horrible, low-down thing to do." Now that the excitement was subsiding, I began to feel queasy. I thought about Lance's crushed head and how the vet was taking his body away, and that I would never get to pet him again. Suddenly, tears sprang to my eyes and I buried my head in Gordy's mattress and cried. Gordy's eyes were already raw and he was hurting even worse than I was, but his big brother impulses seemed to take over. He started patting me on the back.

"There, there," he said. After a while I dried my eyes and went in search of Helen and Stuart to tell them the story. Finding neither, I returned to Gordy's room expecting to see him bawling again. But he surprised me. Once he got the crying out of the way, he got mad; snarling dog mad.

"I'm finding out who did this," he declared. I don't believe I had ever heard Gordy make a declaration before. That had always been my field. "You gonna help?"

"What can I do? Or you? What are you gonna do about it? Go out and arrest somebody?"

"I dunno. It was bad enough that somebody dumped nails in our driveway, but ya can't just let someone kill your dog. Ya gotta do somethin'. I think the same person that dumped the nails killed Lance."

"Why would someone do that? Kill our dog and dump nails in our driveway? It doesn't make any sense," I said. Gordy shrugged his shoulders.

Daddy read Sherlock Holmes mysteries to us whenever he got the chance, so we mulled over our mysteries, wondering what Holmes and Watson might do. And I had my extensive knowledge of Nancy Drew's most intimate thoughts on mystery solving at my disposal. I noticed cars pulling into the driveway. "Whoa, Gordy, there's Stuart and a police car outside."

His eyes got big as dinner plates. "Let's go check it out," he said.

We crept down the stairs, peering over the banister from the second floor. We could see Daddy holding Stuart, who was crying, while the sheriff's deputy stood in the doorway shifting nervously from foot to foot. After removing his hat, the deputy stepped into the house, and adjusted the gun belt around his ample belly. I tingled with the excitement of seeing a real live gun for the first time; and in my own house, no less. Gordy poked me and pointed. "Yeah, neat huh?" I whispered back.

Stuart, still weeping, started for the kitchen, then turned and ran past us on the steps. "Lance is dead," Gordy whispered. Stuart didn't stop. She headed straight to her room and slammed the door after her. I could hear her sobbing. Gordy and I looked at each other, but the scene below had captured our imagination.

Daddy and Big-and-Beefy, the deputy, disappeared from view. Gordy and I inched our way down, step-by-step. We were careful not to make the slightest noise until we reached the spot on the stairs where we could see into the kitchen. We peeped through the rails that separated us from the action. The door leading to the porch was open. It was an awful sight. Ol' Lance lay splayed out on the floor right at the sill. I tried not to look, but couldn't help it. Once I did, I started sniffling again. Gordy shot me a warning look, but I could tell he was on the verge of tears, too. The locker that killed Lance had been pushed out of the way. We couldn't hear what was being said. The deputy and Daddy picked up the body then carried it through the porch and down the stairs. Ethel followed a safe distance behind, wringing her hands in a dishtowel.

We decided to seize the opportunity, so we tore down the stairs. Since the deputy came in the front door, we figured his car must be parked out front. We scurried to the back door, pulled it open slightly, and squeezed through it. Once outside—enthusiasm unbounded—we ran around the corner to position ourselves in a spot that would give us a clear view of the unfolding drama. The trick of good detecting is not to be detected. Ethel, half hidden in the bush herself, shushed us as we plowed into her. "Cain' hear what they sayin'. Hush!"

The deputy grabbed Lance's body by two legs and tossed it into the trunk of his car like it was some litter he'd found on the road. Then he stood with his hand on the trunk hood, his back to us. We couldn't hear a word. Daddy and the deputy looked off down the drive as if they thought that was where the poisoner had come from. Every once in a while one or the other would indicate a direction with his hand. Gordy turned to me and whispered, "What ya think? Maybe it was that old lady that lives on the corner. They're pointing that way. Ya think? Or those guys in that car."

"That ol' lady ain't poisoned nobody's dog," Ethel said. Gordy and I shot each other amazed glances. We had not counted on a coconspirator. We immediately plied Ethel with questions. "I thank it's that mean ol' man down next to the doc's house," she volunteered. "Ya'll know the one I mean?" Neither of us did. "Lives 'round the corner over behind Mattie Bruce's people." I detected some impatience in her voice. Then she said, "What guys in what car?"

"Mr. Gentry? No, he didn't do it," Gordy said. "I cut through his yard all the time. He's as nice as can be." I couldn't tell if he was purposely avoiding Ethel's question. If so, he was brilliant because it worked.

"Wha' ya'll doin' down there? Ya'll ain't s'pose ta be crossin' no streets. I better not catch you doin' that again. G'on git on outta here. I got work ta do."

"Look," Gordy said pointing, "maybe Mr. Dabney did it. He's watching Daddy but he looks like he doesn't want us to…"

"Don' lemme catch ya anywhere near that man, ya hear me?" She glared at Gordy then me. Ethel's vehemence took, us off guard and scared both us a little.

"Yes, ma'am." We said in unison.

We wandered away toward the swings. "Phew, she sure got mad about that," Gordy muttered. Walking aimlessly, but for Ethel's benefit feigning otherwise, we kicked at clumps of wet leaves as we discussed our next move.

"She's gonna be watching us like a hawk now. Why'd you have to mention that car? And Mr. Dabney."

"I got us out of it, so quit griping. Let's go over there and see if we find anything."

"Ethel just said not to."

"Do you wanna find out who killed Lance or not?"

"Well I…"

"Gord-eee, Sal-leee, git in this house afore ya'll catch yo' death o' cold," Ethel called.

"I don't want to go back in there," I moaned. "Out here I at least feel like…well, I don't have to think about what happened to Lance."

"What?" He looked at me like I had two heads.

I groped to explain myself. "I mean the adventure and mystery… Oh, never mind. You're so stupid you wouldn't get it even if I could…" Then the tears started and there was no holding them back. With both of us crying, we bid Ethel's command.

As our search for clues to the mysteries continued, we routinely crept about the house honing our detecting skills. If we had learned one thing growing up with our parents it was that you never knew what adults weren't telling you. The days following Lance's death were wet, cold, and dreary, matching our moods. So snooping around the neighborhood was out of the question. Since I was stuck inside, I did the only thing I could do: I tried my best to spy on my parents and Ethel, even though I'd promised my mother I wouldn't. Thinking I was so clever, I positioned myself in the broom closet one wet afternoon to see if I could pick up any information. Ethel hummed her way to the kitchen, and I quickly closed the door then perched on the vacuum cleaner.

She turned on the water and started a new hymn, one I had never heard before. I pushed the door open a crack to see what she was up to. She sat at the kitchen sink polishing silver. Ethel picked up a fork and rubbed it hard with silver polish, then placed it in the sink half full of water and picked up another one. *This is just great,* I thought. *I'm gonna be stuck here while she polishes silver. How am I gonna get outta here?* I had almost decided on a story I could tell when I heard someone move. Right next to the crack in the door was Daddy. He was so close, I could smell his woodsy-soap, tinged with blood and body heat.. Holding my breath, I sat stock-still. Daddy stood in the doorway watching Ethel. He leaned up against the frame, resting his head on his raised arm. His knuckles on his right hand were scrapped and bloody. He just stood there watching for a long time. Every so often he'd sigh. I could tell Ethel didn't know he was there. She was singing softly to herself. The door to my hideaway was cracked and I didn't want to close it for fear of being detected. As good as I was becoming at making up stories for why I was in strange places, I didn't get the feeling that anyone would be too happy finding me in that closet. Ethel hummed and then stopped. She picked up another fork, started to hum, and then stopped again. No one said a word. My breath roared in and out as I tried to control it. She looked up sharp, right at me. I was sure she saw me looking at her. Then she said, "Lord, Mista Joe, ya scared me! I didn't hear ya come in. You feelin' all right? Ya look 'bout low as a snake belly. Lord, Mista Joe what you done ta yo hand?"

He shifted his weight from one foot to the other, turned to leave, and then stopped; but he didn't say anything. Finally, he went into the kitchen and sat down at the table behind her. Daddy pushed the chair back, got up, went to the refrigerator, and opened the door. He took out a beer, and then another one. Squeezing by Ethel, Daddy opened and shut drawers until he found the can opener. He pried two triangles into the tops of the cans. One of the cans he sat down beside Ethel. Without saying a word, she dumped out the contents of a tin cup into the sink and poured the beer into the empty cup. Sliding off the stool, she lumbered over to the trash. Instead of tossing the empty can in, she placed it very precisely down the side of the trashcan and covered it with a scrap of paper.

He watched her, smiled a sad smile and asked, "Do that often?"

"No, sir, but ain't no use axin' fo' trouble. You know good as me that Miz Ginny would have a fit if'n she saw me drankin' a beer." Back at the sink, Ethel took a long pull from her tin cup, "Goes down mighty fine," she said, smacking her lips. "Be times when a beer just hits the spot." She continued her polishing.

Daddy grunted as he nursed his beer. Neither said anything for a long while. The vacuum cleaner was digging sharply into my left thigh no matter which way I squirmed. After what seemed like an hour, Ethel said, "Ain't like you to be home this time of day. Want me to fix ya some lunch? Miz Ginny out playin' cards, but I kin make you a sandwich if'n you want one."

"No, I'm not hungry. Thanks." He sat at the table, his head down, leaning into his beer. "I just don't know." The telephone rang. He got up to answer it, leaving his half-finished beer on the table. I dozed off waiting for Ethel to finish her polishing. I woke with a start when she bellowed her summons to come home out of the back door. After checking through the crack to see if the coast was clear, I carefully pushed the door open enough to get out undetected.

"Where'd you come from?" she asked, eyeing me suspiciously.

"Upstairs reading," I lied.

"Hmmmm," is all she said.

The living room, dining room, and hallway clear up to the third floor were painted a warm deep green; the kind of color you get when you squint hard while looking at trees on a sunny summer afternoon. My daddy said that color "had balls." My mother seemed pleased that men liked it. "Handsome," is what she called it. A banister started in the front hall and wrapped itself around twice until it ended on the third floor, right at Gordy's door. You could stand outside Gordy's bedroom and see clear to the first floor.

Two days after Lance died, Stuart must have been feeling really low because she hadn't come out of her room once. She asked Helen and me to leave her alone every time we knocked, but had a steady stream of grown-up visitors. My mother stopped in often, and from what Helen and I could tell there was none of the usual shouting. Daddy spent hours with her at night. Ethel brought food up regularly. I heard the springs groan as Ethel sat on Stuart's bed. I couldn't tell what they were saying, but I heard soft murmurs. I could just imagine Ethel stroking Stuart's head and patting her gently like she did me when I was sad.

When Stuart finally emerged from her room, she taught me how to slide down the banister sidesaddle instead of straddling it and going down backward. It was much faster and more fun to see where you were going. She and I practiced on the staircase coming from the second floor. It wasn't as steep, and there was more room to land in the wide front hall. The first couple of times I thought I was going to go straight through the front door when I got to the bottom.

"Right off the bat you have to control yourself at the end, because if you're not careful you shoot right off," she said. She held on to me until I found my balance. I didn't care if I never learned to slide down the banister the way Stuart did. Stuart spending so much time with me was so wonderful, nothing else much mattered. But I wanted her to be proud of me. It took a while to learn how much pressure to use. "It's subtle," she said. "You have to find your own way—like riding a bike." It took the whole afternoon for me to learn how to stop myself at the end of the banister and hop off like the tightrope walkers do. I was so excited to show Daddy my new accomplishment that I'd go to my room every few minutes and check out the front window to see if his car was coming up the drive. Then I'd go back to have another slide, perfecting my skills in order to impress him all the more. He never came home that night.

The next morning Stuart, Gordy, and Helen went to school, but I stayed home. I told Ethel I had a stomachache, and I kind of did. Truth is, I knew my father had to come back at some point and I wanted to be there when he did. I waited in my room for what seemed like forever while my mother hung around the house, chattering distractedly and making a nuisance of herself as Ethel did chores. Finally, my mother left for her bridge meeting. I crept downstairs. Ethel was outside hanging up laundry. Almost without thinking, I ducked in the broom closet, leaving the door ajar. Ethel came back inside. Before long the back door opened and my father walked into the kitchen. It was almost like he'd been waiting for my mother to leave. My first impulse was to run up and hug him and demand to know where he'd been, but the look on his face stopped me. He sat down at the table. He looked tired and worried. Ethel handed him a cup of coffee and started to fix him some toast. He lifted his hand to stop her. "I can't eat," he said.

"Go on, do ya some good." He just shook his head. She wiped the already clean counter. "Mista Joe, ya know she don't mean no harm. She's a good woman; tries as best she can."

Just then, trying to reposition myself to get a little more comfortable, I slipped and knocked up against the vacuum hose. Ethel caught the movement out of the corner of her eye. Our eyes locked for a second. Then she gave me one of her hairy eyeballs and turned back to Daddy.

"She's pregnant. Ethel, I can't do it. Jesus, we've got four children already. Four we can't take care of now. Another baby…" He leaned his elbows on his knees and hung his head. "Oh God, what the hell's a baby gonna help? It's her answer to everything. I don't know what I'm going to do. Can you talk some sense into her?"

"You know I can't. It ain't my place, Mista Joe." Ethel looked over at me. Without a word she conveyed the thought right into my brain that if I didn't get out of that closet and up to my bedroom there was a good chance I would never walk again. I inched the door open, checking with Ethel to see that Daddy couldn't see me. I slipped out of the broom closet and turned to leave, quietly moving into the hall and up the stairs. I was so panicked I hardly knew what to make of the information I had gathered. Then, realizing I might be missing some pretty important information as far as my future was concerned, I crept back down the stairs to listen from the coat closet with the door open.

Ethel was saying, "'Sides, what's there ta do? Too late to take the bull out of the field now."

"There are ways, but she won't even listen. She's acting like she's got me...like I'm in a trap."

"Mista Joe, you don' really mean it."

"What choice do I have? I swear to God, one more thing and I'm afraid I might lose my mind. Where would the kids be then? She spends money like we have the damn United States mint in the backyard. I can't take it. If I leave the kids, God knows what would happen. With that temper of hers, what if she...God, Ethel, she could hurt one of them and then where would we be? I've talked with a lawyer. If you don't testify, Ethel, she'll get the children. He said I didn't stand an iceball's chance in hell of getting custody. Apparently in the state of Virginia, judges don't take children away from their mothers unless there are dire circumstances. You are my only hope. You know her friends and brothers will circle the wagons. I need you to think long and hard about this Ethel. And like a damn bonehead I had to go and get charged with assault. Aw Jesus," he said as he put his head between his hands and looked like was crying.

"What yo mean assault? Who? I mean if 'n ya donne mind me axen."

"Dabney, he mouthed off one time too many and decked him the other day. The bastard swore out a warrant."

"Well sir, I's can't thinka no one mo deservin'. But Lord have mercy."

I could feel my eyes growing wide in the darkness; my head pounded so loudly I was sure they could hear it. I bit my lip hard to keep from crying. Nothing was said for a while. Then Daddy continued, "I've got to clear my head. I'm going to stay at the office for a while. Promise me you'll look after things until I can figure out what to do. I can't take the kids with me right now. I'm going to get some of my things and go. You've got my number. I'll call and check in. You call me if you need me. I hate this," he said. His voice thickened and quavered. "Ethel, I'm serious. You've got to help me."

I sat shell-shocked in the closet, suddenly realizing that I had forgotten to breathe the entire time he'd been speaking. I let out my breath as quietly as I could. A bnvbgnbaby? Daddy leaving? Decking Mr. Dabney? And what did he mean he couldn't take us with him? I was torn: part of me wanted to barge out and put a stop to the nonsense, but the stronger part of me was fearful of being discovered eavesdropping on such a secret exchange. Then I heard Ethel say, "I'd never let nothin' happen to my babies. Mista Joe, you jest got yo'self all riled up. Miz Ginny ain't bad off as all that."

"Yes she is Ethel," he said then pushed himself away from the table and stood to go.

"Don't you worry. Ethel ain't gonna let nothin' happen to my babies," she repeated, but she said it to herself. Daddy left the kitchen and was on his way upstairs. I silently pulled the closet door closed. Through the ceiling I could hear his dresser drawers opening and closing.

When he left the house again, Ethel got up and went upstairs. I eased out of the closet and tiptoed upstairs behind her, intending to sneak into bed before she could scold me. But when I got to my room she was already there, staring at my empty bed. She turned to look at me in the doorway. I was sure I was in for a bawling out and a spanking, but Ethel didn't even look annoyed.

"Lord a mercy," she said as she bustled across the room to wrap me tightly in her arms.

Chapter 10

———

Ethel
1942

Mista Joe and Miz Ginny was happy as cows in fresh clover after they set up housekeepin' in an apartment near the law school. Miz Ginny took to makin' friends like she'd been doin' it her whole life, which I knowed for a fact she hadn'. But she was makin' up for lost time. They had parties might near every weekend, and she always had someone over for dinner during the week.

Cookin' was not a thing Miz Ginny had much interest in, though I have to hand it to her, she did give it a try once or twice. After they come home from their honeymoon, she gushed about how she wanted to cook all of Mista Joe's meals. She said she was going to make bread and soups and roasts every night. So she asked me to help her make up a shoppin' list. That was one thing she was good at—shoppin'.

"So?" she said, lookin' at me like she thought I had the keys to the kingdom.

"First thang ya gotta do is pick what you gon' fix," I said feelin' sorta stupid since it was clear as day to me.

"Oh, of course. Well, we're going to have soup for our first course." She stopped and waited with her pen ready to write.

"Miz Ginny, what kinda soup you gonna have?" I 'bout rolled my eyes at her. I knowed she wasn't *that* stupid.

"I don't know. What do you think?"

"Lord a mercy. I don't even know what ya'll likes to eat. Mushroom?"

She shook her head.

"Why don't we start small and work up to courses later?" I said. "How 'bout a nice roast chicken, mashed potatoes, and green beans?" Even my simple sister Huberta could about handle cookin' that by herself, so I thought Miz Ginny could get by all right. She thought that was a fine idea. She took up her pen again, waiting for me to tell her what to buy. "I tell ya what, I'll jest call down to Mista Maupin's an' his boy can drop it by." She thought that was another fine idea. Maupin's boy brought the groceries by about an hour later. "Miz Ginny, the groceries is here. We best be getting that chicken in the oven if ya wantin' dinner tonight."

"Ethel, would you do it? I'm going over to Miss Charlotte's to play some bridge. When Mr. Joe gets home tell him where I am, won't you?"

And that was pretty much the way it was. Whenever there wasn't some bridge party or tennis game to go to, she would play at cookin'. She made such a mess I quit suggestin' it and fell into fixin' most of the meals myself. The ones I didn't cook, Mista Joe did. I could always tell if she'd been doin' what she called cookin'. When I come into the kitchen in the mornin', the pots an' dishes would be stacked in the sink—that is, the ones that'd fit—the others would be on top of any space that would hold 'em: chairs, tables, books; even the trashcan would have a roaster or pot perched on top it.

Then them Japanese up and bombed Pearl Harbor on Miz Ginny's birthday. She cried the whole livelong day, blubberin' about how her birthday would never be the same. "Everybody from now on will remember it as the day we were attacked and went to war," she wailed.

Mista Joe tried everything he could think of to cheer her up, but she wasn't havin' it. Nothin'—flowers, champagne, chocolates, fancy under things—could make her happy. It was a ruined day for her. Then when Mista Joe told her a few months later he was goin' to war, all she could say was, "You can't go off and leave me alone."

"Lord, Ginny," he said. "Could you think about anybody for one minute besides yourself?" That was the first time Mista Joe raised his voice to her in my hearing. "Hitler is doing dreadful things in Europe. He's bombing the bejeezus out of England. I can't just sit back and hold your hand while the world is going to war." He slammed the door and stomped out of the apartment. I understood what Mista Joe was feelin': Early's boy, Junior, done went off to the war.

Miz Ginny came into the kitchen—face all tearstained and swollen.

"He can't leave me. I don't know what I'll do. Oh God, Ethel, what am I going to do?" She laid her head on my shoulder and sobbed. I patted her on the back.

"We'll get through, and it'll be alrigh', Miz Ginny. I'm sho' it will." I weren't sho' at all, but I didn't know what else to say.

A few days later Mista Joe came home with some excitin' news. He'd been offered a job in an old Charlottesville law firm, and Miz Ginny was tickled. "Oh Joe, that is wonderful news! Now you don't have to go off to that old war. We can settle down and have a great big family and you can fight injustice right here at home. Honey, I'm so happy." She patted her hands together like a little girl, jumpin' 'round and kissin' the man all over his face.

That woman couldn't read her husband no better than she could a recipe book. All you had to do was look at him to see he wasn't gon' take that job. Ever' time she kissed him, his jaw got a little tighter. I decided it was best I go out and get the clothes off the line—I could see that storm comin' a mile away.

Mista Joe didn't go away for almost a year. He spent a lot of time going back and forth to Washington for his trainin'. I don't know for sure what it was. He never said, but I think he was some kind of spy. Miz Ginny was happy as she could be. All her friends' husbands were gone off to the war, so it was like one big hen party. There were knitting parties and card parties and war effort parties. And they wasn't no coffee or tea parties, neither. They was some hard-drinkin' women in that bunch, I'm here to tell you. When Mista Joe came home on leave, Miz Ginny got to show him off to all her friends.

There ain't a whole lot of things to do in a five room apartment, takin' care of one woman; although Miz Ginny could keep a soul busy doin' for her. She would worry a saint into sinnin' askin' silly questions about how she looked and did I think this would look better than that. What kinda fool would axe me questions 'bout fashion? And talk about going through laundry—that woman could make a pile of laundry faster than a nursery full of babies could. I never seen the like. But there was a sweetness 'bout Miz Ginny that I couldn't help but love. She might try on four dresses before she decided on the right one, and there was a good chance she'd toss all the three that didn' make it into a heap so they needed re-ironin', but she made sure to give me all them clothes and shoes when she got tired of 'em. Miz Ginny knowed full well theys wasn' goin' be fittin' me, but Mama and the girls could get a few years outta'em. We goes way back, me and Miz Ginny, and we turned out to be a good fit. She needed motherin' 'bout as much as I needed to mother.

In April of 1943, jus' a week befo' Mista Joe was to ship out (he couldn' tell where, though she hounded 'im hard to say), Miz Ginny come up pregnant. It was the happiest I'd seen them two since the first week of their marriage.

At first it seemed like Miz Ginny was a natural born mother. She sailed through bein' pregnant like it wasn' a thing at all. Her friends had mornin' sickness, swollen ankles, and gained too much weight, but Miz Ginny went to party after party and smoked like a chimney. I don't know if she'd say so, but I would guess them war years was about her best. There was a letter from Mista Joe most ever' day. If a day went by that she didn't get one, she would get two the next day: one in the mornin' post and another in the evenin'. She was good about writin' him too. Ever' day she had a note for the postman. Sometimes after a party, she'd write another for the afternoon; a long one explaining all about the party she went to the day before and how sorry she was she hadn't written more, but she had to get ready. She knew he would understand. Before she would seal the letters she would read 'em to me, skippin' over the private parts. I asked her a few times to write a letter to Junior, which she did. Then it was me that was the stupid one—just the opposite of when I was tryin' to teach her 'bout the meal plannin' and cookin'. She'd hold her pen and ask me what did I want to say to Junior, and I'd look at her dumb as a post. "I dunno," I'd say. "What you think?" Then she'd go and write the sweetest little note and read it back to me and we'd sign it, Love Ethel/Miz Ginny. It made me feel righ' good that Junior was gettin' some mail, an' gettin' it from me, too!

Mista Joe, Stuart, and world peace showed up one right after another, leastwise it seemed that way. Stuart was the first to make her arrival. She was the most beautiful baby I ever did see, and I couldn't have loved her more if she had been my own. From the moment I laid eyes on her I loved her. Miz Ginny was so proud of that baby, I thought she'd pop. She went righ' back to tha size she was befo' the baby in less than a month, and you just know she was happy 'bout that too.

Miz Bess come to help out when Miz Ginny brought Stuart home from the hospital, and I have to say, where Mama and Miz Pansy found sweetness in that woman, I don't know. She was the bossiest old battle-ax I ever run across. Nothin' was good enough. She had me cleanin', washin', and ironin' mornin', noon, and night. She'd find a wrinkle in a crib sheet and she'd ball it up into a knot and throw it in the dirty clothes—for a wrinkle! Babies can put stains on things that no amount of scrubbin' will take out, that don't mean it ain't clean. I was changin' the baby while Miz Bess supervised. It weren't like I didn't know how to change a baby's diaper. I'd been doing it since I was might near five-years-old. I picked up a diaper, newly washed, boiled, line dried, and ironed. Who irons diapers? Miz Bess spotted a stain on that diaper. She looked at me like I had taken my big foot and ground that baby diaper into the dirt. "Don't you ever put a diaper on this baby that looks like that. Do you hear me?"

I nodded. "Yes'm," I said. I found a spotless diaper and put it on the baby, wrapped 'er up good in a new clean blanket, and handed 'er to Miz Bess. Bless that baby's heart: she spit up the whole bottle of milk I'd just fed her all down Miz Bess's back. I took her from the old bag. She fussed like a sour goose on her way out of the room, and when she was gone, I snuggled with that precious child and kissed her all over. I knowed she and I was goin' to be good friends.

When Mista Joe walked through the door three months later, I don't rightly know which of us was happier to see him, Miz Ginny or me. But it was plain as the grin on his face that little Stuart was Mista Joe's hands down favorite girl. That wasn't an observation I made alone, neither. Whatever chance Miz Ginny had of being a good mother to Stuart went out the window when Mista Joe came home from war. Miz Ginny wasn't holdin' any truck with sharin' Mista Joe with nobody, even that po' little baby. Turns out Miz Ginny was a lot more like Miz Bess than anybody knew.

Mista Joe, along with most ever' man I knowed, includin' Junior, was changed after he come back from the war. He stayed on in the army for almost a year. The whole time he'd be goin' back and forth to Washington and stayin' for a week or ten days ever' trip. Miz Ginny had worked out a routine of partyin' with her girlfriends during his time away. That didn't set too well with Mista Joe now that he was back. The parties had begun to wind down some even before Stuart came, since a few of the ladies' husbands had been killed or injured in the war. Some of the others got pregnant and didn't have the healthy constitution Miz Ginny did, so they didn't feel like gettin' out. But there was a few hangers-on who could party with the best of them; ladies Mista Joe didn't cotton to much. Him and Miz Ginny had more than one row about it, too.

Sometimes I wonder if maybe Mista Joe and me hadn't been there, if Miz Ginny and Stuart might've learned to love each other. Every time Miz Ginny picked that baby up, Stuart would start screamin'. Mista Joe would take her and she would start up cooin' like a little dove. On my ha'f days, I worried more than I kin say 'bout that po' lil' baby; 'specially if Mista Joe weren't home. It wasn't like Miz Ginny would have hurt her. I know she loved that baby; she just didn't have the interest. And even when Miz Ginny was interested, you would have to go some to get her attention.

But Miz Ginny was proud that Stuart was beautiful; the most beautiful baby you ever laid eyes on. Nobody could see her and not say so. And Miz Ginny dressed her as pretty as a baby has ever been dressed. She played with that child like she was a doll baby: puttin' on and takin' off dresses just as often as turnin' water on and off at a tap. And every one of them needed to be pressed and starched. An' there was the diapers, an' the formula, an' ster'lizin' the baby bottles when I wasn't pushin' an iron around. It didn't take long for Miz Ginny to move on after the sameness set in. She sorta lost interest in takin' the baby out for walks an' showin' off her new slim figure.

"Ethel, will you take her? I can't stand the crying, not for another minute. Make her stop." She looked at me like she was 'bout to cry herself.

"I'll see what I ken do." I took the hollerin' lil' bundle from her mama and cooed to 'er a little while I bounced 'er in my arms real soft. The baby's cryin' stopped, but Miz Ginny picked up right where it left off, jest boohooin' like she done lost her only friend. "Lord, what's the matter, Miz Ginny?"

"I've been rocking and cooing all morning long," she blubbered. "I've walked her and bounced her just like you showed me. What am I doing wrong?" She slumped in the rockin' chair, covered her face with her hands, and cried softly. My heart like to broke for the po' soul. I had no idea what to say.

There sho' weren't as much joy in the house when Miz Ginny found out that Gordy was on the way. But Baby Gordy sho' loved his mama. Miz Ginny got as close as I ever seen her to bein' a dotin' parent with him. He was a fat, happy baby for ever' body, includin' Stuart, who loved her baby brother. But nobody loved them children more than Mista Joe. He might come home tired and wore out, but the minute he seen them babies, he lit up like a Christmas tree. Stuart would run to him with a book. They would sit and read for as long as Miz Ginny would let 'em.

By the time you—lil' Miss Sallee—was on the way, Mista Joe had got fed up with lawyerin' and was head over heels interested in that shoppin' center. The wave of the future, according to yo' uncle, Mista James. Mista Joe and Mista James would sit on the sofa talkin' 'bout how the downtowns was dyin' and everything was movin' out of town. I didn't have any notion what they was talkin' about. Whatever it was, they was hot on the trail of it. Mista Joe talked about progress and how important it was, and Mista James agreed. After a while Miz Ginny stopped havin' Mista James and his wife, Miz Lisbeth, over to the house. Then she stopped seein' 'em altogether; her own brother, flesh and blood. She blamed Mista James and Miz Lisbeth for leadin' Mista Joe into that dangerous new world of his; one that didn't seem to 'specially include Miz Ginny. But I didn't see Mista Joe shuttin' her out. It was more like she didn't want to go there. Whatever rows Miz Ginny and Mista Joe had before couldn't hold a candle to the ones they havin' now.

Chapter 11

Sallee

"Pregnant," Gordy screwed up his face like he smelled something bad. "She's gonna have a baby?"

"Yeah," I whispered, nodding my head solemnly. No one was around to hear us, but whispering felt appropriate given the gravity of the information I was imparting. "He came home around one o'clock, got some clothes, and then left because Mama's pregnant and he doesn't want it."

"Who doesn't want?"

"Why, Daddy doesn't, on account of his already having us."

"Well, I don't want one, neither," Gordy said, swinging his leg over the tree limb we'd been sitting on and letting himself down to the ground. "What do we need another kid around here for? And why does she have to go and have one if it means Daddy doesn't want to live here anymore?"

His spin on things startled me. "Whaddya mean he doesn't want to live here no more?" I demanded. Up until then it hadn't sunk in that Daddy's stay at the office might be more than a tactic to win the argument. "He's just staying at work. He'll come home when she gives up," I insisted. I wasn't so sure, though. I didn't know the first thing about what it took to talk someone out of being pregnant, or even what that meant; but I did know that my mother rarely budged on any subject.

Gordy shrugged and seemed unwilling to take the matter further. He kicked the grass and looked out toward the street. "We still gotta find out who killed Lance. Come on."

"Not me. I'm not going to sneak around—no more hiding in closets."

"Nobody but a dummy hides in the broom closet to find out clues for who killed their dog. You know Ethel didn't."

"I don't know nothing anymore. Daddy's drinking beer with Ethel. Mama's having a baby. Lance is dead. Oh, oh I can't believe I almost forgot this. Daddy decked Mr. Dabney. Nothing makes any sense anymore."

Gordy spun around. "Daddy decked Mr. Dabney? Are you nuts? How do you know?"

"He said. When he was talking to Ethel. And the time before, I saw his hand was all bloody."

"On my way back from school yesterday I saw a police car driving around going real slow. They stopped at the Dabneys' house."

"Well yeah, He's tryin' to get Daddy arrested for deckin' him. Did the police get out?"

"No, just slowed down and took their time looking into their yard. They must think they did it. Wait, Mr. Dabney's tryin' to arrest Daddy?" He started walking in the direction of the Dabneys' house.

I wasn't as sure as Gordy seemed to be. Mr. Dabney was creepy, but Miz Dabney had always been nice to me. I couldn't picture them as dog killers or people who would try to ruin your tires with a bunch of nails, but then he was trying to arrest Daddy. "Where are you going? You're not going over there, are you?"

"Nope, *we* are. Come on." He slipped under the fence." Don't worry, you won't get in trouble. Nobody will see us cuz we're going to sneak up on them," he whispered loudly as he disappeared into the bamboo that grew wild behind the garage. I ran to catch up. Bamboo is rough stuff to get through without a track. Gordy used to go this way often. His friend George lived four streets away. They had figured out how to visit each other without having to cross streets by cutting through backyards. Gordy's trail had already grown over, but since he knew where he was going, he made much faster progress than I could. "Gordy, wait!" I called, as I plowed through the bamboo, running into dead ends, and doubling back. I searched for a trail or signs that Gordy had passed that way. "Gordy!" I shouted.

I tripped over bamboo shoots and stumbled over their sharp little stumps. The clumps were so thick it was impossible to get through them. It was as if the bamboo plants were directing me deep into a maze. "Where are you? Gordy!"

"Would you shut up?" he said, coming up from behind me. "Jeez, how are we going to sneak around if you're screaming your head off?"

"You went off and left me." I wanted to sob but felt like it was some kind of test. Since I hadn't done well so far, I tried to pull myself together. "Where are we?"

"Look," he said, pointing through a clearing in the bamboo. As I followed his finger, I realized that I could throw a rock through my bedroom window from where I stood.

"Oh."

"Now look, do you want to do this or not? Cuz, if you do you can't be crying and yelling like a ninny. If ol' Dabney killed Lance, he could kill us too." The thought shook us both.

"I don't know if I want to. What if we get caught?"

"We're not going to if you keep quiet. Now come on." Gordy took my hand and led me through the bamboo. Soon we were at the side of the Dabneys' brick house, which, like their yard, was completely covered in ivy. We climbed the picket fence that separated their yard from a neighbor's. The paint peeled off the rotten boards leaving a chalky residue on our hands. I was grateful that the weather was cold. Ivy was creepy enough to walk in without having to worry about snakes.

"Gordy, look—they're here," I said, pointing to the car parked in the driveway.

"That car has been in the same place for the last month. I don't think it works," he whispered back. "They can't see us if we stay on this side of the house."

"How do you know if you haven't ever been inside their house?" I asked. I was impressed by his knowledge. "I have, but I couldn't tell you what they can see from the inside. Besides, they always have the shades drawn." I looked at Gordy like he had amazing magical powers.

"Their house is just like my buddy Bobby's. Look." Again I followed his finger as he pointed to the windows on the house. "See, there's the bathroom and the kitchen and the back steps."

"Wow," I relaxed. "How did you figure that out?"

"All ya gotta do is pay attention," he said offhandedly. "Come on, we've got to get going."

"What are we looking for, anyway?"

"Antifreeze," he hissed.

"I don't know what antifreeze looks like."

"You can read can't you? Just look for a can with a-n-t-i-f-r-e-e-z-e written on it. Let's go over and look around under the back steps."

We scurried from tree to tree as we made our way to the porch. The ivy was so thick in places it was like running through knots of string. I tripped and fell several times. Gordy bent down to help me up, not once calling me a name. Overwhelmed with gratitude, I vowed silently not to let him down. I would find Lance's killer, no matter what it took. We poked around under the steps that climbed up a full story above our heads. I poked Gordy and pointed. The car that scared us so badly the day we were playing with Lil' Early was there, right there. "I knew I'd seen it before. The car. Look, it's the one; the one from that day."

"Yeah, you're right. Gosh." Gordy pursed his lips but moved on.

The wooden garage doors were slightly ajar. I raced inside without a second thought, glad to be out of sight and away from that car. It took a minute or two for my eyes to adjust to the dim light. In front of me was a huge, rusted, blue barrel overflowing with trash. Old oilcans littered the dirt floor. Gordy stumbled in after me just as the door overhead creaked open.

"Who's there?" A man growled from above. The voice sounded like Mr. Dabney's. "Who's down there? I'm going to call the police." The door slammed and we heard the lock bolt shut.

Our snooping around was beginning to make me uncomfortable. "Gordy, why don't we just knock on the door?" I thought about Miz Dabney's muffins and how she'd talked to me about being in love. "I'm sure they'd let us in. Besides, I don't think they killed ol' Lance anyway…"

"Shut up! We've got to get out of here," Gordy whispered. "Come on, run. Go back the way we came. I'll be right behind you." He pushed me out of the door. I started running in the direction Gordy indicated, but my feet got tangled in the ivy. I nearly fell. I realized the best way out was the driveway. I turned around and ran, with little care of being seen, past the house and up the drive. When I got to the street, I hesitated for a second before darting up the sidewalk to our driveway. I sprinted to our house as if the yucky old Mr. Dabney was on my heels, stopping only to catch my breath behind the hemlock tree at the kitchen steps. No Gordy. Creeping around to the back door seemed logical. I rarely used the kitchen steps, and I certainly didn't want to give Ethel something to wonder about. She was putting the last touches on dinner as I casually walked into the kitchen.

"I's jest 'bout ta call ya. Where's Gordy and Helen?"

"I don't know. I think Gordy's outside. You better call him. I'll go see if I can find Helen," I said, darting from the kitchen before she could ask me where I'd been. Although it had become easy to do, I didn't like lying about what I'd been doing or where I had been. Lying seemed like a necessary survival skill—one I preferred to use sparingly.

"Gor—don!" Ethel's hog call rang out the kitchen door. It made me feel better. Ethel's bellow was as sure as the five o'clock whistle. I knew Gordy would be home any minute. All the mothers in the neighborhood would check to see if Gordy were about when Ethel's call rang out.

But Gordy didn't come home for supper. I volunteered to stay with Helen so Ethel could go out to look for him. I was unsure if I should tell where I last saw him. I was not so afraid of getting into trouble as I was worried that I might betray Gordy. Ethel came in the house puffing and blowing. "He ain't out in the yard. None of the neighbors has seen him," she reported to no one. "You know anything?" She glared at me. "Lord a mercy, we don' need no mo' trouble in this house," she muttered as she fidgeted with her rag, wiped clean counters, and straightened already straight chairs. My mother was out. Ethel's agitation increased with every passing moment. When the doorbell rang, she practically jumped in the air. I ran to the window and noticed funny lights in the driveway. Gordy stood on the porch between two policemen. Instead of opening the door,

I turned back to the kitchen, running smack into Ethel who had followed me.

"What the matter wit' you, girl? Go'n, open the do'!"

"Ethel, there's policemen out there."

"Lord a mercy." She hustled to the door and opened it, revealing a tear-and-grease-streaked Gordy sporting a shiner. His clothes were a filthy mess of oil and dirt; his hair sprouting broom bristles. He was accompanied by a mismatched pair of policemen. "Thank ya, Lord!" Ethel said, her hands lifted upward and her eyes rolled up a little, so I guess she was talking to God. "Chile, where you been?" she asked, ignoring the policemen altogether. "Git on in here right dis minute. I oughtta tan yo' hide."

The taller policeman cleared his throat. "Is Mr. Mackey home?"

"No, sir, he ain't," she said, a little taken aback. "Miz Mackey ain't here, neither."

"Is this their son, Gordon Mackey?"

"Yes, sir."

"Where can we git in touch with Mr. Mackey?"

"I don' rightly know. Miz Mackey'll be back soon." Ethel attempted to reach out to Gordy, but the fat little policeman put himself in the way.

"We found him in the Dabneys' garage."

Ethel stood in the doorway with her hands on her hips, glaring at Gordy as if she were Superman and her x-ray vision was going to melt him into a puddle right there on the porch. "Boy, what done got into you? I know one thang: when I git my hands on ya, Imma make it so ya cain' sit fo' a week, hear me?"

"We need to talk to the person responsible for this kid."

"I's responsible fo' des here chil'ren. I raised ever' las' one a 'em."

"The parents, girl. Where are they?" The fat little policeman barked. He reminded me of the big kid down the street who bullied everybody, always hitching up his pants, and strutting around like a pigeon.

"Day's out. I's in charge. What ya'll gotta say ya'll kin says ta me." Ethel puffed up like she was going to take a swing at the mean little policeman. I was pretty sure, judging by the fuzziness of her hairdo, that she had taken a "nip" or two. Gordy had worked it out that you could get a good estimation of Ethel's sobriety by how tightly her hair was arranged. She tended to get cranky when she was drinking, so her hair became our mood barometer. I prayed in this situation that she hadn't launched a full-scale attack on the gin bottle she always seemed to have stashed somewhere these days.

"I ain't telling no nigger nothing 'bout a white boy," the short policeman spat out. "You better get somebody quick, or we're taking him downtown." The tall policeman looked like he was going to say something, but didn't.

I could see anger flash in Ethel's eyes, but she hid it from the policemen by looking down at the floor. She was thinking what to do. "I'm gonna call Mista Joe," she finally said, looking at the short policeman. "Don' be standin' here wit the do' wide open letten' in da cold. I'll go an' call 'im. You stay right here jest a minute." She pointed at the hallway floor.

When the policemen stepped in, she shut the door after them and lumbered down the hall to the phone. She looked back every few steps like she thought they might steal something if she didn't keep an eye out. Gordy looked pale and worried, but he smiled as he watched Ethel's bustling waddle. The mean policeman inched his way farther into the hall, looking after Ethel as she made her way to the phone; the taller one stood by the door with his hat in his hand.

The mean one sort of whistled and said, "Anybody dumb enough that would let a nigger in here by themselves with all this and leave nothin' but a bunch of kids to watch 'em...Shit, that nigger could steal 'em blind and they'd deserve it." I scowled at the little policeman from the dining room. I was too afraid to come out into the hall. Daddy said people who talked like that were ignorant. *Ignorant and stupid must be the same thing*, I thought. I found myself hating this man. Gordy looked like he wanted to kick him.

"Hello, Mista Joe, dis here Ethel," she boomed into the phone. "Day's some po'lease mens here. Day's got Gordy. Day say day found 'em in de Dabneys' garage an' if'in ya'll don' come an' talks ta 'em, day is gonna puts him in da jail house. Yes, sir. Jest a minute."

Ethel bustled back. She said with some pride, "Mista Joe want ta talk to ya'll."

The tall policeman followed her back to the telephone. We weren't able to hear what he said, but when he came back he said to his partner, "Come on, let's go." His partner grunted, leered at us, and left without a word. The tall policeman said to Ethel, "Sorry about all that."

It was lucky for Gordy that the mean little policeman had called Ethel a nigger. That had made her madder than what Gordy had done. I thought she would give him a tongue-lashing hot enough to peel his hide. She huffed and puffed like the big bad wolf, pacing the hall. I think she was so mad she didn't know *what* to do. Finally she said, "Gordy, go'n up to yo' room righ' now. Don' you sit down and get nothin' dirty. You gots oil all over ya. Yo' Daddy comin' over an' he gon' give you a piece a his min'."

I started up the stairs after Gordy. "You git right back he'ah, missy. Don' lemme catch ya anywhere near yo' brother this evenin', hear? Go'n upstairs wit' Helen and take a bath and git ready fo' bed."

The green splatterwear tin cup Ethel used to hide the gin she drank appeared from under the kitchen sink a few days later (never a good sign) from where it had been hidden behind the Joy and Comet. Sometimes she'd conceal a beer in the cabinet where the pots and pans were stored—an oversized Pabst Blue Ribbon bottle wrapped in a brown paper bag. Before a binge really got underway, Ethel would attempt to be discreet. But as time wore on, and her nips turned to gulps, she became as sloppy with her concealment as she was with her person.

Helen and I were sprawled on the floor in the sitting room watching *The Wild, Wild West*. Ethel stormed into the room. One of her buns had come loose and the other three buns were in varying stages of disarray. We had learned from our rapidly accumulating experience that the best approach to Ethel in that condition was to pretend she was not there. We continued to watch the television. Ethel stood just inside the door, swaying menacingly and glaring at us with unfocused eyes. As if someone had turned a switch, she started ranting, "Tha word is 'negro,' not nigger."

Helen and I looked up, bewildered.

"Don' you ever call me a nigger. Look it up in tha dictionary, it'll tell ya." She lunged toward the bookcase, found a dictionary, and fumbled around with it. Then, giving up the search, she began flailing it around like a preacher on Sunday. Three more times she said, "Tha word is negro." Then she left the room.

It was two days before I could get Gordy alone since he was grounded and I was expressly forbidden to go into his room. From a downstairs window I watched him riding his bike up and down the drive. When I could see nobody was around, I scurried outside and got on my bike.

"What happened?" I yelled as I came alongside him. We rolled along in silence. I squinted at him, trying to nudge a response. "Well, what?" He skidded his bike to a stop, dropped it in the dirt, and climbed up to a favorite perch in his tree. I followed silently and sat on the branch below his; my back against the trunk, legs swinging. I waited. He still didn't say anything. "Gordy," I bleated. "What happened?" He just sat there, looking off in the distance.

Then he looked at me. "Just after you left I saw a bowl full of some greenish-looking stuff," he said. "You know how antifreeze is that kinda electricy-yellowish-green? Like that. There was a piece of butcher's paper next to that bowl. I think Mr. Dabney put some meat in it and Lance ate it. I figured that I'd wait until the police came and show them. So they could arrest him."

"Where was Miz Dabney?"

"I don't know. Will you shut up and listen! He called down the steps a couple of times. At first he was trying to sound sorta nice. He said, 'Who's there? I'm going to call the police. You leave or I'm calling the police.'

"'You poisoned my dog, didn't you?' I yelled. I couldn't believe I was talking to him like that, but I knew he did it, I just knew it.

"He said, 'Who's there? You come out right now or I'm calling the police.' I told him, 'Call the police. I'm going to wait. I'm not leaving until they come and take me outta here.' I was sure they would be takin' him out, not me. It was getting dark. I decided the best thing I could do was to just sit down and wait. I didn't want to get into any trouble, but I was pretty sure that when they came and saw the poison in the bowl and the paper, he'd have to go to jail. The garage was all creepy in the dark.

There wasn't any place on the floor not covered in junk and trash. I went to move some stuff so I could sit down. I must have sat on the end of a board or something because the other end went up in the air, knocking a bunch of cans over. Ol' Dabney turned on the light upstairs and started creeping down the stairs. He was carrying a broom. 'I called the police,' he said. 'You're going to be sorry now, buster.'

"When he saw me, he started whaling on me with that broom. 'I know who you are,' he said. 'You're one of them Mackey brats. Go on home to your nigger-loving parents. Get the hell outta my house.'"

My eyebrows shot up. "He hit you with a broom?"

Gordy nodded solemnly. "I screamed at him, 'You killed Lance. You killed my dog.' I tried to get away from that broom, but I tripped and knocked over the bowl of antifreeze. I couldn't get up; there was so much grease and muck. He kept hitting me and yelling, 'All you Mackeys think you're so high and mighty just like your Ma. You ain't nothing but a nigger loving lowlife—breaking into my house.'

"Sallee, I never heard a grown-up talk like he did, except for those men in that car. I'll bet he was one of 'em, ya know?" Gordy shivered, like he was cold. "He just kept banging on me with that broom, yelling all kinds of stuff. When the police finally came, he quit hitting me. 'I found this kid sneaking around,' he said. 'Had his foot on the step going up to our bedroom like he was goin' to rob us. I chased him down here. Probably learned his thieving from that nigger woman next door and that bully father a his.'

"The tall policeman asked me, 'Son, what were you doing in these folks' house?' So I told him, 'He poisoned my dog. Look, there's a bowl of antifreeze and some meat paper right there where he did it.' I pointed. But all the stuff was scattered and the bowl was turned over. 'He's a lying little burglar,' Mr. Dabney screamed, 'And I'm going to press charges. Just like I did on his no count daddy' The tall policeman took me to the car while the fat one talked to Mr. Dabney some more.

"'He killed my dog. I know he did,' I said to the tall one. He started to say something, but the fat guy opened the door and got into the car. He turned and looked at me over the seat. 'Nobody killed your dog, kid,' he said. 'And you're in a powerful lot of trouble. If you know what's good for you, I better not ever find you near this house again. Breaking and entering is a felony. That's what we're talking about there. You could spend a lot of time in jail. It don't make any difference who your parents are.'"

Gordy sniffed hard. I could tell he was trying not to cry. I reached up from my perch on the limb below him and patted his leg. "I'm glad you didn't go to jail," I offered.

"You know, Sallee, I think Mr. Dabney musta known Momma before, like when they were kids or something."

"Why do you say that?" I asked while trying to think of a story that could include two such unlikely characters.

"Something 'bout the way he said we were all just as uppity as her."

The next day the sheriff called our house to report on the autopsy. Lance *had* been poisoned by antifreeze, just as Gordy thought. But the sheriff didn't believe the nails and Lance's death were related—just two accidents, is all. Daddy seemed unhappy with what the sheriff said. He was sitting on the back porch, smoking. I stepped out on the porch and plopped onto his lap. "Sallee!" he snapped, "Go sit over there."

I slunk over to the indicated spot next to Gordy. "Mr. Dabney did it on purpose," Gordy said, looking at Daddy.

Daddy regarded him gravely. "I don't know," Daddy said. "I wouldn't have ever thought it was on purpose..." He pondered for a moment. "Probably they were just accidents. There's no way to tell." He cut Gordy a hard look. "And you had better not even think about trying to find out more, young man."

My mother came through the screen door all giddy and excited, like she had been ever since Daddy left. She looked so pretty; smiling and happy. "I have a little surprise for you," she said to Daddy.

He didn't even look up. He crushed out his cigarette in the ashtray.

"What is it?" Gordy and I asked.

"Where are the rest of you?" my mother asked.

"I'll get 'em," I volunteered and opened the door into the house. "Stuart, Helen! Mama's got a surprise. Hurry up!"

"Dammit, Sallee," Daddy said. "Stop screaming. Go get 'em." Now that he was gone so much of the time, it hurt worse than ever to have him angry with me. I sidled inside and ran upstairs, wishing things were different.

Once I'd gotten Stuart and Helen out on the porch, my mother, who loved to draw things out, said, "Now everybody close your eyes. Don't peek."

"For Christ sake, Ginny, get on with it," Daddy sighed.

I wanted to cry. I squeezed my eyes shut as tightly as I could, trying to stem the tears. I heard the screen door open and shut, then open and shut again. "OK, now open your eyes," my mother said. Her voice was tinny.

"A puppy!" we all shrieked, scaring the poor little creature to death. Daddy got up and went into the house without a word. He took what happiness there was with him. The puppy cowered. My mother hesitated, like a bird on a hot wire, and then followed him inside. Ethel appeared at the door and watched as we tried playing with the puppy. Stuart finally picked up the terrified little dog and snuggled it close. She stopped on her way through the door and laid her head on Ethel's shoulder. Ethel patted her lovingly for a moment. Then Stuart disappeared into the house.

Gordy and I went down the steps into the yard. "It's cute," I said. "It looks like Granny Bess's dog. Remember?" I scanned the yard and let my eyes fall on Lance's old doghouse. The puppy had perfect floppy ears and the softest fur, but still, I felt funny about having a new dog.

"It isn't Lance," Gordy replied gruffly. "He was just too big a dog for a dumb puppy to take his place. I don't even care what she names the ol' thing," he said, kicking at a clump of weeds. "I don't know why she's always trying to ruin things."

"Who? Who tried to ruin something? Mama?" I asked as I ran my foot through a pile of wet leaves. We looked expectantly at the scattered leaves, hoping to find we didn't know what.

"Yeah, Lance hasn't been dead two weeks and she's gone out and bought another dog. It just ain't right. Some things ya just gotta let happen. Give time."

"Hum," I said. I had never known Gordy to have so many opinions. "How'd you get so smart all of a sudden?"

"Shut up. Let's go over to Mr. Gentry's and see if Ethel's right. Maybe the old bastard really did kill Lance."

"Whew, boy, you better not let Ethel hear you talk like that. She'll wash your mouth out with soap sure as you're standing there."

"I don't care if she does," he shot back as he turned to go.

"Hey, wait, you said it was Mr. Dabney who killed Lance."

Gordy weighed this for a moment. "Maybe they all did, damn grown-ups," he concluded then stomped off toward the street.

"Don't go that way," I hissed. "Ethel'll see you. She just told us not to cross the street."

"Are you comin' or not?"

"I don't know. I don't want to get in trouble. It's gettin' dark." I watched Gordy cross the street and disappear into the darkness. I hesitated, wondering whether to follow. I was unsure why I felt so threatened. Finally, I slunk back to the house.

Helen and I went to bed early that night. From their room across the hall, I could hear my mother and father talking as they dressed to go out. My mother loved going to parties. Daddy didn't think much of them. I was glad he was back in their room. When he'd come home to deal with Gordy, he'd brought his suitcase with him. We children all hoped it meant he was back for good.

"Damn it, Ginny, would you lay off?" I heard Daddy bark. "I know what I'm doing. How many times do I have to tell you, you don't need to worry? Nobody is going to hold you responsible. It's not always about your damned ass."

"Joe, the talk is getting more and more unpleasant. With all the things going on, I'm beginning to worry. Why did you think we needed a shopping center, anyway? It's embarrassing. Why couldn't you build something important like a new post office or a library at the university? Maybe a wing on the hospital...Betty told me that Bernard overheard at the club the other night that..."

I heard drawers slamming. It sounded like the ones in my mother's dressing table. I imaged she'd put on her makeup and was looking for jewelry to wear like she always did. She was pretty good at driving home a point by slamming whatever drawer was handy.

"Jesus Christ!" Daddy yelled. His voice sounded like he was near the door. Then, quieter, he said, "As much as you love to shop, you're going to love this new shopping center. You wait. You're gonna feel like a queen when everybody starts using it. You'll see. Besides, what the hell does Betty know? She never had an original thought in her over dyed head. If she had, she wouldn't have married that windbag Chambers who spends his life gossiping—looking for ways to run people down."

"Would you listen? Bernard said that Pete is pulling out of the project. He says you're way behind schedule…losing money…that you're in way over your head."

"Who are you going to believe, me or that sack of shit Chambers? I've told you a thousand times, you don't have anything to worry about. Pete and I played golf yesterday, and he didn't say a word to me about pulling out. We talked a lot about the delays. If he were nervous, I'd know."

"But honey," my mother pushed on, her voice soft and calculated, "what about Lance? Surely you don't think this shopping center is worth putting our family in danger."

My father's voice bellowed so loud I was sure the neighbors could hear it. "Jesus, Ginny! If someone poisoned our dog it didn't have anything to do with the shopping center. Maybe if you paid attention to something other than yourself, you'd realize that." I didn't hear my mother respond. I wondered if she was crying. Then I heard Daddy say, "Go on and get dressed. We gotta hurry up and get to this damn party so we can leave and get home."

She sighed so loudly I could hear it. "If you say so, but you know you always have fun once you get there. Don't be so silly." Things went quiet. Then, just after she asked him to zip her dress, she said, "Honey, another thing: please don't talk about the shopping center. I'd like to have just one nice evening without listening to a debate about 'progress'"

"Stop, goddamn it, Ginny, not another goddamn word," he bellowed.

I turned over and pulled my pillow over my head.

The next morning during breakfast, Daddy wasn't at the dining room table. I thought he must still be in bed, which was something that never happened except when they'd been to parties the night before. As usual, my mother reigned at the head of the table, drinking coffee and her fresh squeezed orange juice. There wasn't another person in the world who could make such a big deal about fresh squeezed orange juice.

In the kitchen Ethel fixed a plate of poached eggs and toast and took it to my mother. "Tell the girls and Gordy to hurry up and get ready," I heard her say. "I'm driving them to school this morning."

Ethel relayed the message when she returned to the kitchen. Stuart groaned loudly. "They tied a big one on last night," she said. "Did you hear 'em?"

She slumped at the table, spooning cornflakes into her face as if she were shoveling sand into a bucket. Then her spoon clattered against the bowl. We heard my mother going upstairs to her room.

"I hate her," Stuart said. "She's so mean to him. I wish he would leave her for good and take me with him."

Ethel shot back, "Ya know you don' mean that, an' don' be callin' yo' mother 'she,' hear me? Miz Ginny *deserve* respect."

"Why would that be? Because she hatched out a bunch of brats? 'Cause all she knows how to do is screw?" Stuart sneered.

Gordy, Helen, and I exchanged shocked looks. I couldn't imagine anyone talking to Ethel like that. I hunkered close to the table in case the fur really began to fly.

Ethel just stood there, eyes bulging. Then her mouth set firm. "You best be watchin' ya mouth, young lady," she thundered. "You ain't too big that I can't turn you over my knee still."

"Go ahead and try," Stuart said. "I'm *so* afraid. Hurry up, you guys. I don't want to be late for school."

Then she turned on me. "Stop sniveling, you little brat. Just shut up."

"I didn't..."

She slammed out of the kitchen.

Ethel let out a long, slow sigh and gave me a pat. "Don' pay her no min', honey," she said. "Stuart jus' done got up on tha wrong side of the bed this mornin'."

Under his breath Gordy added, "And every other morning her whole life." Then he said, "Ethel?"

"What you want, darlin'?"

"I was just wonderin'...They aren't gonna get a divorce, are they?"

"Where you hear such a thang? Ain't no cause fo' you..."

"Gordy, Sallee, hurry up," my mother called as she went out the front door.

In the car she seemed as jovial as Daddy usually was. She even started to sing about the bear going over the mountain. Stuart had gotten in the back seat, so Gordy had to sit up front. As we started down the driveway, Stuart said, "Would you *please* spare us the show?"

Time slowed and every sound amplified. I held my breath, afraid to disturb the air. No one said a word for two long, painful blocks. Then my mother casually asked, "Did you get up on the wrong side of the bed, dear?" From her tone I thought it might be safe to breathe again; but catching a glimpse of her face, I knew otherwise. I cut a sideways glance at Gordy. He too was frozen in fear, staring straight ahead, zombie like.

"Why are you so mean?" Stuart cried. "I heard him leave last night."

I did a mental inventory of the driveway. We were in Daddy's car. I hadn't noticed if hers was there when we left.

"I heard you screaming at him that you had his keys." Stuart was growing hysterical. She began to sob. "How can you be so, so hateful? Is everything just a show to you?"

Chapter 12

The last party I remember my mother having was on a cold, crisp Saturday a few weeks shy of Christmas. The trees in the yard were barren, but garlands and decorations brightened the house. My mother had decided to have *just a few* friends over for a holiday luncheon. As always, she was serving the yummiest things: tiny sandwiches cut into pretty shapes, aspic, cheese soufflé, and Waldorf salad with apples, raisins, and nuts.

Gordy, Helen, and I perched like so many birds in my hemlock tree by the driveway, chattering to each other as we watched the ladies arrive in their pretty hats and fur coats. As they bustled to the house, we giggled from the tree branches, hidden from sight.

"Gosh, I hope she doesn't hit the tree," Gordy hissed, throwing his hands up to protect his head in mock despair as one of the ladies maneuvered her huge Cadillac around the other cars in the drive. Every time she put on the brakes, Gordy would emit an *errch* and then *zroom* when she'd start forward again. Helen and I held on to the branch above us to keep from falling as we snorted and laughed, trying not to be heard. It felt good to laugh. There hadn't been much to laugh about in a long time.

"It's cold out here; let's get something to eat," Helen offered, just as the kitchen door opened. Ethel stuck her head out and gave one of her earsplitting hollers to summon us.

"Ya'll get in here now. I gots to get ya cleaned up and fed before I can serve lunch!" No sooner had Ethel finished her complaint than we were racing each other up the back steps. Gordy *errched* and *vroomed* as he steered his pretend car every which way but straight while Helen and I laughed until tears ran down out cheeks.

"Ya'll stop actin' the fool and wash up," Ethel snapped. "I laid yo' clothes out on yo' beds. I want ya'll to eat this here lunch and go'ne upstairs and put 'em on when you finished eatin'. I ain't gots time to be tellin' ya'll twice, ya hear?" Gordy and I both saw Ethel's green splatterware cup in the kitchen sink. We looked at each other and our laughter stopped.

We knew better than to get crosswise with Ethel when she was drinking. So we sat right down at the table, ate our lunch, and left the kitchen without a word. Upstairs, as we changed into the clean clothes Ethel had lain out, Helen stomped her foot. "I hate it when she drinks," she said. "Don't you?"

No matter the occasion, my mother always looked dressed up to me. Her shoes and purses matched, and routinely she wore gloves. But somehow I was always surprised at how pretty she looked at her parties, this one in particular. I'd heard her complain to Ethel before guests began to arrive that in her condition she felt that she looked as big as a house. To me she looked beautiful. Her new maternity dress was navy blue with white polka dots. The shoes she wore were matching navy blue, with very high heels. They had little holes in them like my father's business shoes.

I felt so much more grown up now than I had the year before. Then, I would've much rather gone to bed without dinner than to make an appearance at one of my mother's parties or luncheons. Now I'd come to the surprising conclusion that some of my mother's friends could be fun. They asked me questions and seemed to want to know the answers. As I helped Ethel pass hors d'oeuvres, I chatted with the guests. I discovered that I loved the attention I was getting. I could retreat behind the big serving plate, so I didn't have to worry about introductions or what to say afterward. In an attempt to stretch my social skills, I mentioned that I had seen a redheaded peckerwood that morning to a lady who'd commented on how many birds she had at her feeder lately. Everyone laughed. I thought I was so clever until my mother corrected me, patting me on the head, "That is a redheaded *woodpecker*, sweetie." She turned to her friends. "It's a fulltime job keeping the children from sounding like Ethel," she said. "She makes me laugh, but honestly, I don't want my children talking like that. What did she say the other day that was so funny...?" Stuart rolled her eyes at my mother. I looked around to see if Ethel was anywhere within earshot. I didn't see her and sighed with relief. My face was burning with the embarrassment of having been corrected in front of everyone.

Our house looked as pretty as my mother: it was full of cheer, flickering candles, and a glittering Christmas tree. It was as if the house was wearing party clothes, too. The crystal, silver, and wood polished to a high shine for the special day added to the magic. Ethel was dressed up as well. Her usual light blue or gray uniform with white collar, white cuffs, and a big white apron was replaced with a black uniform with no apron at all. She looked formal and distant to me. Although it had come a little loose from her nipping at the gin, her hair was fixed in a single large bun at the nape of her neck instead of the four small buns she usually wore that made her head look square. As she bent to serve them, the ladies seated at a table greeted her as an old friend. I overheard someone say to my mother, "You're so lucky to have Ethel. Good help just doesn't come along like that, you know."

"Ethel and I wouldn't know what to do without each other," my mother responded. "We've been together since before Joe and I were married." At the mention of Daddy's name, I thought the room went a little quiet.

Gordy, Helen, and I usually would sneak back to the kitchen to sample a few treats, but we didn't want to spend much time there and risk Ethel's temper. But, like always, we knew that if we seemed to be spending too much time around her friends, my mother would give Ethel the glare and we'd all be hauled out of sight into the kitchen. So we huddled in a corner of the dining room trying our best to be as unobtrusive as possible.

"They're going to eat in a minute. What do you want to do?" I asked. "I don't want to go to the kitchen."

Helen shrugged.

Gordy seethed. "If I see her sneak that bag out of the cabinet again, I might just hit her," he said. Finally, as the guests were being seated in the dining room and Ethel started to serve them, we crept into the kitchen. We snacked from hors d'oeuvres trays and kept out of the way whenever Ethel came back for anything she needed.

When the luncheon was over, the day lost its luster as if it were something my mother's friends brought along with them to the party and then gathered up with their other belongings as they left. Ethel didn't make it into work the day after. It wasn't all that unusual. Parties had a way of doing that to her.

That Christmas season was a strange one. Daddy moved home again for the holidays, and it was just like old times. I think he and my mother made an effort not to fight. Things were going pretty well, and then, just before Christmas day, our new puppy was run over by a car and my mother fell apart. She started crying a lot. You would've thought it was one of us who'd been killed. It was a sad thing. I cried a little, but not as much as when Lance died. I don't think my mother shed a tear about old Lance, but for that puppy we'd had for little more than a month, she wailed like Lassie had died. She'd stand in her bedroom and look out the window at the corner where the dog got hit and cry and cry. Ethel blamed it on her pregnancy. She said pregnant women cry a lot. But the day after New Year's we learned the real reason. Daddy had packed up all his things and put them in his car. Then he called us into the living room and told us he was leaving. This time he wouldn't be moving home again. He and my mother were getting a divorce.

Gordy stood up like a soldier called to attention. "You're getting a divorce?" he shouted, "And you're leaving us here, just like that? Leaving?" He glared at my father who looked away.

Helen and I were crying. I didn't know what to think or to say, though I was very proud of Gordy. I wished I could be so brave. I wanted to go to Daddy and beg him not to leave, or if he had to, at least to take me with him. Then I looked at my mother. She was sitting all bunched up in the sofa like a wad of Kleenex, sobbing and blowing her nose. Somehow

I felt it wouldn't be right to hurt her more, so I didn't say anything. Stuart came into the living room and said she was ready to go.

Helen and I ran from the room. Peering out our bedroom window, we watched Daddy and Stuart drive down the driveway and out of our lives. We collapsed into each other's arms, sobbing.

I assumed that when grown-ups decided to get a divorce it just happened, but I soon learned that it takes a lot of preparation. There were lawyers to hire and court dates to schedule and decisions to make. The whole time we children drifted around the house like ghosts. The lawyers soon made Stuart come back home to my mother. During the months leading up to the hearing, my mother stayed home more than she used to. She trailed after Ethel, not unlike I used to do. I missed my visits with Ethel and sometimes felt a little jealous of my mother for taking up so much of her time. It seemed to me that the mere act of breathing had a way of making my mother mad. I crept around her as if she were a snake ready to strike. Anything could set her off.

"Hey, Gordy. You done your homework yet?" I asked one afternoon in early March hoping to entice him into a game of basketball. Gordy was sitting at the kitchen table struggling over his arithmetic. He was counting on his fingers and mumbling to himself.

"Miz Jones says you're not s'posed to count on your fingers," I helpfully informed him.

"Stop being so impudent, young lady," my mother snapped, appearing from behind me. I didn't know what *impudent* meant, and I was afraid to ask since I got yelled at for almost anything those days. I stole out of the kitchen.

When my mother did leave the house it was usually to run errands. There were no more luncheons or foxhunts or bridge club meetings to go to. When Daddy left, so did the fun. Besides shopping for clothes, the only place my mother went was the grocery store. She'd come home with the car full of groceries and we would all have to help Ethel carry them in. My mother would say to Ethel, "Something told me to buy this."

And Ethel would say, "I thought 'bout that jest after you drove 'way." All of a sudden, it was like Ethel wasn't just someone my mother paid to take care of us; she was my mother's best friend. I guess I should have been happy about that, but the truth was it about made me sick.

They'd chuckle about how they had such a close connection, that all one had to do was to think of something and the other would know it. I didn't think that was true though, because Ethel said lots of things to me that I didn't think my mother would have liked if she knew; like Daddy's talks with Ethel. I bet my mother didn't know anything about those, because if she did, we would've *all* heard about it.

After Daddy left, my mother started putting us children to bed. When she'd have us say our prayers, she would tell us, "Ask God to make Daddy come home." I would, but I always felt sort of dirty afterward, like I'd asked God for something I didn't want. After my mother switched off the light and left the room, Helen and I would whisper about how maybe Daddy should stay where he was. Maybe he was happier there.

If marriage no longer provided structure my mother could count on, social graces still could. There were absolutes at my mother's dining room table: linen, silver, crystal, and china, no matter the meal. When the divorce settlement was finally reached, my mother took some of the money she received and rounded up her silver so that she had a complete service for twelve—luncheon and dinner. Even at nine years old, I thought it was a queer thing, but she seemed so proud of it. I remember her telling me that we would each inherit three full place settings.

Until Daddy left home, I hadn't fully realized how fortunate I was to be a "little kid." Gordy, Helen, and I were allowed to take our meals in the kitchen, but Stuart had to eat in the dining room with my mother. Stuart had been proud of her grown-up status before, but now she hated it. She was expected to sit up straight, hold her fork just so, and converse like a lady. She was allowed to leave the table only after asking to be excused—there were lots and lots of rules. When Stuart started to put on weight, my mother picked at her about it all the time. There seemed to be an argument between them at dinner every night. Usually one, or sometimes both of them, would leave the table in tears. Afterward, I'd help Ethel clear the table. She'd shake her head slowly and say, "Lord, chile, I jest don' know what ta think." I didn't either.

At breakfast my mother sat at the head of the table, reigning like a queen, as though Daddy were still around. Smelling faintly of face powder, Chanel No. 5, and lipstick, she would read the morning paper over a second cup of coffee while she waited for us to get ready for school. Her breakfast of poached eggs and bacon with one slice of toast and strawberry jam that Ethel had prepared for her was finished and cleared. With her reading glasses perched on her nose, she'd peruse the paper. Though she read two papers a day, whatever she read never seemed to have much effect on her—or at least not like it had on Daddy. He held some strong views on the way things in government should be and a discussion about them could get pretty lively.

I don't remember hearing my mother interject a single word into any of those discussions. Nor did I hear her have discussions with her friends that related to the news of the day unless it was about something sensational—like when an acquaintance of my mother's was arrested for embezzlement. I heard her talking on the phone with a friend one day. Her voice was excited, her fingers winding and unwinding the phone cord as she spoke. "I heard the sheriff came straight to his house and took him away in handcuffs," she said. "Can you believe that? I'm surprised that Bernard would have allowed such high handedness. He must be coming up for reelection."

"Ethel, what does *embezzlement* mean?" I asked over a peanut butter and jelly sandwich that noon.

"Have you been lis'nin' to yo' Momma on da phone, again? You best stop that ear droppin'."

Since Daddy no longer lived with us, it was always my mother who drove us to school in the morning: four kids, going to three different schools, and one of the few times Stuart's life intersected with mine. She was spending as much time as she could away from home, but to tell the truth, the trip was far more enjoyable when she decided to catch the bus or ride with friends. Otherwise, Gordy, Helen, and I had to sit in the back of the red woody station wagon and listen to my sister and mother bicker all the way to school.

"Why can't I go the dance?" Stuart would implore. "Dad would let me go," she'd say. "I want to live with him. He said I could."

"The lawyers said…"

"I don't care what any old lawyer says. I'm going back to live with Daddy and you can't stop me." Stuart slammed the car door behind her.

Gordy was lucky: he was the first out, so usually he was dropped off before my mother and Stuart had even started to get worked up. I remember some mornings when my mother wept all the way as she drove Helen and me to our school. Then the routine, unpleasant as it was, changed for a second time that year.

With Daddy out of the household and with expensive lawyers to pay, my mother found she could no longer afford to send us children to private schools. The four of us were switched to public school.

Ethel said one morning while fixing breakfast not long after that, "You know, Miz Ginny, I heard dey is gonna close down da schools here in Charlottesville."

"You heard what? Where?" My mother shook her head like Ethel was all wrong. "Who said such a thing?"

"In church on Sunday, the reverend say we's 'pose ta send our chil'ren to school—ta the white schools—as soon as the law be signed. He say dat no matter what's we hear we is 'pose ta gets 'em ready fo school. And if dey close da schools like dey say dey is, we is 'pose to take 'em anyways. And ta sit outside da school all peaceful like. He say he 'spect dey will too."

"Will too what?" My mother looked puzzled.

"Well," Ethel stated flatly, "close da schools."

Gordy and I were elated to think we wouldn't have schools, but knew enough to stay out of the conversation. It never occurred to us that we would still have to go to school.

No sooner had we started to get accustomed to our local public school, then, for reasons that made no sense to me, we were sent off to attend classes in church basements and old houses. Within a month of our switching schools, the public schools had closed rather than have white and colored kids go to school together. We were relocated to makeshift classrooms and our teachers came with us. More and more often Stuart was getting rides with friends, so that everything seemed to me to be changing at once. It didn't take too many weeks of driving to school every morning to convince my mother that carpooling might be a good idea; that way she'd only have to drive once a week, and if she made Stanley the yardman drive for her, she could avoid the tedium altogether.

I may not have fully understood why the schools had to close, but I knew one thing for sure: I didn't want our yardman driving the car pool for my mother. Stanley was fine in the yard, though a little stinky, but *mothers* were supposed to drive car pools. Three other mothers took turns driving us to school. Jerry's mom was the best. She was always late. She had a car with only two doors and we had to really squeeze ourselves in. I loved to snuggle up to her fuzzy coat in the front seat. She said funny things and made everyone laugh. One cold morning she let me wear her already warm gloves because I had forgotten mine.

When it came time for my mother's turn to drive, Stanley drove in her stead. She said it was because driving made her nauseated now. We weren't so sure about that, though, because she drove plenty of other places when she wanted to. Still, my mother's belly was growing bigger by the week, and whenever anyone wanted to know why our mother didn't drive us, we would blame the baby. Helen, Gordy, and I at least knew Stanley; the other kids in the carpool were even more uncomfortable with the awkward turn of events than we were. We all knew that colored people were somehow responsible for our present school situation.

"My mom says white kids shouldn't be alone in a car with a nigger," one of the Williams boys announced none too quietly as Stanley pulled away from the curb in front of their house. "She said if your mom doesn't get off her high horse and drive us like she ought to, my mom is going to—"

His brother cut in, "'Sides he stinks!" Everyone laughed but us.

"Shhh, he can hear you," I'd whisper, checking the rearview mirror often to see if he was watching us. Every once in a while I'd catch his old eyes scanning the backseat.. I didn't like Stanley driving us anymore than they did, but the stuff they said made me squirm with embarrassment.

Maybe it was my own discomfort, or because I was used to seeing Stanley in the yard—or perhaps he was just one of those men who's too big for confined spaces—but it always seemed like Stanley took up more of the car than he should have. No one else in our carpool had help, black or white, so they didn't understand that having to drive for my mother wasn't Stanley's fault.

Gordy had the great idea one morning to tell Stanley to drop us off blocks before the makeshift school. He said, "We like to walk."

We all said, "Yeah, we like to walk. Drop us off here."

And Jerry added, "You dumb nigger." It was all I could do not to punch him in the mouth.

I don't think Stanley liked driving us to school any more than we liked having him do it. Without a single word of protest, he pulled the car over to the curb and stopped. We all got out. He waved his sweat stained, brown felt hat and drove off.

"I'm going to tell your mother you are using bad language," I told Jerry after Stanley drove away.

"What bad language? Nigger? She won't care."

After that, every time Stanley drove us to school, he'd drop us off at that same place. I think he took special delight when it rained. He never gave us the slightest chance to say, "Never mind." At the end of the day, without fail, Stanley would be waiting in my mother's conspicuous red station wagon at the front of the line of cars, which the whole school would file by. Even when it wasn't particularly warm out, he'd have the windows down so anyone who wanted to could see right in the car. I don't know if he really did wear a red plaid shirt every time he picked us up, or if it just seemed like it.

The car pool disbanded before the school year was out. During recess, Jerry said that his mother "didn't like niggers driving him around." What he didn't say, but I heard him tell someone else, was that she thought my mother was gonna end up paying for being so high and mighty and ought to stop associating with niggers the way she did. To my siblings' and my horror, Stanley continued to drive us every day. The funny thing was, we liked Stanley. Once the neighbors' kids were no longer riding with us, we had nice talks; but I did hate having to get in and out of that car at school.

By the time school started the next year, we didn't have to worry about Stanley driving. He'd stopped coming to work for us. I speculated on the potential scandal of the situation—it seemed there was always a scandal when hired help got laid off—but Gordy informed me quite matter-of-factly that I didn't know anything: we couldn't afford Stanley anymore, and that was that. Before long Ethel was doing everything we'd ever hired out for, and then going home before dusk. Sometimes she'd make our dinner before she departed, but as more and more tasks fell to her, she began leaving the cooking to my mother. It's a bad thing when you can't tell the mashed potatoes from the gravy. Worst of all, we had to start eating in the dining room.

Chapter 13

Ethel
1924

Drinkin' started out as the most fascinatin' thing I ever thought about when I was 'bout fourteen or fifteen. On our afternoons off, Roberta, Alberta, and me would go out behind Freeman's funeral parlor. We'd take a little picnic, play games, and have ourselves a big time and weren't bothered by a soul, 'cept Roberta, who was always makin' out like she was too fancy for picnics out back of a rundown ol' funeral parlor. "I's hot out chere. Ain't enough shade here to cool a ant," she complained one summer Sunday. "Ol' dry mud just vibratin' heat. Less go sit on the porch and pretend we's white folks wit' a fine house that ain't got nothin' to do but sit an' fan ourselves," she said, like it was 'bout the best thing in the whole wide world to do. "Ethel, pick up them sandwiches and brang 'em along." She sashayed over to the porch and plopped herself down on the stoop like she was fine as rain.

"How you gon' preten' to be a fine white lady an' ain't got no chair to sit on?" Alberta asked.

"You is simple as Huberta, po' soul," Roberta said, like she was so much better than our older sister. "That's the point of pretendin': you don't gots to have it to be pretendin'; you make believe."

"I know'd what pretendin' be," Alberta puffed and blew like a dog with a snout full of dust. "Mama would knock you up one side and down the other if she heard you talkin' 'bout Huberta like that. An don' be acting like it be all righ' if you say poor ol' soul afterward. You'll be simple if she catch ya. I be telling ya that sure as I live and breathe."

Funny thing about Alberta and Roberta, they didn' look no more alike than a dog and a donut. Roberta was tall an' light-skinned an' moved like a bird, sort of strutted when she walked, all quick like. Alberta was short, thick, an' dark. She had a mop of hair that stuck straight up no matter what she tried to do to it, which wasn't much. She didn' have the patience to sit for braidin' it, an' she always said she "didn' have time for no mens," either. Maybe that was so.

The three of us sat on that porch all afternoon, actin' like we was fine ladies having ourselves a tea party, laughin' and gossipin' about the white ladies we worked fo'.

"Would you mind pourin' me some mo' tea?"

"Why no, dearie. Like some milk an' sugar wit' it?"

"No thank ya, but I'd powerful like to have another piece of that there chocolate cake." Pretendin', it seemed, came natural to Alberta once she got the hang of it.

Roberta, with her high self, came up with the idea first, but it wasn't like Alberta and me had anything against it, really. "The next Sunday we has off, les bring us some hooch an' pretends we's having a cocktail party," she said, looking at the two of us hard so that we couldn' disagree with her.

"Is we pretendin' we's got the hooch?" Alberta asked. "I spect so, cuz I don' know nowhere to git any." She looked at me like to ask, *Do ya?* I just shook my head and shrugged. I didn't have no idea how ya got it. Prohibition made it 'gainst the law to be drinkin', an' I ain't never broke no law.

Roberta said, "Don' ya'll worry, I know what to do. My lady's got some an' I know where she keep it. I'll jest help myself to a little bit an' bring it 'long wit' me. She don' never notice. I do it all the time. Take me a lil' nip or two when ain't nobody 'round."

"You do what?" Alberta brayed. "Girl, you gonna fine yo'self out in the street if you ain't careful."

"I's careful. You know Miz Boyle ain't got a lick a sense. I don' spect she even knows it's there. Her son be leavin' it. Feels so good—just smooth as silk—it does. Takes all the bumps outta de road. I git my work done twice as fast so I kin sit with my feet up 'til I hear her at the gate. Then I be hummin' a tune as I goes about, lookin' like I been dustin' all afternoon." She said looking proud as punch with herself. "After a while, even tastes pretty good," she added.

"How long you been doin' like that?" Alberta asked, soundin' like she was impressed, but she could have been mad. You never could tell with Alberta. The wind shifted so often. "You know Mama would be on you like a duck on a June bug if she knew. She'll eat you up with that stick o' hers if you lose dat job."

"I ain't gonna be losin' no job," Roberta said, sure as a Bible salesman at a revival.

Alberta and I couldn' disagree, knowin' as little as we did on the subject. The boardin' house where I worked was run by a strict Christian lady who wouldn't even let a single bottle in her house wit'out checkin' to see if there was any hooch in it. I even heard that she got a passel of her friends to close down the saloons afore they was closed for good. I didn't think there was a chance I would run across any hooch at my work, and I knew Mama didn't have none. The one thing you knew 'bout Mama's house was there weren't nothin' there 'cept what you absolutely needed; and sometime not even that. Nobody, Mama knew, needed alcohol; and nobody I knew crossed Mama.

I looked forward to that next Sunday like a new pair of shoes. I don' know why. I ain't never paid no mind to nobody drinkin' whiskey afore then. I didn't know the first thing about it, but Roberta made it sound like magic to me—magic I wanted part of.

It was my turn to bring the sandwiches. I wrapped 'em in some ol' cotton rags while my lady was in the parlor. She didn't pay me much mind on Sunday afternoons after the dishes was done. Didn't even fuss 'bout me makin' the sandwiches, though she only let me use the leftovers she was 'bout to throw to the dogs anyhow.

I slipped out the back door and hightailed it to the funeral parlor. When I got there, the lot was filled with cars, mules, wagons, and carts. People was millin' 'round dressed in their Sunday best. I'd forgot that Clarence Dean had passed. An' when I remembered, I knew we weren't gon' be doin' any drinkin' that day. Roberta, on the other side of the yard, was talking with a boy I knew she liked. She looked like she had already had a taste or two. She waved me over.

"Dewey, you knows my little sister Ethel, don' ya?" she asked, looking all moony eyed. I was sorry she had asked me to come over. She twisted one of those big fat curls 'round her face and batted her eyes. Roberta liked tryin' the latest thing and havin' your hair straightened was the latest. It looked all oily and greasy to me.

"I 'spect I do," Dewey grunted, hardly lookin' at me. "You gonna come with me or not?" he asked, takin' Roberta by the arm. "I know where we can get us lots mo'."

She giggled, turned to me and said, "Go on home. If'n you see Alberta, tell her I got som'thin' else to do."

I couldn' tell ya why I was so disappointed. Roberta was never somebody you could set your watch on, 'specially if there was a man 'round, but that snake oil of a story she told 'bout drinkin' had taken me over. I couldn' imagine workin' so hard that I could make time—time to put my feet up and time to enjoy it to boot. I wanted some of that, and I was bound and determined to get me some.

Alberta bumped up 'gainst the back of my knees with hers like she always do when I don' see her coming. "Where Ro?" she asked.

"She off with that no-count Dewey," I sniffed. "Gots somethin' better ta do, she say."

"Mmhm!" Alberta sneered. "I bet she do. Le's me and you go on over to Clarence's house and pay our respects." She ambled behind the mourners an' I run to catch up.

"Do we has to go to the grave? I hate goin' to the grave," I said, beginnin' to feel a panic set in. "You know how I gets—like I's gon' fall in and cain' get myself out."

Alberta nodded. "No, we don' has to go to no grave. We can just hold back then go on by likes we's there to help out. Early like, ya know. They be glad for the help."

"I don' 'xactly wanna spend my afternoon off workin'," I said.

"You wanna drink hooch or no?" She looked cross at me, waiting for an answer.

I didn' argue. We followed the crowd to the churchyard then passed on to Clarence's ramshackle lil' house. There was a few women settin' up saw horses and boards, making tables out under the trees. Alberta spoke to one of the ladies and then come back to me.

"She say we should go on in the kitchen and help make the sandwiches." The kitchen wasn' big as a shoebox and there must have been ten people crammed in it fryin' chicken, makin' salad, peelin' eggs, and sweatin'. I 'spect it was not one degree less than one hundred and ten in there. One step in the door and the blast of heat hit me smack in the face. I turned myself right around. "You go on, Alberta," I said. "I'm gonna eat my sandwiches I brung and go on home to Mama."

"Wait here," she said, disappearin' into that furnace of a kitchen. Then she come back out, sweat-covered, with a knife tucked under each arm, a loaf of bread, a plate, and some sandwich fixin's all piled on each other up to her chin. She nodded her head toward a rickety ol' table under a tree. "Go'n over there an' clean that up," she said as the sweat jest pourin' offa her face.

While Alberta balanced her load, I pulled a rag out from under the loaf of bread. Then I pumped some water into a bucket from the well and took it over to the table. Them ol' boards had seen better days, but I tried to clean 'em best as I could. Alberta plunked down the bread and fixin's smack on that rotten wet wood. "I ain't finished cleanin' it," I said. "It's still dirty."

"Don' matter. We just makin' sandwiches," she said.

"People gonna eat 'em, ain't they?" I asked. "Ya can't feed nobody dirty food."

She started cuttin' the bread, then handed me a knife an' told me how to make a sandwich; somethin' I been doin' since I was big enough to hold a knife. I did the best I could to pick the dirt off the bread until she said to quit. "Put the white side up and nobody'll notice." Ashamed at myself, I did what she said.

They must have gotten old Clarence buried. Mo' and mo' folks was jest standin' 'round under the trees, talkin'. Afore too long, the yard was filled wit' dozens of laughin', shoutin' people. They covered them tables with sheets and plates of chicken, collards, potato salad, stewed tomatoes, and deviled eggs was set out. I put our plate of sandwiches as far in the middle of the table as I could, hopin' they'd be too hard to reach or to bother wit'. 'Sides, the farther away they was, the harder it was to see them specks of dirt in the bread.

Across from the food tables was a lemonade table with pitchers of water and cups. I noticed the men was takin' cups but not helpin' themselves to the lemonade or the water. Alberta, who had gone over to talk with some folks, come back with a cup in her hand. "Well, you want some?" She held out the cup.

"Lemonade? Don' mind if I do." I took a big pull on that cup and did everything in my power not to spray her and everybody else around with that foul tasting slop. I spluttered like a drownin' man. It burned my throat. Tears welled up in my eyes and I'm not sure smoke didn' come out my ears. I know I looked a fool, coughin' an' hackin' like I was. A few onlookers hurried away. "That ain't no lemonade," I said. "Ya tryin' to poison me?"

Alberta laughed, took the cup back, and tossed the rest of it down. "Want more?" She followed the men folk 'round the other side of the tree. When she walked back, she was holdin' a big glass full of what looked like lemonade. "Try this," she said, holdin' the glass out to me. "It's pretty good. Tastes like lemonade." And it did too, but no lemonade ever made you feel as good. Afore long I had the same goofy grin Alberta was wearin' and I felt like I was floatin' on down the river. We sat by that tree, laughin' an' drankin' that powerful good lemonade, watchin' people doin' what people do; thinkin' it was about the funniest thing we'd ever laid eyes on.

Next thing I knowed, the sun was peepin' up and I felt like I'd been beat with a bag of rocks. Alberta was laid out beside me, mouth wide open; snorin' to beat the band. We was leanin' up 'gainst that tree. Sunlight lit up the trash and tall patches of grass that littered the yard. A rooster was crowin' like to bust his gut, and mine was busy churnin' like nobody's business. I couldn' be late for work. Miz Nancy, the cook at the boardinghouse, would skin me alive if I didn' have the stove lit and water on to boil by the time she got there. I jumped up and made to run, but my legs wouldn' work, and my head felt like fireworks was going off in it. My gut wrenched. I had to lay down before I threw up. "Alberta? You ain't dead, is ya?" I poked my sister who stirred and opened her eyes.

"Oh God, have mercy on me, I wish I was," she whispered. Then she turned and threw up. That started me goin'. We was jest a *mess*. First she'd spew, and then I'd spew. Neither of us had the strength to move. We just laid there in our own vomit. By the time the sun was up good, my head was still swimmin'. Then I look up and see Miz Nancy's black face with her little piggy eyes roundin' the house. She still had a washrag in her hand and a dishtowel tucked into her apron string. She didn' have to tell me who been doin' the dishes. She weren't one bit happy, neither. Under her flat nose, her mouth was twisted up in a scowl. Early as it was, the whole mornin' was goin' to hell in a handbasket. Lookin' at Miz Nancy, I felt like I might spew all over again.

"Now look at you fools," she said, as she stood over us with her hands on her big hips, shaking her head and tutting. "When you ain't come in this morning, Ethel, I knew where you was. I got breakfast done myself and the cleanin' up, too, no thanks to you. Saw you two last night actin' all stupid. Figured you be laid out," she muttered, wagging her finger and sucking her tongue. Then she leaned in real close an' started barkin' out orders so loud me and Alberta both jumped up, even though we could barely see straight. "You betta get yo'selves up and outta here, and Lord God, cleaned up before I tell your mama what you been up to. And don' you let Miz Dupree get a whiff of this or you be outta a job. Come on now, I gots lunch to do!" And then, as if Alberta needed some reminding, she added over her shoulder, "Alberta, you ain't down at the laundry! Theys don' puts up with missing no work. You better get on outta here, girl."

Roberta, Alberta, and I finally had our "pretendin'" cocktail party 'bout a month later. We lazed around on the funeral parlor's porch talkin' 'bout how funny it was watchin' people act a fool. For reasons I can't explain, I remembered the fun I had with Alberta and the lemonade far more clearly than the hangover the day after. Otherwise, I wouldn't have taken another drink.

"That lemonade tasted good," I said, lookin' down at the contents of my glass, "not like this." I made a face as I drank the whiskey Roberta had swiped from Miz Boyle.

"It be good for you to drink this here whiskey, then," Roberta said. "Thata way yo' won't be drankin' too much."

"Sho' 'nough." My face screwed up as I swallowed the last of my cup, but I held it out for a refill. That warm feeling of the edges slidin' off had commenced, and it was worth no end of nasty taste. We were so busy drinkin', we forgot all about pretendin' to be at a white folks' cocktail party. All afternoon long we sat up on that ol' porch drinkin' the little bit of whiskey Roberta brought.

When I complained that there was no more, Roberta asked, "Did ya'll have fun?"

When I nodded yes, she said, "Then they's was just the right amount. You don' be drinkin' just to drink. 'Spose to enjoy yo' self."

Alberta grumbled, "G'on wit' yo' snooty self, girl. Imma get me my own hooch, an' I won' be havin' to listen to you tell me when I done had enough." From then on Alberta and I did most of our drinkin' wit'out Roberta and her big headed self. The porch was ours out of habit. Every Sunday that we had off—when there wasn't a funeral—Alberta and me would be drinkin' on that funeral parlor porch.

One Sunday we was sittin' on the porch, talkin' 'bout how glad we was that the funeral scheduled for that day had been earlier than usual so it didn't take up our drinkin' time. Between the two of us, and a whole lot of trial and error, we'd come close to figurin' out about how much to drink to feel good before we slipped into feelin' some kind of bad. Most times we stayed on the feel good side.

Alberta and I was laughin' over I don't know what, when all of a sudden she stopped short and shushed me. "Did you hear that?" she asked as her head whipped one way then the next. "They somebody in there." She hunkered down like to hide behind the porch rail.

"Why you hidin' like that? If'n they's somebody there, they's gonna see you. That rail ain't gonna do you no good, big as you is." I hadn't heard anything and thought she was just actin' a fool.

Then the front door opened and a real good-lookin' man walked out on the porch carryin' a broom. "Evenin'," he said with a nod to Alberta who busied herself tryin' to straighten up and look dignified. Then he turned and nodded to me.

"Evenin'," I said, suddenly very aware that I did not belong on that porch. But he didn't say nothin' more, just went on 'bout his sweepin' like we was suppose to be there. Alberta leaned back in her chair and took a sip from her cup as natural as could be. All of a sudden, I knew what a bird on a wire felt like. I didn't know whether to fly or sit. I pushed my cup behind the chair leg and fiddled with a button on my dress. After a while Alberta commenced conversin'.

"Nice evenin'," she said. "Was they a good turnout at the funeral today? Who died? I don't recollect hearin'."

"No'm, jest the family. It was Lottie Johnson's baby," he answered. My stomach, which had already commenced ta flip-floppin', dropped like a stone at that. I felt queasy just thinkin' bout a little baby all laid out in a tiny coffin.

"Hm," Alberta said. "Shame 'bout that. I 'spect we be pushin' on then." She heaved herself out the chair tryin' to look sober, but drunk as she was, it was all she could do to get off the porch wit'out fallin' in the dust.

I had to talk myself off that porch and remind myself to breathe. I was so busy concentratin' on walkin', I almost fell over from not breathin'. I left my cup behind the chair leg, too 'shamed to pick it up.

Got near ways to the road and I hear the man callin', "Miz, you forgot yo' cup." His hand was holdin' out my old chipped mug. I liked ta died right there.

"Thanky," is all I could think to say. I took the mug and turned back toward Alberta who was waitin' at the road for me.

"Why you lookin' all mooney eyed?" she asked as she stood swayin' and starin' at me. I cut a quick look back at the funeral home. The porch was empty.

I couldn't get that man's face and voice outta my head. I'd find myself thinkin' back to him when I was doin' my work for Miz Dupree, and I'd find myself lookin' for a glimpse of him whenever I'd pass by the funeral home. I finally worked up the nerve to ask Alberta his name. She told me it was "Early," then she gave me a sharp look like to say, *Not that it's any o' yo' business*. Early was different than any man I ever did see. He had a kindness about him. He looked at you like you was something of value—not like he could get something outta you—but as if he meant to take care of you, like a good pair of shoes. I bet he kept his house neat, too.

One afternoon, a few weeks after I first seen him, Alberta and I was back on the porch of the funeral home. It was gettin' on toward winter, and the gov'ment done said beer was legal again. We had two bottles, each in its own little sack. I kept lookin' around, expecting to see Early. I asked Alberta about him. She got this thinkin' look on her face, like she was tryin' to remember all the things she'd heard about him. Then she said, "He an old lady now. Ain't no fun. Always be working and such. Wouldn' be caught dead in a juke joint. Thing is, I hear he weren't always that way." She leaned toward me and got a mean little sparkle in her eye, then she said, "I hear he was a drunk and dat he beat his wife."

"No!" I said, my mouth gaped. I wasn't sure if I was more upset to learn he'd been married before or that people said he beat his wife.

"Yessum. Beat her near to death! Then she had a baby and some folks say he stopped beatin' on her after that." Her voice softened a little. "But when his wife got pregnant again, she and the baby died in labor. Some folks say he killed her. Others say it was God's way of punishin' him for his drinkin'. But I don't think he killed 'er. After she died, he was so put out he couldn' take care of his little boy. That boy—his name's Junior—I think he's not much younger than you, lives with his mama's people in Washington." She was strokin' her chin like she had a beard, "I think."

I was startin' to feel pretty strong 'bout Early, an' I didn't wanna hear nobody sayin' that kinda thing 'bout im. How could that kind man have done what Alberta say? "How come you know'd so much about it?" I asked, tryin' to sound casual.

She continued on like I hadn't opened my mouth. That was the thing about Alberta: she didn' like to give you information wit'out you askin' for it. She wanted to make sure that if she be talkin', you be listenin'.

But Lord a mercy, once you got her to talkin', it'd be easier to stop a freight train tryin' to make up time than to get a word in edgewise. She kept right on, like she was recitin' the alphabet. "Didn' have enough money to bury her right, she passin' so young an all, so he struck a deal with the undertaker to work off what he couldn' pay up front. Started cleanin' and the like, and in recent times he be helpin' lay the bodies out. Folks says he do lot of the motician' hisself. Suppose to have a license, but it's coloreds so's they don' mind like they do with white folk. People say he could make hisself some good money if'n he go'ed to undertakin' school. Don' know much about all that, but I knows he's cleaned up. He an ol' lady now, though a right handsome one," she chuckled at her own joke. Then she turned and looked hard at me. "Why you want ta know, anyway?"

I shrugged and Alberta changed the subject. "I's cold out here, les go inside." Alberta moved over to the door and tried the handle. "Locked, humf," she grunted like she took it personally.

"Alberta, you know goodness well they wouldn' be leavin' no door unlocked 'round chere. People be livin' in there if'n they did! Shoot, nice house like this be ruined in a blink, too. Jest look at yo'self tryin' to get in, see if'n you cain' see what I'm sayin'." I shook my head and sighed. "I'm goin' on home. Too cold out chere fo' me. You comin'?"

She grumbled behind as I stepped off the porch, pulling my too thin sweater round me to keep off the cold. Buttons was long gone. They wouldn't done much good noways since I was much bigger 'round than the sweater ever had a hope of bein'.

Alberta looked back at the funeral home. "It woulda been colder in there anyway. Stove ain't lit. Look—see, no smoke comin' out the chimley." I was so busy lookin' in the direction Alberta was pointin' that I didn't see Early comin'.

"Evening, ladies," he said and tipped his brown felt hat. He had a nice full head of close-cropped hair and a kind, square-jawed face that looked a little like a bull, but nice; real nice. That head of his perched just about perfect on top of a solid, strong body with sturdy legs that was a little on the short side; had him a nice backside, all the same. Lord a mercy, here I was takin' in a man's hind parts! I couldn't get much of a bead on how old he was. Alberta said he was close to Mama's age, but I couldn't believe he'd be that old. He had a real easy way 'bout 'im. You could tell he was a studious man in his manner, not all slapdash like most of the men Roberta had buzzin' 'round. His round glasses might have made him more studious lookin' than he really was. I'd have to wait and see 'bout that.

I was so wrapped up in my thoughts that it took a minute for it to dawn on me that he'd called me a lady. Nobody'd ever called me a lady. I was struck dumb as a mule. Alberta grunted a greetin' of sorts while I stood dead in the road, lookin' at Early like he fell from the sky.

"Didn' mean to give ya'll no fright," he said. He chuckled; the softest, sweetest little chuckle. It was the kind of chuckle that didn't make ya feel small—just the opposite—it made ya feel you was in on the joke.

"No, sir, you didn'. Justa little surprise, das all," I heard myself sayin'.

"Don' be hurryin' off on my account." He chuckled again as he unlocked the door.

Alberta was full of surprises. She came to life and smiled like she was just seein' him for the first time. "We on our way home," she announced. "It's too cold to be sittin' on a porch in this weather."

"Well, why don' ya'll comes in and makes yo'self comfortable. I'll git a fire goin' direc'ly." He opened the door to a dank, musty entrance hall that smelled of stale smoke and mold.

Alberta didn' wait to be asked twice. She was up on that porch and headin' through the door before that man finished his sentence. "Don' mind if'n I do," she said, brushin' past him. She looked back at him for directions.

"Go'n into the parlor," he said indicatin' to the left with his head while he tried to get the key out the door, "and set a spell. Dat's where da stove be. I'll just be a minute, gotta git some wood out back."

"I'll do dat," I offered, while Alberta sat her big self down like she was a queen or somethin', just waitin' to be waited on. It was the blessedest thing. I felt like I was standin' outside myself, takin' a good hard look, not sure if I liked what I saw. My hair was all tied up in braids. It weren't stylish like Roberta's, but then again, it weren't no rat's nest like Alberta's neither. I still had on my uniform under my shabby, used-to-be-white sweater, and maybe I was a little too stout.

"No'm, I'll git it. You jest set on down and relax yo'self," he said to me like I was a fine-lookin' lady dressed in the latest fashion.

After he left the room, Alberta screwed up her face and shook her head back and forth at me in quick little jerks like she did when she thought people was puttin' on airs. She primped up her hair and cupped her hands to smell her breath.

"What you gots in mind?" I asked.

"Never you mind," she said shooin' me away like a pesky fly. "You jest git on home, now. I'll be along direc'ly."

"I ain't goin' nowhere," I whispered, tryin' to keep Early from hearin'. "He axt us both in here. Why you think I gotta go?"

"Girl, don' ya know nothin'? He jest be lookin' for a little lovin' and I's happy to oblige," she said, givin' me a leer that made her look right comical.

"Stop actin' a fool," I said, offended that Alberta could have such notions 'bout my kind, gentle Early.

Loaded down with a big stack of wood, Early come back inside and carefully filled the small potbellied stove that stood on a metal plate in the middle of the room. He pulled a match out from behind his ear and struck it up against the side of the stove. Afore too long we was gettin' as toasty as you could ever think to be.

"Glad to be seein' you ladies today," Early said, turnin' the damper down. "Ya'll ain't been comin' round much here lately. I's wonderin' if'n you might like…" Alberta was so full of herself, knowin' what she thought she knew, she looked like she might just pop there on that nasty red sofa. She patted the cushion next to her.

"Why don' you set yo' self down here aside me," Alberta said, trying to be jes' as sweet as a flower to a bee but croakin' more like a frog to a fly. I ain't *never* been so embarrassed. I stared up at the peeling wallpaper near the ceiling. The paper, a dirty water brown, was covered in faded bunches of orange and blue flowers.

Early smiled and said, "No, ma'am, I got work to do. But that what I been tryin' to say: Ya'll want some extra work?"

Alberta spluttered and huffed like somebody threw a bucket of cold water on her. She commenced to hitch her skirt down as I rolled my eyes. "What you mean 'work'? You don' think I gots work enough fo' two already? Why you think I wanna do more fo' you?" I think she got so mad 'cause she was mistook 'bout his intentions.

"Com' on Ethel, les git on home," she huffed. She was gettin' spittin' mad by now. "I gots better thangs to do than lookin' fo' mo' work ta do."

"Oh no, Miss, I's gon' pay ya," Early said, lookin' confused. "I's gon' pay ya'll real good!"

Alberta's chin shot up an' it looked like she was mullin' it over. She scratched her head and opened her mouth like she was gon' say somethin'. Then I guess she thought about what a fool she'd looked like pattin' that red cushion next to her. She stood straight up, turned on her heel, an' hollered, "Ethel, you comin'?"

"I ain't," I said. "You go on."

"Suit yer self," she muttered. She stomped down the hall and out the door, slammin' it so hard the windows on the house might near jumped out of their frames. You woulda thought a train was roarin' down the tracks just outside.

"Well, I never," Early said, an' he chuckled that tender warm chuckle. "Did I say somethin' wrong? If'n I did, I sho' is sorry. I didn' mean no harm." He looked down at his chocolate-brown hands, then out in the hall. He took off his gold-rimmed glasses, pulled his hankie outta his trousers, and slowly wiped each lens. He put his hankie back in his pocket and carefully wrapped them glasses back 'round his ears then smiled at me. He had a way of smilin' like it was with his whole body.

"Don' pay her no mind," I said. "She's what they call 'high strung.'"

"As a kite," he said. We both laughed. That laugh of his was like butter on warm bread. I just couldn' get enough. I kept laughin' just to hear him laugh, too.

The work Early had in mind ordinarily would have turned my stomach since I didn' cotton to dead bodies. But I didn' think twice when he said he wanted me to help him lay the bodies out—dress, do the hair, shave—make 'em look like they was alive and jus' sleepin'. "I only gits an afternoon off every other week," I said. "That won' be much help."

"You don' work nights, do ya?"

"I'm free after supper is cleaned up. 'Round 'bout nine-thirty. That won' do ya no good, will it?" I hoped and prayed it would.

"Yea, I jest drop by and lets ya know when I needs ya. Time don' matter none. Dead folk don' cares a lick 'bout time." He chuckled again. I thought if my heart melted any mo' I'd have to scrape it up off the flo' and carry it home in my hand.

Fact was I never studied much 'bout men folk. The ones that visited Mama, colored or white, I steered clear of. I seen enough o' her beat black and blue to know trustin' a snake was a safer bet than trustin' a man. And all that foolishness in the bedroom was just that—foolishness. I wasn' interested in havin' no babies, and didn' see any reason to spin the wheel. Funny thing 'bout Mama, she didn' have men comin' 'round 'cept if money got real tight an' she couldn't stretch the little bit she got from one pay day to the next. Then men started knockin' at the do'. See, Mama never got married; didn' see any sense in saddlin' herself like that. She always said, "When you needs you a man, one gen'ally turn up."

Most time she didn' have no need for one. She kept herself loose, even if she wasn' what you call "fancy free." Mama kept her a cow and some chickens, and she had a good green thumb. She was good at makin' cheese; best you ever put in yo' mouth. There was even a time that she had her a sow. We didn' go wantin' for food. If there was a party or somethin' at the Stuart's, she'd bring home some leftovers. Between workin' up at the Stuart's, cookin', and pocketin' the money them men brought when they come a courtin', Mama took good care of us. Course, she had to sell the sow off to pay for the hospital bill when the horse kicked Huberta in the head. That doctor made house calls for a good long while after Huberta come home, and there was a whole lot more than just doctorin' goin' on.

When I told Mama 'bout working for Early, she said, "You better watch yo' self with dat man. He be old enough to be yo' daddy."

I was thunderstruck. "He ain't that old, is he?" I prayed with my toes and fingers; crossed them for the answer to be no.

"Well, he ain't much younger than me," she said. "You mighty young to be takin' up with a man his age."

"I ain't takin' up. I's jest goin' to be helpin' him out a little, is all." I was hopin' I *would* be takin' up with him.

"Um-humm," was all she said.

At first Early only come by the boardin' house to fetch me when there was a death. I helped him puttin' on makeup an' fixin' the hair of the ladies or shavin' the men just like he said he wanted. First one I had to fix up was ol' Beulah Washington. She wore her hair like mine, up in knots, so it wasn' so bad. I had to laugh to myself, thinkin' as little as I know 'bout fixin' hair and makeup, it'd kill some of them ladies—if they wasn' already dead—to know who was workin' on 'em. But I did a passable job. Kinfolks wasn' all that picky 'bout how the bodies looked, just as long as they didn' look *dead*. I got better at it after I stopped thinkin' 'bout 'em as dead, but more like they was just "resting." I made a point not to touch their skin 'cause no live body is ever that cold. I can tell you, touchin' that cold skin made mine crawl.

One night after we'd finished up, Early pulled out a bottle of gin and asked me if I wanted some. He said, "I noticed that you and yo' sister don' be settin' on de porch no mo' havin' a sip from times to times. Just wondered if you wouldn' mind havin' a few with me." I remembered what Alberta had said about Early getting' drunk an' beatin' his first wife. But he was cleaned up now. I eyed the gin suspiciously. Then, since I was a new convert to the bottle myself, I thought, *Who am I to judge if the man wants to enjoy his self after a long day's work?* He was lookin' at me with all the kindness in the world, waitin' for my answer, and I just knew Alberta and all them people was wrong 'bout him.

Me and Early had us a big time that night in the funeral parlor. We laughed 'til our sides ached at what Alberta had had in mind for Early on the red sofa. His soft eyes glittered with gold as he shuddered and shook like a man with palsy ev'ry time he mimicked Alberta sittin' there, pattin' the seat next to her, and sayin' in a voice with as much appeal as a hog call, "Come on now, honey, set yo'self right here aside me." I almost wet myself laughin'.

Early said, "If she ain'ta got mad at my askin' her 'bout dat job, I swear I don' know what I woulda done." I laughed so hard I couldn' catch my breath, while tears streamed down his face. When I woke up the next morning, I had to hightail it to work with a head as big as all outdoors.

After that, me and Early didn' need nobody to die to see each other. He come by and fetched me 'most ev'ry night. We went to the juke joint and danced 'til I thought my feet would fall off, and all the while we drank and drank. There was always somebody there with some whiskey and we'd drink 'til there wadn't a drop left. I'd go to work sometime after bein' up all night, draggin' my tail 'round like a beat dog. We did have some fun, though. Alberta was dead wrong. Wasn't a thing ladyish 'bout Early. He was a man, and he was mine.

I moved into his house in no time at all. We didn' keep up with the dancin' like we did when we was courtin'. We just couldn't. "Lord, honey, I's an old man. I can't keep up with the likes a you," Early said one night when we had finished the chores. "You gonna have to give this ol' guy a rest." But the drinkin' didn't stop, and I did my best to keep up with him. Early said he didn' see no sense in keepin' on workin' for that shiftless undertaker since his time was more than filled up with me. I don' know where the man got the energy to do what he done afore I come along. He'd been workin' all day as a janitor then at the funeral parlor on weekends and nights when somebody died, and that was on top of keepin' four cows, some chickens, and three hogs; makin' hay in the summertime and keepin' a garden. I did my best to help out, but it seemed like the time I saved him got devoted to drinkin'. Most ev'ry night we drank ourselves to sleep; 'til I got pregnant.

Chapter 14

Sallee

As late winter pressed on, the divorce started affecting our lives more and more. When I stood up for *Show and Tell* and told my class that my mother and daddy were getting a divorce, Miss Bradley, my teacher, took me to the cloakroom. "You don't tell stories like that to your friends." She patted my shoulder with the tips of her fingers like, if she touched too much of me, she might catch something. "The other little children don't need to be frightened. So you just keep your private life to yourself." She looked at me like I had done something terrible. "Do you hear me?" I nodded that I did. "Then say so young lady." I didn't bother to tell anyone at home what happened at school. Things were crazy enough without that.

My mother, or maybe it was Uncle Gordon, had the big idea that Mr. Myers, her lawyer, should talk to us kids about being in court. I don't know what made them think that a person none of us had ever seen before could cast a calming light on the trauma that awaited us; but somehow they decided that the small, peevish man was just the person to make us understand how we should tell the judge we wanted to live with our mother, because that's where children belonged—with their mothers. I guess they also thought that going down to a lawyer's office would make us feel better about the whole thing, like checking in with Santa Claus at the department store before Christmas.

Uncle Gordon came over to our house and drove us downtown to Mr. Myers's office. The whole way there he kept saying, "You're really going to like Mr. Myers. He's a fine man."

We sat in the backseat and rolled our eyes—as if it was going to make a difference whether we liked the man or not. Gordy stuck out his tongue and made a face. Helen and I giggled.

His office smelled just like the public library. And no wonder—there wasn't a wall in the room that didn't have cases stuffed with books. He wore half glasses that he peered over when he looked at you. His hooded gray eyes moved the whole time you talked, like his ears might miss something important. I got the impression that he expected me to lie. None of us did. Not that we got the chance. He'd fire a dumb question at us like, "Do you like living with your mommy?" then sit back and watch us like we were going to answer it. How do you answer a question like that when she's sitting right there? I got the feeling he didn't really care about our answers anyway because he was one of those people who didn't like children. You can tell them a mile away. When they talk to a kid they get all cutesy with a voice that's supposed to sound sweet but just sounds fake because nobody ever talks like that unless they're trying to get a kid to do something. You'd think they'd know.

He sat behind his enormous desk and peered over at us. "You are going to go to the courthouse," he said. "The judge is going to ask you where you want to live."

On the surface, I thought that seemed like a fine thing. It even made me feel a little important, as if I really did have a say in what happened in my life. Except for the fact that I was a kid; how was I supposed to know?

The trial was the only topic of conversation when the lights went out at night. Helen asked me almost every night, "How do you decide where you want to live? Do you know how? Where do you want to live?"

"I don't know!" I wailed into my pillow as I rocked my head up and down. "I can't even think about it," I declared. "I want to die before they do because I can't imagine how I would live without them." What I didn't say, because I didn't know how to articulate it, was that having to choose was the next worse thing. We finally decided we'd choose our Daddy because he played with us and was more fun. The decision had a hollow feel to it. Like many decisions where the stakes are high and the choices onerous, it nestled itself into the recesses of my mind and began to assume a sense of permanence as if it had already gone into effect. Our talks trailed off to solitary musings. I'm sure we both cried ourselves to sleep more than once contemplating our future and the decision we were being forced to make. I know I did. The question loomed over us worse than a trip to the dentist when you just knew he was going to find a cavity because you hadn't brushed since the last time you saw him.

Ethel was no help. For the last couple of weeks she had come to work short-tempered and snappy, and she was gone a lot more than usual. She didn't look much like herself. Her hair was fuzzy and you could tell she hadn't washed it in some time. Plus that splatterware cup of her's was always full by the kitchen sink. She wasn't even trying to hide it anymore. I didn't much like being around her, but I asked her anyway what she thought I should say. She just grumbled and shook her head. "I jest don' know."

The day we went to the courthouse was all jumbled up, mostly because Ethel didn't come to work. I resented that she hadn't come. I grumbled to Helen, "When we need her the most we get this crummy treatment. You'd think we were the ones making them get divorced." She was the closest thing we had to an advocate, and she had left us high and dry. "I can't believe she didn't come today. She knows how we don't wanta go to the dumb ol' court. She promised she'd be there with us and she didn't even show up." I kicked at my pajamas lying in a heap on the floor.

Helen said, "You'd be mad if she was here, too. You're just mad. You like to blame people." She could amaze me sometimes. As I whirled around in a fit of pique over this or that, Helen just went about her life adopting wise insights into the mysterious logic of our elders. It had a remarkably calming effect on me. Whereas I'd argue with Gordy about almost anything, when Helen spoke up, I generally listened.

I considered what she had said. "Yeah, I guess I do." And then I thought, *It's a good thing there are a lot of people to blame.* I rolled it around in my mind like hard candy, savoring the sweetness of its simplicity. Mr.

Myers's talk did nothing to allay our fears. Stuart had her day in court before us, just a few days after our visit to the lawyer's. She filled us in on all the gruesome details. She had a way of making you feel worse under the guise of soothing you.

"It's no big deal. This guy comes in all dressed in black. He's the judge."

"Anybody knows that," Gordy said with a sneer.

"OK smarty pants. If you know so much I won't tell you anymore." She was already gathering her stuff off the bed to leave.

"Go on. I wanta know," I said to her. Helen and I, slack jawed with interest, scowled at Gordy and hissed, "Shut up."

She continued her grisly blow-by-blow description of her trip to see the judge. Gordy was listening mighty carefully, too. "Mother's lawyer told you to tell the judge that you wanted to live with her, but you don't have to. You can say you want to live with me and Daddy. He wants you to. I know he does."

"But what about Ethel? What's gonna happen to Ethel if we go live with Daddy?" Helen asked, and I wondered too.

"I heard Daddy talking to his lawyer the other night. He said that he had talked to Ethel and that she would come work for him and take care of ya'll just like now, except not here." She said all of this like she was describing a trip out in the country—all breathless and breezy. "Don't worry. Ethel is going to testify for Daddy, so the judge will be sure to give you guys to him. So, whatever you say probably doesn't make any difference anyway. It's all going to be fine."

The three of us looked at each other. What was it going to be like in a new house without our mother? What would happen to her?

My mother, never very good at overseeing how we dressed— although detail was everything when it came time to criticize the result—was busy dressing herself for court. The best she could do to help us get ready was to yell; and that she did at full volume. The task of picking out what to wear became ours for the first time. Up until that very instant, Ethel always laid out what we were going to wear. On our own, we wore our pajamas.

"How are you supposed to know what to wear to court if you haven't ever been before?" I wanted to know.

Helen said, "I'm going to wear my Sunday school clothes."

"Well, I'm not. I hate that old dress. 'Sides, I don't want to look like some goody-goody." So declaring, I decided on a red corduroy jumper and white blouse.

As I stripped off my nightclothes, Helen said, "You probably outta…"

"Oh shut up," I snapped, fighting my way into my blouse. "I've about had it with people telling me what I should do." I decided against socks until Helen impressed upon me the need.

"Remember the last time you didn't wear socks? You got one of those big blisters on your heel and it hurt."

Mostly dressed, my mother blew around the house like a plastic bag in a parking lot. She was in our room one minute, and then I heard her up in Gordy's room yelling at him the next. She flew in again and scowled at my choice of attire. Uncle Gordon's car was crunching up the drive. "Hurry up. It's time to go. Give me that brush. Sallee, when are you going to learn how to brush your hair?" She raked my head with the brush. Tears welled up.

"Stop, it hurts."

"Then learn how to do it yourself." She pulled my hair into a pony-tail, yanking at it like it was an old hose stuck around a rock. "Stop," I screamed, pulling away as my face streaked with tears. "It hurts."

Uncle Gordon, the busiest man that ever lived, bustled into the room, his usual jowly red face almost purple. He started to shout, but checked himself in the middle of his question. "What's going on in here? Why is she crying?" he pointed at me like I was something he'd scraped off his shoe. "For God sakes, Ginny, today is not the day to lose your temper with the children. We're supposed to be in court in twenty minutes. Are you trying to lose custody?"

He, who never had a moment to speak to me in the past, put his big, old, bad-breathed face right up to mine and said, "Honey, everything is going to be just fine. Your mommy didn't mean to hurt you. She's just a little upset today. You know how it is. We all are." He glared every so often over my head at my mother who looked like she might cry at any minute. "You," he said, pointing to Helen like he didn't know her name, "go on and find Gordy—we gotta be going."

Still whimpering, I resisted as he took me by the hand. His oversized, sweaty hand squeezed hard on mine as he pushed and prodded the rest of us into his big white car. After letting go of me, Uncle Gordon patted my mother on the arm. "Don't worry," he said. ""It is all going to be just fine." In the back seat of his car I smelled my hand the way you do when you accidentally touch some dog doo, checking to see if the smell was still there, then wiping it on the seat and rechecking. I noticed Gordy's green plaid shirt was buttoned up wrong. He had missed a button, causing the shirt to gap out over his belt showing his undershirt. Then he had skipped another button, making his collar look ridiculously cockeyed. I also noted that a brush had not touched his cowlick, stubborn at the best of times. The way things were going, it just seemed to make sense to keep it to myself.

I had the strangest sensation of feeling smaller than usual, like Alice from *Alice in Wonderland*, only I didn't have a bottle to make me bigger. The courthouse was brick and old. I bet I had probably driven by it a million times in the past and never noticed how enormous it was. The cannons outside were as large as two cars.

The enormous double doors were swept open for us, and we were herded into a green, cavernous room with a desk in front that looked like it went up forever. There were flags all around it. The windows were taller than small houses. Just like on *Perry Mason*, there was a banister that looked like a fence between where regular people and the lawyers and bad guys sat. After walking for what seemed like a mile, we went through the gate. My mother went and sat down with Mr. Myers at one of the tables. My father was sitting at another table with a man I had never seen before. Uncle Gordon stood with us. I gathered up enough courage to look around and saw Ethel sitting with Bertha way in the back of the room. Uncle Gordon and a man who looked like a policeman led us over to the far left-hand corner of the courtroom. Almost hidden in the green paneling was a door.

Big is too small a word to describe the judge. The black robe that he wore was easily as large as one of those holes in space that takes four hundred thousand years to fly through. Like a huge crow, he bent over and put his massive hands—each the size of Ethel's cast iron skillet—on his knees; knees that came up level with my eyes. They called the room we were in "the judge's chamber." It didn't seem big enough for the man; more like his broom closet. He stuck his colossal face in our midst. We could tell he was trying his best not to scare us, but he was failing miserably. His voice had the timbre as I imagined the giant in *Jack and the Beanstalk* had. I half expected him to bellow, "Fee fie foe fum."

"I know what you are going through is very hard," he said. His knees cracked as he eased himself into a chair. "You know where you are and why you are here. And I hope you know that you haven't done anything wrong. Where do you want to live?" he asked staring at each of us in turn with is big hands lying on the chair's arms. He looked like Abraham Lincoln. We stared back at him about as dumb as three kids could, not one of us said a word—too overwhelmed.

I had practiced this moment for weeks. I knew what was expected of me, and I knew that what I wanted to say was "With my daddy." I had thought long and hard about how sad he would be without me. Never in the awful weeks that loomed before that moment had I even once considered how my mother would feel without me. I'd often contemplated how nice it would be to be free from the tyranny that reigned at home. No longer would I have to greet old ladies and learn how to be polite, nor would I have to do what was expected of me. We could eat hot dogs for dinner. But before I knew what was coming out of my mouth I started to cry and blurted out, "With my mommy." The other two followed suit. I kicked myself going out of the courthouse. We all did.

As if the experience at the courthouse hadn't been trial enough, Uncle Gordon had to feed us before he deposited us back at the house. My mother and Ethel stayed behind.

Uncle Gordy said, "Ethel will be back at the house by two-thirty, so we are going to get something to eat before we go home. You all go ahead and get in the car. I'll be along directly."

Uncle Gordon jabbered like a grackle bird as he drove us to a greasy hamburger place. The restaurant smelled like a nasty brew of stale beer, dirty ashtrays, and men—working men. It was blue with smoke and grease. I would rather have licked the sole of my shoe than eat right then, even though we hadn't had breakfast. Uncle Gordon greeted a bunch of men at the bar. He seemed to be at home. I wondered if he ever brought my mother there for lunch. "Whattaya have ol' Gordy boy," he asked, clapping Gordy on the shoulder.

"I dunno. I guess a hamburger. Can I have a coke, Uncle Gordon?"

"Sure, kid, whatever you want. How 'bout you girls?"

"I'm not hungry," I said. Helen started to cry. "I'm going outside with Helen. We'll sit in the car and wait."

"Suit yourself," he said.

Helen and I sat slumped in the backseat and stared at our feet, waiting to go home. "Do you think we'll ever see him again?" she asked. Are they going to put him in jail because of us?"

"No, he's not going to jail. But I bet he'll be really sad." I said feeling more shame than I had ever felt. "I'm sure we'll get to see him. That is, if he wants to see us." I choked up, leaned against Helen, and bawled.

Our kitchen was like a funeral parlor that afternoon. Ethel spilled over one of the ladderback kitchen chairs. Its rush seat groaned with every sigh and sob. Bertha tried in vain to comfort her desolate daughter. Even she looked forlorn. Bertha said to Ethel as she rubbed her on her shoulders, "Honey, ain't nothin' ya coulda done different. Ya had ta stand by Miz Ginny. 'Side Mista Joe had dat assault charge 'ginst 'em. No judge gonna be taken' no child way from they mama, no how. Ya donne did the righ'thing. Ya know as good as me chil'ren belongs with they mamas."

Ethel rocked her head and sighed. Once we realized that there would be no solace to be had in the kitchen, we retreated to our rooms. Miserable, we put ourselves to bed. I felt like I had driven a spike through my father's heart. I wondered if I would ever be able to look him in the eye again.

I don't know if the divorce was finalized, but all the court stuff was over on the sixteenth day of April, 1959 when my baby brother was born. My mother named him Dennis, after her brother, who I don't think I had ever seen, though Stuart said I had once, when I was two. My mother always said he had a delicate disposition and didn't go out much.

Baby Denny wasn't anything but a pain—too young to play with, asleep all the time, and when he wasn't sleeping, he cried. Not that his being asleep was an improvement; you had to creep around like you didn't want to get caught or there was somebody dead in the house. Any time he woke up and cried somebody got blamed for being too loud, usually me. I must not have been the only one who didn't like having him around: Ethel and my mother were as grumpy as two old dogs with a bad case of fleas. To make matters worse, my mother started crying again almost as much as she did after the puppy died. She and her friend Mrs. Chambers talked about how funny it was that my brother looked just like my father. "That ought to show him," my mother said, laughing one of those laughs that people laughed about things that weren't funny. He didn't look like my father to me, but I thought it would be better to keep that to myself. My mother seemed to hold a lot of stock in their looking alike since she said it every chance she got.

One Saturday afternoon, a week or two after my mother and Denny came home from the hospital, Ethel took a day off. The house was quiet. I had been stewing about a bake sale since my teacher had announced it on Friday—the very last one of the school year. I peered into one cabinet after another, looking for what? I wasn't sure.

It all started the week before when Rhonda, the fat pig, opened her big dumb mouth. Ethel had packed some of her marmalade tarts in my lunch. As I was munching away at lunch, Rhonda, who sat next to me, said, "Those look good, can I have one? What are they?"

"Marmalade tarts," I said, showering her with crumbs as I pushed the waxed paper-wrapped confections her way. "You've had them before. I bring them to bake sales all the time. They are one of the first things to sell out. Everybody loves them—one of her specialties."

"Mm they are good. Your mom must be a really good cook," she said, stuffing the last of the tart in her mouth.

"Oh, no, my mother didn't make them, Ethel did. She's our maid."

"She ain't a nigger is she?" she sprayed tart all over me.

"She's colored," I said.

"You eat food touched by a nigger? Gross," she gagged as she wiped the remains out of her mouth, clawing at her tongue with her napkin to wipe out every last crumb. "Better not bring any food she makes to a bake sale again or you'll be taking it home cuz nobody'll buy it."

Though I wanted to smash Rhonda in the face, I remembered what happened when Gordy was sent home for fighting. "Just be quiet, you piece of white trash," I hissed. It was the worst I knew, and I had to be careful using it because I had to stay in from recess once before when I called another girl in my class "white trash" in earshot of my teacher.

So there I was in the kitchen, looking for something to make for the bake sale. No cake mix, no mix of any kind; nothing anyone could just bake. *Why does Ethel have to make everything from scratch?* I grumbled to myself as I looked through yet another cabinet to no avail. Gordy came into the room and flopped into one of the kitchen chairs.

"Whattya doin'?"

"I gotta make something for the bake sale on Monday."

"Why didn't you get Ethel to make something?" he asked as he spun a pencil around on the table in front on him. "You sure don't know how to cook."

"I forgot."

"She's coming tomorrow. She likes baking. She'll do it."

"No I have to, teacher says," I lied.

"Since when? Bake sales are for making money. Who's going to buy anything you make? On the other hand, my fudge—that would bring in some cash."

"I don't know. Go away! Quit bothering me."

"What are you up to?" He eyed me suspiciously.

"Nothing. How come you know how to make fudge?"

"George and I make it all the time. Want me to make some? Look and see if we have baking chocolate. It's in a flat box. Up there." He pointed to the cabinet over my head and added, "The bitter stuff."

I climbed up on the counter and searched around in the cabinet until I found the chocolate. I knocked the yellow confectioners' sugar box over as I pulled out the chocolate from behind it. Sugar spilled on the counter and floor.

"Good, we need some of that stuff too," he said while searching in a cabinet for a bowl. "Don't spill any more though. We might need all of it."

Gordy delivered his orders like a drill sergeant. "Get this...I need one of those..." The chocolate burned until we were down to the last two squares and he remembered that you melted it in a bowl over boiling water. While he stirred, I gathered more supplies and buttered pans. I buttered my way down from a roasting pan, finally settling on a little bitty thing not more than six inches square. The kitchen sink and surrounding counters were littered with numerous buttered pans too large for the job, bowls with chocolate smears on them, several wooden spoons, butter wrappers, and one badly melted plastic spoon. Gordy said he didn't think the plastic melted enough to affect the fudge. Sugar coated the floor like frost. Vanilla pooled on the counter. The chocolate goop he created had the consistency of wet clay. Scraping it into the pan proved to be more of a challenge than melting the chocolate. In the end, I had to hold the hot pot while he poked, prodded, and coaxed the brown mess into the awaiting buttered pan. The potholders covered in chocolate stuck to my hands.

"That is some fine looking fudge," Gordy beamed. He licked his fingers while nodding his approval. "Tastes good too," he added.

We didn't have more than a half inch of chocolate in the small pan. "Do you think this'll be enough to bring to the bake sale?" I asked.

"Bake sale? Who said bake sale? This is my fudge."

"Gordy, you know...Come on, we made this together for the bake sale—you know, come on..."

"I made the fudge. You made the mess." He looked around the kitchen. "A big one, too."

"I've got to take this fudge to the bake sale or she'll tell and then...I don't even know what. Come on Gordy," I whined.

"What are you talking about? Who'll tell? What?"

"Rhonda'll tell. You know the fat one with the stringy black hair? She'll tell that Ethel made stuff for the bake sale."

"So?"

"Well, the way she made it out to be, it was against the law or something; maybe like going to school with colored people. I don't know. I don't want to get Ethel in trouble."

"Are you nuts? How is Ethel going to get in trouble for something she makes for a dumb old bake sale? Sometimes you are so stupid. It's a bake sale! How is that going to get anybody in trouble?"

"But she said nobody would buy them. Nobody would buy them because Ethel—well she didn't say 'Ethel.' She kept saying a nigger made them. 'Nobody wants to eat food a nigger touched,' is what she said. She said I'd have to bring them home and then you know Ethel would want to know why, and then she'd get her feelings hurt."

Gordy spread out his hands and shrugged, "So if nobody buys them, bring them home and we'll eat them, no problem. Ethel doesn't need to know anything. Come on, we better get this place cleaned up. You wash and I'll dry."

The next morning Ethel was mopping the floor when I came down for breakfast. She looked pretty rough. Though her uniform was clean, her hair was sloppy: her four normally tight buns were big and loose, each held together with a hairpin that looked as if it might fall to the floor at any moment. Her tin cup was sitting by the sink. "Someone musta spilled some sugar las night," she slurred softly. "Sugar tracked all over the place. You don' know nothing about that do ya?"

"Uhh, mm uh Gordy…"

"And there was some nasty lookin' stuff in the icebox; I throwed it out. Almos' had to throw out the pan; it was stuck in it like concrete. There's a pound o' butter missin, too, and they is some bowls put away looked like theys not been touched by a lick of soap or water. You know where that plastic spoon is? The one I use for mixin'?"

"Umm, no."

"Hum," she said. "Didn't think so."

I gulped down my breakfast. Even without something for the bake sale, I was glad to be off to school.

Chapter 15

It hardly ever failed that if Ham Bone came on Friday, Ethel didn't come to work on Monday. Gordy and I were watching TV Saturday morning after one of Ham Bone's visits. "I had one of those dreams again," I said as we laid sprawled on the floor in front of the television. I had been having a recurring dream that Ethel was drunk under my bed. If I tried to get out of bed, she would grab at me from under it. Like in the cartoons where there are always pink elephants around drunks, Ethel would be staggering around in my dream in a haze of pink."

Gordy didn't say anything, though he did shutter.

"She smelled. She smelled really bad," I went on, desperate to tell someone the dream in hopes of making it go away. "I was afraid to move. If I did Ethel I knew Ethel would jump out from under the bed and grab me."

Gordy laughed. "She'd get stuck," he said. "Next time you have the dream just think she can't jump out from under the bed she'd get stuck."

"It's a dream, knucklehead. I can't think when it's a dream."

"I don't know then," he shrugged as he got up to change the channel.

I heard my mother complaining to a friend on the telephone after one of Mr. Ham Bone's visits. "Ethel's been drinking again. I don't suppose she'll be here next week. It makes me so mad. I'd get somebody else if I could." In spite of my nightmares, the idea of losing Ethel made my knees weak. I couldn't imagine life without her. I ran upstairs, furious and sick, not caring if my mother knew I'd been eavesdropping.

Helen had the bad luck of being in our room where I had gone to cry. She was scribbling over a picture she had drawn. It felt better to be mad than helpless, so without a word, I pushed her off the bed. She screamed, "Mommy, Mommy."

I grabbed her curls and yanked. "Shut up, you little baby." The betrayal in her eyes stung as bad as if she had hit me. I couldn't help myself. I didn't even know why I was doing what I was doing. I flailed at Helen as if the rage had a mind of its own and the two of us were its helpless victims. Sometimes my hands connected with bone. The sharp shooting pain of contact only fueled my rage. Hot tears burned my cheeks. There was no thought, only an all-consuming urge to give vent to my anger.

"Get off me. Make her stop. Make her stop," she screamed.

My mother descended on me like a chicken on a tick. She grabbed me by the arm and pulled me away from my little sister, smacking at my backside as she dug her fingers into my armpit. "Stop it right now. What has gotten into you?"

I was crying. Helen was crying. With far less inducement, Helen was capable of a pretty good show of tears. Her indignation took her to new heights.

"What is going on? What happened?" my mother demanded of me.

"She pushed me down and I hit her back."

"She pushed me, she pushed me. I didn't do anything!" Helen railed against my duplicity. "I hate you," she gulped for breath between sobs.

"That is enough. You," mother pointed at me, "in bed. I don't want to see you until tomorrow morning, and then only after you apologize to your sister."

"I didn't do anything. She did it." I pointed to Helen, feeling a little guilty, but that was better than what I had been feeling.

"Enough." She left, carrying Helen with her. I hated Helen. I hated my mother. I hated Ethel.

"I hope you all die," I said under my breath as I slammed the door. I flung myself onto my bed and wailed into my pillow. The drawing still on her bed was of a stick lady with an apron and bottle.

I didn't know whether or not my mother thought Ham Bone had anything to do with Ethel's drinking, but I sure did. I wanted to tell her what I thought. I wanted her to fix it to make Ethel better. I wanted to tell her that Ham Bone was bringing Ethel liquor and for her to make him stop. But I didn't want to get Ethel in any more trouble, even though I hated it more than anything when Ethel drank.

Leola and Johnson's daughter, Mazine, stayed with us while my mother was in the hospital for the two weeks after she had the baby. Then she was my baby brother's nursemaid for about two months. I think Ethel appreciated Mazine's help. Ethel couldn't spend the night and didn't have the time since she had to help Early with the farm and still had all the other work to do at our house. When Mazine wasn't seeing to my brother's needs, she would join in on the chats that were becoming a pretty common occurrence in our kitchen.

Mazine took after her father, Johnson. She was real light-skinned and skinny. Where Mazine was lines and angles, her mother was curves and circles. When Leola sat in one of our ladder back kitchen chairs, that chair looked about full. Mazine, Leola, and Ethel would cackle like a bunch of chickens, laughing and talking if my mother wasn't around.

Mazine lived on the third floor in the maid's room. We regularly crept up to Mazine's room before and even after my mother and the baby came home because she would tell us stories. She told us one night in the middle of a lightning storm, "If'n yo house gits struck by lightn' you cain't put it out wit' nothin' but cow's milk." That kept Helen up half the night. Meanwhile I dreamt of cows being airlifted to house fires as I tried to figure out how you'd milk a cow hanging from a helicopter.

Mazine had horror stories for almost any natural occurrence. One of her stories about bats imparted in me a terrible fear of them getting into my hair. I had hair down to the middle of my back. I loved chewing gum. My mother despised the stuff and it was a rare treat when I had any of it. When I did get gum, I didn't spit it out at bedtime. More than once I'd have to sit still while Ethel scraped chewing gum out of the rat's nest that had grown overnight when the gum fell out of my mouth. The pain of Ethel tugging at the gum in my hair was all I could think of as Mazine expounded on the terrors of having a bat caught in your hair. "You jest gotta cut it out," she said. The idea of a live flying mouse trapped in my hair, beating its leathery wings in desperation, left me weak. Never mind that someone would have to have the wherewithal to get close enough to cut the thing loose.

Not long after that, a bat made the huge mistake of flying through Mazine's open window. The shrieks that emanated from the third floor roused the whole house. Cowering in her room, she whooped and hollered as if being tortured.

Helen and I heard my mother run up the stairs calling, "What's the matter?" in a frightened voice. Her question was answered by more whoops. We opened our bedroom door and peeped up at her.

"Isa bat, isa bat! Lord, Miz Ginny, git it. Please, git it," Mazine wailed desperately from her room.

"Sallee, go get a broom," my mother directed. "Hurry."

I tore downstairs to the kitchen, sure that Mazine must be in grave danger, and anxious with the belief that every second might count. The broom was between the wall and the icebox. The difficulty lay in trying to retrieve it. My arms weren't long enough. I squeezed myself as hard as I could into the narrow opening. I just couldn't reach it. I pushed and pushed. I tried to squeeze my head into the space. There was no give in the wall or the refrigerator and my head hurt from the pressure. The broom was just out of my grasp. I could touch the bristles, but could not gain a purchase on them. I raced back upstairs and reported, "I can't get it."

Mazine let loose another shriek. With an exasperated sigh, my mother pushed past me on the steps. Her disapproval burned into me. Desperate to make amends, I steeled myself to confront whatever awaited me within Mazine's room. Just as I opened the door, I heard my mother call from downstairs, "Don't open that door!" The bat flew out and flailed around over my head. Modesty long forgotten, Mazine had pulled her nightgown up over her head and was peering out from under it at me, her rescuer, as I struggled to remain conscious. Mazine's tale of bats getting caught in your hair whirled around in my head as the bat flew over it.

The next morning I awoke to Helen looking at me like I was an exhibit at the zoo. "You must've been tired," she said. "You fell asleep standin' up. Right in front of Mazine's door. I watched. She opened it and one minute you were there, then there you were, asleep on the floor; quick as that. Gordy opened the window. The bat flew out. You missed the whole thing. It was fun."

"Mazine got a job as a grocery store checker," Leola crowed while visiting with Ethel. "Dats why she ain't comin' to work no mo."

"Why you tellin' me? Ain't she growed enough to quit her ownself wit'out her mama doin' it for her? Is I s'posed to be tellin' Miz Ginny or is you?"

Ethel was called on to babysit after that. If she couldn't do it, she'd arrange for someone else to sit for us.

"Ethel, I'm going out tonight. Could you get Roberta to sit?" my mother asked Ethel on Saturday afternoon.

"I's can do it, Miz Ginny. I ain't got no plans."

"I'd rather have Roberta if she's available. She can drive." My mother added, "If Roberta can't do it then you can."

Helen and I were sitting at the kitchen table listening to the conversation. When Ethel left the kitchen to call Roberta we crossed our fingers hoping Roberta would be busy and Ethel could stay with us. Roberta talked really slow with a real deep and raspy voice like she smoked cigars. Everything she said sounded grumpy, even if it wasn't. It didn't help that she was also short tempered. Her broad mouth stayed frozen in a sneer. She was our least favorite sitter.

"Miz Ginny, Roberta say she can sit tonight. What time you want her?"

"Five-thirty would be good."

Helen and I groaned and left the kitchen. "Do you remember the last time she sat and drove Mama to that party way out in the country?" she asked me looking a little sick.

"How could I forget it? I thought we were goners."

Gordy came in and flopped on my bed. "What are you guys doing?"

"Mama's going out tonight and guess who's babysitting?" Helen said.

"Please say it isn't Roberta, please, please." We both nodded are heads up and down. "Oh God, I hate when she sits. Is she driving Mama to a party?" Again we nodded.

I'd rather stay home alone then get in the car with her. "Where's the party?" We both shrugged. "She's gonna kill us one of these days. Somebody oughta tell Mama what a terrible driver she is."

"Go ahead," I said. "I bet she doesn't like how Roberta drives. You notice she never lets Roberta drive to the party. I think I could do a better job driving."

"I know I could," Gordy said.

It was as bad as we thought it was going to be. The party was on a road called Twenty-One Curves. I counted every one of them on the way out there. After my mother got out, Roberta whipped the car out of the driveway and I swear she didn't bother to look to see if anyone was coming. She was just about up to the speed of light when she slammed on the brakes and then creeped along like a bug. The baby rocked around in the car bed that was wedged up against the front seat. I don't know why he wasn't in the front seat when she slammed on the brakes; our heads hit the back of the seat in front of us. The fact that there was one turn after another didn't seem to make a bit of difference to her. As we were going ninety miles an hour around a bend in the road I said, "Roberta, could you slow down a little? I'm scared."

Roberta's temperament was as unpredictable as her driving. "You ain't go nuttin' to be 'fraid of," she assured me—albeit gruffly. "I'll get ya home in no time." We hung on to the armrests and each other while staring ahead wild-eyed; the landscape tearing by us in a blur. As the tires squealed, Helen looked like she was going to cry. My knees shook so badly that when we finally got home, I couldn't get out of the car for a good five minutes. Roberta stood outside the car casting furtive glances toward the Dabney's house. "Come on, honey, you git out ta dis here car. I's got ta gets you chil'ren in de house. Come on." Her coaxing had taken on a harder edge. "Now." She shepherded us up the walk and into the house at a trot. Once in the house she slammed the door and locked it —something I don't remember anyone having ever done before. Then she ran to every outside door in the house and locked them up tight, even the door to the basement.

I went straight to bed. I found Helen staring out the window at my mother's car. "I don't think she pulled up the brake like Momma does," she whispered. "What if it rolls down the hill and crashes?"

"Good. Maybe she'll get arrested and be put in jail. Then we won't have to ride with her anymore," I said as I sank under the covers. Why do you think she was so busy locking all the doors?"

Do you think Mamma will be able to get in when she gets home?" Helen whined

"You worry too much." I said, turned over, and went to sleep.

Ethel had two other stand-ins if she wasn't able to take care of us when my mother went out. One was Mattie Bruce; the other, Ethel's mother, Bertha. I loved Bertha. She looked just like an Indian squaw when she didn't have her hair twisted up around her head. She had skin of the warmest color I ever saw, like if you could mix copper with cream. When she smiled, her face shone as bright as a new penny. She talked really slowly, too, and never once did I ever hear her say an unkind word to anyone. Bertha paid attention to what you said. She'd stop what she was doing and look right at me when I talked to her, like what I was saying was the most important thing in the world.

"Bertha, why does Ethel have a different name?" I asked one afternoon while she was preparing our dinner. Bertha had five daughters with a curious distinction. There was Alberta, the oldest, then Roberta, then there was Ethel, poor, simple Huberta, and Viberta the baby.

"I ran outta Bertas," she said.

"But she was in the middle."

"That's right. I liked the sound so much I made up the other two my own self when the next set of slit tails showed up. But all our names ends in 'a'."

"Hum, that's interesting. Why's that?" I began. Then, before she could answer I protested, "Wait, Ethel's name doesn't end with an 'a'."

"'Cause I liked it that way, I guess. An' it do end wit' an 'a', too. Her name is Ethelia."

"Didn't you get confused when you called 'em?" I asked. "Daddy does with us, and we all have different names," I said as I tried to imagine what it might have sounded like if Bertha called all of her girls to supper like Ethel did us. I tried it for her. "Al-Burrr-da, Roe-burrr-da, Ethel-ya, Hu-burrr-da, Vi-burrr-da. Boy, you'd be tired before you finished," I concluded.

"I'd jest call 'Berta' and dey all answered 'cept Ethel. Thas why I wents back to Berta. Worked right good," she chuckled, obviously pleased with her ingenuity.

Bertha would sit on a chair by my bed, snuggling my baby brother and telling me stories about mother sun and sister moon. Even Denny seemed happier with her; he didn't cry as much—probably because she held him and rocked him any chance she got. "Purdiest chile," she'd croon. I wasn't convinced of that, but I did like him better when Bertha was around.

Bertha stayed with us a whole week once when Ethel was sick or drunk and my mother went to New York shopping with Uncle James and Aunt Lizbeth. That week there was an aurora borealis. Having never seen the northern lights, as vibrant as it was, I was concerned. "Look outside, Bertha, the sky's all red and purple and streaky. Is something the matter?"

"Darlin', chile, thas jest God paintin' you a pitchur in the sky. Don' worry none, honey. I ain't gon let nothin' happen to ya." She wrapped me in her strong arms and sat with me until I fell asleep. That week went by faster than it should have and even though my mother brought us candy gold coins in little sacks, I was sorry to see Bertha's stay come to an end. I could see how Bertha was Ethel's mother, but no matter how hard I tried, I couldn't make out how she was also Roberta the maniac's mother. That was another one of those questions I figured it was best not to ask. One thing I didn't want to do was to find out that Bertha could get mad, especially at me.

While Bertha was by far my favorite sitter, Mattie Bruce gave Roberta a run for worst. Mattie Bruce was a third string babysitter. She was called on when none of the others were available. She worked for Gordy's friend George's mother across the street from us. Mattie Bruce was the closest thing to the Tasmanian devil that there ever was in human form. She made Ethel look tall. Though she wasn't anywhere near as fat as Ethel, she was, as Ethel would say, "stout." While Ethel's body sort of spilled all over soft and unbounded, Mattie Bruce's round and hard body reminded me of a spider with skinny arms and legs. Everything she did, she did double time. I could hardly understand her, she talked so fast. And if Bertha calmed Denny down, Mattie Bruce did the opposite—she'd whirl around the house, rattling off commands a mile a minute, and before you knew it, Denny would be crying; his screams adding to the confusion and making Mattie Bruce shout to be heard.

George grew up listening to Mattie Bruce, so he didn't seem to have much trouble understanding her. As for me, I couldn't so much as read her tone. She always sounded mad to me. It wasn't clear if she stuttered or she thought everything she said bore repeating.

Occasionally George's mother invited us to stay for a peanut butter sandwich. The call for lunch was not like any I had ever heard—more like the mating call of a rare species of bird. Mattie Bruce would come to the kitchen door and in her nervous, high-pitched voice shriek, "Com-ma, com-ma, com-ma."

George translated for us: "It's lunchtime."

He wasn't around to translate when Mattie Bruce babysat. Whenever she called, it fell upon us to guess what she wanted us to do. The challenge of deciphering her words correctly was reason enough to avoid her. We'd played outside long after dinner one night when Mattie Bruce was sitting. She didn't seem to find it strange that three small children were playing outside in the dark.

At nine o'clock sharp, Mattie Bruce yelled out to us, "Com-ma, com-ma, com-ma"

"Do you think she's calling us for lunch?" I asked. "Didn't George say that meant lunchtime?"

Gordy said, "She's probably callin' us into the house. It is dark. I think she means come on."

She asked, "Wheredadishragsat?" while Helen and I were brushing our teeth.

"What? I'm sorry."

"Dishrag. Whereitat?" she asked again at supersonic speed.

"I don't know," I said dumbly.

Mattie Bruce always came and went in a taxi. After she went downstairs, I crept into my mother's room. I pulled out the drawer where the phonebook was kept. I found the number for Pace's taxi and called it. After giving our address, I quietly stole back into our room and waited at the window. Five minutes later a cab drove up our drive. When the driver came to the door, Mattie Brue nearly "Nobody here called" the poor man to death. After he had driven away, she was heard mumbling "Nobody here called" for a good twenty minutes. Helen and I laughed a little, but we were disappointed that she didn't leave in the cab.

Ethel was becoming less and less forthcoming with answers to my questions. Uncle Dennis, the only brother that my mother didn't see regularly, had been in the state hospital. There was a lot of commotion about his coming home, and I wanted to know why. I asked Ethel and she said that I didn't need to know. I asked why he had been in the hospital and she wouldn't answer that either. Sometime in early June when my uncle came home, my mother and her friend, Miz Chambers, planned a party. I heard them talking about what they should drink. Miz Chambers said, "I think beer will be fine, Ginny. It won't make any difference if he has a beer or two."

"Well, maybe just us. We can pour it in glasses. He won't notice," my mother said.

The party was poorly attended. There were only the three of them and it didn't last long. Miz Chambers or my mother kept going into the kitchen and pouring themselves more beer. "Dennis do you want some more ginger ale?" they asked. Even I could tell the difference in color. Uncle Dennis didn't seem to care much that my mother had named her new baby after him. He barely looked at Denny when she had Ethel paraded us all out to meet him. He left early, but before he did he said, "I heard my old buddy CL Dabney lives somewhere around here. You don't know where, do you?" My mother looked as if someone had punched her in the stomach. She slowly shook her head like she had no idea in the world. I was about to pipe up that the Dabneys lived right next door, but she silenced me with a look that would have melted rock. After walking Uncle Dennis to the door, my mother didn't even kiss him goodbye. They both just stood there looking at each other before he turned and walked away. She shut the door awfully hard after him and clucked to herself as she joined Mrs. Chambers on porch. "That ungrateful son of a bitch," she said. "Sallee, what are you doing here? Get to bed." My mother lit a cigarette as I was coming over to kiss her good night and waved me away. "Tell your brother and sister to go to bed too. Good night." I could hear them talking about Uncle Dennis being in the hospital for drinking as I took my time climbing the stairs. But there seemed to be more to it than that because before I got to the top of the stairs they were whispering. As far as I heard, there wasn't another mention of Mr. Dabney.

My uncle's little black station wagon had been parked in our garage for a couple of months. Whenever I asked about the car, I got hazy answers. "He's away," my mother said once. When asked where, she all of a sudden thought of something else she had to do. Another time she said, "He left it here because he didn't need it anymore." Asking why only garnered a vague scowl and an exasperated sigh.

The signs indicated that there was far more to my uncle's hospitalization than anyone was saying. All my years of questioning had taught me what kinds of questions I could ask and how much I could push for an answer, but even my hard earned detective skills were running up against a brick wall when it came to my Uncle Dennis. No amount of finesse could keep adults from shutting down when I broached the topic. I was beginning to realize that people were afraid of my questions. And on some level, I was realizing that questions have power.

"How come Uncle Dennis was in the hospital?" I asked Stuart casually one afternoon when the two of us were lounging on the back porch.

"Can't tell," she said matter-of-factly.

"Don't know?" I asked.

"Yeah, I know, but I'm not supposed to tell."

"Me?"

"Anybody."

"But I heard you talking to Ethel about it."

"She already knew, and she's not going to tell anybody."

"Neither will I."

"Yeah, right, you little brat. You'd ask somebody some question and then they'd figure out I told you."

I involuntarily shuddered. "Must be somethin' big."

"It is. It's really gross. You'd die if you knew."

"Tell me."

She'd been lazily flipping through a magazine, but she closed it now and set it down beside her. "What are you going to do for me if I do?"

"I won't tell that you sneak out at night."

"Old news; I already promised I wouldn't anymore." Stuart, ever so casually, readjusted herself on the chaise and started to pick at her thumbnail.

A few days earlier, Stuart had had an argument (now that they were such fast friends I was always corrected if I referred to them as fights) with my mother about sneaking out. That same night Helen and I, lying in bed, too hot to sleep, were humming and singing softly to each other. While we were speculating on who might move into the new house down the street, a tinny jangle outside our window caught my attention. I got up and peered around the curtains to see what it was. It sounded like someone was on the kitchen porch and had bumped up against Ethel's stack of roasting pans. I knew the sound well.

Ethel used that porch as a staging area for her to-do list and overflow storage for the kitchen. On the floor she parked baskets of unfolded laundry, drying racks, wet mops, and pails of water. On tables and stacks of old newspapers she perched plants to be repotted, piles of coat hangers, and an array of oversized kitchen equipment. Originally, it was just the turkey roaster that was stored on the porch, but over time Ethel had created an amazingly fail-safe burglar alarm. Even in the daytime, it was hard to negotiate her ever widening array of kitchen sprawl.

What I saw was Stuart quietly closing the screen door and creeping down the very far edges of the steps as close to the handrail as she could get. When she reached the bottom, she sprinted off into the neighbor's yard, disappearing into the darkness. Minutes later I heard a car engine start up.

"I not only saw you, I heard you," I said. "It's a wonder Mama didn't hear you. You made such a racket."

"When?"

"Two nights ago. You went out the kitchen door at around eleven-thirty. You bumped into Ethel's tower of pans, and then you went through the Dabneys' yard. And a couple of minutes later I saw Judy's boyfriend's car drive past our house."

"Can't prove it," She said with a smirk. "Ethel really does booby trap that porch, doesn't she?" We both laughed. "OK. Do not tell anyone!"

she said, enunciating every word for emphasis. Then she leaned closer and in hushed tones began, "He was in the state hospital for sexually abusing a little kid, a boy. It's so gross. I didn't tell Judy the whole story. I wouldn't tell anybody. It's just too gross."

"Sexually abusing? What's that mean?"

"Having sex with, you dummy." She sighed a huge sigh and rolled her eyes.

"But he was a boy!"

"Duh, that's the point." She got up, clearly exasperated. "If you tell anyone what I told you, I'll dismember you. You got that?" Then she turned and left in a huff.

Later that day Gordy and I had a conference in his room. He lay on his bed while I draped myself across the other bed on my belly, elbows propped up and head cradled in my hands. From his third story window, we had an excellent view of our front yard. We watched someone walking by on the sidewalk across the street. "She must have been kidding. Boys can't do it with each other," Gordy said.

"She wasn't. I could tell. She was telling the truth." I kicked my feet together, trying out different cadences. "Maybe sexual abusing means something different than doing it." I was way out of my depth. "We could look it up in the dictionary." The dictionary was my best friend. I could find the meanings of words I didn't understand without asking anyone. The dictionary never told me it was none of my business or chastised me for eavesdropping. "There's all kinds of words in there," I said, "like sex and penis and stuff. I even found shit in the big dictionary downstairs."

"Na," he said, dismissing my idea with a wave of his hand. Gordy was never one for reading or looking up words. I decided that I would look up *sexual abusing*. "Remember when his car was here? Remember we found those pants that we thought were mine in the back of his car?"

"So what?" My feet tapped in time to the pedestrian's footfalls.

"So maybe they belong to that kid. Maybe if you told Stuart about the pants she'd tell you more, like what sexual abusing means." Gordy insisted.

"Hey wait, I just remembered, a while back I heard Leola tell Ethel something about CL living next door. She said he r-a-p-e-d a colored boy.

Remember when Uncle Dennis came to that party Mama had for 'em? He said that CL Dabney was a good buddy of his. Mama looked liked she'd about puke when he said that. Like she didn't know or I don't know."

Gordy looked stricken. Do you know what r-a-p-e-d means? He asked.

I shook my head, "no. Maybe Ethel might…" I tried to get the beat of a trot.

"No way. Whatever you do, don't ask her." He made his eyes go out of focus and pretended to take off the lid of a trashcan.

"Yeah, I hate it when she starts rooting around in the trash."

Gordy and I had known for some time that, though Ham Bone had taken to avoiding the house after our mother scolded Ethel for his visits, he hadn't stopped delivering gin to her. He'd put the bottle in an empty trashcan at the bottom of the driveway on trash day. She only brought the trashcans up from the curb when there was a bottle in it.

"I know, I'll ask Mama," I said, my feet tapping now at a fast trot.

"Are you nuts? She's not going to tell you anything," Gordy announced with an incredulous look and a shake of his head that implied that I might become dangerous any minute.

"I'm not to ask about r-a-p-e-d. Leola spelled it. It's gotta be bad. I'm going to ask…Watch." I jumped up and ran down one flight of stairs and mounted the second floor banister sidesaddle, sliding down to the front hall. I heard my mother thank the paperboy as I landed. After I pushed open the door to the porch, I flopped into a wicker chair across from her.

"Can I have the comics?"

"Well, hello to you too. Here." She handed me the local section of the paper.

I checked out the comics and then scanned the front headlines looking for any article that might have the word abuse in it. I couldn't find one, but decided to go ahead with my plan anyway.

"Mama?"

"Yes, dear?"

"What does 'abuse' mean?" The screen door slammed. Gordy plopped down in the chair beside me. He sat back in his chair resting his elbows on the armrests and steepling his fingers. He looked like a prim old lady.

"Why do you ask?" She responded, not looking up from her paper.

"It's in the paper. I don't know what it means. I just wondered."

"Where? What's the article about?" She leaned forward as if to take the paper from me. I pretended not to notice.

I casually continued with my interest in an article that didn't exist.

"It means different things. How is it used?"

Gordy started to giggle.

"What's so funny?" she asked him.

"Nothin'."

"Let me see what you are looking at," she said to me. "Give me the paper."

Gordy started to laugh.

"What is so funny, young man? It's not nice to laugh in front of others and not share the joke. What was the word? Abuse? The paper… here…give it to me."

"Nevermind," I said, deciding it wasn't worth it. "I guess it just means hurt. Right?" I folded the paper neatly, slipped out of my chair and said to Gordy, "Wanna swing? I'll race you."

"Wait. Show me where you saw it. Abuse means different things in different contexts. I need to know the context."

"It's OK. I don't care. I don't even know what context means."

Gordy looked like he was going to pop from stifling his glee. He got up and went into the house. He didn't slam the door this time. He just sort of vaporized through it.

I handed my mother the paper. As she opened it, I saw a headline I'd missed before. *Garden Week: This Week Gardeners are Abuzz.*

She seemed relieved. "That's 'abuzz.' When people are excited; making lots of noise about something like a bee buzzing—not abuse."

"Oh." I too vaporized off the porch.

Gordy was on the swing when I found him. "Pshew, that was close," I said.

"'I'll ask Mama. Watch,'" he mimicked as he hurled himself off the swing into the air.

Chapter 16

Ethel
1930

Five whole years had flown by since Early and me first met. I never worried much 'bout gettin' pregnant—didn' much want no children. I liked things the way they was. Slowly, though, I started to suspect that somethin' wasn't quite the way it had been. Mama wasn't all that free on giving up information. I 'spect she figured I'd work it out on my own, or Roberta would tell me what I needed to know. You could count on Roberta for tellin' what needed to be told. I somehow missed that tellin'. So when I didn't bleed for a time I didn' pay it no mind. I never had paid it much attention.

If I live to be a hundred, I ain't never gon' forget the mornin' I knew for sho' I was pregnant. The last cow was milked. I was washin' up out at the pump tryin' hard to keep breakfast down. Thought I would die sloppin' the hogs; they smelled clear to heaven. Early had slipped into letting me do the mornin' chores since I had to be at work just before daybreak. Miz Nancy had begun grumblin' 'bout my being late most days. I went about getting the stove lit and haulin' water. My head was swimmin' and my stomach was churnin' like a storm at sea. Not like I had ever seen one, but I heard they was mighty rough, and that was how I was feelin'—rough. I had a terrible pain. It felt like a claw had grabbed my belly and commenced to squeeze, like to crack it, and wouldn't let up. It hurt so bad, it knocked me down. I was hanging on to the well pump, sweatin' wit' the chills, my teeth chatterin' and my knees knockin'. I couldn't stand up. Ever' time I went to move, I felt like somebody had punched me in the gut so hard it knocked the air outta me.

Early said he found me up aside the well pump pantin' like a dog. He got me to my feet and half dragged, half carried me into the bedroom, and then he ran fast to get the doctor. Dr. Green said he had no time and sent Early down to Aunt Annie, the colored midwife. By then whatever chance there was for my baby was long gone. They cleaned up the room pretty good. When the doctor finally come in, he and old Aunt Annie huddled out on the stoop talkin' 'bout what had happened. I heard her say, "They was nothing to be done but…"

Dr. Green come into my room. "Miss Ethel," he began. I remember he said "Miss." Most white folk ain't as respectful as Dr. Green was. He was a carin' man; I 'spect that's why he went into doctorin'. "Miss Ethel, you won't have to go through that ever again. That is the good news. As far as having any babies, you won't be able to. I'm sorry." With that he picked up his little black bag, put on his hat, and headed out the door. The screen door slammed after him. Aunt Annie bustled around a bit, straightenin' up this and that, and then she too let the screen door slam on her way out. The call of a whip-poor-will was all the sound there was. Early and I laid together on the bed—after the sad little funeral we had for our dead baby—like two lost souls, holdin' each other and takin' turns cryin' and comfortin'.

When I was able to get on my feet without the world goin' swimmy, I went down to the boardin' house to see Miz Nancy. I was still too weak to be much account at work, but I thought I best put in an appearance. She came out on the porch and just shook her head, lookin' sorry and sad. She said, "Miz Dupree say they no job here for the likes a you. She say she don' want no harlot workin' in her boardinghouse." I heard Miz Dupree call, "Nancy," and Miz Nancy had to turn and go without another word.

I dragged myself on home and went back to bed, miserable as could be. Thing is, losin' that job wasn't nothin' compared to the loss I felt over my child. I had never thought about children much, but suddenly they was all I could think about. I'd fall asleep and dream about my little baby who I'd never even known was growin' inside me. I'd dream he was born and healthy and smilin', and then something awful would happen to him. Sometimes I dropped 'im down the well, hearing his little body go "splash" in the water below. Other times I'd go to pick him up and he'd already be cold as death. Every night that baby would die all over again in my dreams, and I would wake up cryin' and hurtin'. Early would hold me and he'd cry, too. Some nights I don't think either of us slept.

A few days after I lost my job, Mama came by to see me with her new baby, Viberta. She was so proud and I couldn't blame her. Viberta was a sweet looking soul even though she only had three fingers on one hand. "Honey, I'm sorry you feel poorly, an' I ain't been much help to ya, I know." She nodded down to little Viberta. "You wanna hold 'er?"

I shook my head, tears streamin' down my face.

"I'm sorry, honey. I truly is so sorry."

"It's all right, Mama," I said. "I ain't never really want no baby…that is, 'til I found I was havin' one, an' then…" I tried to choke back the tears.

"I know, sugar. I know," she said, patting my hand while gently rocking Viberta.

"Is Early that do; he half crazy with grief. I's don' know what to do. Doctor say I can't have no mo'. Das whats really got Early riled up. He ain't stopped drinkin."

"What's you need is a job, darlin'. I heard Miz Sinclair lookin' for a nursemaid for that boy a her's."

I winced as I thought 'bout taking care of someone else's baby boy.

"It do ya good to spend time wit' a child. You kin love a child wit'out givin' birth to it. A child's love is good for the soul, honey, and you's got a soul thas a hurtin' an' needs that love. Go on down an' talk wit' Miz Sinclair—she a good woman. She know you is, too."

Mama was right. Miz Sinclair hired me the day I went to see her. It took me a week to screw myself up to a place where I wouldn't cry just to look at the baby. Baby Billy Sinclair was the best thing that had happened to me in a good while. He was a sweet baby. The work was easy. I had a half day off ev'ry Sunday, and a full day off once a month; and the pay was better, too. Miz Sinclair was easy to work for, but then I suspect most people would be compared to old Miz Dupree. Every day, Billy got a little bigger and my ache got a little smaller. But even as the hurt softened and faded, I kept right on feeling that loss inside me.

Not three weeks after I came to get that job, Early got fired from his for showin' up drunk. Now with nothin' but time on his hands, he hit that bottle every day 'til the money ran out. Drinkin' like that makes a body hurt, and a man mean. So I stayed 'way as much as I could. I told Miz Sinclair, "Yes'm, I be happy to spend the night 'til the baby gits over his colic. No ma'am, it won' be no problem at all." Every chance I got to get out of the house I took for a good six months.

Havin' no job is doubly hard on a man. The more time went by, the nastier Early got. One night I came home and found him blind drunk in the kitchen, ravin' 'bout how I was a no good, two timin' tramp. He beat me bad. So bad I was laid up for a week.

Roberta came over to see me the next day. When nobody answered the do', she let herself in. "Yoo-hoo, anybody home?" she called as she poked her head first into the sittin' room, and then the room 'cross the hall.

"Git'er outta here," Early groaned.

"How I'm suppose ta do that, me layin' up here in bed beaten bloody?" I hissed. "You the one that got us here; you be the one the git her out."

Roberta stuck her head in the room. She gasped as she looked 'round the room at the mess and began sputterin' "Early Thompson, ya outta be ashamed a yerself! Is true then what people been sayin' bout you and yo' first wife. You best be breakin' that habit, you hear me? Or I got news fo' you: If'n I ever hear 'bout you layin' a hand on my sister again, Imma be comin' for ya." She turned on her heels and stomped out. I never felt so loved by my sister before or after.

Early moaned and turned his head 'way from me to face the wall.

As I lay there in bed achin' 'bout everywhere a body could ache, I thought about what people said 'bout Early when they thought I couldn't hear 'em. *He killed his wife.* I knew that wasn't so. *He beat 'er and that's why the baby came early.* That could be the case. *Befo' his wife died he was a no good drunk. Her dyin' sobered him up.* Now I had never been one for confrontation, but I looked over at that man, who I loved with all my heart, and suddenly I wanted to kill him. Never mind that I was hittin' the bottle pretty hard myself. Suddenly I was mad as hell that he'd let hisself slip with me.

"Look here," I said, not turnin' to look at him, just facing the wall; my voice hard as stone. "I know what they says 'bout you. They says you was a drunk afore. They says you beat yo' wife. They says you cleaned up because she died. Well, you listen good. I's your woman now, and if you can do it for her, you can do it for me, and befo' it's too late this time. I ain't sayin' you cain' drink. But if you lay a hand on me again, Lord, I swear I'll put your sorry self outta yo' misery."

Now, Early hadn't turned around, but I could see his head shakin' back an' forth on the pillow, and I could hear his breath comin' out in sobs as he said, "I cain' be drinkin' at all, I know that now. I'm makin' a solemn promise to you right chere, righ' now." He got outta bed and shook worse than a colicky horse, his right hand on his heart and the other in the air jest like he was standin' befo' the judge. "I ain't never takin' another drop a alcohol. I love ya too much, Ethel. An' thas a promise," he added, "that I aims to keep. I 'spect ya to hol' me to it, too. I 'spect ya to leave me high an' dry if'n I drank another drop."

"You ain't gotta worry 'bout that," I said. He got back in bed. The sheets was rough as sandpaper 'gainst my sore, bruised skin, and the shifting mattress felt like a fast ride on a bumpy road. "I'll do more than be leavin'," I said tryin' my level best not to move any more than I had to.

I sent word to Miz Sinclair that I had broken my leg and wouldn't be able to walk for a good while. She sent word back that she was sorry and would be lookin' forward to my getting back as soon as I was able. After I mended, I helped Early round the farm; did his chores and mine. When Early finally got hisself right, I went back to nursemaidin' Billy Sinclair.

It turned out that quittin' drankin' for Early wasn't simple. He had to do more than just put up wit' a powerful hangover for a day or two. That man suffered worse than starving while he was quitting. He was laid up for days with the heebie-jeebies and throwing up. I'd go out in the mornin' to milk, take care of the stock and vegetable patch. He'd be sleepin' fitful, sweatin' like he done run a race; legs and arms goin ev'ry which way. When I come back 'round lunch time, he barely be done got outta the bed, an' the chamber pot be jest fulla puke and pee 'cause he couldn' make it to the outhouse.

I took to sleepin' in the sittin' room, myself. Between the vomit and sweat, the sour smell coming outta that room made my eyes water—like walkin' into a wall of stink. I had no interest in spending any mo' time than I had to in that room. He was even crazy in the head sometimes, mumbling one minute, yellin' the next. It scared me straight for a good while.

He finally pulled hisself together, and good as his word, he went right out and got that job. He tol' me he didn't ask me to quit drinkin' 'cause he wouldn't make a dog go through that hell. He also said it wouldn't do no good no how because if'n he knew one thang, it was that a body couldn't quit until they was ready, no matter how much beggin' and pleadin' you did.

So I kep' taking little nips now and again. I didn't have the heart to ask Early to get me a drink, but I still had a taste for it, so I would get Ham Bone to get me a pint every now an' again. Early never said nothin'. He knew I was drinkin', but for the most part it was only now and again and only when things just got too hard for me to handle.

I had a rough spell after Miz Sinclair let me go. She said, "Ethel, you don't need to come back to work after next week. Billy is in school now and I really don't have the work for you." It took me by surprise. On the way home from work that night I asked Early to drop me off at the store while he did some errands. I bought myself my firs' bottle an' tucked it into tha groceries so Early wouldn' know. I got pretty tight and stayed that way for 'bout a week. Early might have been a little chilly, but he didn't say a word.

Then one clear April morning Mama came by with news. "Ginny Stuart gettin' married an' she be looking for someone to keep house for her. I tol' her 'bout you, an' she say you to go up there an' talk wit' 'er tomorrow. Lord, honey, don't be going up there like you is. Come on now, less you get cleaned up.

Chapter 17

Sallee

August rolled around and my ninth birthday came and went without much fanfare. My mother invited the usual neighborhood kids over, but fewer of them showed up than in previous years. Then, in the second week of August, the most exciting thing that had ever happened occurred: my mother said yes when Uncle James and Aunt Lizbeth asked me to the beach. I was going to spend two whole weeks with my older cousin by four months whom I got along with better than practically anybody. No four-month-old baby brother to watch when nobody else had the time, none of Gordy's pestering or Helen's—just me and Jilly. Ethel scurried around getting me ready as I got more and more excited. During the two days leading up to my departure, I nearly made myself sick with anticipation—I thought they would never end.

Finally, after what seemed like a whole day of driving, Uncle James's station wagon pulled to a stop, and Jillian James Stuart jumped out of the car before I could reach for the door handle. "Come on, I'll race you to the beach," she shouted behind her. She was already past the cottage. Jilly was dark-haired like her mother with enormous brown eyes. Next to her I looked like a white lab rat.

I struggled with the door. "It's locked, honey. You have to pull that button up," Uncle James instructed. Finally free, I took off. I caught up with Jilly only because she waited for me at the dune. "I won," she declared, laughing.

"No fair. I couldn't get the door open." We stood together on the dune surveying the deserted beach and soaking in the salty sea breeze.

"Finally," she said with a little jump of excitement. "Doesn't that smell good? I can't believe how much I miss the ocean when I'm not here. Isn't it great that Aunt Ginny let you come with us this time by yourself? We are gonna have so much fun." She took my hand and we ran down to the water's edge. As we ran in and out of the surf, my mood lightened a bit.

"I'd forgotten how long it takes to get here. I thought we were going to die of old age before that trip was over." I was only half joking. Aunt Lizbeth, a chronic complainer, found something wrong with every little thing we did or said for the entire trip. She made my mother sound like Mary Poppins—well, maybe not quite like that. I had been spending the night at Jilly's house for years but had never been subjected to Aunt Lizbeth for that long without interruption. I wasn't sure I was looking forward to two weeks of it before the rest of my family arrived to join us. As much as I loved Jilly and being at the beach, I was a little apprehensive about being so far away from home for the very first time by myself.

"You're funny," she said. "It wasn't that long. I think it went faster because I had you to play with."

She must be used to Aunt Lizbeth's complaining, I thought.

"Wasn't it fun when we stumped Daddy at I Spy?"

The way I remembered it, we didn't have anything to do with stumping him. We had been commanded to stop playing because Aunt Lizbeth had a headache. She'd said, "If you don't shut up right now I am going to put you out of the car and leave all of you right here."

I had immediately glanced out the window to get some idea of where we were and how we got there.

Uncle James patted his wife's leg playfully. She pushed his hand away and it didn't look much like she was playing. "Now, honey, you wouldn't want to go and do that. Who would take care of you like I do? Sugarlips, you know you couldn't get along without me and old Jilly Dill."

What about me? I wanted to shout as I pictured myself on the side of the road watching as the car and trailer disappeared into the distance, and kicking myself for not having paid attention to which roads we took to get right here.

Then he added, "And would you want to call my big sister and tell her that you had misplaced her little Sallee? I don't reckon so." I breathed a sigh of relief, though I wasn't completely taken with the idea that Aunt Lizbeth had even thought of leaving us on the side of the road. You never can tell with grown-ups.

"Aunt Lizbeth wouldn't have left us would she?" I ventured.

"No, she was just fooling. She does that sometimes for fun. Let's go see Ben and Carrie," Jilly scampered up the dune.

Some fun, I thought as I followed.

Carrie and Ben worked for, I guess, the house. Before our grandmother died they had worked for her, and after she died they just kept on working at her house. The house belonged to my mother and her three brothers now. Uncle James and Aunt Lizbeth were the only ones who used it, though. They came down every year, sometimes staying all summer. We used to come down and stay with them, but Uncle James and Daddy got mad at each other, so we hadn't been down for a couple of years. Aunt Lizbeth would call Daddy the "arrogant ass" when she thought I couldn't hear her. Even when I was around she wouldn't say his name. She'd just say things like, "What is the AA doing now?"

Ethel told me that, once when Aunt Lizbeth was at our house, she and Daddy got into a fight about the shopping center. He told her to leave. She said, "You can stuff it where the sun don't shine." With that he picked her up, chair and all, put her on the front porch, said, "Go home," and shut the door. She hadn't been back until he left.

When Ben and Carrie weren't working at the beach, they worked at a colored school, I think. Ben was tall and dark-skinned. He had a jolly, easy way about him. He liked teasing and laughing; he was always ready with a chuckle. As Jilly and I rounded the corner of the cottage, we caught sight of him: a huge trunk was hoisted on his shoulders and a big suitcase was in his other hand as he headed for the main part of the cottage. He broke out in a wide grin, leaned over to free himself of the load, and crouched down. Jilly ran into his open arms.

"Well now, Carrie, look at how ol' Jilly Billy has grown. Lord a mercy, girl, you had better stop or you are gonna be as big as me." He wrapped her up in his long arms. "It's so good to see you child. We did miss you so." Ben smiled in my direction over Jilly's shoulder. "I hear we're having a guest, too. Hey there, Sallee, nice to see ya. I don't think I've seen you since you were knee high to a pickle." He and Jilly laughed.

"To a pickle?" she giggled as she hung on to his hand. "Pickles don't have knees."

I smiled back shyly. "Hi," I said.

Carrie came up to me and placed her hand lightly on my shoulder. "Hello there, honey," she said to me, and then to Jilly, "Hi sweetie, Ben is right, you sure have grown. Come on over here and let me give you a hug." She put down the suitcase she was carrying and gave Jilly one of those stiff little hugs that grown-ups give—the kind where they stick their butts out in the air like they don't want to get something on them. Then she picked up my suitcase and said, "Let's put your stuff away. I've got lots of work to do. Ben, take that trunk into Miz Stuart's room and then go back and get the frozen food and put it down in the freezer; the one out in the storeroom. Better hurry up too—you got to unpack the trailer and there's dinner to fix. "She started barking orders like a spoiled terrier on the wrong side of the door. Ben picked up the heavy trunk as if it were filled with nothing but air and yes'umed his way into the cottage.

Jilly, jabbering like a crow, fell in line behind Carrie, and I followed them into our room. As she opened the door, a blast of cool cedar-scented air hit us in the face. "Don't you just love that smell?" she asked then turned to Carrie. "Did you get here this morning?"

"Lord, child, no. We've been here for two days getting this place ready for you."

"Lucky you," she said as she flounced down on the already made bed.

It didn't seem to me that Carrie agreed with Jilly's assessment. Carrie was light-skinned like Ethel and had freckles, but that was where the similarities ended. Her dark brown hair was short and fell in pretty curls around her head. Shorts and a sleeveless blouse were as close as she came to a uniform. She kept her feelings to herself, though she had enough sour opinions to make up for it. Never once did I hear her giggle or chuckle. When she did laugh it had a hard, raw edge to it—and I was never quite sure if we were laughing at the same thing. I guess you could say that Carrie was the housekeeper. She did the laundry and cleaning. She also made sure we went to bed on time, brushed our teeth, and picked up after ourselves mostly by telling us to do it. After dinner, Carrie was on her own time.

"Guess what we're havin' for dinner tonight?" Ben asked as he headed toward the kitchen with Jilly and me skipping behind him.

"Beanies and weanies," Jilly said.

"Nope, you guess, Sallee."

"Fried chicken," I said hopefully, "like Ethel makes."

"Last time I saw Ethel she was the only thing fried." Ben said to Carrie with a chuckle and she laughed. "We're gonna have fried fish and hush puppies. Carrie caught these fish just this morning."

Jilly and I jumped up and down hugging each other, and then Jilly hugged Ben. "We love hush puppies," she said. We ate in the kitchen with Carrie and Ben. I nursed the little dig he took at Ethel. I don't even know why. It just hurt.

Carrie asked, "How's Ethel? She was having a hard time the last time she was here."

Ben twisted up his lips and turned his head to Carrie. "Hard liquor, that's for sure," he said in a low voice. Carrie laughed quietly and slapped Ben's arm lightly while they kept on giggling like it was the best joke in the world.

"She's OK. I don't think she likes the beach much," I said. "She can't swim, and I think she misses Big Early when she's here." I didn't understand why Carrie and Ben didn't like Ethel. It didn't make any sense to me.

"Things haven't been too easy from what I hear."

"Not so good I guess." I started pushing my food around on my plate, wishing we could move on to another topic. My family life had become anything but my favorite topic of conversation.

Jilly piped up. "Are the bikes here yet? Did you bring them over?"

"Ben spent all morning cleaning up your bikes and getting them ready for you. They're out in the carport," Carrie said as she started clearing the table and resetting it for Uncle James and Aunt Lizbeth's dinner. While Ben cooked their meal, we finished clearing the table.

"Aren't they coming?" I asked. "Do you want me to tell them dinner is ready?"

"Who?" Ben asked.

"Uncle James and Aunt Lizbeth."

"No, I just leave it here and they eat when they get ready. I'll come back before I go to bed and clean up."

Ben and Carrie had a room with their own bathroom at the end of the wing. It was a pretty big room with windows on two sides that had views into the carport and the cars on the cement drive. They spent all of their spare time in their room, which made no sense to me because it was hot and a fan pushing around hot air was pretty useless in my book. After dinner we would ride our bikes around the circle while Ben and Carrie played pinochle on the table between their beds. Every time Uncle James and Aunt Lizbeth went out the breeze that had been blocked by the car would waft into their room—the only one without an air conditioner.

That first evening around seven o'clock, the ocean breeze died down and the mosquitos came out in full force. Jilly continued riding her bike, undisturbed by the swarms of invisible, angry insects. But I found myself slapping and scratching my skin like a crazy person. I stowed my bike in the carport and went inside for a warm bath.

Half an hour later I emerged from the bathroom with a towel around my head and a smattering of red welts on my arms. Ben was turning down our beds. "Look," I said, extending one arm to him for inspection.

He shook his head as he took my arm, "Mmm mmm. You must be mighty sweet. Look at them, and they are hot too." He placed his enormous hand on one of the bites. I noticed how pink the inside of his hands were. "Make sure you put some medicine on 'em." I nodded my head in agreement and wondered how on earth I was going to know what kind of medicine to put on them. I wished Ethel was here.

"Well, go on in there and get yourself ready for bed," Ben ordered on his way out the door. "Carrie will be up in a minute."

I got in bed, towel and all. Jilly peeled her clothes off leaving them on the floor in a bunch where they fell. "Aren't you going to brush your teeth?"

"Naw."

"Isn't Carrie gonna get mad?" I asked as I scratched a bite and imagined how much trouble I would be in if I tried to get away with not brushing my teeth when Ethel was on duty.

"No, Carrie doesn't get mad about stuff like that."

"Oh," I said, amazed but feeling like I needed to defend Ethel to my cousin. "I think Ethel gets mad at us because she cares about us."

"Carrie and Ben care about me, too," Jilly protested.

I blushed. "Well, sure," I agreed lamely.

Jilly gave me a funny look. "How come you don't like them much?"

She stumped me. I wanted to like Ben as much as Jilly did. "I do. But I don't know them like you do. I haven't seen 'em in two or three years and besides..." I rolled over and pretended to have fallen asleep. I had to admit Ben was fun. I liked his easy way. I wanted to like him as much as Jilly did, but I felt so disloyal to Ethel.

Early the next morning Ben announced on his way by our window, "If you girls wanna go fishing you'd better be getting up. Your momma left me with a list as long as my arm of things I've gotta get. If I'm gonna get it all done then I'm gonna need your help." He scratched on the screen. "You up in there?" His voice boomed. Had it been anyone else we wouldn't have heard him, but Ben's voice was loud and deep.

"Do you wanna go?" I asked Jilly as I stretched beneath the thin sheet, enjoying the relative cool of the morning. "Don't you want to go swimming first?"

"We can't swim 'til Momma and Daddy get up unless Ben watches us, and he's got errands to run. So we better go cause Carrie'll put us to work if we stay around here." Jilly wisely made her point. "Besides, Ben lets me drive."

"Aren't you too young to be driving? Gordy can't even drive."

"I don't really drive, I just shift the gears," Jilly said as she put on her clothes as fast as she'd taken them off the night before.

As we came into the kitchen, Carrie was fussing with Ben. "What were you thinking, yelling outside like that? You want to wake them folks up? I don't 'spect so."

"Aw they couldn't hear me."

"I heard you down in our room."

"Their air conditioner was on; the windows all shut tight." His logic seemed to calm her down. "You girls gonna come with me or stay here with Carrie?"

"With you," we both said as we jumped together.

"Hurry up and eat your breakfast. We've got lots to do." Bowls, cereal, fresh fruit, and milk were already on the table. "Anybody want some coffee?"

"Oh I do," I said. I was feeling more at home than I had the day before. When my mother wasn't around Ethel would fix me coffee with so much milk and sugar that it tasted more like coffee ice cream, only hot. Momma said coffee was bad for children. I almost fell over when Ben put a cup of black coffee by my place. What was I supposed to do with that? I sipped and doctored and sipped and doctored until I finally got something approximating Ethel's concoction. My saucer was filled with the overflow coffee. The cup was impossible to lift without spilling.

"Child, what are you doing?" Carrie scolded. "Leave that coffee and eat your breakfast." She took the streaming cup and saucer away and grumbled at Ben for giving it to me in the first place.

"Ain't gonna hurt her none," he said good-naturedly. "Come on, let's go. We got miles to go before we sleep."

As we drove down the beach road, Jilly shifted the gears on the old jeep. She did just fine at first. But then she tried to move it to another gear and the car bumped and the engine roared in protest. Ben laughed. "Don't move it up all the way. You got to move like this." He demonstrated the motion in the air. "It's like an 'H'." We stopped in the middle of the road to show her. "The top of the 'H' is first. Then you pull straight down and that's second. Third—and that's the one you're tryin' to get to—is up here on the 'H'." He put his pointer fingers together to make half an 'H' then wiggled his thumb to show what he was talking about. "Now, go back to first and let's start all over." I missed half of what he was saying because I was looking around to make sure no one was coming. "Don't worry so much, Sallee. There ain't no one coming. I've been keeping my eye out."

Our promised fishing trip was fun, though Ben was the only one who caught anything big enough to keep. I caught an eel that writhed like a snake on the line when I finally was able to pull it out of the water. I was so horrified that I let go of the pole. If Ben hadn't been right there to catch it, that eel would have been swimming around for the rest of its life attached to that pole.

The remaining two weeks rolled by in a shimmery haze of sunshine and swimming. Jilly taught me how to ride waves, and when the water was too rough to play in, we'd walk as far down the beach as we were allowed, picking up shells, digging in the wet sand, and looking for clams that disappeared beneath the surface in a trail of bubbles.

"Boy, I bet Gordy and Lil' Early would like this," I said as we dug up a clam.

"Who's Lil' Early?" Jilly asked.

"I thought you came over and played with us once. You know Ethel's grandson."

"A colored boy?" She looked puzzled. "Aunt Ginny lets you play with a colored boy?"

"All of us. You, too. Don't you remember? We played out back in the compost pile behind the garage. Jilly?" I stopped digging and looked at her hard.

"Yeah, I remember now. I just forgot for a minute cuz I never told Mama or Daddy. They wouldna liked it." She looked embarrassed.

I just shook my head. "I don't think I will ever understand grown people," I said and threw the clam I had just found as far into the ocean as I could.

That night after we went to bed, I lay still listening to the ocean and Jilly's soft breathing. I wondered about our conversation. What was the matter with people?

Things changed fast after my family arrived.

I knew Ethel never liked going to the beach. The last time she went I was only three or four, but I gathered from Carrie and Ben that she spent the whole time drunk. I didn't really know what happened, except that Ben always laughed about Ethel's trip. Ethel, I guessed, was lonely being there all by herself. She didn't even have her own room. She had to stay with Helen who was just a baby.

As for Ben and Carrie, I don't imagine they were much company being all educated and acting like they knew more than Ethel. It burned me up when Ben made his snotty comments about Ethel. I knew that she had a different way of talking than I did, but I also knew you weren't supposed to make fun of it. I knew what she meant when she said "de ol' man" or "m'near." I knew, even if I couldn't tell you exactly what the words meant.

So what if she could only write a little and that her signature looked not much better than mine. So what? She only went to school to the fifth grade and then she had to go to work. She didn't have time to study or do her spelling homework. She and Big Early had a little farm and took care of things old Ben and Carrie and all their book smarts wouldn't know the first thing about. People are all kinds of different. But then Ben, with his smarty self, didn't seem to know that.

I sometimes wondered what growing up really meant. It sure didn't mean you were smarter than you were as a kid because I knew lots of adults who weren't half as smart as most kids, and from what I could tell they didn't think nearly as much about stuff. Just like Ben, they'd put people in boxes in their heads and then let them hang there like a fish on a line flapping about "dumb" or "special" or "colored": whatever it was that they had decided some person was or was not.

If I live to be a million years old I'll never forget that morning. Ben, Jilly, and I had just come in from an early morning run to the store when Ethel came shrieking out of her room, crying and stumbling like she had broken out of hell. She was looking over her shoulder, blubbering with snot running down her face.

"He dead! The baby gone, Lord haf mercy...he dead!" She collapsed in a mound on the floor in my mother's old nightgown which barely made her decent, and that was only if you didn't look too close. As bizarre as what she was saying was, the sight of Ethel in a flesh-colored, worn, gossamer nightgown, boobs akimbo was even more so. Lying in a pool of her own flesh, Ethel continued her maniacal rant until Uncle James came out of his room, his robe billowing after him.

"Girl, get up and cover yer self up. What are you saying?"

Ethel blubbered on the floor.

Carrie, who had raced into the room Ethel had just vacated, shrieked, "Oh, my God in heaven. Call the police. What has she done to him?"

My mind, which had been racing to catch up with what was going on, screeched to a halt at Carrie's words. *Done what? Ethel? What was Carrie saying?*

Uncle James disappeared into Ethel's room. "Ben, go get Dr. Wallace next door now!" he boomed. The next thing I knew he was coming out of the room with my brother in his arms. Denny's fat little legs and arms dangled limply like a spider's. I shuddered. Uncle James continued barking orders. "Carrie, find Miz Ginny. Don't tell her anything, just stay with her until the doctor comes. Ben, when you get back do something with this." He pointed to Ethel.

"Mr. Stuart, don't you think she's gonna think it strange, me—," Carrie started to protest.

He cut her off, "Do it! And get these kids outta here."

"Come on, girls," she herded us out of the door, mumbling, "How the hell am I gonna stay with…Poor woman. Lord God Almighty, poor woman. You two stay outta' the way, ya hear me? Out of the way!" She headed off toward my mother's room still mumbling to herself.

"Wait," I stopped her. "What about Ethel?" I was confused and tears were springing to my eyes; but they weren't for Denny. The fact that he was really dead hadn't begun to sink in. Alarming as it was to see him like that, I was more rattled by the image of Ethel on the ground wailing and unable to get up and cover herself.

"Don't you be worrying 'bout her. She's in a heap of trouble and you will be, too, if you don't do what I say. Go find Helen and Gordy and keep'm outta the way, you hear me? Tell Stuart I want to see her. Tell her to come to your momma's room. Now go!" The command was almost as cold as Uncle James's had been.

"Holy shit," Jilly swore. "Do you really think she did it?"

I could scarcely look in her direction, much less answer. We made our way to Stuart's room without another word. Before I banged opened the door I asked Jilly,

"Would you go find Gordy and Helen and bring them here?" The blast of air-conditioned air didn't help the feeling that I had of walking into a crypt. "Stuart, wake up." I grabbed hold of her shoulder and shook her. "Carrie needs you at Momma's room. Denny is dead. Ethel is running around practically naked; the police are coming."

"What?" Stuart's cardinal rule was "Never ever wake me up, no matter what." Things were way beyond no matter what. "What? You're kidding me? It's not funny." she stated as she pulled herself groggy from sleep to one elbow looking at me as if deciding what kind of mayhem she was going to inflict upon me. "He's dead? What do you mean Ethel's running around naked? Jesus Christ!" She shuddered then rubbed her sleep bleary eyes.

I nodded solemnly and said, "Well, almost. She's in a see-through nightgown and her breasts are hanging out and…" I stopped, horrified to realize that I was smiling. Suddenly what had seemed like the collapse of all worldly order sounded funny coming out of my mouth. Ethel naked. Stuart caught my grin and must have thought it sounded funny, too, because she started to laugh. Then we were both laughing uncontrollably. I was gasping, sniffling, and squeezing out all the tears that had been building up over the past few minutes.

Jilly, Gordy, and Helen spilled into the room. "What's so funny?" Jilly asked, perplexed.

Stuart said, "Ethel's running around naked," and the two of us dissolved into another gale of giggles. The three of them just looked at us.

Helen asked, "Are you suppose to laugh when somebody dies?"

Gordy ran to the window and fumbled with the blinds. He threw Helen an irritated glance, "God, we hardly knew him. This place is like a tomb. I can't see anything. Turn the air-conditioner off so we can open the windows." Telling people what to do must be a family trait because Gordy was sounding a lot like Uncle James. "How am I suppose to know what's going on if I can't hear anything?" Then I heard him mutter to himself, "God damn, I wish I had gotten up this morning and gone to the store. I miss everything."

While Gordy fumbled with the window, Stuart dressed. Then she gave each of us a hug and left. As she closed the door Stuart said, "You guys stay here and don't get into any trouble. I'll be back as soon as I can."

Helen sucked her thumb, hugged her bear, and rocked softly on the bed. The rest of us were sitting in front of the door waiting for something to happen. Nobody said anything. The laughter was gone from my belly and its place was slowly being filled with a cold sense of dread. The doctor and Ben were huffing across the sand dune that separated our houses. Dr. Wallace carried a little black bag. Ben looked scared as he ran just behind the doctor sort of shepherding him along. They hustled by us. We pressed our heads up to the screen in order to get a better view.

As he pushed open the screen door, Gordy announced, "I'm not staying here another minute. I'm missing it all." He slipped out of the room with Jilly and me just behind him, and crawled under the bushes alongside of the cottage. The woody branches scraped and stuck our skin creating any number of bloody lacerations well worth crying over any other day. We huddled together at a corner of the house as we peered through the porch screen. The doctor poked around the little body Uncle James had laid on the sofa. He took off the clothes, looked around some more, and then said, "I suspect crib death. You," he turned on Ethel, "tell me, did anything out of the ordinary happen last night? This morning? What did he eat? When?"

Ethel had pulled herself together and was sitting by Denny's body on the sofa. Ben had given her a not-big-enough-for-the-task beach towel that she had wrapped loosely around her shoulders. Though it was an improvement in modesty, it was still sorely lacking. Her gown only came down to mid thigh. "No, sir, I woke up this mornin' like always. He usually be playin' in his crib. Thought it was strange that he weren't. When I went ta pick'm up, he was cold as ice, po' thing. I fed him las night 'round ten I'd say." She started to cry again. "Lord have mercy," she said over and over.

Dr. Wallace snapped, "Calm down you damn fool, this isn't going to help anyone. Go on and get dressed. I'll talk with you later." Turning to Uncle James he asked, "Where's Ginny? And Lizbeth?"

"Lizbeth's still asleep, and for the time being we should leave her that way. Carrie is down with Ginny."

"I'll call the undertaker and then I'll tell her. She doesn't know, does she?" Dr. Wallace sighed as he picked up his black bag and headed toward my mother's room. He passed Stuart in the hall. She had begun to cry. He patted her arm then asked, "The telephone?" Uncle James took the doctor into the study. Stuart didn't come through the living room where Denny's doll-like body still lay on the sofa. She went through the kitchen. After making his call, the doctor walked slowly down the hall toward my mother's room, his head bent over like it was too heavy to hold up. A little while later as Carrie came down the hall, we heard my mother scream. Carrie went over to the baby, picked him up, covered him with a blanket, and took him into Ethel's room. The two women met in the doorway. Ethel, dressed now, looked as if she were going to faint. She made a move as if to take Denny from Carrie then let her arms drop helplessly to her sides as she turned to follow Carrie back into the room.

As we jostled for a more comfortable view, Stuart hissed from behind us, "Get out of there, you idiots. Don't you know anyone that looked could see you? Are you trying to get yourselves killed?" We scrambled out of hiding and plied Stuart with questions.

"Carrie wants me to babysit you knuckleheads," she announced. Stuart sounded tough though her voice quavered as she mussed with Helen's hair. Then she picked her up and held her tight. "Carrie said she went to wake Mother, but couldn't bring herself to do it. 'Poor soul wouldn't ever be able to sleep like that again,' she said. I guess Dr. Wallace is telling her. He's probably going to give her a tranquilizer," Stuart said with a sigh.

A while later a man Stuart said was the undertaker came and took Denny away. There was nothing more to it. My mother and Aunt Lizbeth finally got up around four and started drinking. Carrie and even Ben snapped at us all day. Ethel sat alone in her room. She didn't even come out for meals. I knocked at the door a couple of times.

"Ethel, can I come in?" I asked.

All I got back was a brief response from a husky voice I hardly recognized. "No, darlin', ya can't."

No amount of pleading or crying on my part changed the answer. "Ethel, I'm sorry."

"I know," she said.

I hovered there a minute longer feeling my hot breath bounce off the closed door. I was desperate to help. I made one last attempt. "Ethel, do you want me to bring you a drink?"

I don't know if she heard me or not, but she never answered.

Nothing felt good the rest of that day—not swimming, not anything.

Ethel had probably started to nip at Aunt Lizbeth's gin. I mean, it's not like it wasn't around all the time. The bar was right next to the kitchen door. You had to walk right by it on the way to the kitchen or if you were going out to the beach or the screened porch.

Ethel couldn't swim. Stuck at the beach, she didn't have her cows to milk or a house to clean—all she had to do was hang out with Denny all day. Bored, sad, and lonely, Ethel started taking little nips. She must have known that Carrie and Ben were laughing at her and didn't like her much. She probably worried about Big Early and Lil' Early at home doing all the things she did when she was there, so she drank just a little. It wasn't like she didn't take care of Denny. He just didn't wake up.

Didn't the doctor say it was no one's fault? I didn't blame her. Why did everybody else? She didn't do anything wrong. She just started sipping a little. So what if she didn't do her hair every day like she normally did and her buns got to looking a little shabby. That didn't mean she hurt anybody.

Carrie normally loved to fish and would do so for hours at a time. But we were not on a "fishing for pleasure" trip to the sound. We were on a "get the kids the hell out from under our feet" fishing trip. Later that afternoon Carrie was sitting like a big toad down on the dock, throwing in her line, checking her bait every few minutes, and then throwing the line back. She did not look like she enjoyed it; she was just going through the motions. I never really understood the expression "like a fish out of water" until I saw Ethel plopped down next to Carrie, her body stretching the fabric of my mother's old maternity bathing suit, a big floppy hat on her head, and one of her buns busted out in a corkscrew. She stared out at Carrie's red and white bobber like it was her lifeline. After we assessed the scene halfway down the dock, Jilly and I turned around and skipped right back to land.

It seemed to me that, although the sun was burning bright, there wasn't a single sparkle—no sunlight danced today; not around those two. The water was as dull and lifeless as my baby brother's body. A black hole would have been more inviting. "Yikes, it's creepy here today," Jilly whispered as we neared the boathouse. "You wanna ride bikes? I wish that you didn't have to go home tomorrow. Dumb old funeral." She glanced at me when she said it, like she wasn't sure if I was going to be upset.

I just looked down at the ground. "I know I... God, why did he have to die? You know, don't tell anybody. Promise me you won't ever tell I said this?"

She nodded.

I dropped my voice to a whisper. "I'm kinda glad he's dead. My mother hasn't stopped crying since he was born. Maybe now she can get it over with. But poor old Ethel, I don't think she did anything wrong. Do you?" I was sorry I had asked that question. The expression on my cousin's face shouted her answer. I bit my lip and turned away so that Jilly wouldn't see that I had started to cry.

Two mornings after Denny died we packed up and headed home. Jilly got to stay at the beach with Carrie. She did her best to convince her parents to let me stay too.

"Please," she begged. "Can't Sallee stay here? Why does she need to go to that old funeral? Isn't she too young?"

"That's enough, Jilly," her father said. I had never heard him be short with her. "Sallee needs to be with her mother now. Her mother needs her."

I couldn't see how I was going to be any help. Stuart, yes; me, no. But I wasn't supposed to be listening to that conversation, so I just kept my fingers crossed and my tongue still. I had to go. Uncle James volunteered to take the kids and Ethel in my mother's car while Ben drove my mother and Aunt Lizbeth home. Stuart sat up front with Uncle James, while Ethel sat in the middle seat. Gordy, Helen, and I took turns sitting next to her while the other two sat in the way back. Ethel didn't say two words the whole way. She'd sigh and look out the window. I tried to hold her hand. She'd let me for a minute or two, but then she would move or scratch or just pull away, so I gave up. Helen tapped me on the shoulder when she wanted my seat. I scampered over the back of the seat and Helen crawled up under Ethel's forearm, snuggled into Ethel's great bulk, plugged her thumb in her mouth, and fell fast asleep. Ethel's arm stayed put all the way home. Gordy and I shared whispered speculations about the upcoming funeral until that too held no interest.

"Uncle James, where's Denny?" I asked when we were almost home. Gordy gently kicked my foot and scowled at me with disapproval.

"In heaven, honey," he said.

"No, how did he get back from the beach?" I asked.

Gordy rolled his eyes and mouthed, "Don't ask stupid questions."

"Well, do you know, smartie pants?" I whispered at him. I saw Uncle James's eyes dart at me from the rearview mirror. "I wasn't talking to you, Uncle James. I mean I was asking you about Denny and then Gordy... never mind, I'm sorry." He never did answer my question. But at the funeral Denny was there in a little white casket. Well, at least they said he was in the casket. Daddy was there, too. He sat with us during the service, between Helen and me, and held our hands. He didn't stay long, though. He told Stuart to call him when she needed to be picked up. I don't think Daddy and my mother spoke one word to each other that day.

After the funeral, Ethel didn't come to work for almost a month. She was probably catching up on the stuff she didn't get done while she was away. I remember hearing my mother telling her friends that it was so ridiculous seeing Ethel in her bathing suit. I hated it when she laughed at Ethel. Ethel didn't deserve that. I sometimes thought she knew people were making fun of her and didn't come to work because she was embarrassed about it. I didn't really know, but I sure did hate it when she didn't come to work. Those days, no matter what, the weather seemed dark and the clocks seemed to move in slow motion too. My mother was always grumpy and complaining about Ethel. But when Ethel came back, my mother never said a word about her being gone for so long.

Bourbon bottles got bigger. Even after Daddy left, the bourbon came in regular size bottles; but after Denny died it started appearing in bottles as big as lemonade pitchers, complete with handles. Trips to the ABC Store happened more and more often. I had never been into an ABC Store until after we got back from the beach. Now it seemed every time we went to the grocery store we would make a stop. The first time I was dumbfounded. I had imaged letters of the alphabet painted all over the walls like a nursery school mural. I imagined lambs and other baby animals cavorting around and through elaborately drawn a's and b's; great garlands of flowers festooning the corners and draping the walls; multicolored blocks scattered about in skillfully arranged stacks; and pastel shades and primary colors artfully interwoven. The drab industrial green stood in bitter contrast to my vision, and they didn't even have enough green paint to paint the whole thing; it stopped halfway up the wall. "Well, what does ABC mean, then?" I grumbled as we left the store.

"What? I can't hear you. Stop mumbling, Sallee. I've told you a thousand times not to mumble. If you have something to say, say it," my mother lectured.

"ABC, what does it mean?" I shouted over the traffic and bustle. *Why would you name a store the ABC store if it looked like nothing but an old hallway with a counter cutting it in two and a man standing behind it, plain as pitch?* I wondered to myself.

"Shhh," my mother said then grabbed my hand as we headed to the car.

Having a cocktail before dinner had been a nightly ritual with my parents. Now that Daddy wasn't around, my mother began to entertain more, but with a whole lot less pomp. Her new friends visited while we ate supper in the kitchen. They were mostly ladies who liked to drink as much as she did. It used to be that when people stayed for dinner it was an elaborate affair. Now it seemed that my mother and her friends didn't eat at all. They just stayed holed-up in the living room, talking to each other about Lord knows what. The trips to the bar outside the kitchen were frequent. The first couple of times they'd stick their head round to say "hey." But by the time our dinner was over, they had run out of things to say to us kids. Besides, they had moved on to a place we didn't want to be. Even when she didn't have friends over, my mother's trips to the bar became a nightly occurrence. Ethel would shake her old head, sort of tutting to herself as she wiped up the sticky puddles of bourbon on the counter in the morning. I'd watch her over my breakfast plate as I bit my tongue to keep from asking her, if she disapproved so much, why didn't she lay off the booze herself?

For a while my mother and Ethel seemed to have a tag team approach to drinking. First one would hit it pretty hard, then the other; but never both at once. Ethel would come to work sloppy and unkempt. Her clothes would look as if she had slept in them and she would smell like it too. When she was fuzzy, she was also surly and mean. When she was like that I was grateful for school, our weekends with Daddy, and Stuart's required overnights at our house.

Ethel hadn't come to work for a day or two. My mother had a new friend over. They had been having cocktails for the last two hours and neither of them had made a move to start cooking dinner. Gordy and Helen and I were watching television. My stomach had been growling for a good long time. During a commercial break I went into the kitchen to see if there was anything in the icebox to eat.

"Is anybody else hungry?" I asked.

"Starved" Helen said.

"Yeah me, too," Gordy added. "What are we going to eat?"

"There's nothing in the refrigerator. No hot dogs, bolongna, or cheese." I reported.

"Let's make peanut butter sandwiches," Gordy suggested.

"I thought of that—no bread," I said. "I'm going in there and tell her she's got to make dinner. Now," I announced with more bravado than I really possessed.

"Sure." Gordy said with a sneer. "Let's make pot pies. That's all she'll do anyway. How hard can it be? You have to turn the oven on and put them in there until they're done. It's on the box." He got up and checked the freezer. There were three chicken pot pies. He pulled them out and read the box. "I've got this," he said then flashed a thumbs up. He turned the oven on and put the pot pies on the rack, set the timer for forty minutes, and then strolled out of the kitchen full of self-importance. Thirty minutes later the smell of smoke began to waft from the kitchen. We were panicked. Some gravy had leaked out and was burning on the floor of the oven. Gordy was frantically waving smoke out the back door. I heard ice rattling in a glass behind us.

My mother was standing in the door looking a little tipsy. "What do you think you are up to?" She demanded.

"Fixing our dinner," I announced with pride over Gordy's achievement.

"Don't you talk back to me," she slurred. "Go to your room. No dinner."

I couldn't believe it. "I was just answering your question." I started to argue when she hauled off and slapped me across the face.

Later that night Gordy snuck into my room with an apple. "Here. It's all I could find." He handed me the apple and climbed up on my bed. "I can't believe she did that to you," he said.

I started to whimper again. "I'm telling Daddy."

"Don't," he said. "He can't do anything and it'll make him really sad. Remember how he was at Denny's funeral. It was awful to see."

"Yeah but…" I started to argue.

"Sallee, what's he going to do? If he says anything to her she'll only take it out on us. The judge already said…He can't change what the judge said." We sighed.

"I know. I'll tell Stuart. She got the judge to listen to her. I'm sure she can do something."

Gordy shook his head. "You want to start World War Three?"

"Yeah, I guess you're right." We sighed again.

Chapter 18

It was cold for early October. My mother had gone out, leaving Stuart in charge. Ethel was waiting for Big Early to pick her up, and she was in a particularly prickly mood. Gordy, Helen, and I were under the dining room table watching television. My mother had moved a television into the dining room so that she could eat lunch and watch her soap operas. It turned out to be our favorite place to watch TV. We'd take pillows and blankets under the table, making a little fort. When the chairs were pushed in they formed a compact wall around us making us barely visible to passersby. You got a safe feeling under there, like hiding under the covers during a storm. That night Ethel was prowling around the kitchen, grumbling about her ride. We pulled the chairs in closer and hunkered down on our pillows.

"I wish she'd go home," Helen said. "I hate it when she's drunk. Where's Stuart?"

"She went to Judy's. I'm supposed to call her when Ethel leaves." I couldn't hide my satisfaction at being placed in charge.

Ethel bounced from one wall to the next as she passed the dining room door. Helen and I turned and watched her as she stumbled to the back hall to make a phone call. We moved so that the dining room chairs obscured us from her view in the hallway.

"Go home," Helen hissed after Ethel.

"Shut up. I can't hear," said Gordy. *Wyatt Earp* was his favorite show. He had the ability to block out all kinds of things if he liked the TV program. Helen and I continued to watch out for Ethel. We'd take turns crawling out from our fortress to reconnoiter. We heard Ethel mumbling, then a metallic clunk and sharp knock as the receiver banged against the radiator and the back of the chair smacked up against the wall. Helen and I glanced at each other, both of us hesitant to move. Finally, Helen squeezed out through the chairs and ran to the door to investigate. In an instant she returned and scuttled back under the table. Her eyes were wide with alarm. "She's fallen flat on the floor. Call Stuart. She might be dead."

Horrified, I scrambled out from under the table. Ethel lay sprawled out in the back hall with one shoe kicked off. The telephone receiver dangled above her, clanking against the radiator. A disjointed voice was still talking through it. The chair she had been sitting in was upended behind her. My old dream of Ethel under my bed came back to me. I clambered back under the table. My breathing was fast and furious. "What are we going to do?"

"Shhh," hissed Gordy. He was riveted to the television as he watched the show with the intensity of someone watching a rocket launch.

"She's dead," Helen said. "I'm scared." She started to cry; big, gulping sobs.

"What are we going to do?" I repeated.

Helen cried. Gordy watched TV.

"We've got to do something," I insisted, near panic.

All of a sudden, as if slapped, Gordy came to life although Helen only nudged him, "What? What are we going to do? Go hang up the phone and call the police? You do it. You're so big and in charge," Gordy said.

"Not me. What if she's not dead? What if she gets mad and kills me?" I started to cry, too. "You do it."

He went back to his extreme television watching.

I couldn't stand it. Ethel was dead, my brother was in self-protection mode, and my little sister was bordering on hysteria. I crawled back out from under the table. Somebody had to do something. I ran upstairs hoping the person on the other end of the phone was still there. The extension in my mother's bedroom droned the incessant beep- beep-beep of the busy signal. Fevered clicks would not clear the line. Maybe, I thought, if I take a bath it will all work itself out: Stuart will come home and Ethel will wake up. I almost had myself convinced that taking a bath would be an excellent course of action when one of Mazine's stories came to mind—a story about someone having died at home. When she told the story I thought it was ridiculous, but that was back in a time when I could afford the luxury of rational thought. Back before I had a possible dead body—Ethel's body—lying on the floor in my house. "If'n ya don't tend to 'em right away an' they git hard, then they think ya didn't never care fo' 'em and they will turn into a haint and chase ya fo'ever." The memory of her voice was so clear; it was as if she were standing next to me.

I tiptoed downstairs so as not to wake the dead, and then quietly opened the front door. I slipped outside, leaving my sister and brother under the table. I glanced toward Helen who had stopped crying and was rocking back and forth on her pillow watching *McHale's Navy* with Gordy. The laugh track mocked me as I went out into the rainy night.

My errand, as dire as it was, was strangely mitigated by the horror of being outside at night alone for the first time; as if it were possible to be more terrified. The wind whipped the leaves around in the trees. They cast eerier shadows on the wet street as their branches swayed menacingly under the streetlights. The fallen leaves mashed into a slippery paste on the street and made traction dodgy. I repeated a prayer of thanks that Judy only lived a few blocks away, and in the opposite direction from the Dabneys' house. I knew the neighborhood well enough in the daytime. I could get to her house in less than ten minutes if I cut through backyards. I mapped out the route in my head as I ran down the street. My heart felt like it was going to explode. As my lungs sucked in air, my chest burned. Hot desperate tears ran down my cheeks along with the cold rain.

When I got to my first shortcut, I stopped dead. The alley was as dark as death. The path I had chosen gave me no choice—I either had to go through the alley and the yard beyond it or lose a tremendous amount of time doubling back to follow the road and the streetlights. For what seemed like an hour, but was no more than a few seconds, I stood unable to move. After screwing up my courage, I crept into the darkness just the tiniest bit and then froze again. With my eyes squeezed tightly shut to prevent myself from seeing the imagined terrors awaiting me, I trembled on the edge of the darkness. My imagination proved to be far worse than the reality that faced me, for when I finally opened my eyes, they had already begun to grow accustomed to the inky light. Holding my breath as if I were about to dive into a pool, I leaped into the darkness. I ran so fast I was barely able to breathe. As my legs pumped, my side ached, and my head throbbed. I kept my eyes straight ahead. The gate into the next yard was just ahead. I could just barely make it out in the murky light. Yard after yard blazed by; my attention was focused on the street beyond.

Finally, out on the sidewalk in the safe glow of the streetlight, I doubled over. I panted as I put my head down and my hands on my knees to try to alleviate the cramping in my side. I attempted to calm myself by picturing Judy's house and estimating how much farther I had to go. A car drove by, startling me. Despite the stitch in my side, I ran down the sidewalk, ducking under the low hanging branches that added such charm to the street during the day. A fresh panic set in when I didn't readily recognize Judy's house. An orange front door distinguished her house during the daylight, but at night all the front doors had the same ghoulish gray cast. I noticed a front porch light on farther down the street, much farther than I thought Judy's house was. I heard Stuart's voice. Sopping wet and chilled to the bone, I dashed up to my sister and dissolved into a torrent of sobs and gasps. "Ethel's dead. She fell down while she was on the phone. She was really, really loaded." The words spilled out like floodwater over a bank.

"What?" she asked with a confused gasp. "Oh my God. What? Oh my God, Ethel's dead? What are you talking about?"

Judy disappeared into the house and returned with her parents. Mrs. Jenkins said that she and Judy would stay there with me while her husband and Stuart went back to our house. I insisted, between gasps for air and sobs, that I wanted to go home. "Please don't leave me, Stuart," I pleaded.

She put her arm around me. "You're coming with us, don't worry," Stuart said.

The two of us held on to each other in the back seat of Judy's father's car. For the first time that night, the idea that Ethel was really dead began to take root in my mind. Stuart kept whispering. "She can't be dead. Don't cry, don't cry. It's gonna be all right."

As we drove into the driveway, we saw Big Early's truck parked by the kitchen steps.

"Poor old fellow," Judy's father said with a shake of his head. "That's a tough thing to have to come upon. You girls stay here." He got out of the car.

"I can't," Stuart protested. "Gordy and Helen are in there and I'm supposed to be babysitting." She reached over and opened the back door.

Judy's father raised an eyebrow, but he seemed to think better about saying anything. "Well, come on then. But you get the children and take them upstairs. I'll take care of Ethel."

We walked into the front hall. Helen and Gordy were sitting wide-eyed under the dining room table. The television was still droning on. They didn't make a move to come to us. In the back hall, Bertha knelt over Ethel's body with Big Early who looked like he was pretty mad. They were engaged in a vain attempt to heave Ethel off the floor. "Was a matter, honey, did ya slip?" asked Bertha as she busied herself arranging Ethel's disheveled uniform.

Judy's father started to laugh. He laughed a big ol' rich, deep laugh. Big Early, who I was shocked to discover wasn't much taller than Gordy and Bertha, looked at him as if he were insane. Judy's father laughed and laughed. While still chuckling, he went over and helped them get Ethel upright, which appeared to be an engineering feat. Once righted, it took more massive effort to get her shoe back on her foot.

Ethel didn't come back to work for a good week or two. As far as I know, there was never a word said about the experience. Sure, there was a lot of tittering about it, but I don't believe my mother ever said a thing to Ethel about the incident, and I know I never did. I suspect that my mother couldn't say much considering she was not much better off herself.

A few nights after Ethel's last episode, I was lying in bed listening to Helen's soft breathing and wishing I was asleep. I heard a noise I couldn't place. Light was shining in under the door, so I knew my mother was still up. I listened at the door—nothing. I was about to dismiss it as just my imagination, then I heard it again: shuffling and a tinkling, then a small knock. I knew I had heard that tinkling somewhere before, but there was that small knock, then more shuffling like the noise Lance used to make when he tried to get up off a wooden floor. I carefully opened the door and peered out in the hall—nobody. But, there was that sound again. I looked over the banister and saw my mother crawling up the stairs with her drink on the step above.

Her unfocused eyes were half lidded; I doubt she could have seen me had I been tap dancing at the top of the stairs. I slipped back into my room and quietly shut the door.

In our backyard a week or so later, Helen said, "I sure do wish Ethel would come back. It seems like forever since she's been here." Helen pumped her sturdy little legs for all they were worth, almost as if she was trying to swing herself away: away from the yelling and drinking and complaining; but most of all from the sadness that had enveloped our lives in the past year.

Ever ready to make a correction, Gordy pointed out that Ethel had only been away for a week and a half. "She was here Saturday night, because *Wild Wild West* was on and today is only Wednesday. I heard Mama say she was going to get someone else to work for her. She was talking to Miz Chambers on the phone. She said she was damned tired of all of Ethel's hijinks. She said it was bad enough that Ethel has been getting drunk, but getting drunk and passing out on the phone, that took the cake." Gordy's swing fell out of time with ours. He leapt off the swing and turned to face us with his hand on his hip, and his elbow jutting into the air dramatically. He turned his nose up and began shaking it back and forth, imitating our mother in a high, tinny voice: "Imagine screaming at my children and telling them what they can and cannot say."

Helen giggled at Gordy's imitation of our mother.

"Why do you suppose Mama is being so mean to Ethel?" I asked.

Gordy got back in his swing. "Or us. I don't know, but she actually told Miz Chambers, 'You'd have thought *Ethel* lost a baby.'" I grimaced, knowing that Helen could go off in a second at the mention of Dennis, but Gordy pressed on. "Then she said the worst thing of all: she said maybe it was Ethel's fault."

Helen and I stopped swinging. "What? What did she mean, Ethel's fault? She is crazy. Ethel wouldn't hurt anybody, most of all a baby!" I said this with all of the indignation I could muster.

Helen's face blanched. "What are we going to do?" she asked. "We can't let Mama fire Ethel. We got to do something. If Ethel doesn't come back, I don't want to live here anymore."

"Well, that is just plain dumb," Gordy said. "Where would you live?"

"With Daddy," she said plainly. "Stuart got to."

"Judge already said—" Gordy started to say.

"I don't care what any old dumb judge says," Helen interrupted. "If Ethel isn't going to be around, then I don't want to live here. And I know if I tell Daddy I want to live with him, he'll let me."

"Not if the judge says ya can't," Gordy said like he knew. "Judges get to say, and they would put you in jail if you go against a judge."

"I'm just a kid. They don't put kids in jail. 'Sides, Stuart got to," she insisted.

"Stuart is older, and when you get to be fifteen you get to decide where you live. I can go live with Daddy in three more years." Gordy puffed up like a big old frog ready to croak.

My mother appeared on the back porch with an apron wrapped around her waist and a drink in her hand. She took a sip then yelled, "Gordy, Sallee, Helen." Then she took another sip. "Dinner. Now."

All three of us leaped out of the swings. "You might not have to worry about where you are going to live," I muttered, as we headed toward the house, noticing only then how dark it had become. "That sour cream and zucchini she makes so much could kill us before it really becomes a problem. Please, please, *please* don't make it tonight."

"Sallee, what were you doing out there without a coat? It's cold." She started in on me the minute I walked into the kitchen. I noticed that the gin bottle was out on the counter. Gin always made her mean; a fact with which the three of us were becoming painfully familiar on a daily basis. I looked over at my siblings and shared a knowing look. "Don't you roll your eyes at me, young lady," she said. "Set the table."

"I didn't...," I started to say and then mumbled, "Never mind. I don't feel well. I'm going to bed." Before I could turn to leave, her hand connected with my face.

"Don't you ever talk to me in that tone!" Stunned, I made my way to the cupboard where the plates were kept, trying hard to stem my tears. I didn't want to give her another reason to hit me. My face stung. "Sit down and eat your dinner," she directed the other two. Helen and Gordy had figured out that saying anything was a mistake. They helped me set the table and took their seats while our mother slapped food on our plates. I couldn't look at them; I was too mortified. "Sit up at the table," she snapped. All three of us sat bolt upright. She leaned against the counter and stared through us. The only sound in the kitchen was chewing and the tinkling of ice in her glass.

If dutifully obedient children were what she wanted, my mother had found the perfect solution. Gordy and Helen jumped up to clear the table after asking politely to be excused. A distracted wave was all they got. They sat back down for some time, trying to decide what, if anything, they should do.

"Can I be excused to start washing the pots and pans?" I asked, holding my breath as I waited for her reply. She fixed herself another drink and left the room without a word. Gordy and Helen sprang into action, clearing the table and loading the dishwasher in record time before retreating upstairs out of harm's way. I was grateful that dinner hadn't required many pots. I scraped the leftovers into bowls and prepared to wash up. Did she want dinner? Surely she wouldn't eat fish sticks and tater tots. Still I thought I'd better ask, even though I dreaded having to face her again that night. I walked as soundlessly as I could, looking in rooms along the way until I got to the living room where I found her alone, weeping. My question no longer seemed appropriate. I backed up unseen. Seething with anger and crying at the same time, I decided to run away.

It was important that I kept my decision to myself. Even if they meant well, I didn't need Helen or Gordy trying to talk me out of it, or worse yet, telling someone. I was having enough trouble sticking to my guns. As desperate as the situation felt, I thought I should give myself time to prepare, so I decided to leave on Saturday morning.

Once I had settled on running away, I discovered that the resolution buoyed me. The first two days I floated around the house in a kind of calm. I was nicer to Helen and Gordy than I had been in months. I found myself memorizing the details of my room and gazing on my home with renewed interest, as if it were a museum full of precious artifacts from my life up to now.

By the time I left for school on Friday morning, living at home almost seemed bearable again. And by Friday night with my departure fast approaching, a knot of anxiety began to form in my stomach. I was as irritable and melancholy as ever. All Gordy or Helen had to do was look at me funny and I would just about snap their heads off.

My plan was to leave the house like I was going to play outside as I almost always did. I would just do it a little earlier than usual so that I didn't have Gordy nosing in, or Helen asking questions. I had already stashed some clothes in a backpack under the kitchen porch where I could get them when I was ready to go. I hadn't gotten much further than that. Planning for the future proved to be far more complicated than I had anticipated. Where would I go? Daddy? I knew that wouldn't work some dumb judge had made sure of that. Bertha came to mind, but that was dismissed because I knew she would tell Ethel, and Ethel would make me go home. Besides, the last person I wanted anything to do with was Ethel—she'd deserted us. Jilly, another possibility, was out of the question because Uncle James would drag me home by my hair. Finally, a plausible plan came to me. I could buy a bus ticket to the beach. I could live in the house and no one would think to look for me there. I spent two days checking for loose change in all the spots my mother would leave it. By Friday night, along with the contents of my piggy bank, I had more than fifty dollars. I snuck out after dinner and put the money in my pack under the porch. That last night was excruciatingly painful. I already missed Helen so much that I wanted to crawl in bed with her to soak in her smell so I wouldn't forget her. And I couldn't stop thinking of my terrifying trip to Judy's house three long months ago. I longed to stay, but I couldn't. I hated my mother. I hated Ethel, and I hated the life we were stuck with. The next morning I was surprised to find that it was already seven-thirty when I awoke.

"You're dressed already? Where are you going?" Gordy demanded as he changed channels on the TV.

"Nowhere, I just felt like getting dressed, Mr. Have-to-know-everything. For your information there is no law against being dressed on a Saturday morning," I snapped at him.

"Well, excuse me for living. I just wondered since you are usually the last one dressed. Do you want to watch *The Lone Ranger* or *Looney Tunes?*"

Helen piped up, "Wooney Thunes," with a mouth full of thumb. "What's for breakfast?" she asked after taking her thumb out of her mouth.

"What, do you think I'm going to fix it?" I shot back. "Go get your own cereal. You might as well start learning how to take care of yourself. You're not exactly a baby, you know." I hated myself for being so mean. I just couldn't help it.

Helen looked at Gordy and then back at me. Then she shrugged. She was wearing a vacant look as she hunkered down with her blanket and thumb. Casually I went into the kitchen as I had done a hundred times before and banged open a few cupboards, poured myself some Cocoa Puffs into a bag, and then slipped the bag into my jacket pocket. I searched in the icebox for some bologna. As I drank some milk, I shuddered to think what kind of trouble I would be in if I got caught drinking the milk out of the bottle, and then sort of laughed at myself. Finally, I found the bologna, put it in my pocket, and slipped out the kitchen door. I had just gotten my backpack from under the steps when the door opened above me. Gordy whispered, "What are you doing? Where are you going?" His volume rose with each question. "Can I go? You're not running away, are you?" Finally he yelled, "I'm going to tell."

"Tell what?" I demanded. "That I'm outside on a Saturday morning? Go ahead, tell." I half hoped he would.

"I'm going to…" I couldn't think, "…um, go play," I finished lamely.

Helen was at the door by then. She glanced suspiciously at my face and then my backpack then drew her thumb out of her mouth. "What ya doin'?"

Just then we heard the heavy slam of a truck door, tires on gravel, and Ethel's tuneless whistle coming up the drive as Early's truck chugged and belched its way up the street.

"Ethel!" we all cried together. "You're back!" We ran down the drive to meet her.

Her eyes widened when she saw Helen and Gordy in their pajamas and barefoot. "What are ya doin' out in dis cold with yo' night clothes and no shoes? You betta get in that house afore I tan ya'll good," she said, breaking out in a grin. "You'll catch yo' death a cold out chere. Get on in tha house," she chuckled as she shooed the two of them along. She turned to me. "You dressed mighty early this morning, miss? Where ya off ta?"

Gordon and Helen were happy that Ethel had been restored to her old self, and had begun racing back to the house. But Gordy took it upon himself to answer Ethel's question. "She's trying to run away, Ethel. Don't let her," he shouted over his shoulder before disappearing into the house. Ethel gaped at me. She was speechless for what seemed like the first time. I hesitated, shifted the weight of my backpack, and then looked out toward the street. Before I knew it, I had started to cry. Glad as I was to see Ethel, I couldn't keep the anger from welling up and overcoming me.

"What's the matter, honey chile?" she asked, as innocent as a lamb.

Before I could push it back down again, it swelled up and rolled out of me like a wave. "Don't you know? Don't you know what you do? Do you think it's OK to keep getting drunk and then leave us for weeks with nobody to take care of us, nobody to love us, and then come back here like nothing ever happened? Do you care that Mama beats on us and calls us names? What are we supposed to be doing while you're out getting drunk?"

Ethel just stared at me a moment. Then before I knew it, she had grabbed me up into her arms and held me to her warm chest while I sputtered and coughed into her. Then she let me loose. "You gettin' to be a big girl, an' ol' Ethel can't hol' ya like I used ta." She took me by the hand and we walked back down the drive.

Realizing that I had spoken the unspeakable, I started to blubber an apology. Ethel stopped me. "I's the one tha's sorry, honey. I never been so sick as I been since Dennis died. Big Early, he tol' me that I gotta pull myself together. He say you chil'ren is my responsibility and I'm lettin' ya'll down. And no, honey, I don' think it's OK to get drunk an' leave ya'll."

We had gotten to the end of the drive. She steered us over to the sidewalk, never letting go of my hand. "C'mon, we's goin' for a walk." We walked past the Dabneys' house, down to the end of the street, and then turned to go around the block past the woods Gordy liked playing in past Mr. Gentry's house. Finally she brought us to a stop under a maple tree whose leaves were past yellow and eased her self down onto the grass. She patted her lap for me to sit down too, and then she put her arms around me and began to talk slowly and deliberately. As she talked, it was as if a door, which had always remained just cracked, was flung open wide before me. She had always given me her love. That much I knew because that's what she did: she gave her love—to heal possibly; probably she didn't know how else to be. Now she was offering me her life, too; that was different and I knew it was important. I curled into her, my legs dangling, and listened.

"I was fourteen years old when I come to work for yo' granddaddy's family, Miss Sallee. It was just a few days a week when I didn' have nothin' to do at the boardin'house; helpin' my mother in the kitchen, mostly. Turned out to be one of them little decisions that don't seem like much at the time, but ends up changing yo' life…"

EPILOGUE

———

Ethel

Sho' do wish I could say that I held to that promise I done made to Sallee and myself that day. Lord knows I tried, but I fell off the wagon a time or two, what with my feelin' like I done Mista Joe and the chil'ren a bad turn. Then when I gets to thinkin' 'bout lil' Denny and Miss Ginny, and what I could'da done different—the nights they gets mighty long and lonely. The devil, he commences to whisperin' in my ear, "Just a little will make ya feel better. Go on now, won't hurt none." I listened, called in sick too. The hangover weren't nothin' compared to how I felt when I saw the sufferin' in my babies' eyes. I told ol' Slewfoot to get behind me right then and there. I still have to tell him pretty regular.

Miss Ginny kept up her drinkin'. Try as I might there wasn't nothin' I could do 'bout it. I knew how it felt to lose a baby, though mines never got born, and Denny might as well be mine, for as much as I loved him. Mama say "Feelin' sorry for her or yo' own self ain't gon'na make a lick of difference." Then with that steel in her voice and love in her eyes she say, "It sho ain't gonna help the other chil'ren, so yo' best be gettin' hold'da yo'self."

So when the nights is long, and I start feelin' like I didn't help nobody no way, especially my own self, and ol' Slewfoot starts a whisperin', I reminds myself that my chil'ren needs me more than I needs a drink. Change comes slow, but it do come.

Made in the USA
San Bernardino, CA
13 March 2014